DEAD SKY, BLACK SUN

Hard-hitting action from the pen of
Graham McNeill

EXILED FROM THE Ultramarines Chapter by
Marneus Calgar, Captain Uriel Ventris ventures
deep into the dreaded Eye of Terror to atone for
his disgrace. There, Uriel must unleash the
Emperor's vengeance upon the followers of the
Dark Gods and bring His divine light to this area
of darkness. But a far more terrible foe dwells
within these worlds of insanity – the ancient
Chaos Space Marine Legions! With dishonour
behind him and certain death ahead, Uriel must
gather every ounce of courage if he is to survive
and regain his honour!

A WARHAMMER 40,000 NOVEL

DEAD SKY, BLACK SUN

Graham McNeill

To the Games Dev guys Andy, Ant and Phil. It's a dirty job, keeping me right, but someone's got to do it.

A BLACK LIBRARY PUBLICATION

First published in Great Britain in 2004 by
BL Publishing,
Games Workshop Ltd.,
Willow Road, Nottingham,
NG7 2WS, UK.

10 9 8 7 6 5 4 3 2 1

Cover illustration by Clint Langley.

A CIP record for this book is available from the British Library.

ISBN 1-84416-148-x

Distributed in the US by Simon & Schuster
1230 Avenue of the Americas, New York, NY 10020, US.

Printed and bound in Great Britain by
Bookmarque, Surrey, UK.

See the Black Library on the Internet at
www.blacklibrary.com

Find out more about Games Workshop
and the world of Warhammer 40,000 at
www.games-workshop.com

IT IS THE 41st millennium. For more than a hundred centuries the Emperor has sat immobile on the Golden Throne of Earth. He is the master of mankind by the will of the gods, and master of a million worlds by the might of his inexhaustible armies. He is a rotting carcass writhing invisibly with power from the Dark Age of Technology. He is the Carrion Lord of the Imperium for whom a thousand souls are sacrificed every day, so that he may never truly die.

YET EVEN IN his deathless state, the Emperor continues his eternal vigilance. Mighty battlefleets cross the daemon-infested miasma of the warp, the only route between distant stars, their way lit by the Astronomican, the psychic manifestation of the Emperor's will. Vast armies give battle in his name on uncounted worlds. Greatest amongst his soldiers are the Adeptus Astartes, the Space Marines, bio-engineered super-warriors. Their comrades in arms are legion: the Imperial Guard and countless planetary defence forces, the ever-vigilant Inquisition and the tech-priests of the Adeptus Mechanicus to name only a few. But for all their multitudes, they are barely enough to hold off the ever-present threat from aliens, heretics, mutants – and worse.

TO BE A man in such times is to be one amongst untold billions. It is to live in the cruellest and most bloody regime imaginable. These are the tales of those times. Forget the power of technology and science, for so much has been forgotten, never to be re-learned. Forget the promise of progress and understanding, for in the grim dark future there is only war. There is no peace amongst the stars, only an eternity of carnage and slaughter, and the laughter of thirsting gods.

'He that fights with monsters should look to it that he himself does not become a monster.'

PROLOGUE

DISTANT HAMMER BLOWS from monstrous engines reverberated through the chamber, echoing from the Halls of the Savage Morticians far below, rising alongside noxious tendrils of acrid vapours and agonised screams. Leering gargoyles of pressed and riveted iron ringed the chamber's dizzyingly high, arched ceiling and the tops of impossibly huge, pillar-like pistons, each one wreathed in greasy steam, ground rhythmically up and down through wide, skull-rimmed holes that ran along its edges.

A great chasm in the obsidian floor billowed scalding steam in roiling waves of heat and was crossed by a gantry of studded iron decking that rested upon massively thick girders, which in turn were supported on chains whose oily links were as thick as a man's torso.

Lit by a hot, orange glow from a snaking ribbon of molten metal at the chasm's base, many hundreds of metres below, the chamber reeked of sulphurous fumes and the searing, bitter taste of beaten metal. The gantry led towards a massive, cyclopean wall of dark-veined stone, pierced by a great, iron gate that had been tempered in an ocean of blood during its forging. Studded with jagged black spikes, the inner gate of the fortress of Khalan-Ghol was flanked by two armoured colossi, whose burnished iron hides were scarred by millennia of war. The gate led to the inner halls of the fortress's new master, and both daemon-visaged Titans, hung with the blighted banners of the Legio Mortis, raised fearsome guns – capable of laying waste to cities – to track a dozen figures who dared approach the gate.

The terrible enormity of the chamber did not faze the warriors who marched towards the groaning bridge; they had seen such sights before. Indeed, the leader of this group of warriors hailed from a citadel far more ancient and monolithic than this.

Lord Toramino, warsmith of the Iron Warriors, curled his lip in contempt as he raised his altered eyes to stare down the barrels of the Titans' weapons. If the half-breed thought such a vulgar display of power would intimidate him, then he was even more fool-ish than his inferior lineage would suggest. They had passed through the fortress's gatehouse three days ago, travelling unchallenged by any of the half-breed's warriors, though Toramino had felt supernatural eyes upon them ever since. No doubt warlocks of the kabal were watching them even now, but Toramino could not have cared less, marching with his head held high and hands clasped behind his back.

Alongside him, Lord Berossus growled as he watched the Titans' guns train upon them, spooling up his own weapons. Toramino looked up at Berossus and shook his head at his vassal warsmith's lack of restraint. None here could face a Titan and live, but such were the ingrained responses of Berossus that no other reaction was possible.

Toramino stepped onto the iron bridge, the metal hissing beneath his armoured boot and rippling like mercury, reflecting his massive, armoured form in its glistening lustre. Standing well over two metres tall, Lord Toramino wore a suit of exquisitely tooled power armour, handcrafted on Olympia itself and burnished to a mirror sheen. Its trims were edged with arabesques of carven gold and onyx chevrons and its every surface wrought with terrible sigils of ruin. An ochre cloak of woven metallic thread, stronger than adamantium, billowed around his wide frame, partially obscuring the skull-masked symbol of the Iron Warriors on one shoulder guard and his own personal heraldry of a mailed fist above a plan view of a breached redoubt on the other.

An Iron Warrior from his most trusted retinue carried his elaborately carved helm, and another carried his blasted standard, an eight-pointed star of blackened bone set upon a spiked, brass-rimmed wheel and woven with sinew extracted from a thousand screaming victims. Long white hair, pulled into a tight scalp-lock, trailed down his back and his stern, patrician features were pinched and angular – speaking of long years of bitter experience. His eyes were opalescent orbs of gold, smouldering with suppressed rage beneath thick brows.

As they approached the wall, huge blasts of stinking, oil-streaked gases jetted from the pistons either side of the gate and with a groan and squeal of grinding metalwork, the colossal locks disengaged with percussive booms that shook the dust from the chamber's ceiling.

The Titans lowered their mighty weapons and the upper portions of their bodies twisted around on bronze joints to grip the spiked gateway and pull. Steam jetted from wheezing fibre-bundle muscles, and slowly the awful gate groaned open, spilling an emerald light into the chamber as Toramino and Berossus passed between the mighty death machines and into the sanctum sanctorum of the lord of the fortress.

Toramino remembered this place from the many times he had come to pay homage to Khalan-Ghol's former castellan – a great and terrible warrior who had now ascended to the dark majesty of daemonhood. The walls within were of a plain black stone, threaded with gold and silver and glistening with moisture, despite the heat radiating from the terrazzo floor of powdered bone. Sickly white light reflected as pearlescent streaks on the floor from a score of tall and thin arched windows that pierced the eastern wall, draining the chamber of life and imparting a deathly pallor to its occupants.

A score of Iron Warriors stood to attention at the far end of the chamber, gathered about a polished throne of white and silver upon which sat a warrior in battered power armour.

It galled Toramino that he came before the fortress's new lord as a supposed equal. The half-breed was a bastard mongrel, not fit to wipe the blood from an Iron Warrior's armour, let alone command them in battle. Such an affront to the honour of the Legion was almost more than Toramino could bear, and as he watched the lord of the fortress rise from his throne of fused iron and bone, he felt his hatred rise in a venomous wave of bile.

The half-breed's appearance matched Toramino's opinion of him in that he was unclean and had none of the nobility of the ancients of Olympia. His close-cropped black hair topped a rugged, scarred face with bluntly prosaic features, and his armour was dented and scarred, still marked with the residue of battle. Did the half-breed not care that he was now receiving two of the most ancient and noble warsmiths of Medrengard? That this upstart's warsmith could have appointed such a low mongrel as his successor beggared belief.

'Lord Honsou,' said Toramino, forcing himself to bow before the half-breed while keeping his hands clasped behind his back. His tone was formal and he spoke in low, sibilant tones, though he was careful to include a mocking inflection to his words.

'Lord Toramino,' answered Honsou. 'You honour me with your presence. And you also, Lord Berossus. It has been many years since the walls of Khalan-Ghol shook to the tread of your steps.'

The floor cracked under the weight of Lord Berossus, a hulking monster of dark iron and bronze with a leering skull face. Fully twice the height of Toramino, the living remains of Warsmith Berossus had been fused within the defiled sarcophagus of a dreadnought many thousands of years ago.

The grotesque machine hissed and a grating voice, muffled and distorted by a bronze vox-unit, said, 'Aye, it has, though I feel sullied to stand within its walls knowing a bastard mongrel like you is its new lord.'

Augmented and extensively engineered since his interment, Berossus's mechanical form towered above the other dreadnoughts of his grand company, his leg assemblies strengthened and widened to allow him to carry heavier and heavier breaching equipment. The dreadnought's upper body was scarred and pitted, the testament of uncounted sieges engraved on its adamantium shell. One arm bore a mighty, piston-driven siege hammer, the other a monstrous drill ringed with heavy calibre cannons.

Four thick, iron arms ending in vicious picks, blades, claws and heavy gauge breachers sprouted from behind Berossus's sarcophagus and hung ready for use over his armoured carapace.

Toramino saw Honsou bite back a retort and his soulless, golden eyes sparkled with amusement at the directness of Berossus. Honsou must already know what had brought them both here. There was only one thing that would make both him and Berossus deign to step within the walls of the half-breed's lair and he smiled, easily able to imagine Honsou's chagrin at having to share what his former master had won.

'You must forgive Berossus, Lord Honsou,' said Toramino smoothly, stepping forward and extending his hands before him. Unlike the rest of his armour, his gauntlets were fashioned from a brutal, dark iron, pitted and scarred with innumerable battles. Steeped in carnage, Toramino had long ago vowed never to clean a death from his hands and his gauntlets were gnarled with aeons of blood and suffering. As his armoured gauntlets came into view, the Iron Warriors behind Honsou snapped their bolters upright, every one aiming his weapon at Toramino's head.

Toramino grinned, exposing teeth of gleaming silver, and said, 'I come before you to offer my congratulations on the victory at Hydra Cordatus. Your former master executed a masterful campaign; to carry the walls of such a formidable stronghold was a truly great achievement. And your fellow captains, Forrix and Kroeger? Where are they that I might fete them with honours also?'

'They are dead,' snapped Honsou, and Toramino took pleasure in the vexation the half-breed took from his exclusion from the honours of victory. He scented the mongrel's pathetic desire to be accepted by them and closed on the true purpose of their journey here.

'A pity,' said Toramino, 'but their deaths served a greater purpose, yes? You were successful in capturing the prize that lay beneath the citadel?'

'A pity?' repeated Honsou. 'It is only a pity that I was not able kill them myself, though I did have the pleasure of watching Forrix die. And yes, we took the spoils of war from the cryo-facility beneath the mountains – what the Imperials hadn't managed to destroy at least.'

'Stable gene-seed?' breathed Toramino, unable to keep the hunger from his voice.

'Aye,' agreed Honsou. 'Biologically stable and without mutation. And all of it for the Despoiler. You know that, Toramino.'

Lord Berossus laughed, a grainy wash of feedback-laced static, his massive armoured body leaning down as he said, 'Do not think us fools, half-breed. We know you kept some for yourself. You would be foolish not to have.'

'And if I did, what business is it of yours, Berossus?' snarled Honsou.

'Whelp!' roared the dreadnought, taking a crashing step forward as the clawed servo-arms on his back snapped to life. 'You dare speak in such tones to your betters!'

Before Honsou could reply, Toramino said, 'Though he speaks bluntly, Lord Berossus also speaks true. I know you kept some gene-seed for yourself. So listen well, half-breed: your former master was a sworn ally of Berossus and myself, and we expect you, as his successor, to honour these oaths and share the spoils of victory.'

Honsou said nothing for long seconds then laughed in their faces. Toramino felt his hatred for this insolent half-breed burn hotter than ever.

'Share?' said Honsou, turning and receiving a long, broad-bladed axe from an Iron Warrior behind him and nodding to another, who bent to lift a heavy iron cryo-chest from behind the throne as scores of warriors from Honsou's grand company marched into the hall from behind them.

The Iron Warrior with the cryo-chest held it out before Toramino as Honsou said, 'In that cryo-chest is all that I am willing to share. It is my only offer so I advise you to take it and leave.'

Toramino's eyes narrowed as he reached a battered gauntlet out to lift the lid, wisps of condensing air ghosting from within the chest. His every instinct told him that this was a trap, but he could not show weakness before the half-breed.

He opened the container and stiffened as he saw that it was empty.

'Is this some pathetic attempt at a jest, half-breed?' hissed Toramino. 'You turn your back on your master's oaths?'

Honsou took a step towards Toramino and spat on the warsmith's gleaming breastplate. 'I spit on those oaths as I spit on you,' he said. 'You and your idiot monster. And no, it is no jest. Understand this, Toramino, you will get nothing from me. None of you will. What I took from the Imperials on Hydra Cordatus I fought and bled for, and neither you or any one else, is going to take from me.'

Toramino seethed with anger, but bit it back. The muscles of his neck bunched, and it was all he could do to quell the rage boiling within him. He snarled an oath and nodded to Berossus, who roared and slammed his mighty siege hammer down upon the Iron Warrior carrying the cryo-chest, obliterating him in an explosion of flesh and armour. A blazing corona of electrical discharge flared around the cratered floor and gory matter drooled from the crackling hammer.

Incredulous that this vile half-breed had the nerve to behave in this manner before one such as he, Toramino bellowed, 'You dare insult me like this?'

'I do, and you are no longer welcome in my halls. I give you leave to depart as befits warsmiths of your station, but you will never set foot within this fortress again while I draw breath.'

'To defy me means death,' promised Toramino. 'My armies will tear this place down stone by stone, girder by girder, and I will feed you to the Unfleshed.'

'We shall see,' said Honsou, gripping his axe tightly. 'Send your armies here, Toramino, they will find only death before my walls.'

Without deigning to reply, Lord Toramino spun on his heel and marched from the chamber, his retinue and Lord Berossus following close behind.

If the half-breed wanted war, then Toramino would give him war.

A war that would stir the mighty Perturabo himself from his bitter reveries.

PART ONE
DEATH OATH

CHAPTER ONE

URIEL KEPT HIS breathing smooth as he stepped through the last moves of his attack routine, every action in perfect balance and focus, his body and mind acting in absolute synchronicity. Slowly and deliberately, he performed the strikes, first his elbow then his fist striking an imaginary foe, keeping his movements precise. He kept his eyes closed, his stance light and balanced, with all parts of his body starting and ending their movements at the same time.

Completing his steps, Uriel took an intake of breath as his fists crossed before him, then exhaled, maintaining his concentration as he returned his arms smoothly to his sides, centring his power within himself.

He could feel the potentiality of the lethal force in his limbs, sensing the strength grow within him and feeling a calmness he had not felt in many weeks enfold him as he completed the last of the prescribed movements.

'Ready?' asked Pasanius.

Uriel nodded and shook his limbs loose as he dropped into a fighting crouch, fists raised before him. His former sergeant was much larger than him, hugely muscled and wearing a sparring chiton of blue cotton that left his legs and arms bare. Even though it had been nearly two years since Pasanius had lost his arm fighting beneath the world against an ancient star-god, Uriel still found his eyes drawn to the gleaming, silver-smooth augmetic arm that replaced his lost limb.

Pasanius wore his blond hair tight into his skull and though his face was capable of great warmth and humour, it was set in a deathly serious expression as they prepared to fight. Pasanius launched a slashing right cross towards his head and Uriel swayed aside to avoid the blow. He deflected Pasanius's follow-up punch and spun inside his guard, hammering his elbow towards his opponent's throat. But the big man pivoted smoothly away and deflected Uriel's strike, pulling him off balance.

Uriel ducked beneath a scything punch and leapt backwards in time to dodge a thunderous kick to his groin. Despite his speed, the heel of Pasanius's foot still hammered into his side, and he grunted in pain as the breath was driven from him.

Uriel dodged away from the next blow, bouncing lightly on the balls of his feet as his opponent came at him again, blocking and countering everything Pasanius threw at him. The big man was faster than he looked and Uriel knew he could not avoid being hit forever. And when Pasanius landed a clean blow, very few got back up.

He threw murderous punches towards Pasanius, pivoting his hips and shoulders to get his full weight behind his blows, while ducking in to deliver rapid-fire punches to his opponent's ribs. Pasanius stepped back, untroubled by such strikes, and Uriel swiftly followed him, throwing a hooking punch at his head. It was a risky gambit and easily blocked, but instead of Pasanius's gleaming forearm coming up to block the blow, Uriel's fist smashed home against his right temple.

Pasanius stumbled and dropped to one knee, bright blood weeping from where the skin had split above his right eye. Uriel stepped away from Pasanius, dropping his fists and easing his breathing as he stared in puzzlement at the gash on his former sergeant's forehead.

'Are you all right?' asked Uriel. 'What happened? You could easily have blocked that.'

'You just caught me by surprise,' said Pasanius, wiping away the already clotted blood with his fleshy hand. 'I expected you to go for the legs again.'

Uriel replayed the last few seconds of their bout again in his mind, seeing again his and Pasanius's positions and movements as they sparred.

'The legs? I wasn't in a strong position to attack your legs,' said Uriel. 'If I wanted to attack from that position, I had to go for the head.'

Pasanius shrugged. 'I just didn't get my block up in time.'

'You didn't even try, not even with the other arm.'

'You won. What are you complaining about?'

'It's just that I've never seen you miss such an easy block, that's all.'

Pasanius turned away, picking up a towel from where it hung on the brass rail that ran around the circumference of the geodesic viewing dome Captain

Laskaris had given over to them for sparring and training. The blackness of space filled the view from the dome: stars spread across it like diamond dust on sable. Reflected light from the distant star of Macragge glittered on the dome's many facets and cast a soft pall of ghostly light throughout the viewing bay.

'I'm sorry, Uriel, this whole situation has me a little… off balance,' said Pasanius, draping his towel over his augmetic arm. 'To be exiled from the Chapter…'

'I know, Pasanius, I know,' said Uriel, joining his sergeant at the edge of the dome. He gripped the rail as he stared through the toughened armaglass at what lay beyond.

The gothic, cliff-like hull of the bulk-transporter, *Calth's Pride*, stretched away into the darkness of space and beyond sight as the vessel journeyed from Macragge towards the Masali jump point.

URIEL STEPPED INTO his quarters, throwing his towel onto the gunmetal grey footlocker at the foot of his bed and walking into the small ablutions cubicle set into the steel bulkhead. He pulled off his sweat-stained chiton and hung it from a chrome rail, turning the burnished lever above the chipped ceramic basin and waiting for it to fill. He scooped up a handful of ice-cold water, splashing it over his face and letting it drip from his craggy features.

Uriel stared at the foaming water in the basin, its spray reminding him of his last morning on Macragge, kneeling on Gallan's Rock and watching the glittering spume in the rocky pool at the base of the Falls of Hera. He closed his eyes, picturing again the distant seas, shimmering like a blanket of sapphires beyond the rocky white peaks of the western mountains, themselves sprinkled with scraps of green highland fir. The sun was setting, casting blood-red fingers of dying light and bathing the mountains in gold. It had felt as though the homeworld of his Chapter had been granting him one last vision of its majesty before it was denied to him forever.

He would hold onto that vision each night as he lay down on his simple cot bed, recalling its every nuance of colour, sight and smell, anxious that it should not fade from his memories. The stale, recycled taste to the air made the memory all the more poignant, and the harsh, spartanly furnished quarters he had been allocated aboard the *Pride* were a fond reminder of his captain's chambers back on Macragge.

Uriel lifted his head and stared at the polished steel mirror, watching as droplets trickled like tears down his reflection's cheek. He wiped the last of the water from his face, the grey eyes of his twin watching him, set beneath a heavy, brooding brow and close-cropped black hair. Two golden studs were set upon his brow and his jawline was angular and patrician. His physique dwarfed that of the ordinary human soldiers who filled this enormous starship, genetically enhanced by long-forgotten technologies and honed to the peak of physical perfection by a lifetime of training, discipline and war. His arms and chest were criss-crossed with scars, but greater than them all combined was a mass of pale, discoloured flesh across his stomach where a tyranid Norn-queen had almost slain him on Tarsis Ultra.

He shuddered at the memory, turning and sitting on the edge of his bed, remembering his last sight of Macragge as the shuttle had lifted off from the port facility at the end of the Valley of Laponis. He had watched his adopted homeworld shrink away, becoming a patchwork of glittering, quartz-rich mountains and vast oceans that were soon obscured as the shuttle rose into the lower atmosphere.

Slowly the curve of the world had become visible, together with the pale haze that marked the divide between the planet and the hard vacuum of space. Ahead, *Calth's Pride* had been an ugly, metallic oblong hanging in space above the planet's northern polar reaches.

He had reached out and placed a gauntleted hand against the shuttle's thick viewing block, wondering if he would ever set foot on Macragge again.

'Take a good look, captain,' Pasanius had said gloomily, following Uriel's gaze through the viewing block. 'It's the last time we'll see her.'

'I hope you're wrong, Pasanius,' said Uriel. 'I don't know where our journey will take us, but we may yet see the world of our Chapter again.'

Pasanius shrugged, his massive armoured form dwarfing his former captain. The late Techmarine Sevano Tomasin had forged the armour upon Pasanius's elevation to a full Space Marine, its armoured plates composed of parts scavenged from suits of tactical dreadnought armour that had been irreparably damaged in battle.

'Perhaps, captain, but I know that *I'll* never lay eyes on Macragge again.'

'What makes you so sure? And you don't need to call me "captain" any more, remember?'

'Of course, captain, but I just know I will not return here,' replied Pasanius. 'It's just a feeling I have.'

Uriel shook his head. 'No, I do not believe that Lord Calgar would have placed this death oath upon us if he thought we could not honour it,' he said. 'It may take many years, but there is always hope.'

Uriel had watched his former sergeant, understanding his grim mood as his eyes drifted to the huge shoulder guard where the symbol of the Ultramarines had once been emblazoned. Like his own armour, all insignia of the Ultramarines had been removed following their castigation by a conclave of their peers for breaches of the *Codex Astartes* on Tarsis Ultra and they had taken the March of Shame from the Fortress of Hera.

Uriel sighed as he thought of all that had happened since he had first taken up his former captain's sword to take command of the Ultramarines Fourth Company; so much death and battle that was a Space Marine's lot. Battle-brothers, allies and friends had died fighting renegades, xenos creatures and entire splinter fleets of tyranids.

He sat back against the bulkhead, casting his mind back to the carnage the tyranids had wreaked on Tarsis Ultra. He still had perfect recall of the horrific battles fought on that ice-locked industrial world, the fury of the extra-galactic predators' invasion indelibly etched on his memories. The battles on Ichar IV – another world ravaged by the tyranids – had been terrible, but the gathering of Imperial forces there had been magnificent, whereas those assembled on Tarsis Ultra had been horrifically outnumbered, and only desperate heroism and the intervention of the legendary Inquisitor Lord Kryptman had brought them victory.

But it was a victory won at a cost.

To save the planet, Uriel had taken command of an Ordo Xenos Deathwatch squad – in defiance of his duty to his warriors and the tenets of his primarch's holy tome, the *Codex Astartes* – and fought his way to the heart of a tyranid hive ship. Upon the company's

return to Macragge, Learchus, one of his most courageous sergeants, had reported Uriel's flagrant breaches
of the *Codex's* teachings to the High Masters of the
Chapter.

Tried before the great and good of the Ultramarines,
Uriel and Pasanius had waived their right to defend
themselves, instead accepting the judgement of
Marneus Calgar to prevent their example passing
down the chain of command. The penalty for such
heresy could only be death, but rather than waste the
lives of two courageous warriors who might yet bring
ruin to the enemies of the Emperor, the Chapter Master had bound them to a death oath.

Uriel could vividly remember the evening they had
set out from the Fortress of Hera, accepting the judgement of Lord Calgar and showing the Chapter that the
way chosen by the Ultramarines was true. They were
bound to the death oath that the Chapter might live
on as it always had.

Chaplain Clausel had read verses from the Book of
Dishonour and averted his eyes as Uriel and Pasanius
marched past him towards the doors of the gatehouse.

'Uriel, Pasanius,' said Lord Calgar.

The two Space Marines stopped and bowed to their
former master.

'The Emperor go with you. Die well.'

Uriel nodded as the huge doors swung open. He and
Pasanius had stepped into the purple twilight of
evening. Birds were singing and torchlight flickered from
the high towers of the outermost wall of the fortress.

Before the door closed, Calgar had spoken once
again, his voice hesitant, as though unsure as to
whether he should speak at all.

'Librarian Tigurius spoke with me last night,' he
began, 'of a world that tasted of dark iron, with great

womb factories of daemonic flesh rippling with monstrous, unnatural life. Tigurius told me that savage morticians – like monsters themselves – hacked at these creatures with blades and saws and pulled bloodstained figures from within. Though appearing more dead than alive, these figures lived and breathed, tall and strong, a dark mirror of our own glory. I know not what this means, Uriel, but its evil is plain. Seek this place out. Destroy it.'

'As you command,' said Uriel as he had walked into the night.

The chilling vision of Librarian Tigurius could be anywhere in the galaxy, and though the thought of venturing into such a hideous place filled Uriel's soul with dread, part of him also relished the chance to bring death to such vile monsters.

It had been five days since the bulk lifter had broken orbit with Macragge and used its conventional plasma drives to journey to the Masali jump point.

All Uriel's enemies had been met blade-to-blade and defeated, yet here he and Pasanius were, aboard a vessel rammed to the gunwales with regiments of Imperial Guard bound for Segmentum Obscurus and the wars that had erupted in the wake of the Despoiler's invasion of Imperial space.

'Courage and honour,' he whispered bitterly, but there was no reply.

PASANIUS PRESSED THE point of his knife into the centre of his chest, the skin dimpling under its razor-sharp tip. The skin broke and blood welled from the cut, dripping down his chest before swiftly clotting. Pasanius pushed the blade deeper, dragging the knife across the bulging pectoral muscle on the left side of his chest and cutting a long, horizontal slice in his skin.

He ignored the pain, altering the angle of the blade and cutting diagonally down towards his solar plexus, forming a mirror image of the cuts on the opposite side of his chest. Quick slashes between the heavy cuts formed the final part of his carving and Pasanius dropped the knife onto his bed, falling to his knees before the makeshift shrine set up on the floor beside his bed.

Candles burned with a scented, smoky aroma, flickering in the breeze wafting from the recyc-units and long strips of prayer papers covered in Pasanius's spidery handwriting lay curled at their bases. Pasanius lifted a strip of gilt-edged paper with bloody fingertips, reading the words of penance and confession written there, though he knew them by heart. He raised his gleaming bionic hand, spreading his fingers and placing it palm-down upon his bloody chest, cut with the form of an eagle with outstretched wings.

Pasanius dragged his hand down his chest, smearing the congealed blood across its gleaming metal while mouthing the confessional words written on the paper. As he finished the words, he lowered the paper into the wavering flame of the candle and held it there until it caught light. Hungry flames licked up the length of the prayer paper, greedily consuming the words written there and scorching the tips of his fingers black.

The paper crumbled to flaking, orange-limned embers, disintegrating in his hands and drifting gently to the floor. The last ember fell from his hand and Pasanius slammed his clenched silver fist into the wall of his quarters, punching a deep crater in the bulkhead.

He brought his hand up in front of his face to stare at the terrible damage. His metal fingers were cracked and bent by the force of the impact, but Pasanius wept bitter tears of disgust and self-loathing as he watched the tips of his fingers shimmer and straighten until not so much as a single scratch remained.

'Forgive me...' he whispered.

URIEL EJECTED A spent magazine from his bolter and smoothly slapped a fresh one into the weapon as another enemy came at him from the doorway of the building before him. He rolled aside as a flurry of las-bolts kicked up the sand and rose to a shooting position beside a pile of discarded ammo crates. The movement so natural he was barely conscious of making it, he sighted along the top of his bolter and squeezed off a single round, blasting his target's head off with one well-aimed shot.

Another shooter snapped into view on the building's parapet and he adjusted his aim and put another shell squarely through the chest of this latest threat. Pasanius ran for the building's door as Uriel scanned the upper windows and surrounding rooftops for fresh targets. None presented themselves and he returned his attention to the main door as Pasanius smashed it from its hinges in a shower of splinters.

Uriel broke cover and ran for the building as Pasanius gave him covering fire, hearing the distinctive snap of lasgun shots and the answering roar of a bolter. As he reached the building, he slammed into the wall. Pasanius hurled a grenade through the door before ducking back as the thunder of the explosion blasted from within.

'Go!' shouted Pasanius. Uriel rolled from his position beside the door and plunged within the smoke-filled hell of the room. Bodies littered the floor and acrid smoke billowed from the explosion, but Uriel's armour's auto-senses penetrated the blinding fog with ease, showing him two enemies still standing. He put the first one down and Pasanius shot the second in the head.

Room by room, floor by floor, the two Ultramarines swept through the building, killing another thirty targets before declaring it clear. Since the door had been broken down, all of four minutes had passed.

Uriel removed his helmet and ran a hand across his scalp, his breathing even and regular, despite a training exercise that would have had even the fittest human warrior gulping great draughts of air into their lungs.

'Four minutes,' he said. 'Not good. Chaplain Clausel would have had us fasting for a week after a performance like that.'

'Aye,' agreed Pasanius, also removing his helm. 'It is not the same without his hymnals while we train. We are losing our edge. I do not feel the necessity to excel here.'

'I know what you mean, but it is an honour to have the skills we do and it is our duty to the Chapter to hone them to the highest levels,' said Uriel, checking the action of his bolter and whispering the words of prayer that honoured the weapon's war spirit. Both men had offered prayers, applying the correct oils and rites of firing before even loading them. Such devotion to a weapon was common among the fighting men and women of the Imperium, but to a Space Marine his boltgun was much more than simply a weapon. It was a divine instrument of the Emperor's will, the means by which His wrath was brought to bear upon those who would defy the Imperium.

Despite his words, Uriel knew that Pasanius spoke true when he talked of losing their edge. Four minutes to clear a building of such size was nothing short of amazing, but he knew they could have done it faster, more efficiently, and the idea of not performing as well as he knew he could was galling to him.

Since he had been six years old and inducted to the Agiselus Barracks, he had been the best at everything he had turned his hand to. Only Learchus had equalled him in his achievements and the possibility that he was not the best he could be was a deeply disturbing notion. Pasanius was right – without the constant drilling and training they were used to as part of a Space Marine Chapter, Uriel could feel his skill diminish with every passing day they travelled from Macragge.

'Still,' continued Pasanius. 'Perhaps we need not be the best any more, perhaps we no longer owe the Chapter anything at all.'

Uriel's head snapped up, shocked at the very idea and shocked at the ease with which Pasanius had voiced it.

'What are you talking about?'

'Do you still feel that we are Space Marines of the Emperor?' asked Pasanius.

'Of course I do. Why should we not?'

'Well, we were cast out, disgraced, and are no longer Ultramarines,' continued Pasanius, staring vacantly into space, his voice wavering and unsure. 'But are we still Space Marines? Do we still need to train like this? If we are not Space Marines, then what are we?'

Pasanius lifted his head and met his gaze, and Uriel was surprised at the depths of anguish he saw. His former sergeant's soul was bared and Uriel could see the terrible hurt it bore at their expulsion from the

Chapter. He reached out and placed his hand on Pasanius's unadorned shoulder guard.

Uriel could understand his friend's pain, once again feeling guilty that Pasanius shared the disgrace that should have been his and his alone.

'We will always be Space Marines, my friend,' affirmed Uriel. 'And no matter what occurs, we will continue to observe the battle rituals of our Chapter. Wherever we are or whatever we do, we will always be warriors of the Emperor.'

Pasanius nodded. 'I know that,' he said at last. 'But at night, terrible doubts plague me and there is no one aboard this vessel I can confess to. Chaplain Clausel is not here and I cannot go to the shrine of the primarch and pray for guidance.'

'You can talk to me, Pasanius, always. Are we not comrades in arms, battle-brothers and friends?'

'Aye, Uriel, we will always be that, but you too are condemned alongside me. We are outcast and your words are like dust in the wind to me. I crave the spiritual guidance of one who is pure and unsullied by disgrace. I am sorry.'

Uriel turned away from his friend, wishing he knew what to say, but he was no Chaplain and did not know the right words to bring Pasanius the solace he so obviously yearned for.

But even as he struggled for words of reassurance, a treacherous voice within him wondered if Pasanius might be right.

URIEL AND PASANIUS made their way back down through the bullet-riddled training building and the mangled remains of thirty-seven servitor-controlled opponents, their plastic and mesh bodies torn apart by the Space Marines' mass-reactive bolter shells. Exiting the training building, they made their way through the packed gymnasia, heading towards one of the vessel's many chapels of veneration. With their firing rites complete, their rigidly maintained routine now called for them to make obeisances to their primarch and the Emperor.

The lights in the gymnasia began to dim, telling Uriel that the starship was close to entering its night-cycle, though true night and day were meaningless concepts aboard a starship. Despite that, Captain Laskaris enforced strictly timetabled lights out and reveille calls to more quickly acclimatise the passengers of *Calth's Pride* to the onboard ship time. It was a common phenomenon that many soldiers had trouble adjusting to life aboard a space-faring vessel; the enforced claustrophobia along with dozens of other privations caused by ship-board life resulting in vastly increased instances of violence and disorder.

But the regiments currently being transported within the ship's gargantuan hull had been raised in Ultramar, and those trained within the military barracks of the Ultramarines' realm were used to a far harsher discipline than that enforced by the ship's crew and armsmen.

The gymnasia was a vast, stone columned chamber, fully ninety metres from sanded floor to arched ceiling and at least a thousand wide. An entire regiment or more could comfortably train in shooting, close-quarter combat, infiltration, fighting in jungle terrain or the nightmare of city-fighting. These dedicated arenas were sectioned off throughout the gymnasia, fully realised environments where thousands of soldiers were receiving further training before reaching their intended warzone far in the galactic north-west. Row upon row

of battle-flags hung from the ceiling, and huge
anthracene statues of great heroes of Ultramar lined
the walls. Stained-glass windows, lit from behind by
flickering glow-globes, depicted the life of Roboute
Guilliman as looped prayers in High Gothic echoed
from flaring trumpets blown by alabaster angels
mounted on every column.

'Good men and women,' noted Uriel as he watched
a group of soldiers practising bayonet drills against
one another.

Despite their discipline, Uriel could see many of
the training soldiers casting confused glances their
way. He knew that their armour, bereft of the insignia
of the Ultramarines, would no doubt be causing endless speculation amongst the regiments billeted
within the ship.

'Aye,' nodded Pasanius. 'The Macragge 808th. Most
will have come from Agiselus.'

'Then they will fight well,' said Uriel. 'A shame we
cannot train with them. There is much they could
learn and it would have been an honour for us to pass
on our experience.'

'Perhaps,' said Pasanius. 'Though I do not believe
their officers would have counted it as such. I feel we
may be a disappointment to many of them. A disgraced Space Marine is no hero; he is worthless, less
than nothing.'

Uriel glanced round at Pasanius, surprised by the
venom in his tone.

'Pasanius?' he said.

Pasanius shook his head, as though loosing a quiet
unease, and smiled, though Uriel could see the falsity
of it. 'I am sorry, Uriel, my sleep was troubled. I'm not
used to having so much of it. I keep waiting for a bellowing Chaplain Clausel to sound reveille.'

'Aye,' agreed Uriel, forcing a smile. 'More than three hours of sleep a night is a luxury. Be careful you do not get too used to it, my friend.'

'Not likely,' said Pasanius, gloomily.

URIEL KNELT BEFORE the dark marble statue of the Emperor, the flickering light from the hundreds of candles that filled the chapel reflecting a hundredfold on its smooth-finished surface. A fug of heavily scented smoke filled the upper reaches of the chapel from the many burners that lined the nave, smelling of nalwood and sandarac. Chanting priests, clutching prayer beads and burning tapers, paced the length of the chapel, muttering and raving silently to themselves while albino-skinned cherubs with flickering golden wings and cobalt-blue hair bobbed in the air above them, long lengths of prayer paper trailing from dispensers in their bellies.

Uriel ignored them, holding the wire-wound hilt of his power sword in a two-handed grip while resting his hands on the gold quillons. The sword was unsheathed, point down on the floor, and Uriel rested his forehead on the carven skull of its pommel as he prayed.

The sword was the last gift to him from Captain Idaeus, his former mentor, and though it had been broken on Pavonis – a lifetime ago it seemed now – Uriel had forged a new blade of his own before departing on the crusade to Tarsis Ultra and his eventual disgrace. He wondered what Idaeus would have made of his current situation and gave thanks that he was not here to see what had become of his protégé.

Pasanius knelt beside him, eyes shut and lips moving in a silent benediction. Uriel found it hard to countenance the dark, brooding figure Pasanius had become since leaving the Fortress of Hera. True, they had been cast from the Chapter, their homeworld and battle-brothers, but they still had a duty to perform, an oath to fulfil, and a Space Marine never turned his back on such obligations, especially not an Ultramarine.

Uriel knew that Pasanius was a warrior of courage and honour and just hoped that he had the strength of character to lift himself from this ill disposition, remembering sitting in a chapel not dissimilar to this in one of the medicae buildings on Tarsis Ultra, vexed by torments of his own. He also recalled the beautiful face of the Sister of the Order Hospitaller he had met there. Sister Joaniel Ledoyen she had been called, and she had spoken to him with a wisdom and clarity that had cut through his pain.

Uriel had meant to return to the medicae building after the fighting, but had been too badly injured in the final assault on the hive ship to do anything other than rest as Apothecary Selenus struggled to remove the last traces of the tyranid phage-cell poisoning from his bloodstream.

When he had been well enough to move, it was already time to depart for Macragge, and he had not had the time to thank her for her simple kindness. He wondered what had become of her and how she had fared in the aftermath of the alien invasion. Wherever she was, Uriel wished her well.

He finished his prayers, standing and kissing the blade of his sword before sheathing it in one economical motion. He bowed to the statue of the Emperor and made the sign of the aquila across his chest, glancing down at Pasanius as he continued to pray.

He frowned as he noticed some odd marks protruding from the gorget of Pasanius's armour. Standing above him, Uriel could see that the marks began at the nape of Pasanius's neck before disappearing out of sight beneath his armour. The crusting of scar tissue told Uriel that they were wounds, recent wounds, instantly clotted by the Larraman cells within their bloodstream.

But how had he come by such marks?

Before Uriel could ask, he felt a presence behind him and turned to see one of the priests, a youngish man with haunted eyes, staring at him in rapt fascination.

'Preacher,' said Uriel, respectfully.

'No, not yet!' yelped the priest, twisting his prayer beads round and around his wrists in ever tighter loops. 'No, no preacher am I. A poor cenobite, only, my angel of death.'

Uriel could see the man's palms were slick with blood and wondered what manner of order he belonged to. There were thousands of recognised sects within the Imperium and this man could belong to any one of them. He scanned the man's robes for some clue, but his deep blue chasuble and scapular were unadorned save for their silver fastenings.

'Can I help you with something?' pressed Uriel as Pasanius rose to his feet and stood by his side.

The man shook his head. 'No,' he cackled with a lop-sided grin. 'Already dead am I. The Omphalos Daemonium comes! I feel it pushing out from the inside of my skull. He will take me and everyone else for his infernal engine. Deadmorsels for his furnace, flesh for his table and blood for his chalice.'

Uriel shared a sidelong glance at Pasanius and rolled his eyes, realising that the cenobite was utterly insane, a common complaint amongst the more zealous of the Emperor's followers. Such unfortunates were deemed to exist on a level closer to the divine Emperor and allowed to roam free that their ravings might be grant some clue to the will of the Immortal Master of Mankind.

'I thank you for your words, preacher,' said Uriel, 'but we have completed our devotions and must take our leave.'

'No,' said the cenobite emphatically.

'No? What are you talking about?' asked Uriel, beginning to lose patience with the lunatic priest. Like most of the Adeptus Astartes, the Ultramarines had a strained relationship with the priests of the Ministorum; the Space Marines' belief that the Emperor was the mightiest mortal to bestride the galaxy, but a mortal nonetheless, diametrically opposed to the teachings of their Ecclesiarch.

'Can you not hear it, son of Calth? Juddering along the bloodtracks, its hateful boxcars jolting along behind it?'

'I don't hear anything,' said Uriel, stepping around the cenobite and marching towards the chapel's iron door.

'You will,' promised the man.

Uriel turned as a monotonous servitor's voice crackled from the electrum-plated vox-units mounted in the shadows of the arched ceiling, announcing: 'All hands prepare for warp translation. Warp translation in thirty seconds.'

The cenobite laughed, spittle frothing at the corners of his mouth as he raised his torn forearms above his head. Blood ran from his opened wrists and spattered his face before rolling down his cheeks like ruby tears.

He dropped to his knees and whispered, 'Too late... the Lord of Skulls comes.'

A spasm of sickness sheared along Uriel's spine as the last words left the cenobite's mouth and he stepped towards the man, ready to chastise him for uttering such blasphemies in this sanctified place.

The lights in the chapel dimmed as the ship prepared for warp translation.

Uriel dragged the young preacher to his feet.

And the cenobite's head exploded.

CHAPTER TWO

BLOOD GEYSERED IN slow motion from the ragged stump of the cenobite's neck and Uriel pushed his spasming corpse away in disgust, backing away and wiping the sticky fluid from his face. The body remained upright, jerking and thrashing as though in the grip of a violent seizure. The cenobite's arms flailed wildly, yet more blood flickering from his opened wrists and spattering the statuary and altar.

Even as he stared in horrified fascination at the corpse's lunatic dance, Uriel felt the familiar sensation of his primary stomach flipping as the ship jumped into the treacherous currents of the warp. He gripped one of the chapel's pews as he felt a sudden dizziness, which vanished seconds later as his Lyman's ear adjusted for the sudden spatial differentiation between dimensions.

The hideous corpse continued to thrash and convulse, refusing to fall despite its lack of a head, and

Uriel tasted the unmistakable sensation of warp-spawned witchery on the air. The man's fellow priests wailed in terror, dropping to their knees and spilling prayers of protection and mercy from mouths open wide in horror. Some, made of sterner stuff, drew pistols from beneath their robes and aimed them at the dancing corpse.

'No!' shouted Uriel, drawing his sword and leaping towards the hideous revenant. It lunged towards him, arms outstretched, but a sweeping stroke of Uriel's blade clove it from collarbone to pelvis and the shorn halves of the man fell to the marble floor, twitching, but mercifully free of whatever monstrous animation had possessed it before.

'Guilliman's blood!' swore Pasanius, backing away from the dead cenobite and making the sign of the aquila over his chest. 'What happened to him?'

'I have no idea,' said Uriel, kneeling beside the corpse and wiping his blade on the cenobite's chasuble as the lights in the chapel began flashing urgently. Wailing klaxons and ringing bells could be heard from beyond the chapel door.

Uriel smoothly rose to his feet, saying, 'But I have a feeling we'll find out soon.'

He turned and ran back to the chapel door, grabbing his bolter from the gun rack beside the entrance to the vestry. Pasanius scooped up his flamer and followed him out into the corridor, drawing up sharply as he saw what lay beyond the chapel door.

BOTH MEN STOOD transfixed as the arched passageway before them swelled and rippled, as though in a diabolical heat haze, its dimensions swelling and distorting beyond the three known to man.

'Imperator!' breathed Pasanius in terror. 'The Geller field must be failing. The warp is spilling in!'

'And Emperor alone knows what else,' said Uriel, his dread of the unknown terrors of the warp sending a shiver of fear along his spine. Without the Geller field to protect the ship from the predatory astral and daemonic creatures that swam in the haunted depths of the immaterium, all manner of foul entities would have free rein within the vessel's halls, ethereal horrors and shadowy phantoms that could rip men to shreds before vanishing back into the warp.

'Come on,' shouted Uriel. 'The gymnasia. We need to gather as many soldiers as we can before it's too late.'

Uriel and Pasanius lurched their way along the passageway, stumbling like a pair of drunks as they fought to hold their equilibrium in the face of this spatial insanity. Screams and roars came from ahead, but Uriel found himself unable to pinpoint exactly where ahead was as sounds echoed and distorted wildly around him. The floors and ceilings of the stone passageways seemed to run fluid, swirling as though their very fabric was being unravelled before his eyes.

The sound of a tolling bell rang out, ponderously slow and dolorous one second, tinny and ringing the next. Using the wall as a guide, though it was a treacherous one, the two Space Marines fought their way onwards, each step bringing fresh madness to their surroundings.

Uriel thought he saw a tall mountain, wreathed in smoke, form from the floor before it vanished and was replaced by a roiling sea of snapping mouths. But even that disappeared like a fever dream as soon as he tried to look upon it. He could see Pasanius was having similar difficulties, blinking and rubbing his eyes in disbelief.

A grainy static filled Uriel's vision and an insistent buzzing, like an approaching swarm of insects, filled his skull. He shook his head, trying to clear the distortion and unable to comprehend the things he saw before him.

'How close are we?' yelled Pasanius.

Uriel steadied himself on a bulkhead, grateful for its transitory solidity, and shook his head again, though the movement made him want to vomit. 'How can we tell? Everything changes the moment I look at it.'

'I think we are almost there,' said Pasanius, pointing to where the passageway widened into a marble-flagged atrium, though at present, it appeared that the chamber had been inverted, its domed ceiling swirling below their feet, its dimensions skewed completely out of true.

Uriel nodded and pushed himself forward, an intense and nauseous sensation of vertigo seizing him as they stumbled into the flipped atrium. Uriel's eyes told him he was crossing the floor, but he could tell that his every step found him crossing the shallow concave bowl of the inverted dome. His booted feet trod the shielded glass of the atrium's dome that was all that lay between him and the warp.

Uriel looked down through the dome, the nauseous sensation in his gut surging upwards, and he dropped to his knees, vomiting explosively across the glass. A sickly mass of bruised colours foamed and swirled beyond the glass, the very stuff of the warp itself, noxious and toxic to the eye. Its bilious malevolence went beyond its simple hideous appearance, violating some inner part of the human mind that dared not comprehend its nightmarish potential.

Uriel found his eyes drawn to a loathsome stain of the warp, a vile, filthy sore of ash-stained yellow, he was unable to drag his sight from. Even as he stared at it, the warp shifted, stirred into life by the mere attention and echoes of Uriel's thoughts. Vile, terrible things began shaping themselves from the foul soup of raw creation and Uriel knew that were he to see what horrific thing would be born from its hateful depths, he would go mad.

Gauntleted hands gripped him and hauled him upright, and he could feel the warp's blind, impotent rage at being denied such a morsel as his sanity.

'Don't look at it! Keep your eyes closed!' shouted Pasanius, dragging Uriel over the surface of the dome. Uriel felt its insistent call; the seductions of its fecundity and the promises of power that could be his were he but to surrender to it. His eyes ached to see the awful magnificence of the warp, but Uriel kept them screwed tightly shut, lest they betray his soul to the immaterium.

Breathless and disgusted, Uriel and Pasanius clambered from the atrium and crawled away from the false seductions of the warp, the feelings of sickness diminishing the further they went.

Uriel looked up, coughing stringy, vomit-flecked spittle and said, 'Thank you, my friend.'

Pasanius nodded and said, 'There. The entrance to the gymnasia should be through that cloister!'

'Aye, it should be,' agreed Uriel pushing himself weakly to his feet. 'Let's just hope it is still there.'

Uriel stumbled through the cloister and turned towards the entrance to the gymnasia.

'Oh no...' he whispered as he saw what lay before him.

Where he had expected to find the carven marble archway of the gymnasia, there was now a gargantuan gateway of brazen metal: bronze and laced with razorwire that led into a rectangular, earthen arena which was fully a kilometre wide and twice that in length. More incredible still, there was no roof to this arena, simply a lacerated crimson sky, flecked with cancerous, melanoma clouds. What new madness was this?

Screaming, mad and insane like the wails of the damned in torment, echoed from within and pierced Uriel's skull with lancing, glass shards of pain.

His stomach knotted in horrified disgust as the overpowering reek of fresh blood filled his senses.

The soldiers of the 808th Macragge they had come to find were still here, but where there had once been a proud regiment of men and women ready to fight for the glory of the Emperor, there was now nothing more than the screaming, bloody shreds of those yet to die.

Hundreds of soldiers writhed on the ground, splashing great gouts of blood around them as though fighting some subterranean attacker. Fleshless, bony hands reached up through the dark earth, clawing and grasping at their bodies and dragging them below the surface. Uriel ran through the gate, sword in hand, and felt his boots sink into the soft and loamy ground, crimson liquid oozing from the waterlogged earth.

Bones and grinning skulls gleamed whitely through the red earth and Uriel saw that the ground was not waterlogged at all, but flooded with fresh-spilled blood.

His mind reeled at the prospect. How many must have been drained of their life's blood to irrigate such a vast space so thoroughly? How many arteries had been emptied to slake the vile thirst of this dark, dark earth?

Uriel was shaken from his disgust by the nearby screams of a man half submerged in the earth and weeping tears of agony.

'Help me! For the love of the Emperor help me!' he shrieked.

Uriel sheathed his sword and ran over to help the man, who reached up with pleading arms. The man's gore-slick hands slid from his gauntlets, but Uriel gripped his tunic and hauled him clear of the ground, staggering back in horror as he saw that the man had been stripped of flesh below the waist, his entire lower body flensed of muscle, meat and blood. Even as he watched, the hungry earth swallowed what remained of the dying man, unwilling to be cheated of its fleshy morsel.

A sense of utter helplessness filled Uriel as he watched men and women devoured by the bloody ground, the monstrous sound of marrow being suckled from the bone echoing from the monolithic sides of this gory arena.

'Blessed Emperor, no!' wailed Pasanius, fighting to save a howling woman from a similar fate. Laughing shadows ran like black mercury along the walls of the arena, a capering dance of souls that flared into the blood-red sky as the slaughter of thousands concluded.

A sudden silence descended upon the arena as the last of the bloody ground's helpless victims were dragged beneath its thirsting depths. No sooner had the last body vanished from sight, when a throaty gurgling erupted from the centre of the arena and Uriel saw a long strip of rockcrete slowly rise from the soaking ground. Dull, bloody rail tracks arose with it, running across the middle of the arena and ending at opposite walls.

The hateful silence was broken by a sibilant moaning, as of a thousand voices trapped in a nightmare they know they will never wake from.

'Holy Emperor, protect us from evil, grant us the strength of spirit and body to fight your enemies and smite them with your blessing,' prayed Pasanius.

'Too late,' whispered Uriel, drawing his sword and standing ready to fight whatever new monstrosity the warp might unleash. 'We failed.'

No… you have not yet begun…

Both Uriel and Pasanius spun, searching for the source of the voice.

'Did you hear that?' said Uriel.

'Aye,' nodded Pasanius, 'I think so, but it felt… felt as though it was inside my head. Something terrible is coming, Uriel.'

'I know. But whatever comes, we will fight it with courage and honour.'

'Courage and honour,' agreed Pasanius, firing the igniters on the nozzle of his flamer.

'Let's go,' said Uriel grimly, nodding towards the dripping platform in the centre of the arena. 'Whatever is coming, we'll meet it head on!'

Pasanius followed his former captain as they made their way across the hideously squelching ground towards the platform.

As they mounted its steps, the source of the sibilant moaning was finally revealed.

Each sleeper laid between the rail tracks was a jigsaw of bodies and limbs, writhing in agony and knotted together by some dark sorcery. They screamed in lunatic delirium, their voices piteous and heartbreaking. Though he knew none of the faces, the cast of their features told Uriel that they were of the stock of Ultramar and that the souls of those consumed by this abominable place were suffering still.

Eyes and mouths churning in the fluid matter of each sleeper gave anguished voice to their suffering before being forced from form to formlessness that another soul might vent its endless purgatory.

Uriel's hatred swelled within him at such horror and he closed his eyes...

Splintering crystals of alternate existences clash and jangle, detaching from the walls of one plane and shifting their position to resonate at a different frequency. Echoes in time allow the planes to shift and change; altering the angles of reality to allow the dimensions to unlock, dancing in a ballet of all possibilities.

...then opened them as he felt a sickening vibration deep in his bones and a restlessness ripple through the air. The jagged stumps of bone jutting through the ground retreated into its sanguineous depths and the moaning sleepers wept with renewed anguish.

Where the rail tracks vanished into the walls of this vast courtyard, streamers of multi-coloured matter were oozing from the stonework.

Rippling spirals of reflective light coiled from the mortar, twisting the image behind like a warped lens. The walls seemed to stretch, as though being sucked into an unseen vortex behind, until there was nothing left but a rippling veil of impenetrable darkness, a tunnel into madness ringed with screaming skulls sent out to die.

Warped realms, a universe and lifetimes distant, flow together, joining all points in time on the bronze bloodtracks. On a journey that leads everywhere and begins nowhere, the Omphalos Daemonium pushes itself from nothingness to form. Snaking from its daemonic womb and leaving nothing but barren rape and death in its wake.

And the Omphalos Daemonium came.

THOUGH THE CENOBITE had raved of the might and power of the Omphalos Daemonium's evil, they had been but the merest hints of the thing's diabolical majesty. Roaring from the newly formed tunnel mouth like a brazen juggernaut of the end times, the Omphalos Daemonium shrieked along the bloodtracks towards the horrified Space Marines.

Vast bone-pistons drove it forward, iron and steel flanks heaving with immaterial energies. Bloody steam leaked from every demented, skull-faced rivet as wheels of tortured souls ground the tracks beneath it to feast on the oozing blood of the dead earth.

Deep within its insane structure, it might have once resembled an ancient steam-driven locomotive, but unknown forces and warped energies had transformed it into something else entirely. The thunder of its arrival could be felt by senses beyond the pitiful five known to humankind, echoing through the planes that existed and intersected beyond the veil of reality.

Behind it came a tender of dark iron and a juddering procession of boxcars, their timbers stained with aeons of blood and ordure. Uriel knew without knowing that millions had been carried to their deaths in these hellish containers, carried to whatever loathsome destination this horrifying machine desired before finally being exterminated. The vast daemon engine slowed, the sleepers driven beyond sound in their torment as the towering machine halted at the edge of the platform.

Uriel thought he heard booming laughter and the grinding squeal of warped timber doors sliding open on runners rusted with gore.

Gusts of blood-laced steam hissed from the armoured hide of the Omphalos Daemonium and malevolent laughter rippled through them as they writhed on evil business of their own. Each tendril thickened and became more solid as they wormed towards the Space Marines and Uriel said, 'Stand ready.'

The tendrils of smoke vanished without warning and in their place stood eight figures, each wearing a featureless grey boiler-suit and knee-high boots with rusted buckles along the shins. Each carried a fearsome array of knives, hooks and saws on their leather belts.

Their faces were human in proportion only, flensed of the disguise of skin and glistening with revealed musculature. Crude stitches crisscrossed their skulls, and when they turned their heads as though hunting by scent, Uriel saw they were utterly featureless save for distended and fanged mouths. They had no eyes, nose or ears, only discoloured swellings that bulged and rippled beneath their fleshless skulls.

'Daemons!' shouted Uriel. 'Foul abominations! Come forth and die on my blade.'

A daemon's patchwork face swung towards him, tumourous tissue in its neck bulging with horrid appetite. None of the foul creatures moved, content merely to watch the two Space Marines as a billowing cloud of steam vented from the side of the vast daemon engine. With a clang of locks disengaging, a thick iron door squealed open and a gigantic figure stepped onto the platform.

Standing head and shoulders above them, the giant wore a clanking, mechanical suit of riveted iron plates and thick sheets of melted, vulcanised rubber. Over its rusted armour it wore a charred apron, and a crown of blackened horns sprouted from a conical helmet with a raised visor. For all its crude fabrication and disrepair, Uriel recognised the armour as impossibly ancient power armour, such as had been worn by warriors of legend many thousands of years ago. The stench of scorched meat enfolded it, together with a

crackling sensation of depraved evil and unquench-
able rage.

One shoulder guard was studded with star-shaped
rivets, the other emblazoned with a symbol of ancient
malice that both Ultramarines recalled from the
depths of righteous anger instilled in them by Chaplain Clausel's daily Litanies of Hate. A grinning,
iron-visored skull that once was the heraldry of a
Legion that had fought for the Emperor in hallowed
antiquity, but was now a symbol of unending bitterness and hatred. It was a symbol that now belonged to
the most lethal foes of the Imperium: warriors of unut-
terable evil and malice – the Chaos Space Marines.

'Iron Warriors...' hissed Uriel.

'The Betrayers of Istvaan,' growled Pasanius.

The figure carried a long, iron-hafted billhook, the
broad, curved blade rusted and pitted with reddish
brown stains. A pair of burning yellow eyes, like sickly,
dying suns, shone from beneath the helmet as the figure took a heavy step towards them, the skinless
daemons moving to stand behind it.

'Deadmorsels feed the new fire, blood is supped by
the faceless Sarcomata, and flesh of man will come
with me,' said the figure, its voice like rusted metal on
their skulls.

It gripped its enormous billhook in one blackened,
burned hand and beckoned them impatiently towards
the hissing daemon engine with the other.

'Come!' boomed the giant. 'I have purpose for you.
Obey me or the Slaughterman turn you into deadmorsels! I am the Omphalos Daemonium and my will
drives this suit of flesh, and it will turn you into deadmorsels! Now come!'

Uriel felt sickened even being near this thing of
Chaos. Could it really believe that they would willingly

have truck with such evil? The featureless daemons, which Uriel guessed were the Sarcomata the Omphalos Daemonium spoke of, spread out on the platform, unhooking long, serrated knives from their belts.

'Courage and honour!' yelled Uriel, leaping towards the nearest of the Sarcomata and stabbing for its belly. His sword passed straight through the creature, its form transforming into a cackling pillar of red steam. He pulled up in surprise, grunting in pain as the beast's form coalesced beside him and its blade slashed across his cheek. Another darted in, its rusty blade stabbing into his neck. He twisted free of the weapon before it could penetrate more than a centimetre and swung at his new attacker. Once again, his assailant flashed to steam before his blow could land and Uriel found himself off balance as another knife blade laid his cheek open to the bone.

'Burn, Chaos filth!' roared Pasanius and sprayed a blazing gout of promethium at the giant Iron Warrior. The volatile chemical flames licked hungrily at the giant, but no sooner had the fire taken than it guttered and died.

The creature's booming laughter echoed from the sides of the arena. 'I have been a prisoner in flames for aeons and liveflesh thinks it can burn me!'

Pasanius slung his flamer and reached for his pistol, but, with a speed that belied its ungainly form, the Chaos creature stepped forward, wrapping its blackened fingers around Pasanius's throat and hauling him from his feet.

Uriel slashed at the Sarcomata as they surrounded him, each thrust and sweep of his sword hitting nothing but chuckling tendrils of steam that vanished only to reappear elsewhere to cut him. Clotted blood caked his face and he knew that he could not fight such foes for much longer.

He saw the giant in the rusted armour lift Pasanius from his feet and hurl him through the iron door the Omphalos Daemonium had first stepped from, and surged towards the Chaos creature. He could not fight foes that could disappear at will, but he swore that this traitor from the elder days would die by his hand. He swung his sword towards the Iron Warrior, the blade wreathed in pellucid flames able to cut through armour and flesh with equal ease.

The sword struck his enemy full square on the chest, but the blade simply clanged from the heavy iron plates of his armour. Uriel was amazed, but drew his arm back to attack again. Before he could strike, the Iron Warrior's fist slammed into his face, sending him sprawling across the platform.

He fought to regain his senses, but the Sarcomata surrounded him, their blackened fingers reaching hungrily for him. Their touch felt like rotted meat, wriggling with the suggestion of maggots and freshly hatched larvae. Their dead skin masks were centimetres from his face, their breath like a furnace of cadavers. They moved their undulating faces around his, as though tasting his scent, their fearsome strength pinning him to the ground.

'The Sarcomata favour you, Ultramarine...' laughed the giant, striding across the platform towards him. 'They are corruption of spirit given form and purpose. Perhaps they sense a certain kinship?'

Uriel waited for death as one of the Sarcomata lowered its mouth to his bared neck, but the Omphalos Daemonium had greater purpose for him than mere murder, and roared in impatience.

The skinless daemons hissed in submission, hauling Uriel from the platform and carrying him towards the iron door of the massive daemon engine.

Burning air and the stench of cooked meat gusted from within, and as he was carried inside, Uriel knew that they were truly damned.

CHAPTER THREE

BLOOD. THE STENCH of it filled his nostrils, overpowering and sickening, the bitter, metallic taste catching in the back of his throat. His neuroglottis sifted hundreds of different blood-scents and the searing tang of burning flesh made his eyes water before his occulobe compensated and secreted a protective membrane across the surface of his eye.

He blinked away the moisture, twisting in the grip of the Sarcomata and trying to get a bearing on his surroundings. Despite what his eyes told him, he knew he must be seeing things, for the interior of the daemon engine confounded his senses and flouted any notion of reality. It defied geometry, impossibly arching beyond the limits of vision to either side: a sweltering, red-lit hell cavern. A wide-doored firebox roared and seethed at one end of the chamber and long lines of dangling chains and pulleys, each with a limbless human torso skewered on a rusted hook, hung from the darkened, dripping roof.

He and Pasanius were dragged past scattered mounds of human limbs, each piled higher than a battle tank, the flesh rotten and stinking. Two of the Sarcomata slithered away from Uriel to lift a headless torso and thrust it into the firebox.

They stoked the daemon engine with flesh and blood, its belching stacks spewing ashen bodies into the air. The giant in the armour of the Iron Warriors dragged Pasanius behind it, the mighty sergeant helpless against such power.

'No!' shouted Uriel as the Omphalos Daemonium dropped its billhook and easily lifted Pasanius with one hand while reaching for an empty hook with the other. The iron giant took no notice of him and rammed the rusted hook into the backplate of Pasanius's armour, drawing a grunt of pain from him.

Uriel struggled all the harder as he saw an empty hook hanging beside Pasanius, but the Sarcomata held him firm and he could not break their hold. Fleshy, wriggling hands lifted him high and he gritted his teeth to stop himself from crying out as he too was spitted on a hook, the barbed point went through his armour and pierced his back. The Sarcomata hissed and drew back, the lumpen growths beneath their exposed flesh rippling in monstrous hunger.

The clang of mighty pistons echoed through the impossible structure, hissing spigots belching stinking clouds of oil-streaked steam and iron-grilled furnaces flaring with blue and green flames. Moans and the creaking of molten metal mingled with the chittering glee of the Sarcomata, and Uriel could imagine no more complete a vision of hell.

The Omphalos Daemonium watched their futile struggles and stepped forward, gripping Uriel's jaw in one blackened gauntlet. Uriel could taste the ash on its fingers and smell the cooked meat beneath. The creature… was it an Iron Warrior or some daemonic entity within the flesh of one? Uriel could not tell, and as it leaned close, its breath like the air from an exhumed grave, he kicked out, his boot ringing harmlessly from its ancient breastplate.

'You waste your energy, Ultramarine. It is not within your power or destiny to destroy me. Save your strength for the world of iron. You will need it.'

'Get away from me, you bastard abomination,' shouted Uriel, struggling in his captor's grip, despite the fiery pain from the hook gouging his back.

'It is pointless to resist,' said the Omphalos Daemonium. 'I have travelled the bloodtracks between realities for countless aeons and all things are revealed there. What has been, what is and all the things that might yet be. I have snuffed out lives yet to be born, changed unwritten histories and travelled paths no others may walk. And you think you can defy my will?'

'The Emperor is with us, yea though we walk in the shadows–' began Pasanius.

The Omphalos Daemonium smashed a gauntleted hand across Pasanius's chin, swinging him wildly around and drawing a hiss of pain from him as the hook in his back dug deeper into his flesh.

'Prayers to your corpse of a god mean nothing here. His power has gone out of the world and nothing now remains of him.'

'You lie,' snapped Uriel. 'The power of the Emperor is eternal.'

'Eternal?' snarled the Omphalos Daemonium. 'You would do well not to use such words so lightly until

you have experienced such a span, trapped and helpless and tormented beyond reason.'

The yellow eyes of the Omphalos Daemonium
burned into Uriel's and he saw the depthless rage and
madness within them. Whatever the malign intelligence that lurked within the ancient suit of power
armour was, it was clearly insane, the torments it
spoke of having driven it into a depthless abyss.

'What are you?' said Uriel eventually. 'What do you
want with us?'

The Omphalos Daemonium released its grip and
turned from him as the Sarcomata began gathering up
more body parts and carried them towards the furnace,
hurling legs, arms and heads into the flames.

'That is unimportant for now,' it said, pulling a thick
chain that hung beside the firebox and hauling on a
rusted lever with a thick, rubberised handle. 'All that
matters is that you are here and that, at this time, our
journeys follow the same path.'

Uriel felt the impossible room judder as the lever
was drawn back fully, the iron door they had been carried through shutting with a squeal of tortured metal.
Pain flared in his back as the hook twisted between his
ribs and the massive daemon engine began to move.
Cadavers on other hooks swung on their jangling
chains and Uriel felt the familiar churning sensation in
his belly of a warp translation. Was this infernal engine
somehow capable of traversing the currents of the
warp? Was that how it had managed to intercept
Calth's Pride within the treacherous shoals of the
immaterium?

He knew not to dwell too long on such things. The
asking of such dangerous questions led to the path of
deviation, the very thing that had seen them condemned to this fate.

The churning sensation in Uriel's stomach grew and he gritted his teeth against the growing pain. The Omphalos Daemonium turned from its labours and retrieved its billhook as the Sarcomata continued feeding the fires with corpses.

'Where are you taking us?' hissed Pasanius through gritted teeth.

'Where you need to go,' said the giant. 'I know of your death oath and what has led you here. The Lord of Skulls has more artifice to him than simply the art of death.'

'You are a daemon!' snarled Uriel. 'You are an abomination and I will see you destroyed.'

'Your skull will be laid before the throne of the Blood God before that happens, Space Marine. I have already seen the manner of your death; would you know of it?'

'The words of a daemon are lies!' shouted Pasanius. 'I will believe nothing you say.'

The Omphalos Daemonium slashed its billhook around, the blade flashing towards Pasanius's neck. Blood welled from a shallow cut across the sergeant's throat.

'You seek death, Ultramarine, and I would gladly rend and tear your soul. I would rip your flesh screaming from your bones and garland this body with your entrails, but your death is to be far worse than even one such as I could devise. Your skull will be honoured with a place in one of the bone mountains within sight of the Blood God.'

Another shudder, more intense, passed through the chamber and Uriel felt as though red-hot skewers were being pushed through his skull.

'You should honour me, for you travel in ways no mortal has dared for aeons.'

The Omphalos Daemonium raised its arms to the ceiling and laughed.

'We travel the bloodtracks. The Heart of Blood and the daemonculaba await!'

And the daemon engine roared into realms beyond existence.

URIEL SCREAMED.

Space folded, the currents of the warp vanishing; the arena, the daemon engine, the firebox, Pasanius. All disappeared, ripped away as everything around him turned inside out and became meaningless concepts. He felt himself simultaneously explode into a billion fragments and implode within himself, compressed to a singularity of hollow existence.

Faces floated before him, though as a dense ball of nothingness and a fragmented soul he knew not how he recognised them. Worlds and people, people and worlds, flashing past in a seamless blur, yet each as clear as though he examined each one in detail. Time slowed, yet rushed, splintering crystals sounding from far off as fractured realities ground and shifted like tectonic plates.

He saw the daemon engine spiral through the cracks between dimensions, snaking a path that wound through the shifting glass shards of reality, existing outside of everything, travelling in the slivers of null-space between all that was and all that ever could be.

He saw worlds of choking fumes, people in walking comas shuffling from one banal day to another, grey and dead without even the awareness to scream at the frustration of their pointless lives. Worlds where twisting numbers fell upon mountains of implausibility before running in molten rivers of algorithms to a sea of integers. It was gone in a heartbeat, replaced by a towering world of mountains and seas, white, marble and gold. Flames roared and seethed from every surface as the world burned, its people ashes on the wind, all life extinguished. Uriel, though he could no longer be sure he even knew who that was any more, saw with mounting horror that he knew this world. He saw the Fortress of Hera cast down, her once proud walls splintered and broken, the Temple of Correction no more than a shattered ruin. Daemons made sport in the Shrine of the Primarch, gnawing on his holy bones and defiling his sacred corpse.

He wept at such vileness, furious at his helplessness and incapable of wreaking his vengeance upon those who had visited such wrath upon Macragge.

Black, howling things closed on the daemon engine, unseen, slithering guardians of nothingness worming their way through the cracks to close on them.

The daemon engine had travelled the bloodtracks for millennia and knew that these blind sentinels were no threat to its terrifying power. Such guardian creatures fed on the souls of those unwitting fools who breached this realm by accident; madmen who pored over forgotten lore and forbidden magicks to unlock the gates between dimensions. Mortals who dared to travel to realms not meant for souls were devoured and made into yet more of the dark worms. The bloodtracks carried the daemon engine away from the toothless, questing mouths of the guardian creatures, its evil and power burning those that managed to approach too close.

Clockwork worlds, worlds taken by evil, worlds of elemental madness, worlds of chaos, worlds of insanity and worlds of arcing lightning. Everything was here. Every action that spawned a new realm of possibility could be found here and Uriel felt the knowledge of such things fill him as he hung from his hook, bleeding and raw.

The glue that held his fragile mind from sundering into pieces began to come undone, awful knowledge of the insignificance of being and the pointlessness of action tore at his sense of who he was and he desperately fought to hold onto his identity.

He was Uriel Ventris.

He was a warrior of the Emperor; sworn to defend His realm for as long as he lived.

He was a Space Marine.

His will was stronger, his purpose and determination greater than any other mortal man. He was in the belly of the beast and he would fight its corrupting touch.

He was… who…? His existence flickered and despite the protection of the daemon engine, he knew the madness that claimed the minds of the ignorant fools who sought such places out was enfolding him. He struggled to hold on as shards of his life began spiralling away from him, each spawning fresh realities within this terrifying multiverse.

Visions of potential and unwritten pasts floated past Uriel's eyes and he gasped as he saw alternate histories…

> slide past
>
> his eyes

He saw himself as a wrinkled ancient,
He saw himself as a young man,
Lying prone on a simple cot bed and
but one who was no longer a
surrounded by grieving family members.
Space Marine. He was a lean,
Here was his son, dark haired like him,
muscled farmer, toiling in the

but taller and with the look of a warrior.
cavern farms on his homeworld of
Uriel's heart swelled in pride and regret;
Calth. His features were soft and
pride in his son and regret
tinged with great regret
that this vision of his life could never be...
that this vision of his life could never be...
Both faded from his mind, though he craved to see more of them, to know the consequences of his life having travelled the road not taken. But such was not to be and other visions intruded on his sight.

Pavonis.

Black Bone Road.

Tarsis Ultra.

Medrengard?

What were these? Names of places or people? Memories or invention? Had he journeyed to these places? Was he from them? Were they his friends? He could taste the meaning on every jagged syllable, but none made sense, though he knew he should recognise them. Except... except there was one that did not have the subtle flavour of recognition. One that tasted of dark iron, that reeked of ashen pollutants, burning oil and echoed to the hammer of mountainous pile-drivers and pistons of hellish engines.

This world, that reality, was alien to him. Why now should it then intrude on his fracturing consciousness? It swelled in his perception, growing and filling what remained of his mind before it too vanished and his mind began to collapse inwards.

Nothing made sense any more; all was... dissolvingintamorassofinformation.Hecouldnolonge rholdontoanythingcoherent,feelinghisthoughts-blurandsoften,runninglikeahundredtributariesofa

thousandriversthatempteidintoaseaofoblivio-
nandhewelcomedit,knowingitwouldendthisscrea
mingmadnessinhishead.Aneternityoraninstant-
passedthoughhecouldnottellwhich–timewasnowa
meaninglessconcept,bereftofmeaningandrefer-
ence.

Avoicesoundedamidsttheinsanityandwhatlit-
tleremainedofUrielVentrisclutchedatit,asadrownin
gmangraspsforalifeline

'Fear not, Ultramarine,' it said. 'This journey is like all mortal life.'

The daemon engine roared back into the realm of existence.

'It ends…'

URIEL DREW BREATH, his hearts hammering fit to break his chest, his blood thundering around his body and his face streaked with crimson that wept from his eyes and nose. He had bitten his tongue and his mouth was filled with a coppery taste.

He spat, tasting the reek of fumes and the acrid, iron stench of industry. He lay still for long seconds as he tried to work out where he was. Above him was an unending vista of white, without depth or scale, and he blinked, reaching up to wipe the congealed blood from his face. His hand passed before his face and he was struck by a lurching sense of vertigo. He had a sudden sensation of falling and cried out, scrabbling around him for purchase.

His hands closed on a fine shale of metallic shavings and his vertigo vanished as he realised he was lying on his back and looking up into the sky – a dead sky, featureless and vacant without so much as a single cloud or speck to blight its horrid emptiness. He ached everywhere, his muscles weary to the point of exhaustion and a searing pain in his back from where his flesh had been gouged by the hook. His thoughts tumbled over themselves as he tried to piece together what had just happened.

He pushed himself upright, seeing Pasanius next to him, retching onto the metallic ground. His friend's face was drawn and hollow, as though the weight of the world had settled upon his shoulders.

'Get up,' said a grating voice behind him and a flood of memory filled Uriel's skull. Daemon. Daemon engine. He fought to stand, but his flesh was still adjusting to its return to existence and he could only stumble to his knees.

Before them stood the Omphalos Daemonium, gigantic and monstrous in its blackened and ancient suit of power armour. Behind their captor was a shimmering, impossible rectangle of seething red light, a doorway back to the hellish interior of the daemon engine.

It carried its billhook and stood ankle deep in the powdery shale of the ground. Their weapons, Uriel's sword and bolter together with Pasanius's pistol and flamer rested against the rocks beside it. White reflections of the dead sky glittered on its shoulder guards and it seemed to Uriel that the grinning, visored skull there burned with even more malice than before.

'You will need to restore your equilibrium soon, Ultramarines,' said the daemon thing with an echoing chuckle. 'The delirium spectres will hear the pounding beats of your hearts and such morsels as you shall not go unnoticed for long.'

'The what?' managed Uriel at last.

'Monsters,' said the giant.

'Monsters?' repeated Uriel, gritting his teeth and finally climbing to his feet. Pasanius picked himself up and stood beside him, his face ashen, but angry.

'The skins of murderers stitched across desecrated frames by the Savage Morticians and filled with the mad souls of those who have died by their hands,' explained the Omphalos Daemonium. 'They hunt in these mountains and you will know them by the cries of the damned at your heels.'

'Where are we?' said Pasanius. 'Where have you brought us?'

'This is Medrengard, world of bitter iron,' said the Omphalos Daemonium, pointing at something behind the two Space Marines. 'Domain of the daemon primarch, Perturabo. Can you not feel his presence on the air? The malice of a being who once walked with gods and is now cast down to dwell beyond the realm he once bestrode. Look upon this ashen world and despair!'

Uriel turned to where the Omphalos Daemonium was pointing, the breath catching in his throat as he saw the desolate vista before him.

They stood on a high, rocky plateau above a sweeping, grey hinterland of utter wretchedness. Far below them on the dismal steppe was a world of death. Uriel had thought the sweltering cavern of the daemon engine had been a vision of hell, but it had been no more than a prelude to this soul-destroying desolation. Vast expanses of industrial heartland sprawled across the surface of the world: steel skeletons of factories, mountains of coal and reddish slag and mighty, belching smoke stacks. Flames burned from blasted refineries, the pounding of mighty hammers and the clangourous screech of iron on stone audible from hundreds of kilometres away.

Uriel had seen pollution-choked hive worlds, planets teeming with uncounted billions who toiled ceaselessly in filthy, smog and soot-choked death worlds, but they were garden paradises compared to Medrengard.

He had even set foot on the iron surfaces of Adeptus Mechanicus forge worlds, the hallowed domains of the priests of the Machine God. He had been awed by the scale of their pounding infrastructure, their every surface given over to colossal manufactorum and cathedral forges, but even the mightiest of these worlds was but a village smithy compared to Medrengard.

Rivers of molten metal snaked like channels of lava and evil clouds of smoke wreathed each tall tower and fanged chimney in a halo of lethal fumes.

A vast, dark range of mountains towered over it all, blasted black rock where no living thing had ever lived or ever would. The peaks seemed to scrape the sky itself; the jagged stumps of the mountains a dozen or more times taller than the highest summit of Macragge. Uriel felt his blood chill as his eyes travelled up the terrifying heights of the enormous crags, seeing vile tendrils of noxious black smoke writhing from behind the mountains and clawing impossibly into the sky.

Strange turrets reared beyond the peaks and Uriel knew with awful certainty that some nightmare city lay concealed and brooding in the deep, dark valleys of that damnable mountain range. A city where walls and bastions spread across the ground and distant domes fouled the rock like fungi after the rain. It was a hideous, dead-ringed outpost of malice that was rightly abhorred by all living things. Tarnished steeples and stained walls, deathly weed-tangled spires and empty halls were filled with limping and shuffling ghosts in rags who blindly obeyed the loathsome will of the city's diabolical master: the daemon primarch Perturabo, lord and master of the Iron Warriors.

'The hate…' whispered Uriel. 'So much hate and bitterness.'

'Yes,' said the Omphalos Daemonium. 'Imagine all the rank bitterness I smell within you – poisoned and grown strong by millennia of vengeful brooding, and it is still but the merest fraction of how much a living god can hate.'

Uriel closed his eyes to shut out this nightmare vision, understanding that to take even a single step towards the dreadful city was to die, but its cyclopean immensity was etched forever in his mind such that nothing could ever remove it.

The futility of existence in the face of this nameless horror was almost too great to bear and he raised his eyes to the dead sky, its soul-destroying emptiness preferable to Perturabo's baleful city. The ghostly black tendrils squirmed through the sky and he saw that they poured towards the solitary thing to stain its emptiness.

A vast black sun, its surface so dark that its darkness was not simply the absence of colour and light, but such that its fuliginous depths sucked all life and soul from the world.

Pasanius wept at its horrible, crushing weight and Uriel was not surprised to find that he too shed tears at the sight of such an abomination against nature.

'Emperor protect us,' he whispered. 'This is…'

'Aye,' said the Omphalos Daemonium. 'This is the place you call the Eye of Terror.'

'Why…?' gasped Uriel, tearing his gaze from the morbid sun. 'Why here?'

'This is the end of your journey. The place where you will fulfil your oath.'

'I do not understand.'

'That matters not. The things you seek to destroy, the daemonculaba, are on this world, shuttered away in the darkness, far from the sight of man in a great fastness fashioned from madness and despair.'

'Why would you bring us here?' demanded Uriel, a measure of his self-control returning. 'Why would a creature of Chaos seek to aid us?'

The Omphalos Daemonium laughed its booming, discordant laugh and said, 'Because you are to do my bidding, Uriel Ventris.'

'Never!' snapped Uriel. 'We would die before aiding a beast such as you.'

'Perhaps,' agreed the giant warrior. 'But are you willing to sacrifice all that you have fought to protect by defying me? Everything you have sacrificed and everyone you have bled to save will be washed away in an ocean of blood if you do.'

'You lie,' growled Pasanius.

'Foolish morsels. What need have I of lies? The Architect of Fate has lies enough for this universe; the Lord of Skulls demands no such pretences. I know what you saw as we travelled the bloodtracks, your world afire and your people dead, ashes on the wind as it burned to death.'

The Omphalos Daemonium took a ponderous step towards them, its billhook lowered to aim at Uriel's chest.

'I can make that happen,' it promised. 'All the splintered futures you saw can be shaped and I can ensure that your precious home dies screaming in the flames. Do you believe that?'

Uriel stared into the leprous yellow eyes of the daemon and knew with utter certainty that it could do the things it spoke of – Macragge destroyed, Ultramar gone...

'Yes, I believe you,' he said at last. 'What would you have us do?'

'Uriel!' cried Pasanius.

'I do not believe we have a choice, my friend,' said Uriel slowly.

'Think of what you are saying,' said Pasanius in disbelief. 'Whatever this bastard thing wants us to do can only be for evil. Who knows what we might unleash if we agree to do what it wants?'

'I know that, Pasanius, but what else can we do? Would you see Ultramar destroyed? The Fortress of Hera brought to ruin?'

'No, of course not, but–'

'No, Pasanius,' said Uriel evenly. 'Trust me. You have to trust me. Do you trust me?'

'You know I do,' protested Pasanius. 'I trust you with my life, but this is madness!'

'Then trust me now,' pressed Uriel.

Pasanius opened his mouth to speak once more, but saw the look in Uriel's eyes and simply nodded curtly.

'Very well,' he said sadly.

'Good,' hissed the Omphalos Daemonium, revelling in their defeat. 'There is a fortress many leagues from here, high in the southern mountains, and its master has something deep in his most secret vault that belongs to me. You will retrieve it for me.'

'What is it?' asked Uriel.

'It is the Heart of Blood, and that it is precious to me is all you need know.'

'What does it look like? How will we recognise it?'

The Omphalos Daemonium chuckled. 'You will know it when you see it.'

'Why do you need us for this?' demanded Pasanius. 'If it's so damned important, why the hell don't you just get it yourself?'

The Omphalos Daemonium was silent for a beat, then said, 'I have seen you with it and it is your destiny to do this. That is enough.'

Uriel nodded, hearing a distant, shrill cry on the air.

The Omphalos Daemonium heard the noise too and cocked its head, turning and marching back to the rectangle of red light that led back into the daemon engine and the hissing Sarcomata.

As it reached the shimmering doorway, it said, 'The delirium spectres come. They hear the beat of your hearts and their hunger tears at them. It would be wise not to be found by them.'

'Wait!' said Uriel, but the Omphalos Daemonium stepped through the doorway and he watched helplessly as it faded and vanished from the mountainside, taking their daemonic captor from sight.

A leaden weight of despair settled on Uriel's soul as the Omphalos Daemonium disappeared, and he dropped to his knees as he heard the cries of what sounded like a skirling chorus of air raid sirens.

He looked into the dead sky and saw a flock of hybrid, winged... things, flapping rhythmically on fleshy pinions towards them from the high peaks of the mountains.

'What the hell...?' said Pasanius, squinting into the sky.

'The delirium spectres,' said Uriel, scrambling over the ashen ground to retrieve his weapons.

'What do we do?' said Pasanius, belting on his pistol and slinging his flamer over his shoulder.

'We run,' said Uriel, as the madly screeching flock drew closer.

CHAPTER FOUR

Black shapes against the white sky screeched as they descended from the heights of the mountains and streaked towards the two Space Marines. The delirium spectres filled the air with the wails of murder victims and Uriel could hear their agony in every shriek torn from their bodies.

He scanned the plateau for obvious hiding places, hating the idea of flight, but knowing that the Omphalos Daemonium had not lied when it had told them that it would be wise not to be found by these creatures.

'Uriel,' said Pasanius, pointing further up the steep slopes of the mountain to a narrow defile in the rockface. 'There! I don't think they will be able to get in there.'

'Can we make it?'

'Only one way to find out,' said Pasanius, setting off for the scree slope.

Uriel buckled on his sword and ran after Pasanius, his breath ragged and strained in the toxic atmosphere. His back felt as if it was on fire, but he pushed aside the pain as he reached the slope and began climbing after Pasanius. The slope was rough, composed of dusty iron filings, craggy lumps of coal and twisted scoria. Pasanius's prodigious strength enabled him to scale the slope, albeit with great difficulty, but the loose incline gave Uriel no purchase and the harder he struggled, the further he slid back.

Screeching wails of obscene hunger echoed from behind and he risked a glance over his shoulder as the first of the delirium spectres dived from above.

'Uriel!' shouted Pasanius from a ledge above. 'Go left!'

He rolled to the left as the creature dropped from the sky, welded iron claws on its wings gouging the ground where his head had been.

He kicked out and the creature skidded down the slope, its fleshy wings beating the air in fury as it righted itself. Its shape was like that of some great, ocean-dwelling manta ray, an external skeleton formed of iron struts with its flesh a billowing sheet of patchwork human skin stitched to the metal. Screaming faces bulged across its leathery hide, a vicious 'o' of a mouth edged in hundreds of needle-like teeth.

Another three creatures swooped from above, their jaws stretching across the entire surface of their skin and billowing wings flaring out to arrest their dives as they smashed into Uriel. The creature Uriel had knocked aside leapt into the air with a discordant howl as he struggled with the beasts that enfolded him, their teeth gnashing against his armour.

Pasanius shot the airborn delirium spectre, but his bolt passed clean through its flesh before detonating and it altered its course to swoop further up the slope to attack him with a deafening screech.

Uriel gripped the greasy flesh of the monsters attacking him and wrenched it from his armour, seeing anguished faces bulge from the surface of the skin and reach out to him. He punched through a thrashing jaw, his fist ripping through the taut skin as a flare of heat washed over him from above and he heard Pasanius shout, 'Get back!'

The beast thrashed in his grip as the others snapped and bit at him. He forced his other hand through the wound he had punched, rolling down the slope and dislodging the others. He gripped the flapping skin to either side and tore it from the iron frame, feeling the souls trapped within scream of their release.

Flickering lights and joyous cries erupted from the dying beast, and as the last soul departed, Uriel was left with an inanimate pile of torn flesh and metal in his hands. He hurled its remains aside as yet more of the creatures circled lower. Uriel drew his sword, slashing the energised blade through the flesh of the nearest delirium spectre, drawing a hysterical shriek of freedom from its jaws before it collapsed.

The last beast leapt towards him and he dived forwards, rolling and slashing high with his blade and hacking it into two halves as it passed overhead.

He heard another cry of release and saw a lifeless pile of iron struts and burning skin lying further upslope. Pasanius had his flamer out, spraying burning gouts of promethium into the air to discourage the other creatures from approaching too closely.

'Come on!' shouted Pasanius. 'I don't know how much longer this will hold them!'

Uriel sheathed his sword and stopped to grab two shorn lengths of iron from the corpse of the nearest monster before heading once more for the treacherous slope.

Driving the lengths of iron bar deep into the powdery shale like crude pitons, Uriel was able to climb the slope without too much difficulty while Pasanius kept the delirium spectres at bay with his flamer.

At last he reached the ledge and rolled onto his back as the delirium spectres closed in again. He drew his sword once more and slashed the first apart, feeling a grim satisfaction as it screamed in gratitude before its dissolution. Others burned in the fire, child-like laughter rippling from their blazing flesh as they died.

The two Space Marines edged backwards to the sanctuary of the defile, killing the shrieking, swooping beasts every time they came near. Though they killed dozens of them, Uriel could see hundreds more gathering around the mountaintops and knew that unless they found cover soon, they were as good as dead. They could not hope to hold off that many forever.

The defile was behind them and Uriel glanced along its length as it wound further and deeper into the mountain. Flocks of the delirium spectres circled lower and Uriel prayed they would not be able to follow them.

'I can't tell where it leads!' he said.

'It doesn't matter, does it?' replied Pasanius, bleeding from a patchwork of shallow cuts across the side of his head. 'We don't have much choice.'

'Give them one more blast, then follow me in!'

Pasanius nodded and shouted, 'Go!' and sent another stream of blazing liquid towards the shrieking monsters. Uriel darted into the defile, the narrow basalt walls glassy, black and reflective. It scraped against his shoulder guards, cutting grooves through the paint, and Uriel offered a whispered prayer of forgiveness to the armour's battle-spirit at such careless treatment.

Pasanius backed into the narrow defile, having to force his way sidelong through its narrow length and Uriel had a sickening vision of the pair of them trapped here and waiting to be picked off by these vile creatures.

'Damn, but it's tight,' grunted Pasanius stoically.

Frustrated screeches rang from above and Uriel saw scores of the monstrous beasts flashing overhead across the narrow strip of sky at the top of the defile. He pushed further along its twisting length, the ground sloping upwards and the distance between them and the open sky diminishing with every step.

'We're running out of room!' he called back, as a desperate scrabbling of claws and clanging of metal on stone sounded from above. Hissing beasts, fleshy wings thrashing, forced themselves down into the defile, their screeches echoing deafeningly in the enclosed space. Wails of frantic hunger and longing spat from their bodies and Uriel stabbed upwards, skewering the first of the delirium spectres on his blade.

More forced themselves into the defile, clanging and beating against one another as they struggled to reach their prey.

Unable to fire his flamer in such a confined space, Pasanius ripped them apart with his bare hands, tearing the skin from the desecrated frames with angry bellows. Uriel stabbed and cut blindly, dead flesh enfolding him and sharp teeth snapping at his face. The sound of tearing skin mingled with their grunts of pain and the incongruous noise of joyful souls escaping their hideous torment as each beast died.

'Keep going!' shouted Pasanius in a lull between the ferocious attacks.

'I don't know what's ahead,' answered Uriel.

'It can't be any worse than this!'

Uriel couldn't disagree and forged onwards, wiping clotted blood from his forehead and desperately seeking somewhere that would offer better shelter. The delirium spectres resumed their circling above the defile, patiently waiting for another chance to attack.

The defile twisted and turned, each step winding further into the mountain until at last it turned downwards and led out onto a narrow path that ran along the side of a sheer cliff.

The rockface fell away for hundreds of metres on one side of the path and at its end Uriel could see a narrow cave, its entrance surrounded with a forest of long iron spikes hammered into the rock.

'There's a cave ahead,' said Uriel. 'Looks like someone has used it to hide from these things already.'

'How can you tell?'

'There are spikes around the cave mouth. I doubt these beasts could get near the entrance without fouling their wings.'

'That just begs the question–'

'Who put them there?' finished Uriel.

Pasanius looked towards the sky, hearing the delirium spectres clanging from the rock and their shrill cries drawing closer as they circled down to attack once again.

'We will have to make a break for it,' said Uriel.

'We'll never make it,' pointed out Pasanius. 'They'd be on us before we got halfway.'

'You think I don't know that?' snapped Uriel. 'But we have to try.'

Uriel bit his lip as he wondered how far they could get before the creatures caught them. They might be able to fight some of them off, but not all of them, and even if the monsters didn't kill them, it would be only too easy for them to hurl them from the path.

And to fall such a distance would be fatal, even to one as mighty as a Space Marine.

One of the monsters flew overhead, its blind hunger loathsome and utterly alien.

'Wait...' said Uriel as a memory struggled to the surface of his mind.

'What?'

'When the Omphalos Daemonium spoke of these creatures it said something about how they hunted, something about our hearts and how we wouldn't go unnoticed for long.'

'And?'

'And that's how they are hunting us, they can hear our heartbeats,' said Uriel.

Pasanius was silent for a moment before saying, 'Then we take away what they need to hunt us.'

'You still remember the mantras that trigger the sus-an membrane?'

'Aye, though it's been decades since I've needed to recite them.'

'I know, but we damn well better get them right,' said Uriel. 'I don't want to fall into a coma halfway along that path.'

Pasanius nodded in understanding as Uriel slowly crept to the edge of the defile. The delirium spectres were high above them, but still too close for them to have any hope of reaching the cave entrance unmolested.

Uriel turned to Pasanius and said, 'Go when I go. Slowly, but not too slowly, I don't want you dying on the way.'

'I'll try not to,' replied Pasanius dryly.

Uriel closed his eyes and recited the verses taught to him by Apothecary Selenus that began the hormonal activation of the sus-an membrane, an organ implanted within his brain tissue during his transformation into a Space Marine. He took deep breaths, regulating his breathing and forcing his heart rate to slow. What he was doing was extremely dangerous, normally requiring many hours of meditation and the correct prayers, but Uriel knew they didn't have time for such preparations.

Uriel could feel his hearts pounding in his chest, their rhythmic beats slowing.

Forty beats a minute, thirty, twenty, ten...

He could hear Pasanius repeating the same mantras, knowing that they had to move and reach the cave before the organ activated fully and plunged them into a state of complete suspended animation and their hearts stopped beating completely.

Three beats a minute... two...

Uriel stood, his vision greying at the edges and his limbs feeling leaden.

He nodded to Pasanius and walked from the transient cover of the defile, moving as quickly as he dared along the path towards the cave mouth. Pasanius followed, the piercing shrieks of the daemonic furies above him almost breaking his concentration and icy sweat streaking his pale face. Both Space Marines hugged the cliff face as they inched their way along the path.

The winged beasts swooped towards them, their shrieks ringing from the cliff-face as they circled and climbed in confusion, unable to pinpoint them.

They were almost at the cave as the flocks above wheeled aimlessly in the air.

Two of the delirium spectres flapped noisily past Uriel, their wings flaring as they landed with a scrape of claws on the path before him. Their cries were low and hideous as they turned slowly, their rippling, fleshy skins trying to discern their quarry.

Uriel slowed as he inched his way past the monsters, fighting to hold his body in the limbo between life and a self-induced coma.

He stumbled, his boot scraping against the nearest beast's claws...

He froze.

But whatever other senses it may have possessed, the creature did not register the touch and ignored him.

Uriel edged past the oblivious monster.

The second beast took to the air as he drew near the end of the path and–

One beat...

The delirium spectre twisted in midair, giving voice to an ear-splitting shriek as it heard the thudding beat of his heart. The flocks above ceased their confused wheeling and turned as one towards them, screeching in triumph.

'Move!' shouted Uriel, abandoning all subterfuge and running for the cave mouth, ducking below the first spike and threading his way between the others to reach the entrance. He staggered inside, gasping a great lungful of air. His chest was a raging inferno as his hearts suddenly leapt from a virtual standstill to their normal rhythm in a matter of moments.

He pushed into the stygian darkness of the cave, dropping to his knees as he fought to stabilise his internal organs and willed himself not to slip into a sleep he knew he would not wake from.

Pasanius backed into the cave, his flamer billowing out a cone of blazing fuel.

The delirium spectres flapped noisily around the entrance to the cave, screaming in anger at being denied their prey. Several darted in to attack, but only succeeded in skewering themselves on the sharp spikes protecting the entrance. Their thrashing bodies ripped apart, their torn skins and iron frames tumbling down the cliff as they died.

Uriel let out a juddering breath, knowing how close they had come to death.

'Pasanius, are you all right?' he gasped.

'Barely,' wheezed Pasanius. 'By the Throne, I never want to have to do that again. It felt like I was dying.'

Uriel nodded, pulling himself upright using the walls of the cave. His returning vision easily penetrated the gloom of the cave and he saw that they were in a long, arched tunnel carved into the rockface, but by who or what he could not tell.

'Well, at least we are safe for the moment,' said Uriel.

'Don't be too sure about that,' replied Pasanius, kicking over a cracked human skull that lay on the floor.

THE TWO SPACE Marines made their way carefully along the tunnel, the screeching wails of the delirium spectres fading the further they penetrated into the mountain. Their enhanced eyesight magnified the glow from the hissing nozzle of Pasanius's flamer such that they walked through the utter darkness as though their steps were illuminated by glow-globes.

'Who do you think made these tunnels?' asked Pasanius, staring at the marks of picks and drills cut into the rock.

'I have no idea,' said Uriel. 'Perhaps slaves or the populace of this world before it was taken by Chaos?'

'I still can't believe we have travelled so far,' said Pasanius. 'Do you really think this is Medrengard? Can we really be in the Eye of Terror?'

'You saw the dark city beyond the mountains. Can you doubt that one of the fallen primarchs dwells there?'

Pasanius made the sign of the aquila over his chest to ward off the evil that went with even thinking about such things. 'I suppose not. I felt the evil as a poison in my bones, but to come so far… it is impossible, surely.'

'If this is truly the Eye, then nothing is impossible,' said Uriel.

'I had always believed that the stories of worlds taken by daemons and the Ruinous Powers were nothing more than dark legends, exaggerated tales to scare the unwary into obedience.'

'Would that they were,' replied Uriel. 'But as well as destroying these daemonculaba that Librarian Tigurius saw in his vision, I believe that we have been brought to this place to test the strength of our faith as well.'

'And have we failed already?' muttered Pasanius. 'To truck with a daemon…'

'I know, I have put our very souls at risk, my friend,' said Uriel. 'And for that I am sorry. But I could see no choice other than to make the Omphalos Daemonium believe we would do as it wished.'

'Then you don't plan on getting it this Heart of Blood, whatever that is?'

'Of course not,' said Uriel, appalled. 'Once we find it, I intend to smash the vile thing into a million pieces!'

'Thank the Emperor!' breathed Pasanius.

Uriel stopped suddenly. 'You thought I would acquiesce to the desires of a daemon?'

'No, but given how we ended up here and what it threatened…'

'Breaking faith with the *Codex Astartes* is one thing, but trafficking with daemons is quite another,' snapped Uriel.

'But we have been cast out by the Chapter, banished from the Emperor's sight and are probably trapped forever in the Eye of Terror,' said Pasanius. 'I can see why you might have thought it could have been an option.'

'Really?' demanded Uriel angrily. 'Then pray explain it to me.'

Pasanius did not meet Uriel's gaze as he said, 'Well, it seems likely that the Heart of Blood is some daemonic artefact meant to bring ruin upon an enemy of the Omphalos Daemonium here in the Eye, so might not we be doing the Emperor's work by stealing it from its current master?'

Uriel shook his head. 'No. That way lies madness and the first step on the road to betraying everything we stand for as Space Marines. By such steps are men damned, Pasanius, each tiny heresy excused by some reasonable explanation until their souls are irrevocably blackened and shrivelled. With no Chapter to call our own, some might say that our only loyalty now is to ourselves, but you and I both know that is not true. No matter what becomes of us, we will always be warriors of the Emperor in our hearts. I have told you this before, my friend. Do you still doubt your courage and honour?'

'No, it is not that…' began Pasanius.

'Then what?'

'Nothing,' said Pasanius eventually. 'You are right and I am sorry for even thinking such things.'

Uriel locked his gaze with that of his friend. 'Do you remember the story of the ancient philosopher of Calth who spoke of a stalactite falling in a cave and asked if it would make a sound if no one was there to hear?'

'Aye,' nodded Pasanius. 'It never made sense to me.'

'Nor I, at least until now,' said Uriel. 'Though we have been exiled, we retain our honour and though it is likely that the Chapter will never hear of our deeds, we will continue to fight the enemies of the Emperor until our dying day. Yes?'

'Yes,' agreed Pasanius, slapping his hand on Uriel's shoulder guard. 'And that's why you were captain and I was just a sergeant. You know all the right things to say.'

Uriel chuckled. 'I don't know about that, I mean, look at us, tens of thousands of light years from Macragge and stuck in a cave in the Eye of Terror…'

'…filled with corpses,' finished Pasanius.

Uriel turned and saw that Pasanius was right. The tunnel had widened into a domed cave with rough walls and a number of shadowy passageways leading away. The remains of a long dead fire filled a deep firepit at the centre of the cave, a thin shaft of weak light spearing down from a smoke vent in the roof. Skeletal bodies littered the floor of the cave, splayed and broken, scattered throughout the cave, the bones dusty and cracked.

'Throne! What happened here?' whispered Uriel, circling the firepit and kneeling beside a rag-draped skeleton.

'Looks like they were attacked while they cooked a meal,' said Pasanius, poking around in the remains of the fire with his silver arm. 'There are pots still in the firepit.'

Uriel nodded, examining the bones before him, wondering who they had belonged to and what malicious twist of fate had seen him condemned to such a death.

'Whoever did this was incredibly strong,' said Uriel. 'The bones are snapped cleanly.'

'Aye, and this one has had its skull ripped from its shoulders.'

'Iron Warriors?' asked Uriel.

'No, I don't think so,' said Pasanius. 'There was a madness to this attack. Look at the stains on the walls. It's blood, arterial spray. Whoever killed these people did it in a frenzy, ripping out throats and tearing their victims apart in seconds. They didn't even have time to arm themselves.'

Uriel crossed the chamber to join Pasanius, stepping over the bones of the dead as he noticed something metallic lying partially buried in the dust. He bent down to retrieve it, his fingers closing on a crude, thick-handled knife, the blade long and flexible. He turned to look at the splayed bodies and a sickening realisation came to him.

'They were skinned,' he said.

'What?'

'The bodies,' said Uriel, holding up the knife. 'They were skinned. They were killed and then their killers flayed them.'

Pasanius cursed. 'Is there no end to this world's evil?'

Uriel snapped the blade of the skinning knife and hurled it away from him, the broken pieces clattering from the rocky walls of the cave. What manner of beast would track its prey deep into the mountains to attack with such speed and frenzy before taking the time to remove its victims' hides? He hoped they would not find out, but a sinking feeling in his gut told him that there was a good chance they had already stumbled into its territory.

'There's nothing we can do for them, now, whoever they were,' he said.

'No,' agreed Pasanius. 'So which way onwards?'

Uriel crossed the cave, stopping to examine each passageway and hoping to discern some clue as to which direction offered the most hope of a way out.

'There are tracks leading away at this one,' he said, kneeling and examining the ground at the middle passage. 'A lot of them.'

Pasanius joined him, tracing the outline of a huge footprint in the dust. There was no telling how old it was, but, despite its size, there was no doubt that it was human.

'Are you thinking these might lead to the monsters' lair and that we should avoid it?'

'No, I think that they might lead to a way out of these tunnels,' said Uriel.

'I *knew* you were going to say that,' sighed Pasanius.

URIEL AND PASANIUS set off down the tunnel, its course meandering through the mountains for what felt like many kilometres, until they completely lost track of which way they were headed. As the ground underfoot became rockier, the tracks vanished and Uriel knew they were hopelessly lost.

But just as he began to think that they might never again see the surface – not an unappealing prospect in itself – he caught a hint of something on the air. A breath of motion, the faintest gust of a breeze on his skin.

He held up his hand and quieted Pasanius as he opened his mouth to speak.

Just on the threshold of audibility he could hear a soft rumble, like a distant crackle of white noise. Though it took all his concentration, he followed a twisting path through the tunnels, doubling back, stopping and retracing his steps every now and then as he followed the noise.

As it grew louder, his path became surer and within an hour of first hearing the noise, he saw a bright sliver of white sky ahead.

'I never thought I would be grateful to see that sky again,' said Uriel.

'Nor I, but it is better than that accursed darkness.'

Uriel nodded and the two Space Marines emerged from the tunnel, blinking in the perpetual daylight of Medrengard. As they stepped out onto the mountainside, Uriel saw the source of the noise he had been following.

'Guilliman's oath!' swore Pasanius.

Many kilometres ahead over the mountain was a fortification built from dark madness and standing in defiance of all reason. Its steepled towers and mighty bastions wounded the sky, its massive gateway a snarling void. Its walls were darkened, bloodstained stone, veined with unnatural colours that should not exist and which burned themselves upon the retina.

Lightning leapt between its towers and the clanking of great engines and machines echoed like thunder from beyond its walls.

Pillars of smoke and fire leapt from the walls where explosions blossomed against them, hurling great chunks of black stone from the colossal fortress. The distant rumble of artillery crashed and boomed, bright muzzle flares of innumerable great howitzers and siege guns firing upon the fastness from the jagged rocks below.

The primal battle cries of thousands, tens of thousands of warriors – perhaps even more – were carried on the wind from the distant battle, together with the smell of burnt iron and war.

Clouds of ash and smoke from the blazing pyres surrounding the fortress flickered and twitched with the fury of the siege below, and Uriel felt his soul blacken in the face of such savagery.

Nothing could reach that fortress and live.

But that was exactly what they had to do.

PART TWO
BENEATH A BLACK SUN

CHAPTER FIVE

A BLAST OF superheated air whooshed between the stumps of the merlons, hurling Honsou from his feet and vaporising the top half of one of his Iron Warriors. He rolled to one side as the smoking legs collapsed beside him and leapt to his feet, leaning over the ragged remains of the fortress wall and waving his mighty toothed axe.

'Come on, Berossus, you will need to do better than that!' he shouted.

Far below, the metallic coughs of massed artillery fire echoed from the dark mountains, shelling the lower bastions of Khalan-Ghol to oblivion. The screams of dying men drifted up towards him, but Honsou paid them no mind. They were but slaves and those too badly injured for skinning in the flesh camps, and there were plenty more of them to expend.

He wiped dust from his armour as more Iron Warriors marched forward to plug the gap the stray shot
had blasted in the upper levels of his fortress. It had
been a lucky impact and Honsou felt a thrill of adrenaline course through his body at the near miss. Ever
since the siege on Hydra Cordatus, he had craved the
fire and thunder of battle once more. The fighting on
Perdictor II upon his return to the Eye of Terror had
been desultory and unsatisfying, the warriors of the
Despoiler proving no match for his advance forces.

But now his 'fellow' warsmiths were attacking him,
and this was sure to be a battle worthy of the name.
Once again he was forced to prove his mettle to those
who thought him no better than the Imperial dogs
they fought the Long War against. The bile rose in his
throat at the thought that even though his predecessor
had named him warsmith, he was still not considered
their equal.

'Lord Berossus is thorough in his attentions,' said
Obax Zakayo, his grating, static-laced voice snapping
Honsou from his bitter reverie. 'The lower bastions
will be nothing but dust and bones soon.'

Honsou turned to face his lieutenant, a huge, wide-
shouldered Iron Warrior with yellow and black
chevrons edging the plates of his dented power
armour. Hissing pipes wheezed from every joint, leaking stinking black fluids and venting puffs of steam
with his every step. Like Honsou, he carried a fearsome
war-axe, but he also wielded a crackling energy whip,
writhing on the end of a mechanised claw attached to
his back.

'If Berossus thinks he is achieving anything by killing
such chaff, then he is even stupider than I believed,'
sneered Honsou, wiping grey dust from his visor with
his glossy black augmetic arm. His former master had

gifted the mechanical arm to him after his own had been hewn from his body by the late castellan of Hydra Cordatus. It had once belonged to Kortrish, a mighty champion of ancient days and had been a physical indication of his master's favour.

'What he lacks in imagination, he makes up for with determination,' said Honsou's personal champion, a tall, slender warrior in power armour so dark and non-reflective that he moved like a liquid shadow. His voice was a ghostly monotone, his face a crawling mass of bio-organic circuitry that ran like mercurial fire beneath his dead skin and made his eyes shine with a lifeless, silver sheen.

'Berossus is irrelevant, Onyx. He'll shell the lower bastions to rubble and not be able to move his artillery up. No, it is Toramino that we must keep a careful watch on,' replied Honsou, turning from the battlements as fresh explosions and the roars of charging warriors rippled up from below.

'Agreed,' said Onyx, long bronze talons unsheathing from the grey flesh of his hands. 'Do you wish me to destroy him?'

Honsou had seen some of the most hideous things in this galaxy – having perpetrated a great many of them himself – but even he was unsettled by the malefic presence of Onyx. The Iron Warrior, if he could even still be called such, was a shunned figure, the daemonic presence within him making him outcast even amongst his own warriors. Though his human side still held sway in the symbiotic relationship with the daemon bound to his flesh, its diabolical presence was unmistakable.

'No,' said Honsou. 'Not yet, anyway. I'm going to break these vermin against my walls first. I can defeat Berossus easily enough, but I want Toramino to see this half-breed beat him, to know that the warsmith was right to name me his successor. Then you can kill him.'

'As you wish,' said Onyx, a barely-perceptible haze of power surrounding him.

When the creature had bound itself to Honsou's service, as master of Khalan-Ghol, it had spoken its true name as a sign of its fealty, but its pronunciation had been beyond Honsou, so he had settled for the closest approximation of the part he had been able to understand: Onyx. Honsou had seen, first hand, just how lethal Onyx could be when the warp-spawned part of him rose to the surface and he unleashed the full terror of his inner daemon.

Onyx was his dark shadow, his protector, and he could think of no better a creature to be his champion and bodyguard.

'Berossus is proud though,' said Obax Zakayo, 'and not to be underestimated. He has great strength and many warriors in his grand company.'

'Let them come,' said Honsou.

'They already do,' pointed out Obax Zakayo, gesturing over the edge of the wall.

Honsou followed Obax Zakayo's pointing gauntlet and grinned with feral anticipation.

Tens of thousands of soldiers swarmed across the smoking, cratered hell of the lower bastions, screaming like beasts as they slaughtered the few, mangled survivors of the shelling. Their victims begged for mercy, but their attackers had none to give and the carnage was on a truly grand scale.

Banners with the devotional heraldry of Berossus were raised high and sacred standards that proclaimed the glory of Chaos in its most raw, visceral aspect were planted in the bloody soil. Within minutes, disembowelling racks were set up and the soldiers who were still alive were ritually butchered before the walls to taunt those who watched from above.

'So like Berossus,' scoffed Honsou, shaking his head and watching as another hundred screaming soldiers had their entrails dragged from their bellies and looped around rotating drum mechanisms.

'What?' asked Obax Zakayo.

'He doesn't even have the wit to allow some of his prisoners to live to show his honourable mercy.'

'I fought with Lord Forrix at the side of Lord Berossus before,' said Obax Zakayo wistfully, 'and I know there is no such quality left within him.'

'You know that and I know that, Zakayo, but if Berossus had any sense, he'd try and convince the soldiers of Khalan-Ghol that he does.'

'Why?'

'Because if our soldiers could be made to believe that Berossus would be merciful, the thought of surrender might enter their heads,' answered Onyx. 'But since they now know that only hideous death awaits them should they be taken alive, they will fight all the harder.'

'To breach a fortress you need to break the men inside, not the walls. And to break a besieging army you must wear its warriors down to the point where they would rather turn their guns upon themselves than take another step forward,' said Honsou. 'We must make every one of Berossus's soldiers feel he is living beneath the muzzle of one of our cannons; that he is nothing more than meat for the guns.'

Obax Zakayo nodded in understanding and said, 'We can do that. My guns will sow the ground before the walls with their shredded flesh and the rocks will flow with waterfalls of their blood.'

'To the warp with that, Zakayo, so long as they die!' snarled Honsou, pleased to see the ember of fear smouldering within Obax Zakayo flare to life once more. 'Or else you will be down there with the scum next time. Ever since you lost those slaves bound for my forges to the damned renegades, your promises have been as worthless as the filth I scrape from my boot.'

'I will not fail you again, my lord,' promised Obax Zakayo.

'No, you won't,' said Honsou. 'Just remember that Forrix is no longer your master, I am, and I know that you are a true protégé of his. He may have become so jaded that he tolerated your lack of vision, but do not think for one second that I will.'

Suitably chastened, Obax Zakayo returned his gaze to the slaughter below. 'What will Berossus do now that he has the lower bastions?' he asked.

'He will send the daemon engines,' said Honsou.

As though on cue, the monstrous silhouettes of scores of hulking, spider-legged war engines and clanking dreadnoughts could be seen advancing through the pillars of smoke and blazing wreckage. Berossus's daemonic war engines stalked through the ruined bastions, forcing their way through the fields of corpses, and began clambering across the rocks towards the battered slope of the next level of redoubts.

'Just as you predicted he would,' said Onyx, watching the approach of the daemonic machines.

Honsou nodded, listening as the ululating shrieks of the terrifying war engines echoed towards the next level of defences, hundreds of the clawed and snapping monsters hauling their spiked bulk towards the defenders above them. The next rampart was some five hundred metres above the lower bastions, many levels below where Honsou and his lieutenants watched, but the daemon engines would not take long to reach the defenders. They poured their fire into the climbing machines, but nothing could stop them.

The artillery fire from below resumed with a thunderous crescendo, the first volley exploding against the rock between the defenders and the climbing daemon engines. Boulders the size of tanks tumbled down the sloping rockface, smashing a number of dreadnoughts to flattened hunks of metal as the bombardment continued, the gunners shifting their aim as they found their range.

'Now?' asked Obax Zakayo.

Honsou shook his head. 'No, let the dreadnoughts get closer first.'

Obax Zakayo nodded, watching as the first of the spider-like daemon engines reached the next level, their massive, clawed pincers snatching up soldiers and ripping them apart. They howled as they killed, revelling in the slaughter and hurling the corpses from the battlements.

'Now,' said Honsou.

Obax Zakayo nodded and spoke a single word into his power armour's vox unit.

Honsou watched with relish as the ground of the bastions below shook and trembled as though an earth tremor had struck. Huge, gaping cracks ripped across the bastions, splitting the rock with a hollow boom that rivalled the thunder of the guns. Smoke and flames blasted from the cracks as the ground beneath the entire front half of the bastions sagged and splintered. With a groaning creak, millions of tonnes of rock exploded and detached from the side of Khalan-Gol, sliding ponderously down the face of the mountain.

Thousands of Khalan-Gol's soldiers were carried screaming to their deaths, the avalanche of rubble and debris smashing every one of the daemon engines from the mountainside, crushing them beneath the unstoppable tide of rock. Hundreds were buried beneath the mountain; their shrieking roars billowing from the rubble as their mystical bindings were smashed asunder and the daemons within them were shorn from their iron vessels.

Honsou laughed as he watched the dreadnoughts and the thousands of enemy soldiers below turn to flee the avalanche, knowing that they were already doomed. The tide of rock swept over them all, pouring down the slopes they had fought and bled to capture.

The rumble of grinding rock slowly faded, as did the bellowing roar of the guns, Berossus realising that their fire would be wasted without an escalade.

Honsou turned from the mass destruction he had unleashed.

Now Berossus would know he had a fight on his hands.

THE UNCHANGING SKY and static sun made it impossible to discern the passage of time through their surroundings, and the internal chronometer on Uriel's visor had only displayed a constantly fluctuating readout that he eventually disabled. Days must surely have passed, but how many was a mystery. He had heard that time flowed differently in the Eye of Terror, and supposed he should not have been surprised at such affronts to the laws of nature.

'Emperor, I hate this place,' said Pasanius, picking his way over a pile of twisted iron jutting from the rock of the mountain. 'There is not one natural thing here.'

'No,' agreed Uriel, tired and hungry despite his armour's best efforts at filtering and recycling his bodily excretions into drinkable water and nutrient pastes. 'It is a wasteland of death. Nothing could live here.'

'I think something lives out here,' said Pasanius, glancing at the darkened peaks all about them. 'I'm just not sure what or that I even want to find out.'

'What are you talking about?'

'Haven't you felt it? That we're being watched? Followed.'

'No,' said Uriel, ashamed that his instinct for danger appeared to have deserted him. 'Have you seen anything?'

Pasanius shook his head. 'Nothing for sure, no, but I keep thinking I can see, I don't know, something.'

'Something? What kind of something?'

'I'm not sure, it's like a whisper in the corner of my mind's eye, something that vanishes as soon as I try to look at it,' said Pasanius, darkly. 'Something red...'

'It is this place,' said Uriel. 'The lair of the Enemy will attempt to mislead and betray your senses. We must be strong in our faith and resist its evil magicks.'

Pasanius shook his head. 'No, it is something not of the Enemy, but something that lives here. I think it's what killed those people in the cave.'

'Whatever killed and skinned those people was evil and an enemy of all living things. Let them come, whatever they are, they will find only death.'

'Aye,' agreed Pasanius as they climbed onwards. 'Death.'

The besieged fortress was lost to sight for now, the path from the tunnels leading them down into the rocky gullies and crevasses of the mountains. The white sky beat down upon them, harsher than the fiercest sun, and Uriel deliberately kept his eyes averted from its flat emptiness. Once, he thought he caught a glimpse of the red things Pasanius claimed were following them, but they defied his every attempt to see them properly. Eventually he gave up, unable to catch sight of them, and concentrated on simply putting one foot in front of the other.

The harsh, metallic shale of the mountainside grated beneath his boots and every now and then they saw grilled vents piercing the rock that disgorged a hot steam that tasted of beaten metal. The vents plunged down into the mountain, the darkness impenetrable, even to a Space Marine's enhanced eyesight.

Uriel saw billowing smoke stacks hundreds of metres above them, thousands of blocky chimneys lining the ridge like great pylons that spewed corrosive fumes into the atmosphere. Yet no matter how much black waste was released into the air, the dead sky was always above them, blank and oppressive.

Over the tops of the mountains before them, Uriel could see what looked like bloated dirigibles, drifting above somewhere ahead in the mountains. Long cables drooped from their bellies, but whether these were simply anchoring them to the ground or acting as some form of barrage balloon, Uriel could not tell. Perhaps they were designed to keep the delirium spectres at bay from some facility as yet unseen?

As their weary trudge through the reeking air of the mountains continued, the two Space Marines passed a shorn quarry of shattered stone, where the side of one of these cyclopean smoke stacks was exposed. Reddish-brown stains spilled from the joints between the massive, curved blocks making up the stack and a monstrous heat radiated from the stonework in pulsing waves.

'Where do you think it goes?' said Uriel.

'I don't know. Perhaps there is some manufactory below the mountains.'

Uriel nodded, wondering what diabolical production line was at work beneath their very feet. Were men and women dying even now to forge weapons, armour and materiel for the dread legions of Chaos? It galled him that he could do nothing to prevent such abomination, but what choice did they have? The sacred task of the death oath placed upon them by Marneus Calgar took precedence over all other concerns. The daemonic womb creatures... these daemonculaba were in the besieged fortress they had seen as they climbed from the darkness of the tunnels beneath the mountains and nothing would stand in Uriel's way of reaching that damned place.

Pressing on, Uriel and Pasanius climbed a jagged, saw-toothed ridge, its sides sheer and corrugated, as though gouged by some gargantuan bulldozer blade. A blackened depression of splintered stone and iron, thousands of metres in diameter, fell away from them on the other side, crags of iron columns and twisted girders protruding from the mountain like clawed fingers. The depression appeared to be perfectly circular, though it was difficult to tell, whipping particles of sand and iron filings filling the air and lashing round the circular valley in spiteful, howling vortices. A narrow sliver of white sky was just visible on the far side of the depression, but all Uriel's attention was fixed on the sight that filled the centre of the depression.

'In the name of the Emperor...' breathed Uriel in disgust.

A huge grilled platform filled the centre of the depression. Agglomerated layers of dust coated its every surface and its perforated floor dripped and clogged with jelly-like runnels of fat and viscera. Tall poles jutted from the platform, held in place by quivering steel guys that sang as the unnatural wind whistled through them. Hooked between the poles were billowing sails of flesh, stretched across timber frames that the scouring, wind-borne particles might strip them of the leavings of their former owners.

Monstrous, debased creatures in vulcanised rubber masks with rounded glass eye sockets and ribbed piping running into tanks carried on their backs scraped at the stretched skins with long, bladed polearms. They lurched across the platform with a twisted, mutated gait and gurgled monotone commands to one another.

'What are they doing?' said Pasanius, horrified at the sight before him.

'It looks like they're curing the hides, scraping them clean,' said Uriel.

'But the hides of what?' said Pasanius. 'They can't be human, they're too large.'

'I don't care what they are,' snarled Uriel, setting off down the treacherous slope towards the platform and drawing his golden-hilted sword. 'This ends now.'

Pasanius set off after Uriel, unlimbering his flamer and checking its fuel load.

If the mutant creatures were aware of them they gave no sign, the howling wind and rumble of distant artillery masking the sounds of their approach. But whatever they lacked for in awareness, they made up for in thorough diligence, dragging their bladed polearms up and down the length of the billowing skins to clear them of whatever the lashing winds left behind. Uriel saw a carven set of stone stairs leading to the platform and took them two at a time as his anger continued to build.

The first of the mutants died with a strangled screech on the point of Uriel's sword, the second fell without a sound as Uriel hacked its head from its body with one blow. Now aware of the killers in their midst, the remainder scattered in terror. A sheet of flame incinerated more of the mutants, their screams ululating as their rubber bodysuits melted on their corrupted flesh.

The slaughter was over in a matter of moments, the twisted mutants no match for the power and fury of the Adeptus Astartes. Most turned to flee, but there was nowhere to hide from Uriel's wrath. As the last mutated creature fell beneath his blade, Uriel took a deep breath, taking profound pleasure in the butchery of such worthless wretches. Whatever deviant beasts they had been in life, they were only so much dead flesh now.

He turned as Pasanius said, 'Uriel, look...' and pointed at the nearest of the skins.

Uriel felt his heart tighten in his chest as he saw the dead features of a man atop the huge expanse of skin. Stretched almost beyond recognition, but a man's nonetheless.

'Holy blood. But how could a man become so vast?' said Pasanius.

Uriel shook his head. 'Not by any natural means.'

'But why?'

'The ways of the Enemy are unknown,' said Uriel. 'Better that some remain so.'

'What shall we do?'

Uriel turned in a circle, seeing row upon row of faces in the skins circling the platform – dead, slack features of men and women staring down at him as though he were the subject in an anatomist's theatre.

'Burn it,' he said. 'Burn it all.'

CHAPTER SIX

WITH THE SCORCHED reek of burning flesh still in their nostrils, Uriel and Pasanius left the depression in the rock, leaving the smouldering remains to the scouring wind and whatever passed for carrion on Medrengard. Invigorated and filled with purpose from the slaying of the mutant things, their step was quick and energised, but by the time they passed through the narrow slice in the rock face and began climbing worn steps carved into the rock, the leaden weight of the daemon world had settled upon them once more.

Uriel glanced back down at the blazing sheets of skin, feeling his hate at what had been done to these people burn as brightly. He knew that the image of the skinned man's features would haunt him forever, and was reminded of the horror of the disassembled flesh sculpture created by the loathsome xeno surgeon beneath the estate of Kasimir de Valtos on Pavonis.

Just by being here he felt polluted, as though his very soul was becoming hardened or being drained from his body to nourish the dead rock underfoot, and he was becoming less himself. The emptiness of Medrengard was leaving him hollowed out, a shell of his former self.

'What will be left,' he whispered, 'when this world takes the last of me?'

He could tell Pasanius was feeling the same way, his cheeks hollow and his eyes glazed as he trudged up the winding stairs. Even as he watched, Pasanius stumbled, his silver arm reaching out to arrest his fall, but at the last minute his friend snatched his arm back and he fell to his knees instead.

'Are you all right?' asked Uriel.

'Aye,' nodded Pasanius. 'Just hard to keep focussed without an enemy to fight.'

'Fear not, my friend,' said Uriel. 'Once we reach this fortress, I am sure we will have enemies aplenty. If what the Omphalos Daemonium has told us is true, then we will have a surfeit of them.'

'Do you think a daemon of the Skull Lord is capable of telling the truth?'

'I do not know for sure,' said Uriel honestly, 'but I believe daemons only cloak what they need to in lies, wrapping kernels of truth in shrouds of deceit. Part of what it told us is true, I am sure, but which part... well, who knows?'

'So what do we do?' asked Pasanius, trudging after Uriel.

'Whatever we can, my friend,' said Uriel. 'We will act with courage and honour and hope that that is enough.'

'It will need to be,' said Pasanius. 'It is all we have left.'

* * *

THE HIKE THROUGH the mountains seemed never-ending, their path through the blackened, rocky desolation draining their spirits with every step they took. They saw more of the steam-venting grilles and the acidic reek of the great smoke stacks was their constant companion as they neared the summit of yet another toothed crag of rock.

The further they travelled, the more signs of death they saw. Bleached bones lay strewn all about in the rocks, but Uriel could not discern how they had come to be here. Not a scrap of meat remained on the bones, but it was impossible to tell whether they had been picked clean by scavengers or boiled free of flesh. Toxic clouds of smog and ash hugged the ground; noxious and polluted, lurking in cracks in the rock like predators with coiling tendrils of fog questing through the air like undersea fronds.

Uriel briefly removed his helmet to cough up a mouthful of brackish phlegm, its substance black and stringy. His enhanced metabolism enabled him to survive such pollutants in the air, but didn't make them any less unpleasant.

Several times they had been forced to traverse hissing rivers of molten metal as they flowed along great basalt culverts towards the smelteries and forges on the plains below. The heat of the mountains was growing and great geysers of scalding steam and hot ash spewed from vents and cracks in the rock. Were it not for their blessed power armour and bio-engineered physiology, neither Uriel nor Pasanius could possibly have survived the journey.

Again, Uriel thought he caught sight of the reddish things Pasanius believed were following them, but each time they would vanish into the rocks and remain unseen. Flocks of the delirium spectres wheeled far overhead, but Uriel suspected that only the heat of the lava-hot rivers of metal and spouting plumes of boiling water kept them at bay.

As he passed near a zigzagging crack in the ground, a whooshing tower of boiling liquid suddenly erupted from it. Steam billowed around him, blinding him, and he stumbled away as a rain of objects began clattering around him, falling from somewhere above. Coughing and spluttering, feeling the heat scorch his oesophagus, he wiped moisture from his visor and watched a rain of bones fall upon the mountain, ejected from somewhere deep below the earth by the spouting geysers.

'Well, at least we know where the bones are coming from,' said Pasanius.

The strange objects Uriel had seen in the sky before they had discovered the scouring platform came into sight once more as they neared the summit, swollen leathery balloon-like objects with drooping cables that hovered in the sky over something beyond the ridge of black rock. Now that they were nearer, Uriel could see that his initial assumption that these were some form of crude barrage balloon looked to be accurate. Dozens of them floated ahead, their surfaces a patchwork of uneven fabric and, after what they had seen thus far on Medrengard, Uriel did not want to think too hard as to what they had been fashioned from.

The sound of the siege was not so distant now, the rumble of artillery drawing closer with every step they took.

'Whoever is attempting to take that fortress is determined indeed to keep up such a prodigious expenditure of ordnance,' said Uriel as he clambered up another sheer slab of rock. His gauntlets were battered and scarred, the razor-like rocks of Medrengard tearing at them with every handhold.

Pasanius nodded, his breath heaving as he climbed to join Uriel. The massive sergeant removed his helmet and spat the taste of the world from his mouth. 'Yes, I don't think we're the only ones interested in this Heart of Blood.'

'You think that's what the besieger is after?'

'I don't know, but it's certainly one explanation. Like you said, he's determined.'

'The forces of the Dark Powers make war upon one another for their own amusement. It doesn't necessarily mean anything.'

'True, but all I have learned of the Iron Warriors from Librarian Tigurius leads me to believe that they are consumed by bitterness and malice, not given to capricious whims. Whoever is attacking this fortress is doing so for more than their amusement.'

'You could be right,' agreed Uriel. 'Come on, there is only one way to find out. The summit is near.'

Once again they set off, and after what could have been no more than another hour's climb through drifting banks of stinking steam and yet more piles of bones, they crested the summit before them. Uriel had expected the ground to drop away from them, descending to the plains below, but instead the ground flattened into a rubble-strewn plateau of jagged spikes of rock and snaking cracks that drooled a yellowish fog. One of the bloated balloons was almost directly overhead and Uriel now saw that the cables dangling from it were barbed and as thick as a man's thigh, scraping great furrows in the grey powder of the ground as it drifted.

'Listen,' said Uriel, dropping to one knee.

Pasanius was silent, cocking his head and listening for what Uriel had heard.

Amid the bass rumble of artillery fire and the hammering of distant forges, there was a pulsing, mechanical sound, such as might be made by a host of generators. Though it was hard to pick out any one sound from the omnipresent background noise of Medrengard, Uriel was certain it was coming from up ahead and was near.

'What do you think it is?' he asked.

'Engines perhaps?' suggested Pasanius.

'Maybe,' nodded Uriel.

'Maybe something we can steal.'

'My thoughts exactly,' grinned Uriel, pushing himself to his feet and moving cautiously through the rolling banks of stinking fog while hugging the tall pillars of rock. The noises grew louder as they approached, and as the clouds of smog parted, Uriel saw their source.

A sprawling complex of corrugated metal buildings, each the size of a large warehouse, squatted atop the plateau, surrounded by a high fence of razorwire topped with forests of iron spikes. Bodies hung draped from thick lengths of timber along the fence, their flesh desiccated and their limbs twisted at unnatural angles around the spars. Pillars of ashen smoke curled from a building of black brick near the centre of the camp and a low moaning permeated the air. A greasy, fatty residue coated the rocks and Uriel smelled a loathsome stench that reminded him of spoiled meat.

'This place reeks of death,' he whispered.

In the centre of the camp, a tall, armoured tower reared into the sky, thick iron girders and cable stays supporting a monstrous assembly that resembled the head of some gargantuan daemonic creature. Flames spouted from its eyes and nostrils, and its gaping mouth was filled with long gun barrels. Two bunkers guarded the entrance to the camp, their roofs sloped and festooned with spikes. Uriel could see the glint of heavy guns through the firing slits and knew that to approach this death camp, they would need to cross the interlocking fields of fire of both bunkers.

Beyond the razorwire barrier, Uriel could see warriors in iron grey armour patrolling the interior of the camp, and felt his instinctual hatred rise to the surface.

'Iron Warriors!' hissed Pasanius.

'Iron Warriors,' repeated Uriel, gripping the hilt of his sword tightly.

Traitors. Abominations. Chaos Space Marines... was there any other foe so vile?

These warriors sought the ruination of everything Uriel believed in and the destruction of the Emperor's realm. Every aspect of his soul cried out for vengeance.

'What is this place?' asked Pasanius as the shutter doors of one of the warehouse buildings screeched open and a host of the shambling mutant things they had killed earlier emerged. Behind them came a pathetic, shuffling mass of humanity, their heads cast down and their bodies swathed in baggy, flesh-coloured robes.

'Some kind of prison?' ventured Uriel, as the mutants herded the prisoners towards the gates of the camp. Were all these buildings filled with prisoners? The great daemonic head on the tower turned on grinding cogs to face the hundreds-strong column, huge streams of flame belching from its eyes. A booming voice roared from its mouth, speaking a language Uriel did not understand, but which sent aching spasms through his joints and muscles, as though the sound resonated within the darkest recesses of his brain.

The prisoners marched through the camp, the mutants stabbing at them with crackling prods and beating them with iron-tipped cudgels. The Iron Warriors marched ahead of the column, hideously perverted bolters carried across their breastplates. As they approached, the gate squealed open, the corpses hanging from it jittering in a grotesque imitation of life.

'Where are they taking them?' wondered Uriel.

'Oh, Emperor, no,' whispered Pasanius. 'They're taking them–'

'To be skinned alive...' finished Uriel as he saw that the prisoners were not swathed in baggy robes at all, but were all completely naked to the elements. Their flesh hung in huge flaps from their bodies, stretched beyond all normal proportions by some unknown means. Encrusted dewlaps drooped from emaciated arms, chests, legs and buttocks. Men and women clutched fold upon fold of stretched skin to their bodies for fear it would trip them, sagging bellies and drained teats hanging like empty sacks of dried leather from their wasted frames.

'They're taking them to the skinning platform. No, no...' said Uriel. 'But why?'

'Does it matter?' snarled Pasanius, gripping his flamer tightly, his silver finger hovering over the ignition key. 'We can't let this horror go unpunished!'

Uriel nodded, feeling his hatred for the Iron Warriors reach new heights, but he forced himself to try and remain calm. To attack this column was suicide, they were directly in front of the bunkers and the gun tower, not to mention three Iron Warriors.

But to let such an affront against humanity go unmolested? To allow these traitors to butcher these people as though they were no more than animals?

Pasanius was right, such evil would not stand.

He could see righteous anger in Pasanius's eyes, but also something else, something darker. Uriel saw the light of a zealot in his battle-brother's eyes, the light of one who goes to battle with a death wish, where survival is irrelevant.

Was there more to Pasanius's desire to fight than the obvious reasons of humanity?

It seemed to Uriel that there was, but such were questions for when, or if, they lived through the next few minutes.

Uriel drew his sword, his thumb hovering over the activation rune.

He gripped Pasanius's shoulder guard and said, 'If we do not survive, then it has been an honour to call you my friend.'

Pasanius nodded, but did not reply, his gaze never wavering from the approaching column of slaves, mutants and Iron Warriors.

His eyes suddenly narrowed and he nodded at something over Uriel's shoulder. 'What in the name of the Emperor?'

Uriel turned and saw a number of figures moving stealthily through the high crags that surrounded the camp.

'Are these the things that have been tracking us through the mountains?'

'No,' said Pasanius. 'I don't think so. They look like…'

'Space Marines!' breathed Uriel as he saw two figures in green power armour rise from behind a cluster of boulders and aim missile launchers towards the camp. The Iron Warriors below had not noticed the figures moving above them and Uriel realised with wild enthusiasm that this must surely be an ambush!

A pair of missiles shot from the Space Marines' weapons and slashed towards the leftmost bunker, slamming into the rockcrete and obscuring it in a

bright explosion of fire and smoke. Another flashing
pair of contrails hammered into the opposite bunker
from somewhere high above Uriel and Pasanius and
the second bunker vanished in a fiery explosion.

Prisoners screamed and Iron Warriors bellowed
commands at the mutant herders as more warriors in
power armour emerged from hiding now that the trap
was sprung. Bolter shells stitched an explosive path
through the prisoners, blood and screams filling the
air as they died. More missiles shot out and exploded
against the bunkers, and Uriel heard the crack of
stonework collapsing under the onslaught.

'Let's go!' shouted Uriel, activating his sword and
charging from cover towards the panicked column of
prisoners. Pasanius was quick to follow him, a blue
flame leaping to life on the end of his weapon.

Uriel saw an Iron Warrior clubbing a prisoner with
the butt of his gun and aimed his charge towards him.
The warrior was a full head and shoulders above Uriel,
his armour spiked and daubed with unclean symbols.
A pair of curved and looping horns sprouted from his
helmet and he carried a brutal sword with screaming,
serrated teeth. He spun, hearing Uriel's wild charge
and raised his weapon, but it was already too late.
Uriel slashed his sword through the Iron Warrior's
breastplate, drawing a spray of black blood and a roar
of pain from his foe.

Pasanius sprayed a sheet of flame across a second
Iron Warrior, one with mechanised, snapping claws for
hands and an explosion ripped through the prisoners
as a fuel-filled tank on the Chaos Marine's back detonated.

Uriel heard the roar of bolter fire from above, seeing
scores of warriors in different coloured power armour
charging from their concealment. He swayed aside as

the Iron Warrior swung his sword in a graceless arc meant to behead him and slashed his sword around at his flank, cutting a full handspan into his armour. More missiles speared out from the spires, slamming into the towering daemon head and rocking it back. Thick cable stays snapped and whipped around in slashing arcs as the daemon tower roared.

Heavy calibre shells ripped from its mouth, tearing great gouges in the earth as they sprayed through the camp, striking friend and foe alike. The mutants in rubberised body suits jabbed the prisoners back to the camp, drawing blood and piteous cries from their wretched charges.

The Iron Warrior roared in anger, stepping forward to smash his fist against Uriel's chest. His strength was phenomenal, even for one genetically engineered to be stronger, and Uriel was hurled back, skidding through the ash as his attacker raised his sword two-handed to deliver the deathblow. He drew his pistol and squeezed off two shells, both ricocheting from the Iron Warrior's armour.

'Now you die, renegade!' bellowed the traitor.

Uriel rolled aside as the screaming sword hacked into the ground, kicking out at the Iron Warrior's kneecap. He roared as he struck, putting his entire strength behind the blow, feeling his foe's armour splinter and the knee shatter into fragments. The Iron Warrior howled and dropped to the ground. Uriel didn't give him a chance to recover and stepped in, driving his sword clean through the Iron Warrior's chest.

The warrior seized his neck and chuckled, a throaty death rasp, and Uriel felt the immense strength in the grip. He twisted the blade, spurts of blood spraying his hands as the wound tore wider. The Iron Warrior's grip on his neck tightened and he heard a joint in his gorget pop and crack as his dying foe sought to choke the life from him. Uriel slammed his fist into the side of the warrior's helmet again and again, pounding his skull to destruction until he finally released his grip.

Uriel staggered back from the dead Iron Warrior, seeing the Space Marines storming through the open gateway in the razorwire fence. The bunkers were smoking ruins, their interiors like abattoirs. Gunfire blasted from the daemonic tower, ripping through the ranks of the attacking Space Marines. Some fell, but most picked themselves up before ducking into whatever cover they could find. Mutants fled before the wrath of the attackers, but they were cut down without mercy, hacked to death with swords or beaten to death with armoured gauntlets.

The fire from the tower was punishing the attackers and as its fiery gaze swept across the plateau, Uriel had a sickening sensation that it *saw* him, saw him and recognised him…

Even as he watched, he saw a warrior in midnight black power armour leap from a spire of rock to one side of the camp. A searing fire erupted from his back and Uriel saw the warrior was wearing a jump pack. Smoke and flames fired from its vents, propelling the warrior through the air to land on the head of the daemon tower. Flames burst from its eyes and the tower shook violently, but whether that was in response to the Space Marine landing on it or the daemon's own fury, it was impossible to tell.

The warrior slashed at the daemonic head with lightning sheathed claws, crackling arcs of blue energy flaring where he struck, before swinging one-handed from the side of the head and clamping something to its side. The tower shook violently, as though seeking to dislodge its attacker, but the dark armoured warrior drove his lightning claws into the daemon head and hung on. He swung around the tower, slashing at the thick cables that held it in place before bracing his feet against its cheek and pushing off. His jump jets fired as the melta charge he had placed on the daemon head detonated and he flew clear on the bow wave of an explosion that vaporised the top of the tower in a pluming mushroom cloud of incandescent energy.

With a shrieking roar, the tower swayed drunkenly, the few remaining cable stays twanging loudly as they pulled taut before snapping with the crack of a gun-shot. The tower toppled majestically, crashing through the corrugated tin roof of the nearest warehouse and sending up plumes of dust and smoke.

Gunfire sounded sporadically from the camp as the last of the mutant labourers were rounded up and killed, and Uriel let out a deep breath as he saw that the battle was over.

He dragged his sword from the chest of the body before him, looking around to see an Iron Warrior on his knees, blood flooding down his breastplate as Pasanius slashed at him with his own chainblade. Both his arms had been hacked off and his belly had spilled its contents across the dark earth.

The fight was gone from the Iron Warrior, but still Pasanius took his measure of vengeance from him. A mob of Space Marines had the last Iron Warrior sur-rounded and shot him to death without mercy, their bolts penetrating his torn armour and exploding wetly within his flesh.

Only now, with the battle over, did Uriel really pay close attention to the armour of the Space Marines he had fought alongside. No more than two or three were alike in colour or design, and each bore testament to many hard fights, with ancient battle scars hastily and imperfectly repaired with crude grafts and filler. Almost all bore a different Chapter symbol on their shoulder guards and many had painted over them with jagged red saltires.

Wailing slaves squatted in their folds of flesh or cradled each other in their misery. Uriel ran over to Pasanius as he continued to hack the fallen Iron Warrior into pieces.

'Pasanius!' shouted Uriel.

He grabbed Pasanius's arm as he drew back for another blow. 'Pasanius, he is dead!'

Pasanius's head snapped round, his eyes ablaze with fury. For the briefest second, Uriel feared that something terrible had possessed his friend, then the killing light went out of him and he dropped the Iron Warrior's weapon and let out a deep, shuddering breath. The sergeant dropped to his knees, his face ashen at the fury he had unleashed.

'Your comrade's anger does him credit,' said a voice behind Uriel and he turned to see the warrior in black who had destroyed the tower. His armour was a far cry from the usual gleaming brilliance of a Space Marine's power armour, being ravaged with dents, scars and patches. Hot vapours vented at his shoulders from the nozzles of his jump pack, and a white symbol – a bird of prey of some kind – had been painted over with a jagged red cross. His helmet bore a similar symbol across his visor.

'You kill Iron Warriors well, both of you,' he said.

Uriel took the measure of this Space Marine before answering, seeing a confident, almost arrogant swagger to his posture.

'I am Uriel Ventris of the Ultramarines, and this is Pasanius Lysane. Who are you?'

The warrior sheathed the lightning claws on his gauntlets and reached up to release the vacuum seals on his gorget. He removed his helmet and took a lungful of the stale air of Medrengard before answering.

'My name is Ardaric Vaanes, formerly of the Raven Guard,' he said, running a hand over his scalp. Vaanes's hair was long and dark, bound in a tight scalp lock; his features angular and pale, with deep-set hooded eyes of violet. His cheeks were scarred and he bore a trio of round scars on his forehead above his left eye, where it looked as though long service studs had been removed.

'Formerly?' asked Uriel warily.

'Aye, formerly,' said Vaanes, stepping forward and offering his hand to Uriel.

Uriel eyed the proffered hand and said, 'You are renegade.'

Vaanes held his hand out for a second longer before accepting that Uriel was not going to take it and dropped it to his side. He nodded. 'Some call us that, yes.'

Pasanius stood next to Uriel and said, 'Others call you traitor.'

Vaanes's eyes narrowed. 'Perhaps they do, but only once.'

The three Space Marines stared at one another in silence for long seconds before Vaanes shrugged and walked past them towards the wrecked camp.

'Wait,' said Uriel, turning and following the renegade. 'I don't understand. How is it you come to be here?'

'That, Uriel Ventris, is a long story,' replied Vaanes, as they passed through the gate into the blazing camp. 'But we should destroy this place and be gone from here soon. The Unfleshed are close and the scent of death will draw them here quickly.'

'What about all these people?' asked Pasanius, sweeping his arm around to encompass the weeping prisoners outside the camp.

'What about them?'

'How are we going to get them out of here?'

'We're not,' said Vaanes.

'You're not?' snapped Uriel. 'Then why did you come to rescue them?'

'Rescue them?' said Vaanes, gesturing to his warriors, who began methodically working their way around the warehouse buildings and placing explosive charges. 'We didn't come to rescue them, we came to destroy this camp and that is all. These people are nothing to me.'

'How can you say that? Look at them!'

'If you want to rescue them, then good luck to you, Uriel Ventris. You will need it.'

'Damn you, Vaanes, have you no honour?'

'None to speak of, no,' snapped Vaanes. 'Look at them, these precious people you want to save. They are worthless. Most do not survive to reach the skinning chasm anyway and the ones that do soon wish they had not.'

'But you can't just abandon them,' pressed Uriel.

'I can and I will.'

'What is this camp anyway?' asked Pasanius. 'A prison? A death camp?'

Vaanes shook his head. 'No, nothing so mundane. It is much worse than that.'

'Then what?'

Vaanes grabbed the handles of the roller shutter door of the nearest warehouse and hauled it open, saying, 'Why don't you find out?'

Uriel shared a wary glance with Pasanius as Ardaric Vaanes gestured that they should enter the building. A powerful reek of human waste gusted from within, mixed with the stench of rotted flesh and the stink of desperation. Flickering lights sputtered within and a low sobbing drifted on the stinking air.

Uriel stepped into the brick building, his eyes quickly adjusting to the gloom within. Inside, the warehouse was revealed to be a mechanised factory facility, with iron girders running the length of the building fitted with dangling chains and heavy pulley mechanisms on greased runners. Mesh cages on raised platforms ran along the left-hand side of the building, a mass of pale flesh filling each one, with gurgling pipes and tubes drooping from bulging feed sacks suspended from the roof.

A trough that reeked of human faeces ran beneath the cages, clogged and buzzing with waste-eating insects. Uriel covered his mouth and nose, even his prodigious metabolism struggling to protect him from the awful stench. He walked forwards, his boots ringing on the grilled floor as he approached the first cage.

Inside was a naked man, though to call him such was surely to stretch the term. His form was immense, bloated and flabby, and his skin had the colour and texture of bile, with a horrid, clammy gleam to it. Rusted clamps held his jaw open while ribbed tubing pulsed with a grotesque peristaltic motion as nutrients and foodstuffs laced with growth hormones were pumped into him as another tube carried away his waste. Coloured wires and augmetic plugs pierced the flesh of his sagging chest, no doubt artificially regulating his heart and preventing the cardiac arrest that his vast bulk should have long ago brought on.

His limbs were thick, doughy lumps of grey flesh, held immobile by tight snares of wire, his features lost in the flabby immensity of his skull, his eyes telling of a mind that had long since taken refuge in madness. Uriel felt an immense sadness and horror at the man's plight – what manner of monster could do this to a human being?

He moved on to the next cage, finding a similar sight within, this time a naked woman, her body also bloated and obscene, her belly scarred and ravaged by what looked like repeated and unnecessary surgery. Unlike the occupant of the previous cage, her eyes had a vestige of sanity and they spoke eloquently to Uriel of her torment.

He turned away, appalled at such hideousness, seeing that there were hundreds of such cages within this darkened hell. Repulsed beyond words, yet drawn to explore further, he crossed the chamber to see what lay on the other side of the building. More cages occupied the right-hand side of the building, but these were narrower, occupied by splayed individuals who looked like the poor wretches Uriel had once seen on a hive world that had been cut off from the agri world it had relied upon for foodstuffs. Starving men and women were hung from iron hooks, wired to machines that kept them in a hellish limbo between life and death as their body fat was forcibly sucked from them by hissing pumps and industrial irrigation equipment.

Their skin hung loose on their bodies and drooped from their emaciated frames in purulent sheets. Uriel now knew the fate of those in the cages behind him. Fattened up artificially so the skin might stretch to obscene proportions, then ultra-rapidly divested of their bulk that they might be skinned to provide swathes of fresh skin.

But why? Why would anyone go to such lengths to harvest such vast quantities of human skin? The answer eluded Uriel and he felt an all-consuming pity well up within him at the plight of these prisoners.

'You see?' said Ardaric Vaanes, standing behind him. 'There is nothing you can do for them. Freeing these… things is pointless and their death will be a blessed release.'

'Sweet Emperor,' whispered Uriel. 'What purpose does this cruelty serve?'

Vaanes shrugged. 'I do not know, nor do I care. The Iron Warriors have built dozens of these camps in the mountains over the last few months. They are of importance to the Iron Warriors, so I destroy them. The "why" of it is irrelevant.'

'Are all the buildings like this one?' asked Pasanius, his face lined with sorrow.

'They are,' confirmed Vaanes. 'We have already destroyed two such camps, and they were all like this. We must destroy it now, for if we do not, the Unfleshed will come and there will be a feasting and a slaughter the likes of which you cannot imagine.'

'I do not understand,' said Uriel. 'The Unfleshed? What are they?'

'Beasts from your worst nightmares,' said Vaanes. 'They are the by-blows of the Iron Warriors, abortions given life who escaped the vivisectoria of the Savage Morticians to roam the mountains. They are many and we are few. Now, come, it is time we were gone.'

Uriel nodded wearily, barely listening to Vaanes, and followed the renegade back out into the remains of the camp. Numbly he took in the scale of the camp: two dozen of these buildings filled it, each one a darkened hell for those farmed within them. For all that he hated to admit it, Vaanes was right, the sooner this facility and all within it were destroyed the better.

A Space Marine in the grey livery of a Chapter Uriel did not recognise jogged up to Vaanes and said, 'They're here. Brother Svoljard just caught their scent!'

'How far?' demanded Vaanes, clamping on his helmet and calling to the remainder of his warriors over his armour's vox.

'Close, perhaps three or four hundred metres,' answered the warrior. 'They approached from downwind.'

'Damn, but they're learning,' hissed Vaanes. 'Everyone clear out. Head south into the mountains and make your own way back to the sanctuary.'

'What is it?' asked Uriel.

'The Unfleshed,' said Vaanes.

CHAPTER SEVEN

GALVANISED BY THE urgency in the renegade's tone, Uriel quickly followed him through the camp as the first of the charges detonated with a hollow boom. Debris and flesh rained down as one of the human battery farms exploded, freeing the prisoners from their agonies in a fiery wash of release.

More charges blew and more of the infernal buildings collapsed inwards. Uriel prayed that the souls within them would forgive them and find their way to the Emperor's side. Flames and smoke billowed from the blazing wreckage of the camp as it was destroyed and the Space Marines ran for the safety of the mountains.

Uriel and Pasanius followed Ardaric Vaanes and his renegades southwards, climbing away from the camp as Uriel heard a mad chorus of howls from the mountains either side of them.

The breath caught in his throat and his pace slowed at the sight of the Unfleshed as they shambled from the mountains towards the burning camp with a twisted, lop-sided gait. Monstrously huge, they were a riot of anatomies, a carnival of the grotesque with no two alike in size or shape. Hugely built and massively tall, they were grossly swollen, glistening red and wet, the rippling form of their exposed musculature out of all proportion to their bodies. Uriel saw that, over and above their enormity and lack of skin, every one of them was deformed in other nightmarish ways, resembling the leavings from a mad sculptor-surgeon's table.

Here was a creature with two heads, fused at the jawbone, with a quartet of cataracted eyes that had run together into one misshapen orb. Another bore a monstrous foetal twin from its stomach, withered, and metastasised arms gripping its parent tightly.

Yet another shambled downhill using piston-like arms, its legs atrophied to little more than grasping claws. A trio of beasts, perhaps related somehow, shared a similarity in their deformities, with each clad in flapping sheets of leathery skin. Their skulls were swollen and distended with long fangs, and bony crests erupted from their flesh all across their bodies.

But supreme amongst the tide of roaring horrors charging towards the camp was a gargantuan beast that led them. Taller and broader than all the others, its physique was greater even than the largest of its monstrous followers, its lumpen head hunched low between its shoulders. Though some distance from Uriel, its skinless features bore the unmistakable gleam of feral intelligence, and the thought of such a creature possessing even the barest glimmer of self-awareness repulsed Uriel beyond reason.

'Come on, Ultramarine,' shouted Vaanes. 'No time to gawp at the monsters!'

Uriel ignored Vaanes and stared at the creatures as they smashed their way through the razorwire fence, unheeding of the barbs that tore at their red-wet bodies. Were they impervious to pain, wondered Uriel?

'What are they?' he said.

'I told you,' shouted back Vaanes. 'Come on! There's enough meat down there to keep them busy for a while, but once they've eaten their fill, they'll try to hunt us. If you don't come now, we will leave you here for them.'

Uriel continued to stare at the grisly spectacle below with morbid fascination, watching as the Unfleshed ripped their way through the ruins of the warehouses, tossing aside massive girders like matchwood and gorging on the scorched meat within. Horrific sounds of snapping bone and tearing flesh sounded from below as the Unfleshed fell upon the prisoners who had remained outside the camp when the renegades had first attacked.

Most died in the first instants of the attack, torn to pieces in a frenzy by the Unfleshed. Others were devoured alive, limbs and slabs of meat flying as the monsters fought for every morsel, their terrible roars of loathsome appetite echoing from the mountains.

Pasanius gripped his arm and said, 'We have to go, Uriel!'

'We let them die,' said Uriel darkly. 'We abandoned them. We might as well have killed them ourselves.'

'We couldn't have saved them, but we can avenge them.'

'How?' said Uriel.

'By living,' answered Pasanius.

Uriel nodded and turned away from the hideous spectacle below, shutting out the roaring feasting and orgiastic howls of pleasure, and feeling a part of his heart grow colder and harder as he left these people to die.

KHALAN-GHOL WAS in flames. Its spires were in ruins and its bastions pounded to dust by the relentless bombardment. Square kilometres burned in the fires of Berossus's shelling, but it was still the merest fraction of the scale of the fortress. Unnatural darkness swathed the fortress, black clouds of lightning-shot smoke hanging low and blotting out the dead whiteness of the sky for leagues around. Snaking kilometres of trenches topped with razorwire surrounded the darkened peak, newly constructed redoubts, bunkers, pillboxes and towers whose mighty guns deafeningly shelled Honsou's fastness, strobing the landscape with their red fire.

Belching manufactorum had been erected on the plains and the pounding clang of industry was a constant refrain in the air. Glowing, orange-lit forges constantly churned out shells, guns and the materiel of war, and Honsou knew that their production rates would put the finest Imperial forge world to shame. He saw the huge silhouettes of Titans on the horizon, their diabolical forms dwarfing everything around them. They could do little but act as gun platforms for now, the leviathans unable to climb the mountainous slopes of Khalan-Ghol until the massive ramp Berossus was building was complete.

He and a hand-picked cadre of his finest warriors clambered down the jagged slopes towards the forces arrayed below them. Honsou slid down a fallen pile of broken boulders, rotted, skeletal arms jutting from the cracks between them, but whether they belonged to one of his warriors or one of his foes he neither knew nor cared.

Berossus had been nothing if not thorough in his attentions; the lower bastions were gone, shelled until it was as though they had never existed, and the outer ring of forts had fallen before his onslaught.

Tens of thousands had already died in the battle, but Berossus had not been so stupid as to waste his best warriors in the battle thus far. Chaff, slaves and rabble bound to the service of Chaos, had charged his walls only to be met and hurled back by fire and steel.

Combined with the soldiery of Toramino's grand company, the two warsmiths had enough manpower to drag down the walls of Khalan-Ghol eventually; it was simply a matter of time.

Time Honsou did not intend to give them.

'Berossus is a fool,' he had said, when broaching the plan that now saw him cautiously approaching the sentry lines of the enemy's furthest advanced trenches. 'We will take the fight to him.'

'Beyond the walls?' asked Obax Zakayo.

'Aye,' replied Honsou. 'Right to the very heart of his army.'

'Madness,' said Zakayo.

'Exactly,' grinned Honsou. 'Which is why Berossus will never expect it. You know Berossus! To him, sieges are simply a matter of logistics. As a former vassal of Forrix, I would have thought you would have appreciated that, Zakayo.'

'I do, but to leave the protection of our walls…'

'Berossus is a slave to the mechanics of a siege. *This* course of action results in *that* result – that's how he thinks. He is too hidebound by the grand tradition of battle from the ancient days to think beyond the purity of an escalade, to expect the unexpected.'

'It has not failed him before,' pointed out Obax Zakayo.

'He hasn't fought me before,' said Honsou.

The trenches ahead were lit by drumfires, and the clang of digging shovels and the rumble of earth-moving machines was all but obscured by the thunder of guns.

'Onyx,' whispered Honsou, unsheathing his black bladed axe. 'Go.'

Onyx nodded, a fluid shadow and all but invisible in the darkness, slithering on his belly towards the trenchline, his outline blurring and merging with the night. Obax Zakayo said, 'If he is discovered, we will all die here.'

'Then we die,' snarled Honsou. 'Now be silent or I will kill you myself.'

Suitably chastened, Obax Zakayo said nothing more as he heard the sound of gurgling cries and slashing blades from ahead. Honsou saw a fountain of blood spurt above the line of the trench and knew that it was now safe to approach.

He crawled to where Onyx had cut a path through the razorwire and dropped into the trench. A score of corpses filled the trench and adjacent dugout, blood, glistening and oily in the firelight, coating the walls and seeping between the well laid duckboards. Each body lay sprawled at an unnatural angle, as though every bone had been broken. Each bore a long gash up the centre of their backs where their spinal column had been ripped out. Onyx himself stood immobile in the centre of the trench, slowly sheathing bronze claws into the grey flesh of his hands as the silver fire of his veins burned even brighter than normal. The daemon within him revelled in the slaughter and allowed the human part of him to return to the surface once more.

'Good kills,' said Honsou as his Iron Warriors dropped into the trench, spreading out and securing their entry point. He ran over to the communications trench at the back of this widened area and ducked his head around the corner. Just as he had expected, he could only see partway along it, the trench following a standard zigzagging course. Further down its length, he could see red-liveried soldiers and slaves.

'Have you no imagination, Berossus?' he chuckled to himself. 'You make this too easy.'

He turned away and gathered his warriors about him. 'It is time. Let's go, and remember, as far as anyone here knows, we are loyal Iron Warriors of Berossus. Let no one challenge that.'

His warriors nodded and, with Honsou in the lead, they set off down the communication trench. They walked with the confident, easy swagger of warriors who know they are without equal, and all the human and mutant labourers of Berossus abased themselves before them as they passed.

They passed dugouts filled with twisted mutant creatures gathered in chanting groups around shrines to the Dark Gods, their mutterings overseen by sorcerers in golden robes. None questioned them, none had any reason to, honoured to have ancient warriors of Chaos pass by. Honsou saw bright arc lights suspended on baroque towers of iron that reared into the night and were hung with all manner of bloody trophies. Chanting groups of robed figures surrounded them,

Honsou stopped and asked, 'Zakayo, what are these towers? This doesn't look like something Berossus would do.'

'I am not sure,' replied Obax Zakayo. 'I have never seen their like.'

'They seek to break the walls of Khalan-Ghol with sorcery,' said Onyx. 'The towers are saturated with mystical energy. I can feel it, and the daemon within me bathes in it.'

'What?' hissed Honsou, suddenly wary. 'Are their magicks strong enough to overcome the kabal and the Heart of Blood?'

'No,' said Onyx. 'Not even close. There is great power here, but the Heart of Blood has endured for an eternity and no power wielded by a mortal can defeat it.'

Honsou nodded, reassured that the mystical defences of his fortress would hold. He glanced at the towers.

'This smells of Toramino,' he said. 'Berossus would not have thought of it.'

'Aye,' agreed Obax Zakayo. 'Lord Toramino has great cunning.'

'That he does, but I'll see that arrogant bastard dead before he takes Khalan-Ghol, sorcery or not.'

Passing beyond the towers, Honsou and his warriors emerged from the trench lines without incident, watching as the sweating, straining army of Berossus sought to bring his fortress to ruin. Tracked dozers laden with shells rumbled past behind high earthworks and Honsou was forced to admire the thorough completeness of the siegeworks. Forrix himself would have been proud.

Plumes of fire shot up from an iron refinery. The thunder of processing plants producing explosives and the hammering of forges filled the plains; millions of men working to bring him down. Stockpiles of ammunition and brass-cased shells were stored in armoured magazines and as they passed each one, Obax Zakayo would enter and place an explosive charge from the dispenser on his back. Honsou knew that Obax Zakayo was, in all likelihood, a liability, too entrenched in the old ways of his former master to be part of Honsou's cadre of lieutenants, but no one knew demolitions and explosives like he did.

And he had a cruelty to him that appealed to Honsou's sense for mayhem.

The further back they travelled from the front trenches, the greater the risk of discovery became. He saw sturdily constructed barrack-bunkers and great artillery pits that had obviously been built by Iron Warriors, and heard roaring bellows of madness that could only mean the cage-pits of the dreadnoughts were near.

'It is folly to continue, my lord, we should retreat now,' said Obax Zakayo. 'We have placed enough explosives to disrupt Berossus for months.'

'No, not yet,' said Honsou, a reckless sense of abandon driving him onwards as he caught sight of a familiar banner flapping in the wind atop an armoured pavilion. It squatted in the shadow of one of the colossal Titans, beyond a forest of razorwire and a staggered series of bunkers. 'Not when we have a chance to deliver something a little more personal to Lord Berossus himself.'

Obax Zakayo saw the banner and said, 'Great gods of Chaos, you cannot be serious!'

'You know I am, Zakayo,' said Honsou. 'I never joke about killing.'

DUG SEVEN METRES down into the rock, the sides of the artillery pit were reinforced with steel-laced rockcrete, at least two metres thick. Angled parapets, designed to deflect enemy artillery strikes swept up over the embrasure the huge siege gun would fire through. Honsou knew that none of his artillery pieces could reach this far and that such endeavour was wasted effort, but it was so like Berossus to have them built anyway.

The mighty cannon's bronze barrel was silhouetted against the roiling clouds above, etched with great spells of ruin and hung with thick, drooling chains of desecrated iron. It sat at the base of an incline on rails, so that after each shot it would roll back into its firing position.

Perhaps a hundred human soldiers surrounded the huge cannon, guards to protect the mighty siege gun. Honsou and his warriors brazenly marched towards the artillery pit, daring the soldiers to stop them. Though he and his warriors proudly displayed the heraldry of the Iron Warriors, it would not take the soldiers long to realise that they did not belong here and raise the alarm.

Honsou could see they were attracting stares, but pressed on, pushing the bluff to the limit as an Iron Warrior with a heavily augmented head and arms climbed from the artillery pit. Red lights winked on his helmet, fitted with range-finders, trajectorum and cogitators, and Honsou knew he looked upon one of Berossus's Chirumeks. More machine to him than man, the practitioner of the black arts of technology scanned him up and down before a huge gun affixed to his back swung around on a hissing armature and aimed at them.

Onyx never gave him a chance to fire the weapon, leaping forward with the speed of a striking snake. His outline blurred, becoming oily and indistinct as he moved. A flash of bronze claws and a rip of flesh and the Chirumek collapsed, his spinal column held aloft by the daemonic symbiote.

'Hurry!' shouted Honsou, running for the artillery pit now that all hopes of subterfuge were gone. He dropped into the artillery pit, firing his bolter at its other occupants. Loader slaves died in the hail of fire, blasted apart by his explosive shells and Chirumeks dived for cover as the Iron Warriors stormed in.

Yells and shouts of warning sounded from the human soldiers, but as the bark of gunfire continued, most were soon silenced. Honsou knew they didn't have much time and shouted, 'Zakayo, get down here!'

The lumbering giant climbed down into the pit as Honsou and his warriors slaughtered the remainder of the gun's crew. The huge cannon hissed and rumbled, revelling in the bloodshed around it and he could sense the daemonic urge to kill bound within it. Obax Zakayo climbed to the gunner's mount and began hauling at the bronze levers there.

Laughing at the irony of the moment, Honsou also climbed the ladder to the gunner's position as the turret emitted a bass groan and the barrel began turning from Khalan-Ghol towards the pavilion of Berossus.

The growling barrel depressed until it was virtually horizontal as bolter fire rattled from the sides of the artillery pit and Iron Warriors from Berossus's grand company poured from their barracks – together with their human auxiliaries – to launch a counterattack.

'Can't you hurry this up?' snapped Honsou.

'Not really, no!' shouted Obax Zakayo, pulling thick levers and heavy chains fitted to the daemon gun's breech. Honsou leaned over the railings of the gunnery platform and shouted down to his warriors. 'Get ready to reload this gun when we fire! I want at least a couple of shots before we have to escape!'

Four warriors broke from the defence of the gun pit and began hauling on the pulley chains that led down through a great iron portal in the floor of the artillery pit to the armoured magazine below. Within seconds, the iron gate groaned open and an enormous shell emerged. Grunting with the effort, the Iron Warriors manhandled the shell onto the gurney that would deliver it to the gun. It was extremely dangerous to have the magazine open while firing, but Honsou figured that since it wasn't their gun anyway, it didn't matter whether it got blown up or not.

'Ready to fire!' shouted Obax Zakayo.

Honsou sighted along the aiming reticule and laughed, seeing the roof of Berossus's pavilion and the gold and black heraldry of his banner.

'Fire!' he yelled and Obax Zakayo yanked the firing chain. Honsou swayed as the gun's massive recoil almost hurled him from the gunnery platform, the roar of its firing nearly deafening him. Thick, acrid smoke belched from the barrel as the great cannon screamed in pleasure. The daemonic breech clanged open of its own accord and his Iron Warriors ran the next shell along the rails and into the weapon.

As they fetched another shell from the magazine, Honsou saw that the first shot had been uncannily accurate. The banner of Berossus was no more, destroyed utterly by the explosion. The top portion of the pavilion was gone, nothing but a saw-toothed ruin left of its upper half. Even as he watched the debris rain down, secondary explosions were touched off by the burning wreckage as the gun fired again.

This time he was ready, but even so, was again almost dislodged by the recoil. Once more the pavilion vanished in a sheet of flame as their second shell impacted. Another shell was rammed home, but as the breech clanged shut, Honsou felt a huge tremor pass through the earth, swiftly followed by a second.

He looked up through the murk in time to see a massive shadow moving through the darkness and saw with a thrill of fear that one of the Titans was making for them. The ground shook to its tread, the footsteps of an angry god of war come to destroy them.

'Come on!' he shouted to Obax Zakayo. 'One more shot, then it's time we were gone!'

Obax Zakayo nodded, casting fearful glances over the gunner's mantlet with each booming footstep of the approaching Titan. Once again the mighty daemon gun fired, this time striking the barrack block beside the pavilion and reducing it to flaming rubble.

'Everyone out!' shouted Honsou, leaping from the gun and running towards the ladders that led from the artillery pit. Honsou wrenched open the iron door to the magazine as he passed and lobbed a handful of grenades inside. He leapt for the ladder as a huge shadow enveloped the artillery pit and looked up in time to see the massive, clawed foot of the Titan descending upon him.

He scrambled up the ladder and rolled aside as its thunderous footstep slammed down, obliterating the daemonic gun in a heartbeat and missing him by less than a metre. He rolled away and lurched to his feet, still dazed from the concussive impact of the Titan's foot when the grenades he had dropped into the magazine detonated.

The ground heaved and bellowed, huge geysers of flame and smoke ripping from the ground as hundreds of tonnes of buried ordnance exploded in a terrifyingly powerful conflagration. Honsou was lifted into the air and swatted for a hundred metres or more by the blast, slamming into an earthen rampart and rolling into a pile of excavated soil.

He picked himself up, coughing and reeling from the impact to take stock of his surroundings. He turned as he heard a groaning sound and saw the Titan that had destroyed the gun pit sway like a drunk, its leg destroyed from the knee down by the magazine's explosion. Sparks and plasma fire vented from shattered conduits and sparking cables. Even as he watched, the massive daemon engine began to slowly topple over, its piston-driven arms flailing for balance as it fell.

He turned away, laughing as dismayed soldiers and horrified Iron Warriors watched one of their mightiest daemon machines destroyed before their very eyes. The ground shook as the Titan hit the ground and was smashed asunder, but Honsou was already making his way back to Khalan-Ghol. He had no way of knowing what had become of the rest of his warriors, but trusted that they were experienced and resourceful enough to get back to Khalan-Ghol on their own in all this confusion.

A dark form emerged from the smoke beside him and he recognised the sinuous form of Onyx. The daemonic symbiote's claws were unsheathed and bloody, the glittering fire of his eyes shining with a deathly lustre. He had hunted well.

'A successful foray,' said Onyx with typical understatement.

'Aye,' agreed Honsou. 'Not bad. Not bad at all.'

THE SANCTUARY ARDARIC Vaanes had spoken of turned out to be secreted in a shadowed valley overlooking the plains before the mighty fortress shrouded in dark clouds and explosions. The sounds of battle still raged from below and Uriel could see a tremendous blaze deep in the besieger's camp. Their flight from the Unfleshed had been a helter-skelter journey of false trails and looping attempts to prevent the beasts from following their tracks.

Uriel could not shake the sound of the Unfleshed feasting on the prisoners, but was surprised at how little it bothered him now. Perhaps Vaanes had been right, there was nothing anyone could have done for those poor unfortunates, and death was the best thing for them.

The renegades had split up once clear of the death camp and now returned to their base in ones and twos, climbing down the valley sides or hiking up from below.

'Our sanctuary,' said Vaanes, pointing towards a series of crumbling bunkers and blockhouses that had fallen into disrepair and had clearly seen better days. Partially filled-in trenches and rusted coils of razorwire were angled before the dilapidated constructions, but Uriel's practiced eye could see that this place was not without its defences. Barely visible gun nests over-looked the approaches and he doubted that anyone could approach without some warning being given.

'What was this place used for?' asked Pasanius.

Vaanes shrugged. 'An old ammunition store, a barracks, a construction exercise? Who knows? All I know is that when we found this place it was abandoned and no one ever came near it. That's good enough for me.'

Uriel nodded as they crossed a trench via a series of iron sheets and Vaanes moved ahead of them towards the blockhouse beyond the bunkers.

Pasanius leaned close to Uriel and whispered, 'What are we doing? These Space Marines are renegades! Are we to damn ourselves even more in the sight of the Emperor?'

'I know,' said Uriel bitterly, 'but what choice do we have?'

'We can strike out on our own.'

'Aye, and maybe we will, but they have been here longer than us and we may learn something of this world and its dangers.'

Pasanius looked unconvinced, but said nothing more as they reached the armoured doors to the blockhouse. Whatever mechanism had once opened and closed them obviously no longer operated and Vaanes hauled them open with brute strength before disappearing within and indicating that they should follow.

Uriel ducked inside the blockhouse, the interior surprisingly well-lit by numerous holes pierced in the roof. Shafts of dead white light pooled on the rockcrete floor and reflected from the peeling, flakboard walls.

'I realise that this might be a little more luxury than you're used to as Ultramarines, but it's the nearest thing we have to a home just now,' grinned Vaanes as he walked ahead of them into the blockhouse's main chamber.

Light streamed in through the firing slits and Uriel could see that the chamber was full of the same Space Marines who had attacked the camp earlier. Most were engaged in cleaning their weapons or repairing their armour and Uriel was shocked at the sheer number of different Chapter symbols he saw on display.

Howling Griffons, White Consuls, Wolf Brothers, Crimson Fists and many others he did not recognise.

But most surprising of all were two figures crouched in the corner of the main chamber cleaning lasrifles. Dressed in the battered fatigues and torn uniform jackets of the Imperial Guard, they looked up as Uriel and Pasanius entered. Both men were so filthy and dishevelled that it was impossible to tell what regiment they had belonged to, but both wore expressions of tired, proud courage.

'Two new warriors for our band!' called Vaanes before slumping against one wall and removing his helmet.

Uriel refrained from qualifying that statement as the leaner of the two Guardsmen rose to his feet and limped towards Uriel. His skin was pale and wasted looking, blotchy and unhealthy, his eyes bloodshot.

The man extended a palsied hand and said, 'Lieutenant Colonel Mikhail Leonid of the 383rd Jouran Dragoons.'

'Uriel Ventris, and this is Pasanius Lysane.'

'What kind of Space Marines are you?' asked Leonid, stifling a cough. 'I don't see any markings.'

'We are Ultramarines,' replied Uriel. 'Sent from our Chapter to fulfil a death oath.'

Leonid shrugged. 'A better reason than most for being here.'

'Perhaps,' nodded Uriel. 'And how is it that a colonel of the Imperial Guard comes to be here?'

'That,' said Leonid, 'is a long story...'

CHAPTER EIGHT

Leonid and Sergeant Ellard, the softly spoken companion of the colonel, spent the next hour and a half regaling Uriel and Pasanius of how they had ended up in slavery on the bleak daemon world of Medrengard, beginning with the devastating assault of the Iron Warriors on the world of Hydra Cordatus just prior to the Despoiler's invasion through the Cadian Gate.

He spoke of weeks of constant shelling, of tanks and Titans and of the lethal cancers that base treachery had infected the men and women of his regiment with. But more than this, he spoke of noble courage. He spoke of a warrior named Eshara, a Space Marine of the Imperial Fists, and the sacrifice he and his men had made before the Valedictor Gate. Uriel felt a fierce pride well within him at the thought of such a noble warrior standing before impossible odds, and wished he could have met such a brave hero.

But ultimately, the story did not end well. The Iron Warriors finally took the citadel before Imperial reinforcements could arrive and Leonid wept as he spoke of the brutal slaughter that took place upon its final fall.

'It was a nightmare,' said Leonid. 'They showed no mercy.'

'The Iron Warriors serve the Ruinous Powers,' said Uriel. 'They do not know the meaning of the word.'

'Captain Eshara bought us some time, but it wasn't enough. The cavern below was too large and there was too much gene-seed to destroy. We–'

'Wait,' interrupted Uriel. 'Gene-seed? There was Space Marine gene-seed beneath your citadel?'

'Yes,' nodded Leonid. 'An Adeptus Mechanicus magos told me that it was one of the few places in the galaxy where it could be stored. The Warsmith Honsou stole it and brought it to this world along with the slaves he took for his forges at the battle's end.'

'Who is Honsou?' asked Pasanius.

'He is the warlord who dwells in the fortress you saw as we came into this valley,' said Ardaric Vaanes.

'It is this Honsou's fortress that is besieged?' said Uriel, unable to mask his interest.

'It is,' confirmed Vaanes, wandering over to join the conversation and squatting down on his haunches. 'Why are you so interested in Honsou?'

'We have to get to that fortress.'

Vaanes laughed. 'Then you truly are here on a death oath. Why do you need to get to Honsou's fortress?'

Uriel paused, unsure as to how much he could trust Vaanes, but realised he had no choice and said, 'Our Chief Librarian was granted a vision from the Emperor, a vision of Medrengard and bloated, daemonic womb creatures called daemonculaba giving birth to corrupt, debased Space Marines. We are here to destroy them and I think that more than mere happenstance has brought us to this place.'

'How so?' asked Vaanes.

'Can it be coincidence that this Honsou has returned here with quantities of gene-seed for these daemonculaba and that we should learn of it from a man who was there to see him take it?'

Vaanes looked Ellard and Leonid up and down. 'I wondered why I hadn't left you to die with the other slaves on the Omphalos Daemonium. Perhaps something other than curiosity stayed my hand.'

Uriel started. 'You know of the Omphalos Daemonium?'

'Of course,' said Vaanes. 'There are few on Medrengard who do not. How is it you know of it?'

'It brought us here,' said Pasanius. 'It appeared within our ship when we made the translation to the immaterium. It killed everyone on board and then brought us here.'

'You willingly travelled within the Omphalos Daemonium?' said Vaanes, aghast.

'Of course not,' snapped Uriel. 'Its daemon creatures overcame us.'

'The Sarcomata…' nodded Vaanes.

'Aye, then the iron giant within the daemon engine brought us here.'

'The iron giant?' asked Leonid. 'The Slaughterman?'

'Slaughterman? No, it said that it only wore the flesh of the Slaughterman, that it was the will of the Omphalos Daemonium that commanded.'

'Then the daemon is free!' breathed Vaanes.

'What is it anyway?' asked Uriel.

'No one knows for sure,' began a sallow-skinned Space Marine of great age wearing armour of deep red and bone, with a raven's head on his shoulder guard. 'But there are tales aplenty, oh yes, tales aplenty.'

'And would you care to share any of them?' asked Vaanes, impatiently.

'I was just about to,' growled the Space Marine, 'if you'd given me half a chance.'

The Space Marine turned to Uriel and said, 'I am Seraphys of the Blood Ravens, and I served in my Chapter's Librarium in the years before my disgrace. One of the greatest driving forces of my Chapter is the seeking out of dark knowledge and forbidden lore, and over the millennia of our existence we have discovered much, and all of it gathered it aboard our Chapter fortress.'

'Your Chapter knew of the Omphalos Daemonium?'

'Indeed we did. In fact, it was a source of particular interest to many of our secret masters. Over the centuries I read much of this daemonic entity, and though much of what was said I believe to be false, there are some things I believe are true. It is said that once it was an ancient and powerful daemon prince, a servant of the Blood God that existed only for slaughter. The skulls it piled before its dark master were legion, but always one creature ever outdid it, one of the Blood God's most favoured avatars, a daemon known as the Heart of Blood; so terrible it was said to have the power to summon bloodstorms and drain the vital fluid from its victims without even laying a blade to their flesh.'

Uriel and Pasanius shared a start of recognition as Seraphys continued. 'This avatar was a daemon of deadly artifice who forged for itself a suit of armour into which it poured all of its malice, all of its hate and all of its cunning, that even the blows of its enemies would strike them down.'

'What became of these daemons?' said Uriel.

Seraphys leaned closer, warming to his tale. 'Some say they fought a great battle that sundered the very fabric of the universe, hurling the debris across the firmament and thus were the galaxies and planets born. Others say that the avatar of the Blood God outwitted the Omphalos Daemonium, and trapped it within the fiery heart of a mighty daemon engine bound to the service of the Iron Warriors, becoming the dread chariot of the Slaughterman – ever to hunger in torment for vengeance.'

'Then how is it that it is free?'

'Ah, well, that the ancient legends do not tell,' said Seraphys sadly.

'I think I might know,' said Leonid.

'You?' said Seraphys. 'How could a lowly Guardsman know of such things?'

Leonid ignored the Blood Raven's patronising tone. 'Perhaps because when Ardaric Vaanes and his warriors freed us from captivity, we were able to defeat the Slaughterman and drive him into the firebox of the daemon engine. We thought we had destroyed him.'

'But all it did was free the daemon within the firebox to take the Slaughterman's flesh for its own,' said Vaanes.

'Does anyone know what became of the Omphalos Daemonium's rival, the avatar?' asked Sergeant Ellard hesitantly.

'There is nothing in the tales I have read of its ultimate fate,' said Seraphys. 'Why?'

'Because I think I have seen it.'

'What? When?' asked Leonid.

'On Hydra Cordatus,' explained Ellard. 'Sir, do you remember the stories that went around when the Mori Bastion fell?'

'Yes,' nodded Leonid. 'Mad stuff, ravings about a giant warrior killing everything in the bastion by his voice alone and a whirlwind that… fed on blood.'

By now a sizeable crowd had gathered to hear these tales and the synchronicity of these revelations was lost on no one.

Ellard nodded. 'I saw it too, but… I didn't say anything. I thought they'd section me for sure if I said what I'd seen.'

'Don't keep us in suspense, sergeant, what happened to it?' demanded Vaanes.

'I don't know for sure,' said Ellard, 'but once it killed Librarian Corwin, it opened up some kind of… gateway… I think. I'm not sure exactly. It was some kind of black thing that it stepped through and vanished. That was the last I saw of it.'

Vaanes rose from his squatting position and said, 'I think you bring trouble with you, Uriel Ventris of the Ultramarines. This is a deadly world, but we can survive here. We steal what we need from the Iron Warriors, and they in turn try to hunt us. It is a fine game, but I think your coming to Medrengard has just skewed that game.'

'Then perhaps that is a good thing,' pointed out Uriel.

'I wouldn't bet on it,' cautioned Vaanes.

PASANIUS SAT ALONE on the rocks outside the blockhouse, more tired than he could ever remember being. He had been awake now for… days, weeks? He couldn't tell, but he knew it had been a long time. The sky above was still that damnable white, and how anyone could live on such a world, where there was no change to mark the passing of time, was beyond him. The crushing monotony of such a bleak vista made him want to weep.

He held his arms out before his chest, turning both hands before his face. His left gauntlet was torn and scarred, ruined by the constant climbing over razor-sharp rocks, but his right was as unblemished as the day it had been grafted to the flesh and bone of his elbow. Thus far he had been able to keep its unique ability to repair itself secret from his battle-brothers, but he knew it was only a matter of time before its miraculous powers became known. Pasanius hammered his fist into the ground, pounding a powdered crater in the rock, smashing his fingers to oblivion then watching in disgust as they reknitted themselves once more.

The shame of concealing such evil from his brethren had almost been too much to bear and the thought of disappointing Uriel terrified him. But to admit to such weakness was as great a shame, and the guilt of this secret had torn a hole in his heart that he could not absolve.

There was no doubt in his mind that it had been beneath the surface of Pavonis, facing the ancient star god known as the Nightbringer, that he had been cursed. He remembered the aching cold of the blow from its scythe that had severed his arm, the crawling sensation of dead flesh where once there had been living tissue. Was it possible that some corruption had been passed to him by the Nightbringer's weapon and infected his body with this terrible sickness?

The adepts of Pavonis had been quick to provide a replacement arm, the very best their world could produce, for Techmarine Harkus and Apothecary Selenus to reattach. He had never been comfortable with the idea of an augmetic arm, but it was not until the battles aboard the *Death of Virtue* that he had begun to suspect that there was more to his new limb than met the eye.

What crime had he committed to be so punished? Why had he been visited by such an affliction? He knew not, but as he removed his breastplate and took out his knife, he vowed he would pay for it in blood.

URIEL LAY BACK and tried to sleep, his eyelids drooping and heavy. At least in the blockhouse there were areas out of the perpetual light of the dead sky, where darkness and sleep could be sought. But sleep was proving to be elusive, his thoughts tumbling through his head in a jumble.

Uriel now felt sure that there was more to this quest than he had initially thought. He knew he should not have been surprised to learn that the Heart of Blood was more than just an artefact, that the schemes of daemons were never straightforward. Were he and Pasanius part of some elaborate vengeance the Omphalos Daemonium had planned for its ancient rival? Who knew, but Uriel vowed that he would not allow himself to be used in such a way. Dark designs were afoot and a confluence of events had come together to bring them to this point. Despite the dangers around him, he felt on some instinctual level that the will of the Emperor was working through him.

Why then did he feel so empty, so hollow?

Uriel had read of the many saints of the Imperium and had heard numerous sermons delivered with impassioned oratory from the pulpit of how the Emperor's power was like a fire within that burned hotter than the brightest star. But Uriel felt no such fire, no light burned within his breast and he had never felt so alone.

Sermons always spoke of heroes as shining examples of virtue: pure of heart, untainted by doubt and unsullied by self aggrandisement.

Given such qualifications, he knew he was no hero, he was outcast, denied even the name of his Chapter and cast within the Eye of Terror with renegades and traitors. Where was the bright light of the Emperor within him here?

He shifted his position, trying to get comfortable on the hard rockcrete floor so that he might be rested enough to press on to the fortress. He knew that the chances of their surviving the journey to the fortress of Honsou were minimal, but perhaps there was some way to entice these renegades to join them. In all likelihood they would all die, but who would miss such worthless specimens as them anyway?

As he turned over, he caught sight of a silhouetted Space Marine in the doorway and pushed himself into a sitting position as Ardaric Vaanes entered and sat resting his back on the wall opposite Uriel.

Thin light spilled in through the doorway, a fine mist of dust floating in the air where Vaanes's footsteps had disturbed them. The two Space Marines sat in silence for long minutes.

'Why are you here, Ventris?' said Vaanes, eventually.

'I told you. We are here to destroy the daemonculaba.'

Vaanes nodded. 'Aye, you said that, but there's more isn't there?'

'What do you mean?'

'I saw the way you and your sergeant looked at one another when Seraphys mentioned the Heart of Blood. That name has some meaning for you doesn't it?'

'Perhaps it does. What of it?'

'Like I said, I think you bring trouble with you, but I can't decide whether it is trouble I want to be part of yet.'

'Should I trust you, Vaanes?'

'Probably not,' admitted Vaanes with a smile. 'And another thing. I noticed that you very deliberately

shied away from explaining why the Omphalos Daemonium went to such lengths to bring you here.'

'It is a daemon creature, who can say what its
motives were?' said Uriel, reluctant to reveal the
pact, even a false pact, he had made with the
Omphalos Daemonium.

'How convenient,' said Vaanes, dryly. 'But I still
want an answer.'

'I have none to give you.'

'Very well, keep your secrets, Ventris, but I want
you gone once you have rested.'

Uriel pushed himself to his feet and crossed the
room to crouch beside Vaanes.

'I know that you have no reason to, but trust me. I
know we are all here on the Emperor's business –
too much is happening to be mere accident. Come
with us, we could use your help. Your men fight well
and together we can regain our honour.'

'Regain our honour?' said Vaanes. 'I had no honour to lose, why do you think I am here and not
with the battle-brothers of my Chapter?'

'I don't know,' replied Uriel. 'Why? Tell me.'

Vaanes shook his head. 'No. You and I are not
friends enough to share such shames. Suffice to say,
we will not go with you. It is a suicide mission.'

'Do you speak for everyone here?' demanded
Uriel.

'More or less.'

'And you would turn your back on a brother Space
Marine in need of your strength?'

'Yes,' said Vaanes. 'I would.'

Suddenly angry, Uriel rose and snapped, 'I should
have expected no less from a damned renegade.'

'Don't forget,' laughed Vaanes, getting to his feet
and turning to leave, 'that you too are a renegade.

You're no longer one of the Emperor's soldiers and it's time you realised that.'

Uriel opened his mouth to reply, but said nothing as he remembered a line from the last sermon he had heard Chaplain Clausel deliver outside the Temple of Correction.

Softly he whispered that line as Vaanes left the room: 'He must put a white cloak upon his soul, that he might climb down into the filth to fight, yet may he die a saint.'

URIEL AWOKE WITH a start, startled and disorientated. He had not been aware of falling asleep, an awareness of his surroundings giving him a strange sense of dislocation as he blinked away sleep. He pushed himself upright, repeating a prayer of thanks for a new day and feeling his mind focus and sharpen as the Catalepsean node of his brain reawakened his full cognitive functions.

Allowing a Space Marine to sleep and remain awake at the same time by influencing the circadian rhythms of sleep and his body's response to sleep deprivation, the Catalepsean node 'switched off' areas of the brain sequentially. Such a process did not replace normal sleep entirely, but allowed a Space Marine to continue to perceive his environment whilst resting.

He ran a hand across his scalp and left the shadowed room, catching the mouth-watering scent of hot food. He entered the blockhouse's main chamber, the same lifeless light spilling in through the firing slits and groups of Space Marines gathered around a cookfire upon which bubbled a large pot of a thick gruel-like porridge. It looked like poor food at best, but right now it was as desirable as the tenderest morsel of roast boar.

Several figures lay sprawled around the chamber, Space Marines resting and Leonid and Ellard asleep beneath the firing slit, using their rifles as pillows.

'I'd say "good morning", but that's not really a term I can use on this world,' said Ardaric Vaanes, spooning some porridge into a crude bowl of beaten metal and handing it to Uriel. 'It's not much, just some stolen ration packs made to go a long way.'

'It's fine. Thank you,' said Uriel, accepting the bowl and sitting next to Pasanius, who nodded a greeting as he scooped the greyish food into his mouth. 'Aren't you worried about the smoke of the fire being seen?'

'On Medrengard? No, rising smoke isn't anything unusual on this planet.'

'No, I suppose it isn't,' said Uriel between mouthfuls. The porridge was thin and he could taste watered down nutrients, the gruel barely enough to stave off starvation, let alone provide any nourishment. But still, it had more taste than the recycled paste his armour provided him.

'Have you thought any more about what I asked before?' said Uriel, finishing the bowl of porridge and setting it down beside him.

'I have,' nodded Vaanes.

'And?'

'You intrigue me, Ventris. There is more to you than meets the eye, but I'm damned if I know what. You say you are here to fulfil a death oath, and I believe you. But there is something else you are not telling me and I fear it will be the death of us all.'

'You're right,' said Uriel, seeing that he had no choice but to tell these renegades the truth. 'There is more and I will tell you all of it. Gather your warriors together outside and I will speak to you all.'

Vaanes narrowed his eyes, wary at letting Uriel speak directly to his men, but realising that he could not refuse. 'Very well. Let's hear what you have to say.'

Uriel nodded and followed Vaanes and his men into the still air and burning glare of the black sun. Space Marines filed out of the blockhouse and descended from their posts in the peaks surrounding the bunker complex as they were called down. Yawning and blinking, Leonid and Ellard stepped into the brightness of the valley, cradling their lasguns over their shoulders.

When the entirety of the renegade warrior band had gathered, some thirty Space Marines of various Chapters, Vaanes said, 'The floor is yours, Ventris.'

Uriel took a deep breath as Pasanius whispered, 'Are you sure this is wise?'

'We don't have a choice, my friend,' replied Uriel. 'It has to be this way.'

Pasanius shrugged as Uriel moved to the centre of the circle of Space Marines and began to speak, his voice strong and clear. 'My name is Uriel Ventris and until recently I was a captain of the Ultramarines. I commanded the Fourth Company and Pasanius was my senior sergeant. We were cast from our Chapter for breaking faith with the *Codex Astartes* and to our brethren we are no longer Ultramarines.'

Uriel paced around the circumference of the circle and raised his voice. 'We are no longer Ultramarines, but we are still Space Marines, warriors of the Emperor, and we will remain so until the day we die. As are you, and you and you!'

Uriel jabbed his fist at Space Marines around the circle as he spoke. 'I do not know why any of you are here, what circumstances drove you from your Chapters and led you to this place, and nor do I need to know. But I offer you a chance to regain your honour, to prove that you are true warriors of purpose.'

'What is it you are asking of us?' said a huge Space Marine in the livery of the Crimson Fists, his battered skull scarred and shaven.

'What is your name, brother?'

'Kyama Shae,' said the Crimson Fist.

'I am asking you to join us in our quest, Brother Shae,' said Uriel. 'To penetrate the fortress of Honsou and destroy the daemonculaba. Some of you already know that, but there is more. The Omphalos Daemonium, the daemon that brought us here did so for a reason. It spoke to us of the Heart of Blood and told us that it resides within the secret vaults of Honsou's fortress.'

A muttered ripple of horrified surprise travelled the circle as Uriel continued. 'It charged us with retrieving the Heart of Blood for it, and we agreed.'

'Traitors!' hissed a White Consul. 'You consort with daemons!'

Pasanius surged to his feet and shouted, 'Never! Say such a thing again and I will kill you!'

Uriel stepped between the two Space Marines and said, 'We agreed because our homeworlds were threatened with destruction, brother, but fear not, we have no intention of honouring such an agreement. When I find this Heart of Blood in that fortress I will destroy it. You have my word on that.'

'How can we trust you?' asked Vaanes.

'I have only my word to offer you, Vaanes, but think on this. The warlord Honsou has recently returned from campaign and is laden with stolen gene-seed. What do you think he is using it for? How do you think the daemonculaba are producing these newly-birthed abominations? With enough gene-seed, Honsou can create hundreds, perhaps even thousands, of new warriors for his armies. Soon they will come and destroy you. You know this, so why not strike now before they are able to?'

Uriel could see that his words were reaching the assembled Space Marines and pressed on. 'You say that what hurts the Iron Warriors is at the heart of all you do, well what will hurt them more than this, to have their newest warriors destroyed before they can fight? At the very least, we can cause the Iron Warriors such grief that they will not soon forget us. If we are to die in this, then at least it will be with our honour!'

'What use is honour if we are all dead?' asked Vaanes.

'Death and honour,' said Uriel. 'If one brings the other, then it is a good death.'

'Easy for you to say, Ventris.'

Uriel shook his head. 'No, Vaanes, it is not. You think I *want* to die? I do not. I wish to live for a long time and bring death to my enemies for many years to come, but if I am to die, I can think of no better an end than fighting alongside brother Space Marines for a noble cause.'

'Noble? Who do you think cares?' snapped Vaanes. 'If we die on this suicide mission of yours, what will any of this matter? Who will even know of your precious honour?'

'I will,' said Uriel softly. 'And that will be enough.'

Silence fell and Uriel could see that the renegade Space Marines were torn between the status quo of their current existence and this chance for redemption. He could not yet tell which way they would lean.

Just as he was beginning to believe that no one would rise to the challenge he had offered them, Colonel Leonid and Sergeant Ellard stood and crossed the circle towards him.

Leonid saluted him and said, 'We will fight alongside you, Captain Ventris. We're dying anyway and if we can kill Iron Warriors before that happens, then so much the better.'

Uriel smiled and accepted Leonid's hand. 'You are a brave man, colonel.'

'Perhaps,' said Leonid, 'or a man with nothing to lose.'

'I thank you both anyway,' said Uriel as Brother Seraphys also came forward to join them.

'I will come with you, Uriel,' said Seraphys. 'If I can learn more of the machinations of the Ruinous Powers then that can only be for the good.'

Uriel nodded his thanks as first one Space Marine, then others came forward to join him. They came in ones and twos, until every one of the renegade Space Marines stood beside Uriel and Pasanius save Ardaric Vaanes.

The former Raven Guards Space Marine chuckled to himself and said, 'You have a way with words, Ventris, I'll give you that.'

'Join us, Vaanes!' urged Uriel. 'Take this chance for honour. Remember who you are, what you were created to do!'

Vaanes rose and approached Uriel. 'I know that well enough, Ventris.'

'Then join us!'

The renegade sighed, casting his gaze around the ruined bunker complex he had called home and the Space Marines who now stood with Uriel.

'Very well, I will help you get into the fortress, but I'm not getting killed to help you carry out your death oath. So long as you understand that.'

'I understand that,' assured Uriel.

Vaanes suddenly grinned and shook his head. 'Damn, but I knew you were trouble...'

CHAPTER NINE

THE WARRIOR BAND gathered up their weapons and equipment, filled with a new sense of purpose as they prepared to leave the sanctuary. Uriel cleaned his armour as best he could and knelt to give thanks to his battle gear, placing his gun and sword before him and asking them to help him do the Emperor's bidding.

Pasanius filled his flamer with the last of his promethium and though it pained him, he knew he was going to have to leave it behind soon. A weapon with no ammunition was no weapon at all.

At last the warriors were ready and Uriel proudly led the ragtag band of Space Marines away from the crumbling bunkers towards the mouth of the shadowed valley. Ardaric Vaanes marched alongside him and said, 'You realise you're probably going to get every one of us killed.'

'That is a distinct possibility,' admitted Uriel.

'Good, I just wanted to make sure you understood that.'

THE SKY DARKENED when they finally reached the end of the valley, an unnatural darkness of low, threatening smoke clouds. Briefly Uriel wondered if there were such a thing as weather on Medrengard, but dismissed the notion. What need had the Iron Warriors of weather? Nothing grew here or needed nourishment from the heavens.

Ahead was their ultimate destination, and now that Uriel could see it clearly, he understood Vaanes's assertion that to attempt to penetrate the defences of such a fastness was a suicide mission.

The fortress of Honsou was a nightmarish black fang against the sky, ebony towers of dark, bloodstained stone piercing the clouds of ash and crackling with dark lightning. The towers and arched halls of the fortress were surrounded by scarred bastions with walls hundreds of metres tall. The upper levels stood inviolate against the besieging army below, but the lower reaches were a cratered hell of flames and war. A haze of powerful energies surrounded the fortress as though it were not quite real. Uriel had to blink away stinging moisture from his eyes if he gazed too long at its lunatic architecture.

The world itself echoed to the snarl of mighty machines, and the rhythmic drumming of hammers sounded like the beat of some monstrous mechanical heart. Like a malignant fungus, the armies of Honsou's attackers were spread around the fortress in jagged lines of circumvallation, zigzagging approach saps snaking through the lower foothills of the fortress and ending in heavily fortified parallels, studded with enormous bunkers and redoubts. Blooms of explosions swathed the fortress and the plains before it flickered and flashed with the constant muzzle flares of monstrous cannons and howitzers.

A huge ramp was under construction from kilometres back that would allow heavy tanks and Titans access to the upper levels of the fortress and Uriel could see that the plain was teeming with millions of warriors. Sprawling camps and entire cities had been built to barrack these soldiers, and how they were going to successfully get through so many enemies to reach the fortress was beyond him.

'Having second thoughts?' asked Vaanes.

'No,' said Uriel.

'Sure?'

'I'm sure, Vaanes. We can do this. It will not be easy, but we can do it.'

Vaanes looked unconvinced, but pointed to where the plateau narrowed to become a near-vertical shear in the rock that carved a path down the flank of the mountain, 'That's the way down that leads to the plains below. It's steep, very steep, and if you fall you're dead.'

'How the hell are we meant to get down that?' breathed Leonid.

'Very carefully,' said Vaanes. 'So don't fall.'

'It's all right for you,' said Ellard, slinging his lasgun and making his way towards the path. 'If you fall you have a jump pack!'

'What? You want me to announce our presence here?' returned Vaanes.

Uriel followed the renegade and was seized by a dizzying lurch of vertigo as he saw the route they must take.

The plain was thousands of metres below them, steaming waterfalls of molten metal splashing along basalt channels towards lakes of glowing orange below.

'You need to go down facing the rock,' explained Vaanes, edging onto the path, barely half a metre across and gripping onto cracks in the rock for handholds. Gingerly, he edged out onto the path, leaning into the rockface and sliding sideways along and down.

Uriel went next, gripping the rockface and easing himself out onto the narrow path. He kept his weight forward, knowing that to overbalance even a little would send him plummeting thousands of metres to his death. Cold wind whipped at him and he felt his heartbeats hammering in his chest.

He edged out, following Vaanes's example and utilising the same handholds wherever he could. Within the space of a few hours, his muscles ached, his fingers burned with fatigue and they were barely half way down. His breath came in short, hard gasps and it was all he could do to not look down.

Hand over hand followed hand over hand and shuffling step to the side followed shuffling step to the side until they reached a point where the slope became shallower and it was possible to climb directly downwards for a short distance.

As Uriel climbed down to a narrow ledge, he flexed his fingers, the textured pads of his gauntlets torn and useless. His arms were leaden weights and he hoped he had the strength to make it to the bottom. With a little more room to manoeuvre on the ledge he carefully eased round and gazed at the terrifying scale of the siegeworks below.

What had brought this siege about anyway? Was it some internecine conflict or was there some other, darker purpose to the slaughter going on below?

Did the attackers have some knowledge of the Heart of Blood or the daemonculaba?

He supposed it didn't matter why the followers of the Dark Powers made war upon one another; the more they killed each other, the fewer were left to attack the Emperor's realm.

A startled cry from above snapped him from his reverie and he looked up in time to see a hail of stones skitter down the slope, closely followed by Colonel Leonid, who screamed in terror as he tumbled downwards.

Uriel pressed himself flat against the rockface and leaned dangerously to one side to snatch at Leonid as he plummeted past.

His fingers closed on Leonid's uniform jacket and he gritted his teeth, gripping the rocks tightly as the colonel's weight threatened to pull them both from the ledge. Under normal circumstances, Uriel would have had no problem with catching Leonid like this, but off balance on the edge of a crumbling corbel of rock he felt himself being pulled from the cliff as his agonised fingers slipped from their transient handhold.

'I can't hold on!' he yelled. The ledge crumbled at the edge, dirt and pebbles spiralling downwards to the plains far below.

'Don't let go!' screamed Leonid. 'Please!'

Uriel fought to hold on, but knew that he could not. Should he just let go? Surely the presence of Leonid would not affect their mission one way or another. He was a normal man amongst Space Marines, what good could he possibly do?

But before he could release his grip he felt a hand take hold of his shoulder guard and pull him back. Above him, Sergeant Ellard had hold of his armour and strained to pull him back. Uriel was too heavy for him to hold, but Ellard's strength was prodigious and held Uriel long enough for him to shift his grip to a better handhold with firmer balance. Centimetre by centimetre, Uriel eased himself back onto the firmer ground of the ledge and was able to deposit Leonid back onto the slope.

The colonel was hyperventilating, his face pallid from shock and terror.

'You are safe now, Mikhail,' said Uriel, deliberately using the colonel's first name.

Leonid took great gulps of air, keeping his eyes averted from the drop behind him. His body shook, but he said, 'Thank you.'

Uriel did not reply, but looked up to see a breathless Sergeant Ellard clinging to the rockface by what looked like his fingernails. Uriel respectfully nodded at the man, who nodded back.

'Sir, are you able to go on?' asked Ellard.

'Aye…' wheezed Leonid. 'I'll be all right, just give me a minute or two.'

The three of them waited as long as they dared before moving onwards, Uriel in the lead with Ellard bringing up the rear. The colonel's steps were hesitant and unsure at first, but eventually his confidence returned and he made good time.

The journey down the mountains blurred into a painful series of vignettes: traverses across terrifyingly narrow spurs of rock and heart-pounding drops onto splintered ledges. Uriel continued down the slope of the mountain, pressing himself flat against the rock until he felt a tap on his shoulder and looked around to see that he had reached the base of the shear in the rock, that he was on a wide, screed slope of ash and iron debris. A churned mass of broken earth sloped gently to the darkened plains below.

The warrior band were spread around, breathless from their climb, and as Uriel looked up to see Leonid and Ellard completing the descent, his admiration for their endurance and courage soared as did his shame at the thought of even considering letting Leonid fall to his death.

Ardaric Vaanes approached him and said, 'You made it then.'

'You were right,' said Uriel. 'That was not easy.'

'No, but we're all here. Now what?'

That was a very good question. They were still many kilometres from the fortress, and Uriel could not even begin to guess how many enemy soldiers lay between them and its lower slopes. He scanned the ground below him, picking out scores of work parties and earth-moving machines hauling hundreds of tonnes of earth to build the ramp that led towards the fortress. A hissing lake of molten metal pooled at the base of the slope, bathing everything in a hellish orange glow and the rumble of engines and cursing voices drifted up from the construction sites.

'You know there's no way we can just walk through that many soldiers. Even if the vast majority are only human.'

'I know,' replied Uriel, eyeing the huge bulk-haulers. 'But perhaps we will not need to.'

THE HEAT RADIATING from the molten lake was stifling, filling the air with stinking fumes and making each breath hot and painful. Uriel edged around a tall mound of piled steel sheeting and waited for the latest work party to shuffle past, chained together at the neck by spiked collars and dressed in filthy rags. Servants of the Iron Warriors in all-enclosing vacuum suits shouted gurgled commands to the slaves, beating and whipping them as they pleased.

The rumble of heavy, tracked bulk-haulers and booming gunfire covered the Space Marines' approach down the lower slopes of the mountain, the darkness of the smoky clouds only helping them to approach the construction site unobserved. The huge machines were bigger than the largest super-heavy tank Uriel had ever seen, controlled via a cab mounted high on a massive, tracked engine unit that pulled a huge container on wheels with the diameter of three tall men.

Laden with tonnes of earth and rock, they plied their stately way up the ramp before depositing their cargo on its forward slope and then turning around and making their way back down again to refill. Millions of tonnes had already been poured out, yet the ramp was barely halfway towards the upper levels of the fortress. Uriel watched as a trio of bulk-haulers made their way towards the bottom of the ramp, and turned to Pasanius.

'They're coming,' he whispered through his armour's vox unit.

'I see them,' confirmed Vaanes.

Across the construction site from Uriel, he could see Vaanes climbing the side of the ramp, gaining height from where he could use his jump pack to better effect. Other Space Marines were poised ready for the word to attack.

The first of the bulk-haulers completed its wide turn and ground off into the smoke for more earth and Uriel bit his lip in nervous anticipation.

'Second one's almost round,' said Pasanius, and Uriel could sense the anticipation in his sergeant's voice.

'Aye,' he nodded. 'Ready?'

'As I'll ever be.'

'At times like this, I wish Idaeus was still here,' said Uriel.

Pasanius chuckled and said, 'This attack would be just his kind of thing.'

'What? Against impossible odds and with no recourse to the *Codex Astartes*?'

'Precisely,' said Pasanius, nodding in the direction of the ramp. 'Last one's down.'

Uriel returned his gaze to the hauler as it described a wide arc at the bottom of the ramp and the massive machine turned towards the fortress. When the cab had levelled out, but the huge trailer portion was still curved around, he rose to his feet and shouted, 'Go! Go!' over the vox and ran out into the open.

Scattered groups of slaves looked up at them as they ran for the enormous machine, but otherwise paid them no mind. Up close, the bulk-hauler was even larger than it had first appeared, fully nine metres tall and constructed of dented sheets of thick iron and bronze girders. Its wheels were solid and tore deep furrows in the ground as it rumbled onwards. Fortunately, it was still moving slowly enough to catch and Uriel leapt for the iron ladder that led to the cab above.

Space Marines jogged alongside the bulk-hauler and clambered onto the running boards, beginning to climb the craggy sides of the trailer. Uriel swiftly ascended the ladder towards the platform bolted to the side of the driver's cabin, hearing a heavy thump of something landing on the cab's roof. Metal tore and he heard screams.

He continued climbing, seeing the door above him burst open and a creature in a vacuum suit and leather harness emerge from the interior of the cab. Harsh, static trills of fear emitted from a copper faceplate as it saw Uriel, but he didn't give it time to react, reaching up and gripping its harness.

It tried to draw a pistol, but Uriel pulled hard and sent it spinning from the driver's cab to the ground below. Kyama Shae, the Crimson Fists Space Marine riding the running boards, shot the mutant in the head and the groups of slaves clustered around this part of the ramp cheered as it died.

Uriel scrambled up the ladder and swung into the driver's cabin, ready to fight, but saw that there would be no need. Another two creatures, clad in the same black vacuum suits as the one Uriel had thrown to the ground, lay dead in their bucket seats, torn open from neck to groin by Ardaric Vaanes's lightning claws.

The renegade sat awkwardly before a control panel, the bulk of his jump pack almost filling the cabin. He struggled with an array of levers and a giant wheel beneath a great rent in the steel roof, and said, 'Do you know how to drive this thing?'

'No,' said Uriel. 'But how hard can it be?'

'Well, we're about to find out,' said Vaanes.

Uriel wiped a hand across the blood-smeared windscreen and peered through at the rear ends of the two bulk-haulers in front of them.

'Just keep it straight, and try to stay with the two ahead for as long as you can.'

Vaanes nodded, too intent on working out the controls to the bulk-hauler to reply. Uriel left him to it and swung out onto the platform on the side of the cab.

The Space Marines of the warrior band were making their way along the running boards to the ladders at the sides and rear of the bulk-hauler, climbing up towards concealment within the empty trailer.

Satisfied they could actually get close without significant risk of discovery, Uriel clambered back into the driver's cab and dragged out the dead bodies of the mutant drivers. He hurled them from the cab, those slaves chained nearest to where the bodies fell tearing them apart with wanton abandon.

'It's not actually that difficult,' said Vaanes as Uriel closed the door behind him.

'No?'

'No, a Rhino's harder to control than this. It's just a little bigger.'

'Just a little,' agreed Uriel.

He left Vaanes to wrestle with the controls and stared through the dirty windscreen at the siegeworks beyond, the scale of the battle taking his breath away.

They passed great artillery pits, enormous guns, bigger by many times than the heaviest artillery pieces of the Imperial Guard, hurling tank-sized shells towards the fortress. Tall towers hung with bodies and spiked bunkers were spread throughout the camp and a sprawling infrastructure had arisen to support the massive effort of taking Honsou's fortress. Dark wonders and monstrous sights greeted them at every turn, the myriad horrors of a daemon world at war.

The bulk-haulers drove along corpse-hung roads, skull-paved plazas where naked madmen capered around tall idols hung with entrails and pillars of iron that crackled with powerful energy. They watched mutants hurl crippled slaves into bubbling pools of molten metal, laughing as they did so, and Uriel turned away. He could not save them all, so he would save none of them. It scarred his soul to let such atrocities go unpunished, but he was coming to believe that Vaanes was right – better to let them die than to be killed trying and failing to save them.

As the bulk-hauler swallowed up the distance between the outskirts of the camp and the siege lines, they drove over great bridges of iron that crossed deep trenches, through kilometres of razorwire and around deep pits containing screaming mechanical monsters. Shadows of great, clawed limbs swayed in the firelight and Uriel felt a shiver of dread at the thought of even laying eyes on such daemon engines.

The heat in the cab was oppressive, but he didn't dare open the door for fear of discovery. So far they had been able to continue following the bulk-haulers ahead of them, but as soon as the lead hauler turned away from the fortress, it would only be a matter of time before their ruse was discovered.

The bulk-haulers rolled onwards through the Iron Warriors' camp, driving through great shanty towns of red-garbed soldiers and blazing drumfires. Soldiers chanted in praise of their masters and fired off shots into the air as they danced around the flames.

'These are the warriors of Lord Berossus,' said Vaanes, pointing to a gold and black standard raised high at the edge of the camp.

'And who is he? A rival of Honsou's?'

'So it would seem. He is the leader of a grand company of the Iron Warriors, a vassal of Lord Toramino, one of their most powerful warlords.'

'How do you know all this?' asked Uriel.

'We have sometimes taken prisoners,' replied Vaanes, 'and did not shirk from their interrogation. If Berossus is here, then so too is Toramino. Whatever the reason they lay siege to Honsou's fortress, it must be powerful indeed.'

'Perhaps they know what Honsou brought back from Hydra Cordatus and desire a share in his spoils of victory.'

'Gene-seed? Yes, that would probably do it.'

'We can't let that happen.'

Vaanes laughed. 'We are but thirty warriors and you would have us topple this world.'

'Why not?' said Uriel. 'We are Space Marines of the Emperor. There is nothing we cannot do.'

'I don't know why, since you are probably going to get me killed, but I like you, Uriel Ventris. You have an absurd sense for attempting the impossible that appeals to me.'

Uriel returned his gaze to the siegeworks outside, pleased at the compliment, as the lead truck reached a wide crossroads and began making a wide turn towards a huge spoil heap.

'Damn it, they're turning,' cursed Vaanes as he saw the same thing.

'We are too far away to make it on foot,' said Uriel. 'There are whole regiments ahead of us.'

'What do you think?'

'Push it!' said Uriel. 'Head straight for the fortress and we will kill anyone that gets in our way. We'll drive over them or shoot them, just get us as close to that fortress as you can.'

'I'll try!' shouted Vaanes, pushing the hauler into high gear and slamming his foot to the floor. 'We won't get far before we run into trouble, so get ready to give me some covering fire.'

Uriel nodded and left the driver's cab, calling to the other Space Marines in their band and alerting them to their plight. Acknowledgements flickered on his visor and Uriel readied his sword and bolter as the bulk-hauler rumbled towards the crossroads. The main route travelled by the bulk-haulers was clearly visible, curving off to the left, but instead of slowing to take the turn, their transport increased speed and roared straight ahead, bucking madly on surfaces not designed for such a heavy vehicle.

Screams and shouts of alarm rose in their wake as tents, stores and prefabricated huts were flattened beneath their tracks. Red-liveried soldiers, slaves and mutants scattered before them, those not quick enough crushed to death by their wild charge.

Shots ricocheted from the sides of the bulk-hauler, but they were sporadic, hastily aimed and Uriel knew that they need not be concerned about such small-arms fire. It would be when word was passed on ahead that they would need to worry.

Sure enough, he could see fire teams ahead of them, swinging round static weapon platforms that would tear their vehicle to shreds.

'Warriors, engage!' he shouted over the vox.

Space Marines who had been waiting for his command rose from behind the shelter of the trailer's sides and opened fire, bolter shells raking the gunners of the weapon teams and ripping their guns to pieces. The bulk-hauler crashed into the trench lines, ploughing a huge furrow in its wake as it slowed going across the softer ground.

Yelling soldiers leapt into their trenches, but there was no refuge to be found there, as the massive weight of the hauler collapsed their trenches and buried scores of men beneath tonnes of earth and rubble. Uriel watched without compassion, relishing the destruction they were causing. He fired his weapon into the soldiers, yelling encouragement to the other Space Marines of their warrior band as they killed the enemy.

He looked up in time to see a brilliant flash of light and ducked as a huge explosion hammered the ground beside them. The bulk-hauler swayed, and for a moment Uriel felt sure it would tip over.

But the Emperor was with them and the hauler righted itself, slamming back to the ground with teeth-loosening force. Uriel pulled himself upright and saw several artillery pieces aiming for them with their gun barrels lowered. Another explosion burst next to them, showering the hauler with debris and earth and smoke. The gunners were finding their range, heedless of however many of their own men they killed to get it, and Uriel knew that they had seconds at best before one of the guns got lucky and blew them to atoms.

'Everybody off!' he shouted. 'Now!'

After two such close calls, none of the Space Marines needed any encouragement. They clambered over the sides of the bulk-hauler and leapt from the vehicle. Uriel saw Pasanius hit the ground and roll, and hauled open the driver's cab.

'Vaanes! Come on, let's go!' he shouted over the din of gunfire and explosions.

'Go!' he shouted. 'I'm right behind you!'

Uriel nodded and vaulted from the platform outside the cab. He hit the ground hard and rolled, smashing a dozen soldiers aside as he landed. In a heartbeat he was on his feet, slashing with his sword and running for the mountain. Shots kicked up dust around him and ricocheted from his armour as he ran.

He saw Ardaric Vaanes leap from the driver's cab as a shell from one of the guns finally struck the bulk-hauler. The engine section vanished in a sheet of flame and the wreckage ploughed onwards for another few seconds before slamming through a razorwire fence and exploding with the force of a cluster of demolition charges. Secondary explosions quickly followed as fuel bladders and siege shells cooked off in the huge blast. Uriel realised Vaanes must have used those last few seconds to guide the hauler towards a valuable target before escaping the cab.

The earth shook as shells arced through the air and burning sheets of fuel sprayed in all directions. Enemy soldiers ducked and ran for cover in the maelstrom of exploding shells and blazing plumes of scorching fires, but Uriel and the Space Marines kept running.

Ahead, he saw the lower reaches of the mountain, where Berossus's engineers had constructed vast funicular rails onto the rock that climbed towards the higher peaks of the mountains. A giant, angled car, bounded by iron railings, ascended the rails, bearing hundreds of the Iron Warriors' soldiers towards the battle high above.

Thousands of soldiers clustered at the base of the mountain, awaiting their turn to travel up the mountainside and join the assault. The sounds of explosions and gunfire were nothing new to them and they had not yet noticed the charging Space Marines behind them. Uriel saw Pasanius and Vaanes up ahead and called to them over the vox.

'The platform on the right!' he called. 'There's an empty car just coming down. We need to take it!'

'I see it,' replied Vaanes.

The Space Marines of the warrior band struck the milling soldiers like a freight train, cutting down scores in the first seconds of their attack. Grimly they forced their way onward, hacking, cutting and slaying their way forward in an orgy of bloodshed.

Caught unawares by the killers in their midst, the soldiers fought to get out of their way and Uriel soon found himself with a clear run to the platform. Vaanes was there before him and had already killed them a path up to the approaching funicular car.

Uriel took the steps up to the platform two at a time, glancing over his shoulder to see the rest of their warriors right behind him, keeping low to avoid the worst of the gunfire directed at them. The car docked at the platform with a huge, ringing clang and barely had it done so before the Space Marines swarmed over it.

The car was empty save for a grey-fleshed servitor creature, fused with the mechanism of its controls, whose only function appeared to be pulling the levers that sent it up or down the mountain. Uriel and Pasanius, together with Kyama Shae, moved to the edge of the platform and fired into the approaching enemy soldiers whose courage now began to return.

'Ventris!' shouted Vaanes. 'Come on, the car's leaving!'

Uriel slung his bolter and slapped the shoulder guards of his two companions before running for the funicular car. Grinding cogs and wheezing engines lifted it from the platform, but it was slow to get moving and Uriel clambered aboard before it had climbed more than a metre. He turned to help Pasanius, gripping his silver arm and hauling him up, noticing with surprise that it was utterly pristine, without so much as a scratch on it. How could that be, when his own gauntlets were torn and battered to the point of uselessness?

Pasanius moved past him to take up a firing position at the railings and Uriel turned to help Kyama Shae aboard the moving car.

Small-arms fire spanged from the sides of the car and the railings, but as it rapidly picked up speed they were soon beyond the range of the soldiers' rifles.

Uriel glanced over at Pasanius before transferring his gaze to the mountain above. Black, smoky clouds wreathed the higher slopes, lightning and explosions flaring in the darkness from the battle above.

'Well, we're here,' said a breathless Vaanes.

Uriel turned to watch the swiftly diminishing ground as they rose into the clouds and darkness swallowed them.

'Getting here was the easy part,' said Uriel. 'Now we have to storm the fortress.'

CHAPTER TEN

'IT WOULD SEEM your attempt to antagonise Lord Berossus by shelling his pavilion was successful,' said Obax Zakayo needlessly, as another flurry of shells impacted against the walls. Plumes of flame and smoke soared skyward and Honsou laughed as he watched bodies rain down amid the rubble. Dust enveloped them, chunks of debris clattering down on the cobbled ramparts, and Honsou coughed as he swallowed a mouthful of ash. It was perhaps foolish to be this close to the front lines, but he was not so far removed from the sharp end of battle that he did not relish the cannon's roar in his ear.

'Yes, it does, doesn't it? He's so predictable it almost takes the fun out of crushing him.'

'But, my lord, he is within days of breaching the inner walls of Khalan-Ghol,' said Onyx, standing slightly behind Honsou. 'How can this be to our advantage?'

'Because he is dancing to my tune, Onyx, not his own. Get an enemy to react to your designs and he is as good as lost. I almost have him exactly where I want him. But Toramino... Toramino is not so easy. He is the one we need to be wary of. I don't know what he is doing.'

'Our scryers have seen nothing of note regarding Toramino,' said Obax Zakayo. 'It seems he waits, simply husbanding his warriors while Berossus grinds his men to dust against our walls.'

'I know, and that's what worries me,' snapped Honsou, waving his arms at the carnage taking place on the walls below him. 'Toramino is too clever to simply hurl his men at us like this. He knows that Berossus has no other stratagems and is waiting for his moment to strike. We must anticipate that and pre-empt him. Or else we are lost.'

Onyx leaned over the parapet and cast his gleaming silver eyes to either side of where he, Honsou and Obax Zakayo stood. Iron Warriors were ready to defend the ramparts should the bastions below fall, which if the projected strength of the assault below was correct, was entirely likely.

'We are too close to the battle,' he said.

Honsou shook his head. 'No, I need to be here.'

'I can protect you from an assassin's blade or a killer's bullet,' said Onyx, 'but I cannot say the same for an artillery shell. An eternity of torment awaits my essence should I allow you to die while under my protection.'

'Why should I care about your eternal torment?'

'You wouldn't, you'd be dead.'

Honsou considered this for a second and said, 'You may have a point there, Onyx.'

The daemonic symbiote nodded respectfully as more screaming shells exploded against the walls below. Honsou turned, content that the bastion here was as secure as he could want. The warriors he had chosen to accompany him into the camp of Berossus commanded this section of the walls, and there were no better warriors in his grand company.

He had taken one step when a flash of dark prescience made him look up and he yelled, 'Down!'

Whether it was by sheer luck or great artifice, Honsou would never know, but a salvo of shells from the guns below impacted on the edge of the ramparts upon which he and his warriors stood, shearing the rock clean from its supports in a cataclysmic hammerblow. Honsou picked himself up and desperately scrambled for the safety of the esplanade behind the ramparts, but it was already too late.

With a grinding crack of splintered stone, he and hundreds of his finest warriors were swept down the mountainside in a raining avalanche of rubble and blocks of sundered stone.

EMERGING FROM THE smoke was like being born into hell, thought Uriel. At first he had been frustrated not being able to see their ultimate destination, but upon passing through the dark clouds of the mountain and seeing it up close for the first time, he soon wished for the sight of it to be snatched away from him.

Stretching up to pierce the dead sky, the fortress of Honsou was a madman's conceit made real, stone laid upon stone so that each angle was subtly *wrong* and violated the senses on a deep, instinctual level. Its dark veined walls reared up in defiance of the laws of perspective, looming and huge with pierced garrets leaning from the wallhead and spiralling, lightning-sheathed spires. Blades and spikes stabbed from its glistening fabric, and black rain, like the very lifeblood of the fortress, spilled from where artillery shells had struck. Fast-flowing rivers of molten metal poured from glowing culverts and ran down the mountainside like streams of lava from an erupting volcano.

Guns fired from daemon-visaged portals and burning, daemonic blood spilled from vast iron cauldrons onto the screaming soldiers below. Flames danced on the ramparts and in the mass of struggling soldiers. Death and destruction stalked the battlefield this day, and they hunted well.

Tens of thousands of soldiers thronged the rubble-strewn reaches of the fortress, fighting their way up a ruined screed slope that had once been a bastion. Explosions tossed corpses through the air as buried mines swept hundreds to their deaths and the monstrous forms of a pair of Titans struggled in the rubble, crushing men and machines beneath their great footsteps as they fought amid the flames.

Uriel and the Space Marines watched the terrifying battle rage above them, the car grinding as it approached the upper platform where it would deposit them and begin the journey back down the mountain.

'Emperor protect us,' breathed Vaanes. 'It's like nothing I've ever seen before.'

'I know…' agreed Uriel, drawing his sword as the car clanged home against the platform and the bronze gate in the railings squealed open.

'How can we hope to survive this?'

Uriel turned to Vaanes and said, 'Remember what I told you: death and honour. If one brings the other then it is a good death.'

'No…' hissed Vaanes. 'No death is a good one. Not like this.'

None of the Space Marines moved, too in awe at the terrible and magnificent spectacle of war on a scale few had ever experienced. Uriel realised he had to get them moving before the vastness of this battle and their impulse for survival overcame the newly-rekindled sense of honour and duty he had instilled in them.

He was saved when Pasanius shouted, 'Come on, get moving! Everybody off!'

Ingrained reflexes took over and the Space Marines swiftly debarked from the funicular car, chivvied all the way by a bellowing Pasanius. Only Uriel and Ardaric Vaanes remained on board.

'Come on,' said Uriel. 'We have work to do.'

Vaanes said nothing, but nodded and followed Uriel from the car, climbing up past the platform and unsheathing the crackling claws from his gauntlet.

'What are you doing?' called Uriel.

'Funicular cars work on the principle of counterbalancing one another,' explained Vaanes, slicing his claws clean through the thick cables that held the car.

The platform groaned and the cable snapped with a metallic twang, whipping around and sending the car plummeting back downhill through the smoke. The sound of screeching metal and showers of fat orange sparks followed it down.

'No one will be coming up here in a while,' said Vaanes, climbing back to join Uriel.

'Clever,' said Uriel.

The two Space Marines jogged over to where the rest of the warrior band had sequestered themselves, hidden in a fold in the rock below an overhanging bastion where they could observe the battle in relative safety. Missiles and shells crisscrossed the air, and the noise of explosions and gunfire was deafening. The mountain trembled to the footsteps of the Titans, both of which lurched heedlessly through the battle as they grappled and struck at one another. Snarling daemon heads slammed together and massive blades tore at each other's armour as whipping, barbed tails brought down whole swathes of the wall.

'Now what?' shouted Pasanius, barely audible over the cacophony.

'Now we have to get in!' said Uriel.

'You mean we join the assault?' asked Vaanes. 'Impossible!'

'What choice do we have?' yelled Uriel.

'We can get the hell off this mountain! I told you I'd help you get in, Ventris, but I also told you I wasn't going to get killed for your death oath!'

'Damn it, Vaanes, we're here now! We have to keep going!'

Vaanes looked set to reply when a salvo of shells streaked overhead and struck the lip of the overhanging bastion directly above them. Dust and debris showered them, rocks tumbling down the slopes as it split from the mountain with a splintering crack.

'Look out!' shouted Uriel as the bastion crumbled and toppled, falling towards them in an avalanche of rubble and blocks of sundered stone.

HONSOU FELT ROCKS pummelling him as he fell, battering him and threatening to crush him utterly. He tumbled end over end, his senses whirling in a kaleidoscopic flurry of noise and light. The breath was driven from him as he landed, and he rolled aside as huge, tank-sized blocks of rubble smashed down around him. Choking clouds of black dust and smoke billowed, and though he felt painfully battered by the fall, he didn't feel any broken bones or ruptured organs.

'Onyx!' he yelled hoarsely. 'Zakayo!'

'Here!' coughed Zakayo. 'I am alive!'

'As am I,' said Onyx, 'but I require assistance.'

Honsou struggled over to where his champion lay almost completely buried beneath a pile of jagged lumps of rockcrete with twisted iron bars protruding from them. Onyx's torso and lower body were trapped beneath a volume of rubble that would have crushed even a power-armoured warrior flat, but immaterial energies had saturated the daemonic symbiote's flesh and it was proof against such things.

Honsou gripped the debris and strained against its massive weight, but it was too great even for one as enhanced as he. Obax Zakayo joined him, the hissing mechanical arms sprouting from the armature of his back to grip the reinforcement bars.

Iron Warriors began picking themselves up from the rubble, those who hadn't been crushed beneath falling masonry or otherwise killed in the bastion's collapse lending their strength to freeing Onyx.

Honsou moved out of the way and looked around him as glowing afterimages of the battle flashed on his visor. He shook his head to clear it and get a better idea of where their fall from the fortress had brought them.

More rubble had been dislodged from above by the thunderous battle of the nearby Titans and Honsou saw that they would have little difficulty in getting back to the fortress. The lucky artillery strike had collapsed a good portion of the wall beneath the bastion that now formed a ready-made slope that led straight to the walls.

That was if they survived to get back to the fortress, he thought, watching as blurry shapes approached through the swirling clouds of dust and smoke.

* * *

URIEL TORE OFF his helmet, its visor cracked and useless; the pressure seals that clamped it to his gorget smashed and irreparable. He muttered a prayer of unction for the helmet's spirit and placed it on the ground. Without his auto-senses, he could only see hazy outlines through the smoke and debris of the bastion's fall, but blinking away motes of dust from his eyes, he saw that the Emperor had blessed them once more.

'There!' he shouted, pointing to the great gash torn in the side of the fortress where the bastion had fallen. A steep but practicable slope of rubble and rebar-laced rockcrete led upwards towards the ramparts. Uriel knew they would never get a better chance than this to penetrate the fortress.

Leading the way, he picked his way upwards, seeing indistinct, power-armoured forms also clambering to their feet. At first he assumed that these were the Space Marines of the warrior band, but as the dust began to settle, he saw they were not.

They were Iron Warriors.

HONSOU WATCHED A Space Marine emerge from the smoke, his blue armour dust covered and battered. His heart lurched as the warrior snarled and drew a shimmering blade. One of the False Emperor's warriors? Here? His surprise almost cost him his life as the blade sang for his neck and he was barely able to parry it with his axe, dodging away from the return stroke of the Space Marine's blade.

His axe screamed as its warrior soul roared to life and Honsou saw that the attacking warrior's blue armour was devoid of all insignia or markings. A renegade? A mercenary?

Was this Toramino's doing? Rallying the renegade scum that skulked in the mountains to his cause? But he had no more time to wonder at the warrior's origins as his blade stabbed for him once more.

'Iron Warriors!' he bellowed. 'With me!'

URIEL SLASHED AT the Iron Warrior again, but his every stroke was parried by a huge war-axe with a glossy, black-toothed blade. His foe shouted to his warriors and more shapes emerged from the dust, swords and axes raised and bolters piercing the smoke with barking muzzle flashes.

'Emperor guide my blade!' he shouted as he attacked again.

'He has no power here,' retorted the Iron Warrior as he spun his axe and attacked.

Uriel sidestepped and brought his sword around in a beheading stroke, but his opponent was not there, rolling beneath the blow and swinging his axe for his back. Uriel hurled himself flat, the screaming axe blade slashing centimetres from his armour. He rolled aside as the axe hammered down, the earth shaking in fury at its impact.

Uriel kicked out, driving the Iron Warrior to his knees and slicing his sword in a wide arc towards his head. The tip of his blade caught the Iron Warrior's helm and sent him tumbling down the slope. He scrambled to his feet as more Space Marines joined the fray and the vast shadow of the battling Titans engulfed them. The fury of the devil machines' combat dwarfed this one, but for all that, it was equally brutal and merciless. Vicious, short-range firefights and melees broke out, bolters roaring and grunts of pain and anger sounding as explosive shells cracked open armour and blades tore at flesh. He drew back his sword to gut an Iron Warrior, but a lashing coil of energy snaked out and ensnared his arm.

Pain roared up his arm and it was all he could do to keep hold of his sword as flaring bursts of agony coursed along the length of the energy coil. Uriel dropped to his knees as a giant, wide shouldered Iron Warrior drew near, massive mechanised arms snapping from his shoulders and the snaking whip of energy attached to yet another of his hunched claws.

'You dare attack the master of Khalan-Ghol! You will die!' roared the warrior, his voice ugly and crackling. A wash of flame shot through the combat and Uriel caught the sickening stench of cooked meat. Once again the earth heaved and a gargantuan foot slammed down against the mountainside not three metres from Uriel, leaving a deep crater in its wake.

He saw the massive Titans towering above them as he fought against the crippling pain lashing in waves from the energy whip. While the whip-armed claw held him immobile with agony, the lumbering Iron Warrior's free hands unsheathed a crude, brutal, but no doubt effective chainsaw-bladed axe.

'Obax Zakayo!' screamed a voice, but Uriel could not see who shouted through the pain screeching around his nervous system. Gunshots burst against the Iron Warrior's armour and he lashed out with his axe.

'You?' laughed the Iron Warrior. 'You were under my blade once, slave, and escaped. You will not do so again.'

For the briefest second, his attention shifted from Uriel and it was all the distraction he needed. He swept up his sword, hacking through the energy whip, and the pain vanished, leaving him drained, but free of its incapacitating agony. Uriel pushed himself to his feet, seeing Colonel Leonid and Sergeant Ellard facing off against the Iron Warrior.

Lasbolts hammered his bulky body, but his debased power armour could withstand such trifles and he roared, swinging his axe for Leonid's midriff. The colonel jumped back, stumbling on loose rubble, and fell to the ground. Obax Zakayo closed for the kill, but Ellard leapt upon the Iron Warrior, pummelling his fists against his head.

Ellard was a big man, but next to the Iron Warrior he was a child, and Obax Zakayo ripped him from his back and hurled him away. Uriel stepped in and hammered his sword across the Iron Warrior's shoulders. The blade crackled as it hacked though the ceramite plates of his armour, but slid free before connecting with flesh.

Obax Zakayo swung his axe in a vicious arc at Uriel's groin, but the blow never landed as the ground shook and cracked, molten metal spewing up as the crashing footsteps of the battling Titans finally split the mountain. White hot metal hissed and spat as it spilled out onto the rocks, rendering them down to slag in seconds. Uriel scrambled away from the widening crack in the ground, sheathing his sword as he saw that there was no way his opponent could reach him across the gulf of liquid metal.

Roiling clouds of bitter smoke gusted from the river of molten metal and Uriel scrambled away from its intolerable heat, Leonid and Ellard clambering over the rocks to join him.

'This is Uriel Ventris!' he shouted, hoping that the vox-bead attached to his larynx was still functioning. 'If anyone can still hear me, make for the breach above us now!'

Bolters roared behind him and the crash of explosions almost drowned his order, but as he climbed through the blinding clouds of steam and smoke, he could see the shadowy forms of the warrior band climbing towards him.

The breach was above them, barely thirty metres away, the rubble-strewn sides of the fortress a beacon that called him onwards.

They had done it. They had found a way in.

BLOOD BLINDED HIM and a grating static filled his senses. Honsou removed his helmet, tossing it aside in anger, and wiped blood from his eyes. Banks of hot steam sent runnels of moisture down his face and he pushed himself upright as the thunder of battle returned to him with all its fury.

'What in the name of the Dark Gods is happening?' he shouted to no one in particular.

'My lord!' returned Obax Zakayo, picking his way carefully through the rocks. Moisture and blood ran from his armour, his energy whip crackling with sparks where it had been severed. 'The–'

'Renegades!' roared Honsou. 'Is this what Toramino has been reduced to?'

'Aye, renegades,' agreed Obax Zakayo. 'Renegades and runaway slaves, they–'

'I was wrong to fear him, Obax Zakayo,' said Honsou, a measure of calm returning to him. 'They are all dead?'

'No, my lord. The mountain sundered and we were separated.'

Honsou looked up sharply. 'Then where are they?'

'That is what I am trying to tell you. They broke past us and made for the breach!'

'Damn!' cursed Honsou. 'Then why in the name of Chaos are you still standing here?'

'My lord, a river of molten metal separates us. For now, there is no way across.'

'For you, perhaps,' sneered Honsou, striding through the battle to where he had left his trapped champion. 'Onyx!'

Iron Warriors still struggled with the debris that buried the symbiote, but seeing their master's fury and urgency, redoubled their efforts. Within minutes, they had shifted enough of the rubble to allow Onyx to pull himself free of the debris. Lithe, supple and showing no signs of having been almost crushed to death, Onyx made his way gracefully towards Honsou. His black armour bore not a single scratch and Honsou saw Onyx's daemonic powers rippling just below the surface of his crawling, silver-etched skin. His eyes blazed with deadlights as Honsou pointed to the breach.

'Find the renegades,' he ordered Onyx. 'Find them and bring them to me.'

The daemon creature nodded and set off up the slopes of the mountain.

THE SHATTERED REMNANTS of this part of the ramparts were eerily deserted, the noise of battle muted from here, as Uriel pulled himself over the tattered lip of stone with the aid of the orange-steel rebars. He rolled to his feet, alert for danger, but finding none. The brooding presence of the fortress still towered above him, but he kept his eyes averted from its monstrous geometries for now, turning and helping the remainder of their force onto the battlements.

The walls swept around the mountain, curving and angled, seemingly at random, hordes of human soldiers and mutants firing from the embattled ramparts into the masses of attackers below. Thousands of warriors fought in the breach, looking from here like some great serpent that heaved and convulsed as it pushed its way, metre by metre, up the rubble slopes.

Pasanius and Vaanes climbed up, followed by Leonid and Ellard and the rest of the warrior band. Uriel could scarce believe it. They were within the walls of the fortress!

'Throne of Terra,' breathed Pasanius. 'That was bloody work!'

'It's not over yet,' cautioned Uriel, turning and more fully surveying their surroundings. A row of great archways led deeper into the fortress, each one as tall as a battle Titan and ringed with grotesque carvings that squirmed within the rock, as though the unquiet matter of the blocks was reshaping itself as they watched.

'Which way?' asked Vaanes as the last of the Space Marines climbed to the ramparts.

'I don't know,' admitted Uriel. 'There is nothing to choose between them.'

'Then we've nothing to lose, whichever one we take,' pointed out Vaanes, heading towards the middle archway.

'I suppose,' said Uriel, though a gut feeling told him that there *was* something different about this archway. He could not put his finger on what, but since he had no better idea of which one to take, he set off after Vaanes. The Space Marines followed him, bolters levelled in cautious apprehension.

Vaanes waited for him at the entrance to the archway, and as Uriel passed beneath its stygian immensity, he sketched the sign of the aquila across his chest, hearing a distant pounding, like the slow heartbeat of a sleeping monster.

'We are in the belly of the beast once more, Uriel,' said Pasanius, the guttering blue tip of his flamer throwing their faces into stark relief and causing the carvings on the inner faces of the archway to leer and dance across the walls.

'I know,' nodded Uriel, praying that the white cloak he had put over his soul would protect it from the vile things they were sure to see in the heart of the Enemy's lair.

ONYX GHOSTED OVER the lip of the ruined bastion, his bronze claws sliding slowly from his flesh. His silver eyes scanned the battlements for any sign of the renegades, but they were nowhere to be seen. Moving like a shadow, Onyx tasted the air, the crawling silver veins beneath his skin burning brighter as he channelled the daemonic energy within him into tracking the intruders.

His vision shifted into realms of sight beyond the ken of mortal men, where that which had already come to pass could be seen by listening to the echoes in the air. He watched as shadowy forms climbed over the ramparts, in much the same way as he had just done: many warriors, led by one whose soul burned brightly with purpose and another whose soul was withered and dead.

As though formed from swirling particles of smoke, their forms were ethereal and insubstantial, but Onyx could see them as clearly as though he had been here to watch them arrive. They had passed this way but minutes ago, their phantasmal echoes walking from the battlements and heading in the direction of the monstrous archways carved into the mountainside.

Onyx watched as the ghostly figures were swallowed up by the whispering darkness of the archways and sheathed his claws. He would need to take another route into the fortress to hunt the intruders, for if Khalan-Ghol had lured them into the bedlam portals, there was a good chance they were already dead.

CHAPTER ELEVEN

THE JOURNEY THROUGH the darkened archway was one that Uriel knew he would never forget. The sensation of being spied upon by every square centimetre of wall was intolerable and he was sure he could hear a susurration of whispered voices, just on the threshold of hearing. Their words, if such they were, were unintelligible, but on some primal level, Uriel knew that they whispered of vile, terrible things.

…dishonour, disgrace and failure…

This at least he felt he could bear, having already seen the most terrible things imaginable in the presence of the Nightbringer, but still…

The twilit darkness seemed to go on forever and Uriel soon lost track of how long they had been travelling along the damnable tunnel.

…it doesn't ever stop, it goes on and on…

197

'Imperator! Does this ever end?' growled Vaanes as they delved further and further into the never-ending darkness.

'I know,' said Uriel. 'I get the feeling that we do not travel normal paths here. We can trust nothing, not even the evidence of our own senses.'

'Then how will we find what we're looking for?'

…you won't…

'We will have to trust that the Emperor will show us the way,' said Uriel, irritated by Vaanes's constant questions.

Vaanes shook his head in exasperation. 'I knew I should have never come on this mission. It was doomed from the start.'

…yes, doomed, only death awaits…

'Then why did you come?' snapped Uriel, rounding on the former Raven Guard, his temper fraying.

…he hates you and will betray you…

'Damned if I can remember,' snarled Vaanes, his face centimetres from Uriel's. 'Perhaps I thought you had more of an idea about how you planned to get in here and find what we came for!'

…he doesn't, he will see you dead soon…

'Damn you, Vaanes. Why must you always undermine me?' said Uriel, hearing soft, malicious laughter and the whispers of the walls growing louder in his ears. 'Every step of this journey you have done nothing but tell us that we are on a fool's errand. That may be so, but we are Space Marines trapped on a daemon world and it is our sacred task to fight the enemies of mankind wherever they may be.'

…not any more. Give in, you are worthless…

'Don't you understand? We are not Space Marines,' shouted Vaanes, the reflected blue light of the tunnel glittering in his eyes. 'Not any more. We are all outcasts, shunned and banished from our Chapters. We owe neither them nor the Emperor anything any more. And I, for one, am getting sick of hearing your sanctimonious voice telling me what I ought to be doing.'

…yes, kill him, what is he to you anyway…?

Uriel shook his head as Vaanes slapped a gauntleted hand on his shoulder guards and said, 'Where is your Chapter badge, Ventris? I don't see it, does anyone else?'

'What happened to you, Vaanes?' asked Uriel, angrily shrugging off the hands on his shoulders and gripping the hilt of his sword. 'How did you become so damaged?'

…because he has no honour, he deserves to die…!

'Because I let myself get put in situations like this once too often,' hissed Vaanes. 'And I swore I would not blindly follow another to my death. Damn me, but I let myself get fooled again.'

Uriel drew his sword, his anger boiling over when he heard the soft susurration of the whispering walls once more and the words and feelings behind them wormed their way into his brain.

…more, say more, give vent to all your secret doubts and fears and frustrations…

The voices insinuated themselves within his head and lodged upon his tongue, just *aching* to be said for the sake of malice and spite. Uriel clamped his hands to his ears as a measure of understanding forced its way past the fog of bitterness that filled his mind.

The voices clouded his head, louder now that their subterfuge was unmasked. Uriel stumbled and reached out to steady himself, his hand brushing against the wall, its undulating substance wet and fluid. He dropped to his knees and shouted, 'Get out of my head!'

…no, worthless you, meaningless you, insignificant you, unremembered you…

'Uriel? Are you all right? What's going on?' shouted Pasanius, running over to where his captain knelt. Vaanes backed away from Uriel, shaking his head and clutching his temples in pain.

'What the hell is going on?' he yelled as the roar of voices, thousands of them, swelled in volume and filled the tunnel.

…kill, it's such a friendly word… it's the only way…

'Don't listen to them!' shouted Uriel. 'Shut them out!'

The other Space Marines now felt the full power of the lunatic voices, dropping their weapons as the urge to turn them upon themselves grew unbearable. A shot rang out and one of their warrior band, a Doom Eagle, toppled forwards, his skull little more than a charred blood basin, spilling brain and skull fragments as he fell.

Uriel threw away his gun as he felt the muscles of his arm twitch in response to the voices, fighting their urgings

…it is hopeless, no point in fighting, nothing can stand against the majesty of Chaos…

He squeezed his eyes shut, repeating the Litanies of Hate as preached by Chaplain Clausel from his umbersap pulpit; catechisms of loathing and the Rites of Detestation he had been taught when in the service of the Ordo Xenos.

…it is pointless to resist the inevitable. Join us! Give in and kill yourself…

Uriel fought the urge to curl up and give in, remembering past glories where victory *had* meant something concrete, where the defeat of terrible foes had achieved something meaningful. He pictured the great victory on Tarsis Ultra, the defeat of Kasimir de Valtos and the capture of the alpha psyker on Epsilon Regalis. With each victory remembered, the power of the voices diminished, the despair they fostered kept at bay by his powerful sense of worth and purpose.

He staggered to his feet, seeing Pasanius disengage the promethium unit from his flamer and flip a fragmentation grenade from his dispenser into his hand.

'No!' shouted Uriel and kicked the grenade from his sergeant's hand.

Pasanius rose up to his full height, his face twisted in a snarl of anger and tears coursing down his face.

'Why?' he yelled. 'Why won't you let me die? I deserve to die.'

...he does! Let him die, you hate him anyway...!

'No!' gasped Uriel, fighting the deadly power of the voices. 'You have to fight it!'

'I can't!' wailed Pasanius, holding his silver arm up before him. 'Don't you see? I have to die.'

Uriel gripped his friend's shoulders as another shot echoed in the tunnel and another warrior succumbed to the suicidal lure of the voices.

'Remember how you got that arm?' shouted Uriel. 'You helped save the world of Pavonis. You stood before a star god and defied it. You are a hero, Pasanius! All of you, you are heroes! You are the greatest warriors this galaxy has ever seen! You are stronger, more courageous and more resourceful than any mortal man!'

...no, no, no, no, no, no, no, no, no, no, no, no, no, no, no, no, no, no, no...

Uriel released Pasanius and moved from warrior to warrior, shouting at them as he went, his voice growing louder as he warmed to his theme.

'Do not forget who you are!' he yelled over the furious whispers. 'You are Space Marines. Warriors of the

Emperor of Mankind and you fight the Dark Powers wherever you find them. You are strong, proud and you are warriors. You have fought for centuries and your honour is your life, let none dispute it!'

He drew his sword and activated the blade, which rippled with fiery energies, and raised it high.

'Every foe we slay means something!' shouted Uriel, slashing at the walls of the tunnel with every word. 'Every battle we win means something. *We* mean something! Remember every battle you have fought, every foe vanquished, every honour won. They stand for everything we were created to serve. Remember them all and the voices will have no power over you!'

The slithering carvings within the walls screeched in frustration, retreating into the depths of the rock before Uriel's bright blade as his words undid their masquerades. A new sound arose to banish the hateful whispers: the sound of voices being raised in honour of great victories of the Imperium.

The Storming of Corinth, the Iron Cage, Phoenix Island, the Liberation of Vogen, Armageddon, the Fall of Sharendus, the Eleggan Salient, the Battle of Macragge... and a hundred others rang out against the foul temptations of the voices, the walls becoming dark and solid as the volume of the warrior band's shouts grew.

Uriel almost wept in triumph as the darkness of the walls retreated and the illusory nature of the tunnel fell away to reveal the softly glowing exit before them. The soulless light of Medrengard filled the tunnel and though it promised nothing but death and emptiness, Uriel rejoiced to see it.

'This way!' shouted Uriel, scooping up his bolter before staggering exhaustedly towards the tunnel's exit.

The warrior band gathered their weapons and followed him from the hellish mouth of madness.

ONCE CLEAR OF the tunnels of despair, Uriel saw that they had barely penetrated the walls of the fortress at all. The Iron Warrior with the coruscating energy whip had called this place Khalan-Ghol, and as Uriel cast a wary glance towards the hungry maw of the tunnel they had just left, he wondered if it was a name given to the fortress or one it had taken for itself. A potent malice saturated the air, a sense of ancient sentience lurking in the very rocks and mortar of this place.

The Space Marines, Colonel Leonid and Sergeant Ellard collapsed as they fled the dark of the mountain, shaking their heads clear of the last vestiges of the tunnel's evil. It had led them out onto a high ledge at the head of a long, winding set of carven black stairs overlooking the madness of the interior of Honsou's fastness.

Sprawling towers, manufactories and darkly arched cloisters jostled for space amid tall statues and spike-fringed redoubts. Dark-tiled roofs and insane structures of non-Euclidian geometries that hurt the eyes and violated the senses were crammed within the jagged, hostile architecture of the fortress, twisting, and gibbet-hung boulevards winding between them in impossible ways. A wan emerald light held court over it all, pierced with streamers of sickly orange fires burning from forges and melancholy temples. Streams of liquid metal ran in basalt troughs through the fortress, the reflected heat bathing everything in droplets of glistening, metallic condensation.

Copper, verdigris-stained gargoyles vented clouds of steam and tall, crooked towers of black brick spewed choking clouds of pollutants into the atmosphere from great, piston-heaving power plants. Grey figures shuffled through the city and dark, slithering things slipped like shadows through the nightmare streets of the fortress towards the heart of the mountain, where a single, rearing tower of iron stood, its dimensions immense and impossible.

It speared the clouds above, a swirling mass of bruised vaporous energies circling its tallest peak. Thousands of arched firing slits pierced the tower, its base out of sight behind the belching forges clustered before it. Uriel knew that the master of this horrible place must dwell within that awful tower and understood with utter certainty that this was their ultimate destination.

Flocks of the delirium spectres wheeled above the dread tower, their raucous cries echoing weirdly from its tall spires and nameless garrets. Tall peaks of the black mountains swooped high above them, and though it had seemed they walked for many kilometres through the rock of the mountain, the noise of the battle was close, as though they had travelled only a little way.

'How can that be?' said Vaanes, guessing Uriel's thoughts.

'I don't know,' replied Uriel. 'We cannot trust that our senses are not deceived at every turn in this dark place.'

'Uriel, listen, about that tunnel and the things that were said…'

'It doesn't matter. It was the voices, they got inside us and made us say these things.'

Vaanes shook his head. 'What were they? Daemons? Ghosts?'

'I do not know, but we defeated them, Vaanes.'

'*You* defeated them. You saw through what they were trying to do to us. I almost gave in… I wanted to.'

'But you had the strength to defeat them,' said Uriel. 'That came from inside *you*, I just reminded you of it.'

'Maybe,' said Vaanes, in a rare moment of confession. 'But I am weak, Ventris. I have not been a Space Marine of the Emperor for many decades now and I do not think I have the strength to be one again.'

'I believe you are wrong,' said Uriel, placing his hand in the centre of Vaanes's breastplate. 'You have heart, and I see courage and honour within you, Vaanes. You have just forgotten who you really are.'

Vaanes nodded curtly, pulling away from his touch without replying, and Uriel just hoped he had been able to convince the former Raven Guard of his own worth. This hellish place would test them all to the very limits of their courage and would seek out any chink in their armour and destroy them if they let it.

He caught Pasanius's eye, but his friend broke the contact just as quickly, turning his back upon Uriel.

'Pasanius,' said Uriel. 'Are you ready to move on?'

The sergeant nodded. 'Aye, there's no telling what might follow us through those tunnels. The sooner we're gone the better.'

Uriel reached up to stop Pasanius as he moved off. 'Are you all right, my friend?'

'Of course,' snapped Pasanius, pushing past Uriel and marching to the top of the winding, uneven stairs. Smooth, black and glassy, they would require careful negotiation if they were to avoid slipping and breaking their necks.

Pasanius led the way down, the Space Marines and the two Guardsmen following gingerly in single file. The clanking workshops of the fortress spat flames and smoke; the pounding of hammers the size of tanks echoing from the blackened walls of the windowless buildings. But over everything hung the leaden weight of the spirit of the iron tower, its dead-windowed stare crushing the soul by its very existence.

As they descended into the fortress, Uriel saw strange creatures of light moving between the vast structures, tall, elegant beings walking on golden stilts that trailed streamers of lambent amber fire. Bizarre carriages were suspended between them, filled with glowing ripples of light and a swirling latticework of cogs and pistons. A procession of these creatures passed through the fortress, but they were soon lost to sight in the illogical maze of the streets.

Huge bulldozers, similar to the bulk-hauler they had commandeered, rumbled through the wider thoroughfares, red and hateful, with tall banner poles hung with eight-pointed stars and iron tenders hitched behind them. Blood sloshed from the tenders, leaving a filthy stream of red in their wake as they made their way from the fighting on the walls to the tower at the centre of the fortress. Twisted limbs jutted from the blood-filled tenders, the corpses in each one jostling against one another as the bulldozers ploughed onwards. As the bodies moved, it was clear from their size and muscle mass, that they were those of Iron Warriors.

'Where are they taking them?' said Leonid.

'For burial perhaps,' suggested Uriel.

'I didn't think the Iron Warriors cared too much about honouring the dead.'

'Nor did I, but why else bring the fallen back inside the walls?'

'Who knows, but I have a feeling we'll be finding out soon,' said Vaanes, gloomily.

'If it is connected to our mission, then yes, you're right,' said Uriel continuing down the stairs to the interior of the fortress. The stone steps reflected the light from the purple clouds above the iron tower and Uriel wondered what dark practices and plans had been hatched within its cold depths. The stairs curled down the cliffside of the mountain, widening until they formed a long processional that opened into a bone-flagged esplanade with iron execution poles spaced at regular intervals.

Corpses hung from three of the poles, dry and desiccated, their skin sagging and blotchy. Uriel ignored them, staring into the dark mass of hammering buildings and winding, haunted streets that led towards the tower.

The same emerald glow that suffused the mountain's interior from above was stronger now that they had reached the bottom of the stairs though, the source of its sickly glow was invisible. The manufactories towered above them, the noise of grinding pistons, hissing valves and clanging hammers echoing from all around them and Uriel tasted ash and hot metal on the air.

'Let's go,' said Uriel, as much to galvanise himself into action as to issue an order.

He set off with his bolter at the ready, the Space Marines of the warrior band following close behind him, instinctively falling into a defensive formation with Leonid and Ellard at their centre and all their guns pointing outwards.

A chill of the soul pierced every warrior as they entered the evil shadows of Khalan-Ghol, the chill of plunging into the black waters of an underground lake that has never known the warming touch of a sun. Uriel shivered, feeling a thousand eyes upon him, but seeing nothing and no one moving around them.

'Where are all the people we saw from above?' asked Vaanes.

'I was wondering the same thing,' said Pasanius. 'This place looked well occupied.'

'Perhaps they are hiding from us,' replied Ellard.

'Or perhaps it just seemed occupied,' suggested Uriel, casting wary glances all around him, catching fleeting snatches of movement from in the shadows. 'This place will confound our senses and try to mislead us with illusions and falsehoods. Remember what happened in the tunnel.'

The streets and narrow alleys of Khalan-Ghol twisted at random, zigzagging and twisting around until Uriel could not say for sure which way they were even heading any more. He wished he still had his helmet, but wasn't sure that even its direction finding auspex would be any use here. He couldn't see the iron tower in the cramped streets and had to trust that his instincts were leading them towards it.

Tall shadows danced on the walls, capering along the sides of the black brick buildings, as though racing them through the interior of the fortress. The darkness pressed in around them, and Uriel found himself absurdly grateful for fleeting snatches of the white sky above them. He could feel the power of the black sun above him, but kept his eyes averted for fear of the madness it promised in its fuliginous depths.

Tinny laughter, like a child's, seeped from the walls and shadows and Uriel could see the Space Marines were greatly unsettled by such a plaintive sound. He was reminded of the joyous cries the delirium spectres emitted on their death and wondered if there were similar creatures lurking somewhere nearby.

It seemed that for hours they wandered, lost and misdirected by the insanities of the daemon city. Uriel could find no landmarks upon which to base his choice of direction, the iron tower obscured by the looming sides of the windowless forges and the impenetrable shadows cast by the black sun.

Eventually, he called a halt to their march and ran a hand across his sweat-streaked scalp. There was no rhyme or reason to the layout of the fortress, if even such a thing truly existed. Travelling down the same street was no guarantee of arriving at the same place and doubling back did not return them to whence they had begun.

Impossible physics misdirected them at every turn and Uriel was at a loss as to how to proceed. He squatted on his haunches and placed his gun across his thighs, resting his head against the crumbling brickwork of the building behind him.

He could feel the pounding of heavy industry through the building's fabric, but of all the weirdly angled structures they had passed, they had seen neither window nor entrance to them, simply smoking chimneys and steaming vents.

'What now?' asked Vaanes. 'We're lost aren't we?'

Uriel nodded, too weary and soul sick to even reply.

Vaanes, slung his bolter across his shoulder, as though he had expected no other answer. He looked towards either end of the narrow, enclosing street, its surface black and oily, with the rainbow sheen of spilt promethium to it.

'Is it just me or is it getting darker here?' he asked.

'How can it be getting darker, Vaanes?' snapped Uriel. 'That damned black sun never sets, never even so much as moves in the sky. So I ask you, how can it be getting darker?'

'I don't know,' hissed Vaanes. 'But it is. Look!'

Uriel rolled his head around and saw that Vaanes was right. Creeping liquid shadows were slithering up the walls, swallowing the light and obscuring the surfaces of the buildings they climbed. Inky black, the shadows rippled from the walls, spreading like slicks across the ground and rearing up at the ends of the cobbled street to enclose them.

'What the hell is going on?' gasped Uriel as the sinister, impossible shadows began to coalesce before them, nightmare pools of foetid black iridescence that crept across the walls and street towards them from both front and back.

They drove stinking clouds of vapours straight from the abyss itself before them, vile toxic fumes and indescribable pollutants. Shapeless congeries of protoplasmic bubbles erupted across their amorphous forms, and Uriel now saw the source of the pallid, emerald glow that suffused the city as myriad temporary eyes formed and unformed in the hideous depths, glowing with their own luminescence.

'What are they?' he cried as the slithering mass of filthy, stinking creatures – or creature – oozed forwards.

'What does it matter?' shouted Vaanes. 'Kill them!'

Bolters fired explosive bolts into the heaving mass of corruption, exploding within the jelly-like mass of the things' bodies and the overpowering stench of chemical and biological pollutants gusted from the wounds.

Uriel caught a breath of the fumes and immediately dropped to his knees and vomited copiously across the ground. Even the formidable biological enhancements of a Space Marine were unable to overcome the sickening, horrific stench their bolters had unleashed.

More and more Space Marines dropped to the ground, retching and convulsing at the foulness of the creatures.

'Pasanius!' gasped Uriel. 'Use your flamer!'

He could not tell whether his battle-brother had heard his exclamation, but seconds later Pasanius bathed the advancing beasts in sheets of flame from his hissing weapon. The fires engulfed the beasts, leaping high and burning with terrifying force, as though they contained every flammable substance known to man.

Crackling ooze burned with a white flame and Pasanius switched his aim to the approaching shadow creatures behind them. More liquid flame sprayed and the deafening cries of the burning creatures reached new heights as they burned. Insensate eyes immolated and new ones formed in the fluid flesh of the beasts as the flames burned them. Eye-watering fumes were released from the conflagration, but even though it seemed the beasts were in pain, they did not retreat, holding them trapped within the narrow street.

The heat was intense, but protected by power armour, the Space Marines were immune to the lethal temperatures. The Space Marines sheltered the two Guardsmen as best they could from the killing heat, but Uriel could see that both Leonid and Ellard were on the verge of collapse. The fires killed the worst of the stench and Uriel pulled himself to his feet using the wall.

'Why don't they die?' cursed Vaanes. He held his bolter at the ready and Uriel could see he desperately wanted to fire, but kept his finger clear of the trigger guard, having seen how little effect their initial volley had had. Space Marines picked themselves up, forming a defensive cordon between the walls of flame at either end of the street.

'And why aren't they attacking?' wondered Pasanius. 'Until they went up in flames, it looked like they were ready to overrun us.'

'I'm not sure,' answered Uriel, as an unsettling suspicion began to settle in his gut. 'I think that maybe they never intended to kill us, that maybe they intended something else.'

'What?' asked Vaanes.

'Maybe they just intended to trap us here,' said Uriel, watching as a warrior in glossy black power armour and glowing silver traceries for veins marched through the leaping flames, the oozing matter of the beasts parting before him.

Bronze claws unsheathed from both his grey-fleshed hands and his eyes burned with a soulless silver light.

'Found you,' said the warrior.

CHAPTER TWELVE

'You survived the bedlam portals,' said the warrior, sounding faintly impressed as he walked towards the Space Marines. His armour was utterly black, not even the bright flames reflecting on its mirror-smooth surfaces. Uriel saw that the warrior did not carry a gun, but that did not put him any more at ease. After all, how supremely confident must a warrior be to come before more than two-dozen Space Marines unarmed?

Though to call this warrior unarmed was a misnomer, thought Uriel, seeing his long, glittering bronze claws.

'Who are you?' called Uriel.

The warrior smiled, dull silver light spilling from his mouth as he spoke. 'You have not the aural or vocal configurations to hear or speak my name, so you will know me as Onyx.'

The Space Marines turned their guns on Onyx, the crackling flames beginning to die as more ripples of shadow slithered into the street and quenched them in darkness.

'Are these your creatures?' asked Uriel, raising his own weapon.

'The Exuviae? No, they are nothing more than the polluted filth of Khalan-Ghol, waste matter shed by its industry that mutated to idiot life. They infest this place, but they have their uses.'

'You would do well to let us pass,' snarled Vaanes.

Onyx shook his head. 'No, my master has commanded me to bring you to him.'

'Your master?' said Uriel. 'Honsou?'

'Indeed,' said Onyx.

Uriel could see that there was no they were going to get past Onyx without violence. He had no idea how fearsome the enemy warrior Onyx was in blade-to-blade combat and had no desire to find out.

Calmly, he said, 'Kill him.'

Bolter fire ripped along the street, but Onyx moved like quicksilver, a darting shadow that slipped between the shells and pirouetted above the hail of gunfire. Bronze claws slashed for Uriel's belly and he threw himself back against the wall, only just avoiding being disembowelled by Onyx's stroke.

Pasanius stepped in and hammered his boot towards Onyx, but the black warrior spun away and cracked his elbow into Pasanius's face before leaping over him and delivering a spinning kick to Ardaric Vaanes. Kyama Shae fired his bolter at point blank range, the shells ricocheting from the gleaming black armour of his target.

Onyx lunged close and hammered his fist into Shae's gut, the bronze claws tearing through the Crimson

Fist's armour and ripping upwards. Onyx spun away from his victim with a tortured crack of bone, Shae's spinal column clenched in his fist. The Space Marine collapsed to his knees, blood flooding from the great wound torn in his body. His eyes stared in horrid fascination at his spinal column in another's hands for the briefest second before he pitched face first to the ground.

Uriel's jaw dropped open in horror at the sight, as the dripping, bloody spinal column was enveloped within the glassy darkness of Onyx's armour, and the silver-eyed killer leapt upwards as more bolter fire raked the wall behind him. He pushed off from the wall, twisting in midair to lash out with his claws and feet, crushing windpipes and decapitating Space Marines with every blow.

As he landed, he plunged his bloodstained blades into each victim, ripping their spines out with the awful sound of splintering bone. Five Space Marines were down and they hadn't managed to shed a drop of this thing's blood. Uriel sprayed bolts towards Onyx, but no matter how he anticipated the killer's movements, he was always just that little bit too slow to hit him.

'Emperor save us, he's too fast!' shouted Vaanes.

Another Space Marine fell, ripped open from groin to sternum and Uriel could see that Onyx was not going to be too particular in how he carried out his master's wishes. The black-armoured warrior spun through the air, his blazing silver veins and eyes leaving molten trails as he moved with preternatural speed.

Uriel raised his bolter as Onyx leapt for him, but knew that he wouldn't be quick enough. Onyx's fist hammered into his throat, the claws on the furthest extremities of his fists pinning him to the wall behind. Uriel's head cracked painfully against the brickwork and he felt blood matt his hair. He saw that Onyx's middle claw was partially retracted into his flesh, the point pricking the skin of Uriel's throat.

'Anyone else moves and your leader dies!' shouted Onyx, bathing Uriel in silver light as he spoke. The flames from the burning Exuviae had died and the renewed oily, shadow beasts slithered forward, rearing up on amorphous bodies that now achieved a semblance of solidity. The survivors of the warrior band surrounded Onyx and Uriel, their weapons aimed squarely at the symbiote's back.

'I thought you said your master wanted you to bring us to him,' gasped Uriel.

'He did,' nodded Onyx. 'But he didn't say if you were to be alive.'

'He's not our leader,' said Vaanes. 'So go ahead and kill him, but you will follow him into death!'

'I beg to differ,' said Onyx. 'I can see his soul burning with the light of purpose.'

'Vaanes, shoot him!' shouted Uriel, twisting in Onyx's grip and closing his eyes as bolter shells filled the air around him with a deafening roar. He felt Onyx shudder as the bolts struck him. Amid the gunfire, he heard the warrior laugh, and cried out in pain as he felt Onyx's middle talon stab forwards to punch through his throat and embed itself the wall.

The talon was ripped free and he slid down the wall, blood pouring from his neck and armour in a scarlet wash before the Larraman cells were able to clot his blood and stem the wound. Uriel gasped, the breath rasping in his throat, and he realised his trachea had been completely severed. Uriel closed his eyes as his vision greyed and his body fought for oxygen, his chest

hiking convulsively. He fought to stay focussed, knowing that to slip into unconsciousness was to die, and
shifted his breathing to the third lung grafted to his
pulmonary system. His altered breathing pattern shut
off the sphincter muscle that normally took in air and
he gulped down a great breath as his enhanced physiology took over.

Onyx spun beyond the hail of shells, landing behind
the Space Marines with an atavistic howl of bloodlust.
His claws swelled to become monstrous golden swords
and three Space Marines were hacked apart in as many
blows. His face swelled and rippled, black horns curling from his temples and gleaming lines of augmetic
body parts becoming visible within his form as the
daemonic entity within Onyx took complete command of his body.

His eyes blazed and Uriel could see the beast he had
become was eager to do them more harm, but before
he could enact it, his entire body shuddered and the
daemon-thing Onyx had become retreated back into
his flesh, the golden swords writhing and sliding back
into his hands.

Even as Uriel watched, Onyx's original form was
restored before his eyes.

Onyx let out a long breath and dropped to one
knee, but before any of the warrior band could take
advantage of his momentary vulnerability, the undulating forms of the Exuviae roared like black tidal
waves and bore down upon them. Uriel struggled to
rise, but the bubbling, animated pollutants swept over
him, pinning his arms and holding him fast within
their grip.

Dull, mindless eyes ruptured from the toxin-flecked
matter, blinking idiotically at him and he heard the
repulsed cries of the surviving Space Marines as the

Exuviae swallowed them in their stinking, foetid embrace.

WITH ONYX LEADING the way through the interior of Khalan-Ghol, the delirious architecture seemed to resolve itself in response to his very presence. Where the chaotic nature of its plan had led Uriel and his battle-brothers a merry dance through its shadow-haunted streets, it eased the path of the daemonic creature and his shambling, slithering following. The Exuviae roiled along the cobbled streets with a grotesque, rippling motion, bearing their immobile charges within their odious, fluid bodies.

Only Uriel, Pasanius, Vaanes, Seraphys, Leonid, Ellard and nine other Space Marines had survived to reach this far within the fortress, but Uriel knew that so long as he drew breath he could not forgo his death oath. The soot-stained thoroughfares of the fortress soon fell away to reveal their ultimate destination: the centre of the fortress and the great tower of iron.

Whether it had been a trick of perspective or the illusory power of Chaos, Uriel did not know, but he was shocked speechless by its sheer immensity. Its summit was lost to sight beyond the writhing purple clouds above and it was impossible to see the entirety of its width. Twisting, crooked towers sprouted from its sides, overhanging forges spewed thick toxins into the air, swooping winged things clustered around dark rookeries and evil lightning crackled from slitted windows. A high wall surrounded the base of the tower, its ramparts thick with Iron Warriors and gun turrets.

A huge gate of black iron with a tall, armoured barbican to either side defended the entrance to the tower and as Onyx led them towards it, the dread portal swung open with a scream of deathly anguish. The

Exuviae carried them through the dark gate, and as they were borne along the passageway, Uriel saw scalding steam gusting from the spiked murder holes in the roof.

Emerging from the oppression of the gateway, Uriel gaped in dark wonderment as he saw that the tower did not sit upon the rock of the mountain at all, but was impossibly suspended over a giant void that mirrored the dead sky above on hundreds of immense chains. Each link was as thick as the columns that supported the great portico before the Temple of Correction and as they were carried towards a bridge, Uriel saw that the tower also plunged deep into the void for thousands of metres.

'Emperor protect us...' breathed Uriel.

'You waste your breath,' said Onyx. 'You think *he* has any power in this place?'

Uriel disdained to reply, unwilling to further bandy words with one touched by the fell powers of the immaterium. A long basalt slab spanned the void, its surface worn smooth by the passage of uncounted marching feet, leading to an enormous gateway that pierced the tower itself. As they crossed the bridge, Uriel saw that it was fashioned from some deathly material, hissing and spitting as though fresh from the forge. Its scale was colossal: entire regiments would be able to march through and the tallest of Titans could pass beneath it without fear.

Onyx led them towards the gate, a smaller, rivet-studded postern granting them access to the tower's echoing interior. Uriel felt the power of ages past within the tower and its ancient malice was a potent breath on the air.

'Khalan-Ghol,' said Onyx proudly. 'The power and majesty of a living god helped forge this fortress, shaping it into a form pleasing to him, unfettered by any of the laws of nature.'

'It is an abomination!' snarled Pasanius.

'No,' said the daemonic symbiote. 'It is the future.'

THE INTERIOR OF the tower was no less horrifying than its exterior – vast dusty halls of bronze statues, huge, sweating forges that spat sparks and orange rivers of metal. A parching, stifling heat infused the tower, black moisture dripping from the shadowed vaults of the ceiling. Uriel could hear distant screams and heavy hammer-blows far below, louder and more powerful than he had heard thus far on Medrengard.

Crawling shadows, perhaps more of the Exuviae, lurked in the high cloisters, though the most numerous inhabitants of the tower appeared to be figures swathed in black robes, walking with a wheezing mechanical gait.

Red augmetic eyes scanned them with interest as Onyx led his coterie of Exuviae deeper into the tower, clicking brass limbs grasping towards them with a hissing hunger. Warped cog symbols combined with the eight-pointed star of Chaos were burned into their robes and gurgling algorithmic voices clicked between them as they tended to vast, dusty machines whose purpose was lost on Uriel.

As they passed a hulking, bronze construction with pumping, greased pistons and an armature-mounted pict-slate, a huge, hissing monster stepped from the shadow of the great machine to bar their way.

Onyx stiffened as the black-robed creature shuffled painfully into a pool of light and Uriel felt a creeping horror scrape its way up his spine at the sight of it. It moved awkwardly on six, spider-like legs of riveted iron, its body braced within an oil-stained exo-skeleton at its centre. Where its flesh was exposed, Uriel could see that it was withered and dead, a patchwork of sutures running along raised ridges of bone. Its head was heavy and hung low on its shoulders, brass rods piercing the width of its skull and scaffolded by a cage of brass bolted to its temples. Its hooded face was a loathsome, parchment-coloured skull, the lower half gleaming metal and flensed of skin, its eyes replaced with whirring mechanical optical feeds.

Myriad transparent tubes pierced its flesh, running in gurgling loops around its body and hissing valves released noxious gusts as its chest heaved with the effort of breath. It reached forward to lift Uriel with long, augmetic arms, bulky with scalpels, drills and blowtorches.

Onyx stepped in front of the creature, his claws unsheathing.

'No,' he said. 'These ones are for the master of Khalan-Ghol.'

The beast hissed in anger, its clawed hands snapping in frustration and its drill bits whirring dangerously close to Onyx's head. It reached down to push Onyx out of its way, but the black-armoured warrior refused to be moved.

'I said no,' he repeated. 'It may be that the Savage Morticians will have them in time, but that time is not now.'

The creature appeared to consider this for a moment, before its hideous skull face nodded and it retreated into the shadow of the machine once more.

Onyx watched it go and, while his attention was elsewhere, Uriel struggled within the stinking prison of the beast that bore him, Pasanius and Vaanes, but it was no use, they were held utterly immobile. At last, sure the Savage Mortician was not waiting in ambush,

Onyx sheathed his claws and led the Exuviae bearing his prisoners onwards.

Uriel's frustration grew with every darkened hall they traversed and every impossibly angled staircase they climbed or descended, unable to move so much as a single muscle. The maddening sound of hammering grew louder the further they travelled and the same emerald light that permeated the city beyond the tower grew brighter as their journey led them from passages and chambers raised by the hands of men into a vast fiery cavern edged with great steam-venting pistons.

A gleaming silver bridge crossed a great chasm in the floor, through which rose banks of hot, sulphurous fumes and the taste of beaten metal. Beyond the bridge was a colossal wall of dark, green-veined stone pierced by a great, iron gate. Studded with jagged black spikes, the gate was flanked by two daemon-visaged Titans, their armoured plates scarred by millennia of war. Uriel saw with loathing that the rippling kill banners hanging from their weapons bore the damnable symbol of the Legio Mortis.

'Behold, the inner sanctum of the fortress of Khalan-Ghol! You are honoured indeed!' cried Onyx, leading them across the bridge spanning the chasm. As they drew near the gate, it unlocked with a reverberating boom that shook the dust from the leering gargoyles clustered around the chamber's roof, and the Titans reached around to open the spiked portal.

Onyx led them through the gateway and at last Uriel and his companions came face to face with the master of Khalan-Ghol.

THE WALLS WITHIN the inner sanctum of the fortress were of a dressed black stone, threaded with gold and silver and glistening with moisture. A score of tall, arched windows pierced one wall and the dead light of the sky was reflected as milky lines on the floor.

Surrounded by two score Iron Warriors and seated on a throne of silvery white sat a scarred warrior with close-cropped black hair, clad in a dented and heavily battle-scarred suit of armour. His face was cruel, set in an expression of arch interest, a long, recently healed scar on his right temple. Behind him stood the giant Iron Warrior who had incapacitated Uriel with the writhing energy whip.

'Get rid of the Exuviae, Onyx,' said the warrior.

Onyx nodded and turned to face the slithering monsters, the silver lines on his face flaring brightly and a silver sheened hiss escaping his mouth. Uriel felt the solidity of the creatures become less constrictive and toppled to the floor as their form became sticky and liquid once more. Their substance retreated from the light on the floor, reverting to their sinuous shadow forms. Like whipped dogs, they slipped into the dark corners of the hall before sliding out of sight through the great gateway and back into the mordant darkness of the fortress.

Briefly Uriel considered reaching for his sword, but when he looked up, he stared into the barrels of some forty bolters, their plated sides carved with obscene sigils and decorated with the eight-pointed star of Chaos. The Iron Warriors divested them of their weapons and indicated that they should approach the warrior on the throne.

As they neared, Uriel saw that the warrior carried a huge black war-axe across his lap and recognised him as the Iron Warrior he had first fought on his ascent up the breach. His sword had come within centimetres of beheading this fiend.

'I know you,' said the warrior, recognising him also.

'You are Honsou?' said Uriel.

An Iron Warrior stepped in and hammered the butt of his weapon across the back of Uriel's skull. He dropped to one knee, the wound on the back of his head opening once more and fresh blood soaking his armour.

Honsou nodded. 'You know of me, but I do not know you. What are you called?'

'You will learn nothing from us by force,' said Uriel, rising to his feet and massaging the back of his head.

'It is a simple question,' said Honsou, rubbing his fingers across the scar on his temple. 'I would know the name of the warrior who drew my blood.'

'Very well. I am Uriel Ventris and these are my warriors.'

Honsou looked beyond Uriel. 'You keep strange company, Uriel Ventris – renegades, traitors and runaway slaves.'

Uriel did not reply, realising that Honsou believed him to be nothing more than a renegade himself. Without insignia or markings, there was nothing to indicate that he was still a warrior of the true Emperor of Mankind.

His mind raced as he tried to think of some way to exploit the traitor's mistake as Honsou continued: 'How is it you know of me? Did Toramino tell you?'

'Who?'

'Do not play the innocent with me,' cautioned Honsou. 'You'll find I have no patience for it. You know who Toramino is.'

Still Uriel did not reply and Honsou sighed. 'There is no point in trying to be noble, I will learn what I want to know. If not now, then the Savage Morticians will extract it from you soon enough. Trust me, you would do better to tell me what I want to know now than to suffer at their hands.'

'I learned of you from Toramino, yes,' Uriel said at last.

Honsou chuckled. 'See Zakayo, Toramino has sunk so low that he stoops to the employ of mercenaries. So much for his high ideals of purity, eh?'

'Indeed,' said Obax Zakayo, circling Honsou's throne and lifting Leonid and Ellard with the powerful, hissing claws that hunched over his shoulders. Both men struggled in his grip, but were powerless to resist the giant's strength.

'I told you that you would be beneath my blade again, slaves.'

'Put them down, Zakayo, their blood is not worth spilling here. Put them to work in the forges.'

Obax Zakayo nodded and dropped the two Guardsmen, but remained beside them, his desire to wreak bloody harm upon them plain.

'Why are you within the walls of my fortress, Ventris?' said Honsou.

'As you say, we are mercenaries,' replied Uriel.

'They had passed through the bedlam portals and were attempting to make for the inner keep when I found them,' said Onyx. 'I believe them to be assassins.'

'Is that it, Ventris? Are you an assassin?'

'I am but a simple soldier.'

'No, you are not,' stated Honsou, rising from his throne and walking towards Uriel with a relaxed, confident stride. 'A simple soldier would not have brought his warriors alive through the bedlam portals or penetrated this far into Khalan-Ghol.'

Honsou took hold of Uriel's chin, turning his head from side to side, and Uriel saw that the traitor's arm was a black metal augmetic, its surfaces smooth like an insect's carapace. Its touch felt loathsome on his skin.

'Why are you on Medrengard?' asked Honsou, looking into Uriel's eyes.

Uriel met Honsou's gaze and the two warriors stared at one another, each daring the other to break the contact first. Uriel was a warrior of the Emperor of Mankind and Honsou a traitor; one just over a century old, the other having bestrode battlefields thousands of years past. Though a gulf of time and faith separated them, Uriel saw a warrior spirit within Honsou and a core of bitterness that was unsettlingly familiar.

Whether his presence in the Eye of Terror had heightened his senses or he felt some form of dark kinship with the master of Khalan-Ghol, he didn't know, but he saw with horror that there was not so great a difference between them as he might have thought.

He saw the same drive to prove himself the equal of his peers, the same frustration at being denied his rightful place through the blindness of others. Part of him admired Honsou's single-mindedness at pursuing his goals.

But for an accident of birth, might they have stood together on the battlefield as brothers? Might Uriel have fought in the Black Crusades or might Honsou have stood shoulder to shoulder with brother Space Marines in defence of Tarsis Ultra?

He saw the recognition and admiration in Honsou's face, seeing that he too had understood their shared heritage.

'We are on Medrengard to fight,' said Uriel simply.

'So I see,' nodded Honsou. 'You fought well before my walls. I take it I have you and your warriors to thank for destroying Berossus's troop elevators?'

'Aye,' said Vaanes proudly. 'I cut the cable.'

'Then it is certain you do not serve Berossus, perhaps only Toramino...' said Honsou with relish. 'In any case, you have done me a great service! Without reinforcements, Berossus was unable to carry the walls. But for you, Khalan-Ghol might now be in his damn fool hands.'

Honsou circled the warrior band of Space Marines, taking the measure of each of them in turn. He stopped beside Pasanius and lifted his silver arm to more carefully examine its unblemished surfaces.

'This is fine workmanship,' he said. 'Your own?'

'No,' said Pasanius through gritted teeth. 'The adepts of Pavonis fashioned it for me.'

'Pavonis? I have not heard of that world. Is it a world of the Mechanicum?'

'No.'

Honsou smiled. 'You hate me, don't you?'

Pasanius turned to stare at Honsou. 'I hate you, yes. You and all your traitorous, bastard kin.'

Honsou circled behind Pasanius and wiped black dust and the filthy residue of the Exuviae from his armour, taking a closer look at the colour of the plates below. He returned to Uriel's side and examined his armour too.

'I see no insignia,' he said. 'What Chapter were you from?'

'What does that matter here?' said Uriel.

'I like the way you answered that.'

'How did I answer it?'

'Very carefully,' chuckled Honsou. 'Shall I tell you what I think?'

'Would it matter if I said no?'

'Not really, no. For what it is worth, then, I think you are Ultramarines, though I dread to think what heinous crime an Ultramarine must commit to be banished to the Eye of Terror. Did you turn left instead of right on the parade ground? Forget to say your prayers in the morning?'

Uriel felt his anger grow, but forced himself not to react to Honsou's mockery. 'Yes, we are Ultramarines, but the reasons we are here are unimportant. We are here to fight.'

'Then do you care who you fight for?'

Uriel considered the question before answering. 'Not particularly,' he said.

'Then I could use warriors like you,' said Honsou, extending his hand. 'I can offer you so much more than Toramino or Berossus. Will you join me?'

Uriel stared at the Iron Warrior's hand, a tumble of emotions racing through his head. He and Honsou shared many qualities as warriors, but they could never reconcile their differences in faith... could they?

With no Chapter to call his own, might he not be better served by finding a warrior leader of courage and vision he could fight alongside?

Everything he had been brought up to believe and everything he had been trained in as a Space Marine warred with the bitterness at their expulsion from the Ultramarines, and as he locked eyes with Honsou once again, he saw the only course open to him.

PART THREE

IN THE REALM OF THE UNFLESHED

CHAPTER THIRTEEN

Uriel lunged to the side and hammered his elbow into the throat of the Iron Warrior holding his sword and caught the falling scabbard as the traitor clutched for his shattered windpipe. The blade hissed from its sheath as he shouted, 'I am a warrior of the Emperor of Mankind and a Space Marine. I will never join the likes of you!'

Honsou didn't move and Uriel's blade sang for his neck, but the bronze claws of Onyx were there first, intercepting the blow. Onyx's other fist hammered into Uriel's chest, sending him sprawling across the powdered bone floor and driving the breath from him. He dropped his sword and gasped for breath as he momentarily tried to take oxygen in through his severed trachea before his autonomic functions reverted to his third lung.

He reached for his fallen sword, but a booted foot slammed down on the blade.

'How stupid do you think I am, Ventris?' snarled Honsou. 'Do you think I became the master of this fortress by blind luck? No, I earned this by being better than everyone who tried to take it from me!'

Honsou's boot lashed out, smashing into his jaw and cracking the bone. Uriel rolled away from Honsou's kicks, the Iron Warriors closing on the warrior band with their bolters raised as they made to come to Uriel's assistance.

Uriel struggled to rise, but Honsou was giving him no chance, dropping his knee into the small of his back and hammering hard, economical punches into his ribs. Honsou gripped the back of his head and slammed Uriel's face into the floor. Uriel felt his nose break and his cheekbone crack under the assault, twisting his head to try and avoid the worst of the blows. But Honsou was a gutter fighter and trapped his head with his elbow while pounding his face in fury.

'Damn, but you will wish you had accepted my offer!' raged Honsou as he stood and wiped Uriel's spattered blood from his face. 'I will give you to the Savage Morticians and they will rape your flesh and show you agony like you have never known. Your body will be their canvas and once they are d**** violating you, they will render you down to flesh their wasted frames.'

Uriel rolled onto his back, blood filling his mouth, and he coughed, spattering his armour with red. He pushed himself onto one elbow and said, 'I am Uriel Ventris of the Ultramarines, loyal servant of the beneficent Emperor of Mankind and foe to all the traitorous followers of the Ruinous Powers. Nothing you can do will change that.'

Honsou snarled and crouched over Uriel's breastplate, hammering his fists against Uriel's face once more. Blood sprayed the floor as he yelled. 'Damn you, how dare you refuse me! You are nothing, no one. Your Chapter has disowned you! You are nothing to them. What can you possibly have to gain by honouring them?'

Uriel's hand shot out and caught Honsou's descending fist.

'I would have my honour and my faith!' he spat, lashing out with his other fist and smashing Honsou aside. Uriel rolled to his feet and staggered to join the remainder of the warrior band. The Space Marines and the two Guardsmen formed a circle of defiance before the Iron Warriors. Uriel spat blood and teeth, leaning on Pasanius for support.

'You had me worried there for a moment,' said Pasanius. His tone was light, but even in his battered state, Uriel caught the concern in his friend's tone.

'I am a warrior of the Emperor, my friend,' he gasped. 'I would never turn to the Dark Powers, you know that.'

'I know that,' agreed Pasanius.

'Well you certainly had that bastard fooled,' said Vaanes, moving to stand beside them, his lightning claws sliding from his gauntlet. 'And me too. Damn it, Ventris, I won't die like this!'

'Neither will I, if I can help it,' said Uriel.

The Iron Warriors surrounded them, bolters aimed at their hearts as Honsou rose, wiping blood from his face.

'I'll make sure you're broken in two, Ventris,' he promised. 'I'll let them feed you the filth of the daemonculaba then have you thrown to the Unfleshed. Let's see how your precious ideals hold up then.'

'Nothing you can do will ever break my faith in the Emperor,' said Uriel.

'Faith?' scoffed Honsou. 'What is that but hopeful ignorance? The Iron Warriors once had faith, but where did that get them? Betrayed by the Emperor and cast into the Eye of Terror. If that's what faith in the Emperor gets you, then to hell with it, you're welcome to it!'

Pasanius roared in anger and leapt for Honsou's throat, but again Onyx darted in to protect his master, hammering his bronze claws towards his throat. For such a big man, Pasanius moved surprisingly swiftly and he batted aside Onyx's blow, backhanding his massive fist into the daemon symbiote's face.

Onyx roared and fell back, silver fire spurting from his ruptured flesh. Pasanius gripped Honsou's armour, drawing back his gleaming fist to deliver a killing blow.

But before he could strike, a biting claw closed on his arm and Obax Zakayo wrenched him back. The hydraulic claw snapped shut on Pasanius's forearm, crushing the limb and virtually severing it completely. Obax Zakayo lashed out with his sledgehammer fist and smashed the sergeant from his feet, closing to finish the fallen sergeant with his own dread axe. He raised the weapon high, but the blow never landed, the Iron Warrior incredulous as what he saw before him.

Uriel watched in horror and amazement as the crushed and mangled metal of Pasanius's arm ran like liquid mercury and the destruction Obax Zakayo had done to it vanished utterly, every single dent, scrape and imperfection renewed until the arm was as unblemished as the day it had first been grafted to the sergeant's stump of an elbow.

'Pasanius...' breathed Uriel. 'What... how?'

His friend rolled onto his side, hiding his newly healed silver arm from Uriel's sight.

'I'm so sorry...' he wept. 'I should have...'

Honsou loomed over Pasanius, pulling the sergeant's silver arm away from his chest where he cradled it. He slid his own augmetic fingers across the silver perfection of Pasanius's mechanised arm and looked at his own glossy, mechanical limb in leering anticipation.

'Take them to the Halls of the Savage Morticians and give them to the Savage Morticians, but tell them to keep this one alive… I want this arm.'

Honsou rose and walked over to Uriel, his features twisted in betrayed anger. 'But give Ventris to the daemonculaba, he's not worth anything else. Let them abuse his body and take what they want from him before shitting him out.'

THE JOURNEY TO the Halls of the Savage Morticians was as fraught with insane visions and delirious apparitions as the one towards its inner sanctum. The interior of the tower flaunted the laws of nature and physics with nauseating perspectives and impossible angles that fought the evidence of Uriel's senses.

They descended winding spiral stairs that looped around others in a dizzying double helix pattern, with shuffling slaves, gold-robed acolytes and Iron Warriors climbing or descending – Uriel wasn't sure which – above them in defiance of gravity.

Obax Zakayo, Onyx and the forty Iron Warriors had marched the warrior band from Honsou's chambers, back through the chasm-split chamber and Titans towards the dirge-echoing cloisters of the tower. Beyond that, Uriel could not say what route their captors led them, the chaotic architecture of the tower defeating his every attempt to remember their route of travel.

Battered, without weapons and heads bowed in defeat, the Space Marines and Guardsmen were herded through darkened, dusty corridors – though Pasanius kept his distance from Uriel and would not meet his eyes. Such passivity chafed on Uriel's sense of honour, but to attack their captors now would see them all slaughtered. And while he still had a death oath to fulfil and continued to draw breath, he knew there would be time enough to fight.

Their march led ever onwards to what Honsou had called the Halls of the Savage Morticians, where dwelt the Savage Morticians. Uriel had caught more than a little fear at the mention of these individuals, and did not relish discovering the reason for that fear. Was the creature that had tried to take them from Onyx as they had entered the tower one of these beings? Uriel had a horrible suspicion they would find out all too soon.

Their march came to an abrupt end when Obax Zakayo hesitantly approached a low, red-lit archway, its edges delineated with hooks, long needles and gory meat racks hung with cuts of dressed human flesh. Plaintive cries and the hiss of sizzling meat gusted from within, carried upon the stench of blood and despair. Something moved within the glowing arch, a shambling, misshapen thing.

Obax Zakayo hesitated before passing beneath the archway, the click, click of metal claws on stone and the echoes of a booming heartbeat echoing from the dripping archway ahead. The Iron Warriors' apprehension was plain to see. Onyx displayed no such hesitancy, passing the threshold into the domain of the Savage Morticians without fear.

Uriel felt foetid warmth as he passed through the arch, glancing around to see what could so discomfit the Iron Warriors. The silver fire of Onyx's eyes and veins cast a faint glow around the chamber, and Uriel was suddenly grateful for the dimness of the light as he saw macabre hints of all manner of grotesque experimentation hung from the walls and displayed within jars of milky fluid. The chamber's occupant limped towards Obax Zakayo, its every step obviously painful.

Uriel saw its naked body was a mélange of limbs and appendages from Emperor alone knew how many other bodies. Its head was stitched on backwards, with rusted copper augmetics replacing its eyes and ears. It bore itself up on legs that had obviously belonged to two people of greatly differing size and its torso was a spiderweb of poorly healed surgical scars. Perhaps it had once had a gender, but nothing remained of its groin to tell. The thing's arms dangled before its chest in an asymmetrical loop, its hands grafted together in one lumpen mass of fused flesh and bone.

'What want you?' it slurred from a mouth thick with ropes of drool. 'Not welcome.'

'Sabatier,' said Onyx. 'We bring offerings for your masters. New flesh.'

The creature named Sabatier transferred its gaze from Onyx to the warrior band and dragged itself painfully towards Ardaric Vaanes. It reached up to rub its fused fists against his face, but Vaanes pulled away from its bruised flesh before it could touch him.

'Don't touch me, you monster,' he snarled.

Sabatier chuckled – or gargled, it was hard to be sure – and turned back to Onyx.

'Defiant,' it said as Vaanes lunged forwards and grabbed its neck, twisting its head around with a loud crack of bone. It sighed once and dropped to the ground. Obax Zakayo stepped in and gripped Vaanes's armour with his mechanised claws, lifting him from the ground with a roar of anger.

'And strong…' said Sabatier from the ground as it awkwardly picked itself up. Its head lolled on its shoulders, a sharp-edged shard of bone jutting from its patchwork skin.

It waved the fleshy loop of its arms at Obax Zakayo. 'Leave him be, masters always prefer flesh be strong, than weak, starved things normally get. Maybe defiant one get lucky and masters make him like me. Dead, but not cold in ground.'

'He should be so lucky,' said Obax Zakayo, dropping Vaanes back to the ground.

'No, will not be,' said Sabatier, raising its head and speaking a guttural incantation.

At the sound of its phlegm-filled voice, the far wall of the archway shimmered and vanished, the noise of screams and the pounding heartbeat filling the chamber. A great, iron-meshed cage lay beyond, and the Iron Warriors pushed them into its centre with brutal clubbings from their bolters.

Once they and their captors had entered the cage, Sabatier looped its arms around a yellow and black chevroned bar and, with some difficulty, pulled it shut across the cage's door. As the door clanged shut, the cage lurched and a grinding squeal built from above as ancient mechanisms engaged and the cage began to descend into the depths of the tower.

Uriel looked down through the grilled floor of the cage, seeing only a dimly glowing shaft constructed of oily sheets of beaten iron. The bottom was lost to perspective, and Uriel saw that there was no way that this shaft could be physically contained within the tower. The fact of the shaft's spatial impossibility did not surprise him any more.

Vaanes sidled close to Uriel as the shaft continued its descent, gaining speed as it went until the metal sides were screaming past.

'We have to get out of here soon. I don't like the sound of these Savage Morticians.'

'Nor I,' agreed Uriel. 'Anything that worries an Iron Warrior cannot be good.'

'Perhaps your sergeant with that self-repairing arm can fight his way clear. Where in the hell did he get that?'

'I wish I knew…' said Uriel as the speeding cage finally slowed before coming to a juddering halt. Sabatier hauled open the doors on the opposite side of the cage.

The Iron Warriors beat them from the cage into a gradually widening tunnel hacked through the rock. At its end was a pulsing red glow, a chorus of screams, hissing, clanging and thumping engines. But drowning everything beneath its thudding, regular hammering was the pounding of a deafening heartbeat.

The red glow and hateful cacophony of noise swelled until they passed into the colossal cavern beyond.

'Oh, no…' breathed Uriel as he finally laid eyes upon the Halls of the Savage Morticians.

'What the hell…?' said Vaanes, his face lit by the diabolical, blood-red glow of the cavern.

Its far side was lost to sight, the ribbed iron walls soaring to distant heights where throbbing machines and mighty turbines roared and seethed. Great cables and looping tubes ran across the walls and curving ceiling, dripping a fine mist of bodily fluids to the stinking rocky floor. Tiered levels of darkened cages, similar to the ones Uriel had seen in the mountain flesh camp, circled the walls of the cavern, troughs

running below each one and pipes running from
heavy bladders suspended from the roof.

As he was forced into the cavern, Uriel felt a sudden
dullness assault his senses, feeling as though under the
effects of a massively powerful pain balm. Everything
seemed bleached of its colour and taste and smell, as
though every sensory apparatus of his body was being
smothered.

The floor of the cavern was rough and irregular, random structures and gibbets built upon one another
with mortuary tables – some occupied, some not –
scattered in a haphazard fashion around the chamber.
Drawn by the noise of the elevator cage, black-robed
monsters threaded their way through the cavern, scut-
tling forwards on an assortment of wildly differing
forms of locomotion. Some came on spidery limbs,
others on long assemblies of stilts, while others rumbled forwards on spiked track units. Their waving arms
were an eclectic mix of blades, claws, clamps, bone
saws and whirring cranial drills. No two were alike, but
each one bore the scars of massive, self-inflicted surgeries, their forms repugnant and evil.

Each displayed a corrupted version of the skull and
cog symbol of the Adeptus Mechanicus upon its robes,
though Uriel found it hard to reconcile these abominations with the priests of the Machine God. Their
skins were dead and they babbled in a series of unintelligible clicks that sounded like gibberish to Uriel.

Onyx stepped into the cavern, closely followed by
Sabatier. The Savage Morticians quickly surrounded
them, prodding Onyx with pincer arms and stabbing
at him with needles.

'A gift from Lord Honsou,' said the daemon symbiote, ignoring the examination. Finding nothing of
worth on his daemonic frame, the fell surgeons moved

on, approaching the warrior band with a sick, skeletal lust in their soulless eyes. One of the nightmare monsters turned back to Onyx and Uriel recognised it as the one they had seen upon entering the tower. Its mouth opened and a hissing, clicking language emerged.

'Your gift acceptable,' translated Sabatier. 'You get to leave unsurgeried.'

Onyx nodded, as Uriel took in more of the dark wonders displayed throughout the cavern. But immediate and terrifying as the forms of the Savage Morticians were, it was to the centre of the chamber that Uriel's gaze was irresistibly drawn.

Held suspended over a bubbling lake of blood by a trio of thick chains and gleaming silver awls piercing its chest and torso was a bloated red daemon, ancient and swollen with crackling energies. The flesh of its body was scaled and thick tufts of shaggy, matted hair ran from its horned skull down the length of its back. Its cloven hooves clawed the air and as it thrashed impotently against its fetters, Uriel could see great wounds on its back where a pair of wings had been surgically removed. Its chest heaved violently in time with the booming echo that filled the chamber and Uriel knew that this imprisoned daemon must be the source of the noise.

'"You will know it when you see it…"' said Pasanius.

'What?'

'That's what the Omphalos Daemonium told us, isn't it?'

'About what?' asked Uriel.

'The Heart of Blood,' said Pasanius. '"You will know it when you see it."'

Uriel looked up at the bound daemon, realising that Pasanius was right. This could be none other than the

Heart of Blood, the daemon thing that according to the tale Seraphys had told, had outwitted the Omphalos Daemonium and bound it to an eternity of torment within the firebox of a terrifying daemon engine.

Surrounding the lake of blood were hundreds of upright coffins of black iron with gurgling red tubes piercing their tops. In each coffin lay a chanting, gold-robed sorcerer, their withering bodies pierced by scores of exsanguination needles that fed the hissing lake beneath the imprisoned daemon with their blood. A pulsing tube rose from the lake, penetrating the daemon's chest as the psykers' blood was forced into its immaterial flesh. The daemon writhed in agony above the lake, a rippling haze of psychically dead air rising from the warp entity's skull and filling the pinnacle of the chamber. The daemon's torment at its confinement was plain and now that he focussed on it, Uriel could clearly see that this was the source of his deadened senses.

'Lord Honsou requests that this one,' said Onyx, indicating Uriel, 'be fed to the daemonculaba, while the one with the silver arm has it removed and brought to his inner sanctum. Is this acceptable?'

The creature lurched forwards, lifting Pasanius with a hissing claw that sprouted from its pneumatic leg assembly. A whining blade snapped from the armature on its wrist and with brutally efficient cuts, sawed the armour from Pasanius's upper arm, exposing the muscled flesh of his bicep and the junction of flesh and metal.

'Put me down, Chaos filth!' yelled Pasanius, kicking out at the withered chest of the Savage Mortician. It hissed, as though unused to such defiance and a thick needle extended from beneath the saw-blade and stabbed through Pasanius's breastplate. Within seconds the sergeant's struggles had ceased and the monster handed him on to another of its surgical brethren.

Uriel surged forward as Pasanius was borne away, but his lethargic senses slowed him and Onyx stopped him with a bronze blade at his neck.

'Don't,' he said simply. 'His fate will be nothing next to yours.'

Uriel said nothing as the Savage Morticians surrounded them and gathered them up in their mechanical claws.

'I will kill you,' promised Uriel as he was lifted, struggling, from the ground. 'You had best shoot me now, for I will see you dead if you do not.'

'If the powers decree that is my fate, then so be it, but I think you are wrong. You will die in this place, Uriel Ventris,' shrugged Onyx before turning on his heel and re-entering the tunnel that led to the elevator cage with a grateful-looking Obax Zakayo.

Uriel fought uselessly against the claws of the Savage Mortician, but its strength was enormous and he could not move. Its dead face hissed as it examined his body in detail. Gleaming arms of bronze held him immobile while pincers and needles pierced his flesh.

A clicking arrangement of spindly rods extended from the monster's hood, telescoping outwards and bearing a meshed mouthpiece that snicked into place before its toothy jaws. Sharp drill-bits clicked from the mouthpiece and burrowed into the Savage Mortician's metal jaw, sending dusty flurries of metallic flesh flying.

The mesh unit hissed with static and the Savage Mortician said, 'You are to be fed to daemonculaba. Waste of flesh. Much surgeries could be done with you. Things unknown become known. Others will do.'

'What are you going to do with us?' shouted Vaanes, struggling helplessly in the grip of a tall, black-robed monster that travelled on hissing mechanical legs, reverse jointed like those of a Sentinel.

'We are the surgeons of demise,' said the monster. 'Monarchs to the kingdom of the dead. Will show you the meaning of pain. Abacinate you then open you up with knives. Take what we want. Make your flesh our own.'

The dark priests of flesh and machine stalked off through the red-lit cavern, carrying the members of the warrior band towards the experimentation tables, animatedly discussing their proposed surgeries with one another in their clicking, machine language.

The Savage Mortician holding Uriel set off in a different direction entirely, its rolling, multi-legged stride carrying it swiftly through the chamber. Uriel saw horrific sights as he was borne through the hellish cavern; stripped down bodies, chains of prisoners sewn together, screaming madmen with their skulls pumped full of fluid, the internal pressure forcing it through their bulging eyes.

Men and women turned above slow-roasting fires, burning flesh dripping away and hissing on the iron skillets below. More mutants like Sabatier, deformed and reassembled without reason or recourse to the laws of anatomy, tended to the more mundane experiments, feeding on the screams of their subjects and recording every aspect of their suffering on long sheaves of parchment.

Several times they were forced to make diversions through the cavern to avoid the hateful red bulldozers he had seen from atop the stairs that led down into the fortress. They still hauled the blood-sloshing tenders filled with the corpses of Iron Warriors behind them, and threaded their way through the experimentation chamber taking the bodies to some unknown destination.

Uriel lost sight of the bulldozers as the Savage Mortician climbed a long grilled ramp that led up to the first tier of cages that ran around the circumference of the chamber. A number of conduits suspended on cruel iron hooks followed the curve of the cavern walls, laden with groaning, spitting pipes, crackling electrical cables and a clear tube filled with a viscous, gristly substance. As they reached the top of the ramp, Uriel saw that the cages were indeed filled with hideous victims that resembled those poor unfortunates who had died in the flesh camp in the mountains. But as horrific as that had been, this was a horror beyond anything he had seen before.

Each vast, bloated creature in these cages was female, their bodies swollen beyond all resemblance to humanity. Shackled into their cages, they gurgled and drooled in voiceless madness and torment, their vocal chords having long since been cut. Engorged as they were by unnatural means, Uriel saw that their size was not simply due to monstrous infusions of growth hormones and dark magicks.

These gargantuan females were pregnant.

No normal pregnancies though, saw Uriel. Their swollen bellies rippled with numerous tumescent growths, giant squirming things, easily the size of a Space Marine…

With repulsed horror, Uriel realised that he looked on the daemonculaba, vile, terrible, daemonic wombs from which were ripped newly created Chaos Space Marines. Each cage was filled with these horribly pregnant monsters and Uriel wept at their terrible fate.

Here was the ultimate goal of his death oath, the destruction of which would see him restored in the grace of his Chapter. He struggled harder in the grip of the Savage Mortician as it began cutting his armour from his body with a brutally efficient mix of blades and plasma cutters.

This was no delicate surgery, and he screamed as his flesh was cut, pierced and burned black by the procedure. Shards of his armour clanged to the floor and he wept for the violation done to its spirit. First his breastplate was split apart, his gorget torn off and his shoulder guards broken in two before being ripped asunder.

'Not struggle,' warned the monster. 'You be fed to daemonculaba.'

'Get your damn, dirty hands off me, daemon spawn!' shouted Uriel.

The irritated beast slammed a heavy fist against Uriel's head and blood streamed down his forehead, bright flashes of pain bursting before his eyes. The robed creature carried him further around the tier of battery cages, blood dripping into his eyes as he was turned around to find himself looking through the mesh floor.

Below him, he saw a great rumbling machine with a blood-smeared conveyor laden with bullet-riddled bodies or corpses with limbs missing. Great rollers and crushers awaited the bodies of the fallen Iron Warriors and each was ground to a thick paste within the machine before being carried along pulsing pipes to the cages of the daemonculaba.

Together with the gene-seed Honsou had taken from Hydra Cordatus, Uriel saw that this must be how the traitors managed to reharvest their gene-seed for rebirth. This blasphemy against such a sacred and precious symbol of the Space Marines was almost too much to bear and he swore he would kill Honsou with his bare hands.

At last he was turned upright once more, seeing a number of other black-robed morticians working on convulsing daemonculaba. These sorry specimens had their bellies cut open and spread wide, pale pink folds of fatty flesh held open with clamps as the deformed mutants placed the panicked bodies of adolescent children within the opened wombs.

Where the genetic material fed to the daemonculaba would pass to the implanted children within...

The children screamed at the monsters, begging for their lives or their mothers, but the black-robed monsters paid them no heed and continued their macabre procedures.

Uriel twisted in his captor's grip, fighting desperately as he saw the opened belly of a daemonculaba before him.

'No!' he roared. 'Don't!'

Another of the Savage Morticians assisted its fellow surgeon with the ovariotomy procedure and Uriel bellowed in anger as he felt a blunt needle punch through the ossified bone shield that protected the organs within his chest cavity.

His struggles grew weaker as the powerful soporific sped around his body and overcame his fearsomely resistant metabolism. He felt rough hands laying him within the soft, wet embrace of the daemonculaba's womb and warmth enfolded him as he felt his limbs sutured into its bloody interior.

He felt pulsing organs around him and the rapid tattoo of a heart beating too fast above his head.

'You die now,' said the Savage Mortician. 'Too old to become Iron Warrior. Gene-seed will foster new growths to rupture your flesh. Mutant growths and unknown results ensue. You will be in pieces soon. In jars.'

'No…' slurred Uriel, struggling feebly against the incapacitating drug. 'Kill you…'

But the swathes of the daemonculaba's blubbery flesh were already being folded over his supine body to leave him trapped in darkness. Moist, blood-rich flesh smothered his face and he fought to free his hands, but a warm numbness suffused his body.

The last thing Uriel heard before he slipped into unconsciousness was the sound of the daemon womb's thick, leathery skin being stitched shut above him.

CHAPTER FOURTEEN

ARDARIC VAANES FOUGHT the Savage Mortician all the way, though it did little good. It had a firm a grip of him in its bronze claws, his limbs held immobile and only his head able to move. The monstrous surgeon loped through the screaming chamber on long, stilt-like legs, its stride smooth and long, despite the unevenness of the ground. It towered over the abominable hybrid creations that toiled at blood-slick experimentation tables, making its way towards some hideous destination of its own.

'Pasanius!' he shouted. 'Can you hear me?'

The Ultramarines sergeant nodded dumbly, his head rolling slackly on numbed muscles, and Vaanes knew there would be no help from him until the drug he had been given wore off. With the exception of Ventris, he could see that the black-robed monsters were taking all of them to the same place, a procession of the grotesque creatures bearing them towards their doom. Pasanius was near as damn unconscious behind him, closely followed by Seraphys, the Blood Raven and the two Guardsmen. The remaining nine members of their warrior band were there as well.

Not for the first time since they'd begun the journey to Khalan-Ghol, Vaanes cursed Ventris for deluding them into believing they could pull this suicide mission off. But more than that, he cursed himself for falling for his fine words of courage. Vaanes was under no illusions as to his lack of honour, and should have known better than to believe the same tired old lie.

Honsou had been right when he talked of where honour got you. Vaanes had given up believing in such things long ago and all it had earned him were decades of wandering the stars as a rootless mercenary until he had ended up on this miserable hellhole of a world.

He had dared to believe that Ventris represented his final opportunity for redemption, that by taking this one, last chance, he would be redeemed and renewed in the sight of the Emperor. Now he knew better, as that promise turned to bitter ashes.

He shut out the cries and moans of those poor unfortunates who suffered in the Savage Morticians' lust for knowledge, their piteous cries unable to penetrate his bitter heart of stone. They were weak, allowing themselves to feel. To feel pain, remorse, anguish and pity. Vaanes had long ago shut himself off to those emotions and knew that it made him stronger.

'The strong are strongest alone,' he whispered, remembering those words when he first heard them from the mouth of one of his former paymasters.

At last their hellish journey came to an end as they entered a wide, circular arena with a dozen, rusted steel mortuary tables around its circumference, deep blood gutters running down the length of each one. An arrangement of iron poles, like the framework for some great gazebo, encompassed the anatomist's theatre, supporting a heavy block and tackle arrangement of meat hooks above each table. Large tubs and barrels for blood and waste trimmings were placed at convenient intervals, together with a long trough of dark water. A soiled workbench sat in the centre of the theatre, strewn with an assortment of short and long-bladed knives, cleavers, hatchets and hacksaws.

Swiftly, the Savage Morticians deposited each of the warrior band on one of the tables, securing their limbs with thick bands of iron and heavy bolts. Vaanes kicked out as the beast carrying him hacked off his jump pack with one blow and slammed him down on the table. A bronze claw slashed out, and Vaanes blinked away blood as the blade laid his face open to the bone.

The creature's dead features leaned in close to his own, hissing its crackling, unintelligible language in anger, and he spat blood in its eye. Its claw drew back to strike him again, but another of the Savage Morticians angrily hissed something and the blow never landed. Instead, it secured him to the table, ensuring that his hands were bound such that he could not unsheathe his lightning claws.

Vaanes watched as a robed monster on spiked tracks carried their weapons to an examination table and a pair of the Morticians began cataloguing them with studied interest. He tugged at the bindings on the table, looking to free himself and kill his enemies.

He didn't expect to escape alive, but perhaps he could take a few of these bastards with him before he died. Pasanius was bolted onto another table; his silver arm bound above the junction of metal and flesh, his forearm dangling over the sharp-edged sides. Their charges secured, most of the Savage Morticians departed, each of them eager to be about their own particular macabre experimentation.

Only two remained and Vaanes knew that if there was ever going to be a time to try and escape, this was it. The mutant creature their daemonic captor had called Sabatier limped into the theatre, nodding in satisfaction as he saw that the Space Marines were securely restrained.

'Not so defiant now,' it said to Vaanes, its malformed head still resting on its shoulder.

'When I get loose, I'm going to tear that head clean off and see if you still get back up, you damn freak!' shouted Vaanes.

Sabatier laughed his gurgling laugh. 'No. I going to watch you hoisted up on hooks and butchered. You and all your fellows.'

'Damn, you. I'll kill you!' screamed Vaanes, thrashing ineffectually at his bonds.

Sabatier leaned closer, its snapped neck causing its head to lurch and sway. 'I will enjoy watching you die. Watch you weep and soil yourself as they open you up and your innards spill out in front of you.'

Vaanes heard Leonid's familiar hacking cough, and twisted his head, his frustrations spilling out in an exclamation of rage. 'Will you shut up!' he yelled. 'Shut up or just die and stop making such a pathetic noise!'

But Leonid's cough was soon obscured as he heard the sharp whine of a sawblade powering up. Vaanes twisted his head to watch as the Savage Morticians bent over Pasanius, one extending steel clamps to hold his arm firm, while the other lowered a shrieking saw towards the flesh just above the sergeant's elbow.

Horrified, but morbidly fascinated, Vaanes watched as the saw bit into the meat of Pasanius's arm, sending arcing sprays of blood across the mortuary theatre. Pasanius yelled as the Savage Mortician worked the blade deep into his convulsing arm, the pain cutting through the fog of the sedative. The pitch of the slicing saw changed and Vaanes smelled the burning tang of seared bone as the blade cut into the humerus.

Blood flooded from the wound onto the floor, draining through a partially clogged sinkhole in the centre of the theatre with a horrid gurgling. Vaanes heard the two Guardsmen weep in terror at what was happening, but pushed them from his mind as he continued to watch the grisly amputation.

Within moments, the gruesome procedure was complete and the Savage Mortician who held the limb clamped tight lifted it clear of its former owner. Pasanius, the pain clearing his senses, rolled his head to see the horrific damage done to him and, though the light in this dreadful place was dim, Vaanes swore he could see the ghost of a smile crease the sergeant's features.

A gleaming cryo-chest was brought forth, wisps of condensing air gusting from within as it was opened, and the severed limb was placed carefully within.

The Savage Morticians straightened from their labours and moved around the theatre to the next body laid out before them: Seraphys.

'You will watch your men die one by one,' rasped Sabatier. 'Then you will join them.'

HE FELT NO pain and that was good.

The air was balmy, and condensation fell in a pleasantly warm drizzle from the cavern roof high above him. Uriel knew he should be working to gather in the long, gently waving sheaves of the harvest, but his limbs felt as though warm syrup flowed through his veins and he could not summon the effort to move.

A sense of peaceful contentment filled him and he opened his eyes, watching the stalks above him and knowing that he would be in for a hiding from his father if he didn't fill enough baskets, but, strangely, not caring. The sweet smell of moist crop sap filled his nostrils and he took a deep breath of the familiar aroma.

Eventually, he sat up, massaging the back of his neck where it had stiffened while he had been dozing, rolling his head back and forth on his shoulders. His muscles burned from his earlier exertion and he knew that he would need to stretch properly if he was to avoid painful cramps later. Pastor Cantilus's evening callisthenics at the end of the day should be enough to stave off such cramps though.

The soft, wet rain felt good on his clammy skin and he gave thanks to the Emperor for blessing him with such a peaceful life. Calth might not be the most exciting of worlds to grow up on, but with the entry trials for Agiselus Barracks coming up soon, he knew he would soon get the chance to show that he was ready for great things.

Perhaps if he did well he might…

Trials…

What?

He looked down at his limbs, seeing the powerfully muscled arms of a Space Marine and not the wiry arms of the six year old boy he had been when he had dreamed of entering the martial academy where Roboute Guilliman himself had trained. He pushed himself to his feet, standing head and shoulders above the harvest crop that had seemed so tall to him back then.

The people of his collective farm filled the underground fields, dressed in simple chitons of a pale blue as they worked hard, but contentedly, to gather the harvest. The field filled the cavern, stretching away in a gentle curve and following the line of the rocky walls of the underground haven. Silver irrigation machinery hummed and sprayed periodic bursts of a fine spray across the crop and Uriel smiled as he remembered many happy days spent industriously in this very cavern as a child.

But this had been before…

Before he had travelled to Macragge and begun his journey towards becoming a warrior of the Adeptus Astartes. That had been a lifetime ago and he was surprised at how vividly this scene, which he had long thought vanished from his memory, was etched upon his consciousness.

How then was he here, standing within a memory of a time long passed?

Uriel set off along the line of crops towards a series of simple white buildings arranged in an elegant, symmetrical pattern. His home had been situated in this collective farm, and the thought of venturing there once again filled him with a number of emotions he thought long-suppressed.

The air darkened as he walked and Uriel shivered as an unnatural chill travelled up his spine.

'I wouldn't go down there,' said a voice behind him. 'You'll accept that this is real if you do, and you might never come back.'

Uriel turned to see a fellow Space Marine, clad in the same pale blue chiton as the workers in the field, and his face split apart in a smile of recognition.

'Captain Idaeus,' he said joyfully. 'You are alive!'

Idaeus shook his scarred and hairless head. 'No, I'm not. I died on Thracia, remember?'

'Yes, I remember,' nodded Uriel sadly. 'You destroyed the bridge across the gorge.'

'That's right, I did. I died fulfilling our mission,' said Idaeus pointedly.

'Then why are you here? Though I am not even sure I know where here is.'

'Of course you do, it's Calth, the week before you took the first steps on the road that has ultimately led you back here,' said Idaeus, strolling leisurely along the path that led away from the farm towards one of the silver irrigation machines.

Uriel trotted after his former captain. 'But why am I here? Why are *you* here? And why shouldn't I go down to the farm?'

Idaeus shrugged. 'As full of questions as ever you were,' he chuckled. 'I can't say for sure why we're here, it's your mind after all. It was you that dredged up this memory and brought me here.'

'But why here?'

'Perhaps because it's a safe place to retreat to,' suggested Idaeus, lifting a wineskin slung at his waist and taking a long drink. He handed the skin to Uriel, who also drank, enjoying the taste of genuine Calth vintage.

'Retreat to?' he said, handing the wineskin back. 'I don't understand. Retreat from what?'

'The pain.'

'What pain? I don't feel any pain,' said Uriel.

'You don't?' snapped Idaeus. 'You can't feel the pain? The pain of failure?'

'No,' said Uriel, glancing up as the dark shadows of clouds began to gather in the topmost reaches of the cave and evil thoughts began intruding on this pastoral scene.

Dead skies, the taste of iron. Horrors unnamed and abominations too terrible to bear…

A distant rumble of thunder sent a tremor through the clouds and Uriel looked up in confusion. This wasn't part of his memory. The underground caverns of Calth did not suffer such storms. More clouds began forming above him and he felt a suffocating fear rise up within him as they gathered with greater speed and ferocity.

Idaeus stepped in close to Uriel and said, 'You're dying Uriel. They're stealing the very things that make you who you are… can't you feel it?'

'I can't feel anything.'

'Try!' urged Idaeus. 'You have to go back to the pain.'

'No,' cried Uriel, as a heavy, dark rain began to fall, hard and thick droplets sending up tall spumes of mud.

Suffocating, cloying, questing hands within his flesh, a horrific sense of violation…

'I do not want to go back!' shouted Uriel.

'You have to, it's the only way you can save yourself.'

'I don't understand!'

'Think! Did my death teach you nothing?' said Idaeus as the rain beat down harder, melting the skin on his bones. 'A Space Marine never accepts defeat, never stops fighting and he never turns his back on his battle-brothers.'

The rain pounded the fields flat, the workers running in fear towards the farm. Uriel felt an almost uncontrollable desire to join them, but Idaeus placed a palm on his chest and struggled to speak in the face of his dissolution. 'No. The warrior I passed my sword to would not retreat. He would turn and face the pain.'

Uriel looked down, feeling the weight of a perfectly balanced sword settle in his hand, the blade a gleaming silver and its golden hilt shining like the sun. Its weight felt good, natural, and he closed his eyes as he fondly remembered forging its blade in the balmy heat of the Macragge night.

'What awaits me if I go back?' he asked.

'Suffering and death,' admitted Idaeus. 'Pain and anguish.'

Uriel nodded. 'I cannot abandon my friends...'

'That's my boy,' smiled Idaeus, his voice fading and his form almost totally washed away by the hard rain. 'But before you go... I have one last gift for you.'

'What?' said Uriel, feeling his grip on this fantasy slipping and his perceptions growing dimmer. As the vision of his captain diminished, Uriel thought he heard him say one last thing, a whispered warning that vanished like morning mist... beware your black... sun? But the words faded before he could hold onto the sense of them.

Uriel opened his eyes, feeling the sting of amniotic fluids on his skin and hearing the heartbeat of the daemonculaba above him as reality rushed in once again. He roared in anger, feeling questing, umbilical tendrils invading his flesh. They burrowed in through the sockets cored into his body where the monitoring systems of his armour interfaced directly with his internal organs.

Suckling, feeding parasites wormed inside him, feeding and sampling his flesh.

CHAINS CLANKED AS a pair of dangling hooks connected by a horizontal iron bar were lowered from the framework that encompassed the anatomist's arena. Connected to sturdy block and tackle, the heavy hooks were dragged onto the metal gurney upon which Seraphys lay. As one Savage Mortician prepared the hooks, the other cut his armour from his body with practiced ease. Lastly, it removed the helmet from the Space Marine and produced a heavy iron mallet from the whirring mechanisms of its arm.

Before Seraphys could do more than shout a denial, it smashed the mallet repeatedly against his skull.

Seraphys grunted in pain, but after the sixth blow, his eyes glazed over and his head rolled slack. The Mortician nodded to its compatriot, who lifted the unconscious Space Marine's legs and sliced a heavy blade across his Achilles tendons then thrust a hook into each ankle for hanging support. Seraphys's legs were spread so that his feet hung outside the shoulders, and, satisfied his body was secure, the Savage Mortician hauled on the rattling pulley and dragged the body into the air.

'What are you doing?' shouted Vaanes. 'For the love of the Emperor just kill him and be done with it!'

'No,' hissed Sabatier. 'Not kill him. Not when he has such succulent meat on him. See how they keep arms parallel to legs? This provides access to the pelvis, and keeps his arms out of the way in a position for easy removal.'

Sabatier chuckled as it continued its gruesome narration. 'Observing anatomy and skeleton, you can see that you humans not built or bred for meat. Your large central pelvis and broad shoulder blades interfere with achieving perfect cuts too much. You are too lean as well, no fat. You see, some fat, though not too much, is desirable as "marbling" to add a juicy, flavourful quality to meat.'

'Damn you,' cursed Vaanes as he watched the Savage Mortician bend to the insensible Blood Raven. Red streams caked his face where it ran from the portions caved-in by the iron mallet. A long-bladed knife cut a deep, ear-to-ear slice through the hanging Space Marine's neck and larynx, severing his internal and external carotid arteries.

Blood sprayed from the cut before Seraphys's enhanced metabolism began clotting the flow. But Sabatier limped over and prevented the wound from closing completely by jamming the fused meat of his fists in the cut and allowing the bright, arterial blood to splash into a stained iron barrel.

Unable to bear the sight of the savage glee his captors took from his comrade being butchered like an animal, Vaanes turned his head away from the sickening surgery as a Savage Mortician prepared to remove his victim's head.

Vaanes heard the grotesque sound of muscle and ligaments being sliced and the ripping of tendon and skin as the Savage Mortician gripped Seraphys's head on either side and twisted it off where the spinal cord met the skull.

He squeezed his eyes tightly shut, straining at the thick fetters that held him immobile on the table. His face purpled and veins bulged taut against his skin as he fought.

'No use fighting, so do not,' called Sabatier, seeing his struggles. 'Just make meat tougher. Damage skin too, but no one cares about that, we get enough of that from flesh camps in mountains, despite what you destroy and burn.'

Despite the horror, Vaanes felt a sudden rush of interest. 'What do you need the skins for anyway?'

'To clothe the newborns!' said Sabatier proudly. 'The brood of the daemonculaba are expelled from the womb as mewling, skinless things. Those that survive have new skin to bind their flesh and make them whole, ready to become one of the iron masters!'

Vaanes felt his own skin crawl at this latest vileness. That the camps in the mountains were used to produce masses of skin to flesh newborn soldiers of the Iron Warriors was an abomination too far. He opened his eyes in time to see Pasanius rolling his eyes at him, desperately indicating that Vaanes should continue talking. For a second he was at a loss as to why, then saw that, without the length of his forearm, Pasanius had almost worked his cauterised stump from the iron clamp securing the limb to the table.

He forced himself to return his gaze to the horrific gutting. 'You said that the ones who survive have the skin bound to their flesh. What happens to the ones who don't survive?'

Sabatier rasped in laughter, fixing its attention squarely on Vaanes. 'Newborns too badly deformed or mutated are flushed away with rest of filth of Khalan-Ghol into mountains. Your bones and torn skin will join them soon.'

'The Unfleshed...' said Vaanes, recognising the terrible, red monsters that roamed the mountains from Sabatier's brief description. 'They are the failed births...'

'Yes,' hissed Sabatier. 'Most die in minutes, but some survive.'

'You will pay for this,' promised Vaanes, seeing Pasanius finally slide his arm from the restraint as the Savage Morticians continued their noisy work on the hanging carcass.

URIEL TRIED TO scream, but stinging birth fluids filled his mouth and his body spasmed as his weakened respiratory system fought to sift as much oxygen as it could from the liquid that filled his lung. He floated in the loathsome amniotic jelly of the daemonculaba's womb, his skin burning from leaking gastric fluids and the virulence of the flesh magicks used to warp and mutate the woman's body.

He struggled against the sutures that held him fast, feeling his strength grow with each one he felt rip from the blubbery flesh. His determination to free himself burned with a white heat in his breast and he thrashed like a mindless beast, tearing his bindings loose and leaving him floating and unbound in the womb.

Uriel clawed and bit at rippling folds of flesh, tasting blood and fatty tissue in his mouth as he tore his way upward, each breath a spike of fire in his lung. His vision was greying and his heartbeats sounded like thunder in his ears, thudding booms that echoed strangely, as though it was more than just his own heart he was hearing within this prison of flesh.

He twisted and kicked, always pushing up and stabbing forward with his hands.

Suddenly, his right hand burst into dryness, tearing through the drum-taut skin of the daemonculaba's belly. Galvanised by the prospect of near freedom, Uriel doubled his efforts, pressing his other hand into the tear and pulling it wider. The skin tore along the line of the stitches and frothing fluids drained from the beast's belly as it poured out onto the grilled walkway. Uriel pushed his head clear of the daemonculaba, vomiting up the foul birth juices and gasping in a great lungful of air. Stagnant and blood-soaked though the atmosphere in the chamber was, it still felt like the clearest mountain air of Macragge compared to the inside of the womb.

Twisting and turning, Uriel extricated his wide shoulders, using the additional leverage that granted to pull his bruised torso from the daemonculaba. And in a stinking wash of birth fluids, blood and viscera, Uriel fell from the creature's belly to the iron floor.

He lay coughing and gasping for breath, hearing cries of alarm nearby and looked up to see a pair of the hunched mutants in black rubber bodysuits racing towards him. They carried long halberds with curved blades and Uriel's fury surged around his body at the sight of them.

He pushed himself wearily to his feet as they came at him, stabbing their weapons towards his belly. Uriel dodged the first blade, swaying aside as the second jabbed for his groin.

Uriel gripped the haft of the first mutant's halberd, slamming his fist into its glass faceplate and pulverising its skull. He quickly reversed the weapon, easily blocking a clumsy swipe at his head, and stabbed his own blade through the second mutant's midriff, driving the haft clean through its body. The mutant shrieked in agony and Uriel kicked it from the weapon without pity.

He dropped to his knees beside the mutants, weeping and howling in blind rage, curling into a ball as anger and horror threatened to overwhelm him. He spat a mouthful of greasy fluid from his mouth, hearing a cursing, shouting voice.

Uriel forced himself to take a tight hold on the emotions surging within him as he recognised the voice as belonging to Ardaric Vaanes. He couldn't make out the renegade's words, but he could easily read the bitterness and fury in his tone.

His heart hardened with righteous anger, Uriel pulled himself unsteadily to his feet with the aid of the long halberd and set off in the direction of the shouting.

CHAPTER FIFTEEN

'EMPEROR DAMN YOU all to the depths of hell!' shouted Vaanes as Seraphys's dismembered corpse was taken down from the hooks on the block and tackle. Those hunks of meat not harvested for consumption were disposed of in the same barrels that overflowed with blood, and the clattering assembly was moved around the circumference of the theatre to the next Space Marine.

The Savage Morticians ignored his ravings and Sabatier just laughed, but their attention was fixed either on him or their next victim. And that was all that mattered.

He risked a glance towards Pasanius, and fought to keep a vengeful smile from his face as he watched the sergeant lean across the mortuary table. Using the ragged stump, he pushed the bolt from the restraint holding his other arm and the clanking of chains,

Vaanes's shouting and the great booming of the Heart of Blood easily swallowed the squeal of rusty metal as the bolt slid through the clamp.

With his good arm free, he easily loosed the bolts holding his midsection and legs.

Vaanes shouted, 'Sabatier! The Unfleshed, what becomes of them?'

Sabatier looked up from dragging away the remains of Seraphys, his drooling features twisted in irritation. 'You ask too many questions! Cut out your tongue first!'

Vaanes saw Pasanius climb to his feet on the mortuary table and he shouted, 'Come here and do it then, Chaos filth!' as he saw the disgusting mutant corpse finally realise that Pasanius was free. It screeched a warning to the Savage Morticians, who spun to face him, surprisingly agile for such ungainly looking creatures. They shrieked in apoplectic fury, sounding more outraged than anything else.

Sabatier cowered behind the barrel of blood, but the Savage Morticians sped across the arena, bladed arms and pistoning legs carrying them with fearsome speed. 'Pasanius, watch out!' shouted Vaanes, but the sergeant had no intention of avoiding the incoming monsters. Instead, he leapt, feet first towards the nearest, and Vaanes heard metal and bone snap beneath his bootheels. It flailed for Pasanius, whirring drills and slashing blades cutting its own dead flesh as it struck at him.

Vaanes struggled uselessly once more as he watched the unequal battle, Pasanius gripping the black robes of the Savage Mortician with one hand as it tried to prise him from its body. The sergeant transferred his grip to the mesh scaffolding that supported its skull and slammed his forehead into its face. Even over the screaming Morticians, Vaanes heard the crunch of bone.

The Savage Mortician collapsed, its spider-like legs folding under it as it reeled from the impact. As it dropped, Pasanius released his grip on its body and dropped lightly to his feet beside it. The second creature tried to snap at him, but Pasanius kept the stunned creature between him and its slashing blades.

It backed away, unfolding longer, more deadly blades from the sheaths of its arms and Pasanius took the opportunity to step in and deliver a thunderous punch to the creature before him as it struggled to push itself to its feet. It howled in pain and Pasanius took hold of its quivering, beweaponed armature, alive with shrieking cutting implements, and rammed it into the monster's face.

Dead fluids and long-decayed skin flew as its own fist ripped its head to rotten shards. Desiccated flesh and bone sprayed, and its howls were silenced as it slumped forward with a long death rasp.

'Pasanius!' shouted Vaanes. 'Release me! Hurry!'

Pasanius looked as though he were about to take on the second Mortician alone, but nodded, backing away towards Vaanes as it leapt forwards on its long legs. He dodged the first slash of its blades, ducking below a high sweep of a second. Its leg hammered out and slammed into his stomach, doubling him up with a whooshing intake of breath.

Pasanius rolled aside as its blades stabbed the bloody ground and Vaanes saw that the sergeant would not be able to avoid its attacks for much longer. Sabatier ran from the dissection theatre as fast as his mutated gait allowed him. It screamed for aid and Vaanes knew that unless Pasanius could free him quickly, they were as good as dead.

Pasanius surged to his feet, leaping for the restraints holding Vaanes to the mortuary table. He lunged for the bolt at Vaanes's arm, his fingers connecting with the bolt and closing on the metal as another thumping blow sent him flying through the air. Pasanius landed with a steel crash on the table of saws, scalpels and their weapons, scattering bolters and Uriel's golden-hilted sword to the floor.

But Vaanes saw that the sergeant's effort had been enough. The bolt had been hauled clear as Pasanius had been kicked away and, with a feral roar of hate, Vaanes ripped his arm free and unsheathed his crackling lightning claws. With a few quick blows, the remainder of his restraints were hacked clear and he dropped from the mortuary table, bellowing a challenge to the Savage Mortician as it towered over Pasanius's battered form.

But before he could do more than take a single step towards the looming monster, a bloody, reeking figure vaulted onto an empty mortuary table and leapt for its terrible form. The figure held a long halberd above its head, with the wickedly hooked blade aimed towards the Savage Mortician's torso. He landed on the creature's back, driving the halberd deep into the monster's spine, the blade erupting in a flood of stinking, yellow fluids and gasses from its chest.

As terrible a wound as it was, the creature made no sound, but twisted on some internal axis to dislodge its gore-smeared attacker, while leaving the halberd embedded in its body.

'Uriel!' shouted Pasanius, hurling the golden-bladed sword towards him, and Vaanes was shocked to see that this wild, animalistic figure was none other than the former Ultramarines captain.

Ventris caught the sword on its downward arc, the blade flaring to life as he thumbed the activation rune. Without words, Uriel and Vaanes moved left and right, the Savage Mortician ripping the halberd from its body and tossing it aside, a blaring shriek of warning blasting from the vox-units on its throat.

'We have to finish this thing!' shouted Vaanes.

Ventris did not reply, darting in to slash at the Mortician's legs. It dodged back, stabbing for him with a roaring saw blade, longer than the largest eviscerator. Ventris rolled beneath its screaming arc and hacked his sword upwards through the arm, severing it in a wash of blue sparks.

Vaanes also leapt to attack, jumping onto the creature's arched back as it reared away from Uriel's blow. He hammered one clawed fist through its neck and held on with the other as the thrashing monster attempted to dislodge him. Hooks hanging from the structure surrounding the arena slammed into him, but he grimly held on, stabbing his claws through the Savage Mortician's body again and again.

The Savage Mortician shrieked in pain and he tumbled from the beast's back as Ventris chopped its convulsing legs from under it. Vaanes rolled away from its monstrous body as it thrashed and jerked on the ground, dying in agony as Ventris stabbed and stabbed and stabbed at its loathsome corpse.

'Ventris!' he called. 'It's dead. Come on, let's get the hell out of here!'

The Ultramarine stabbed the creature's chest one last time, taking huge, rasping breaths and looking more like one of the followers of the Blood God as he revelled in the slaughter he had just perpetrated.

'Uriel, come on!' urged Pasanius. 'We have to go now. There's bound to be more of these things coming!'

Ventris nodded, joining Vaanes and Pasanius and gathering up their weapons from where the Savage Morticians had dumped them. The bloody Space Marine sheathed his sword and hefted his bolter when Leonid shouted, 'Wait! Don't go, don't leave us!'

'Why?' asked Vaanes.

'What?' snapped Ellard, amazed that such a question had even been asked. 'We'll die otherwise!'

'What's the use in freeing you? You're going to die anyway,' said Vaanes, turning away and gathering up his own guns.

'Uriel!' cried Leonid. 'You can't mean to leave us here? Please!'

Ventris said nothing for long seconds, his chest still heaving with the thrill and adrenaline of combat. Vaanes moved past him, but Ventris gripped his arm and locked eyes with him, slowly shaking his head.

'We leave no one behind,' he said firmly.

'We don't have time for this!' snapped Vaanes. 'They won't make it, but we might!'

'I think I was wrong about you, Vaanes,' said Uriel sadly. 'I thought you still had courage and honour, but your heart is dead inside. This place has destroyed your soul.'

'If we don't go now, we'll all die, Ventris, cut to bloody rags by more of those things!'

'Everyone who serves the Emperor dies bloody, Vaanes,' said Uriel. 'All we get to do is choose how and where. Every warrior deserves that, and I'm not leaving without them.'

Ventris turned and ran back into the arena, and with Pasanius's help, began freeing the pitiful remainder of their once-proud warrior band.

'If they don't kill you, follow my tracks!' called Vaanes. 'Sabatier said something about all the filth of

Khalan-Ghol being flushed out into the mountains, so there's got to be a way out of here!'

Ventris nodded, too busy to answer, as the shrieks of approaching enemies drew nearer.

Cursing the Ultramarine for a fool, Vaanes set off into the depths of the cavern.

URIEL FREED LEONID and Ellard, the coughing Guardsmen nodding their thanks as they clambered free and gathered up their own weapons. Soon they had freed the surviving members of the warrior band and set off into the macabre wilderness of the chamber, the great heartbeat and the screams of both victims and pursuers echoing weirdly from the rocky walls of the cavern.

Vaanes's trail was not hard to follow; the cloven bodies of mutants and overturned surgical tables clearly marking his passage through the cavern. The sounds of pursuit drew ever closer, their ragtag band weary to the point of collapse through a combination of sheer physical exhaustion and terror.

The sound of rushing fluids came from ahead and Uriel staggered into a vast, open sluice chamber filled with a multitude of filth-encrusted chutes and aqueducts that either pierced the walls of the cavern, rose up from below the ground or sluiced down from the upper tiers of the daemonculaba. The roaring noise of tonnes of excrement, waste matter and dead flesh rivalled the thudding of the Heart of Blood. Everything washed into a pool of stinking effluent that in turn poured through a colossal pipeway in the cavern wall.

A waterfall of filth, body parts, corpses and decomposing foetal matter poured from the cavern and away from the fortress. A way out...

Dead mutants littered the chamber, hacked in two by Vaanes's mad dash for freedom, and Uriel saw that there was only one way they would get out of this damnable place.

'We cannot fight them here! Into the tunnel!' he shouted and set off through the pool, wading thigh-deep in the bobbing detritus of surgical waste matter. He had no idea where the wide tunnel led or even if their situation would be improved by jumping in, but it had to be better than this.

The going was slow, but as he looked back over his shoulder to see a dozen or more of the Savage Morticians emerge into the sluice chamber, he pushed forward through the sludge with renewed vigour, sheathing his sword as he went.

The warrior band reached the churning, roaring waterfall of the tunnel and, one by one, leapt into its stinking darkness. Uriel heard the splash of thick, mechanical limbs entering the water behind him, and without a backwards glance, leapt in after his warriors.

Rushing filth enfolded him, its repulsive contents buffeting him as he tumbled downwards. Darkness and half-light warred with one another, and as he slipped beneath the surface of the scummy fluid, he was grateful for the shadows that hid the dead horrors flushed from the Halls of the Savage Morticians.

The roar of the tunnel was deafening, its slope too precipitous and the waters too deep to gain any hand-holds. He fought to the surface, gasping for breath and swallowing mouthfuls of foetid, frothing matter. The thunder of great pumps and the whining of enormous filters echoed from the encrusted walls and Uriel felt his skin burning with the pollutants and toxic discharge.

He slammed into the tunnel wall as it bent to one side, losing his grip on his bolter and watching as it spun off into the water. His fingers scrabbled for purchase, but he was being carried along too fast to find any kind of grip. Huge blades churned the water, hurling severed body parts and disembowelled carcasses into the air and Uriel desperately kicked out to avoid them. A rusted spar of sharpened metal slashed the water next to him and stinging water blinded him as he was carried along by the torrent, spinning him beneath the water.

As his head broke the surface, Uriel saw a huge foaming mass of spuming effluent ahead and heard the thunderous crash of water falling hundreds of metres. Jagged archipelagos of ruined flesh and foetal islands had agglomerated into decaying masses at the edge of a waterfall, and Uriel fought against the immense flow of the river of waste to direct his frenetic course towards one.

The roar of the waterfall and the stench of rotten flesh and organic waste matter filled his senses, threatening to overwhelm him. As the current hurled him onwards, he gave one last desperate kick and thrust his hands out to grip the mass of body parts before him. His hands closed on the clammy, greasy flesh, his fingers breaking the surface and spilling a mass of rotted innards into the water. Dead eyes and glassy features stared at him from the lifeless mounds as the sodden flesh disintegrated beneath his grip. He tumbled away, spinning around and cried out as he was swept over the edge of the waterfall.

Suddenly Uriel was in freefall, hurtling downwards through the air and tumbling end over end into the unknown depths. His limbs flailed uselessly as he fell and he roared in defiance at the darkness below. Was this how it was to end? Dying, broken to pieces within the refuse of the Iron Warriors?

He caught a glimmer of light on the fractured glass surface of water below and straightened his body to reduce the coming impact. His body knifed into the water, the filthy murk closing over him as he plunged into its inky black depths. Drowned corpses swirled in the cold darkness with him, rotted arms wrapping around him and eyeless skulls mocking him with their sightless gazes.

Uriel kicked for the surface, the breath hot in his supernumerary lung, fighting against the dead of the Savage Morticians who were dragging him down to lie with them forever.

His head broke the surface and he heaved a great breath of air, the dank stench of the rushing, water-filled tunnel welcome after the stinking depths. Swirling filth foamed around him and, as he shook his head clear, he heard and saw giant, churning blades chopping the water ahead of him, smashing the water and debris ahead to a fleshy morass.

Uriel fought against the current, spitting effluent from his mouth as he struggled against the worsening flow of water. The great fan blades spun too fast to dodge, but as he was carried ever closer, he saw that the leading edges of the fan did not quite reach the roof of the cavern…

Was it possible they didn't reach the bottom of the tunnel also?

Knowing he had only once chance of survival, Uriel took a deep breath and dived beneath the surface of the corpse-filled water, feeling the pressure waves of the huge blades buffet him from side to side as they foamed with water stained red with flesh and blood. The pounding pressure wave of the fan blades was a fierce force dragging him onwards, but with powerful strokes and kicks, Uriel swam downwards towards the bottom of the tunnel.

His lung burned with fire and his vision greyed, but through the murk of the water, he saw the soiled rockcrete base of the tunnel. Ahead, a thrashing mass of bubbles obscured the lethal edges of the fan blades, and he couldn't tell whether there was enough room for him to pass beneath. With no other choice before him, he pulled himself along the bottom of the tunnel, feeling the enormous beat of the blades.

He cried out, a breath of bubbles bursting from his mouth as he felt a searing slash across his back. Instinctively he pulled himself down and forward, letting what little air remained in his lungs pull him towards the surface as he cleared the blades. Uriel's struggles and kicks grew weaker and weaker, his limbs leaden as oxygen starvation took its toll on his already weakened physique.

And then his head broke the surface once more and he vomited up polluted matter, retching in a reeking lungful of air. The current beyond the fan blades was still strong, but he found that he could keep his head above the water with a little effort.

Amazed that he still lived, he circled in the water, searching for other members of the warrior band.

'Pasanius!' he yelled. 'Vaanes!'

His voice echoed from the dripping walls of the tunnel, but there was no response to his call and he despaired at seeing any survivors. Had they all been chopped to unrecognisable hunks of meat by the filtering blades of the tunnel?

Now that his immediate danger had passed, Uriel wondered where this tunnel eventually led. He had no way of knowing for sure, but felt that he must have travelled for many kilometres through these hellish passages. Where then did it empty?

Even as he formed the thought, he felt the speed of the water increase and saw a bright dot of white light up ahead. Once more, he heard the roaring crash of a waterfall, but this time there were no potentially life-saving archipelagos to cling to and Uriel was carried towards the tunnel mouth at greater and greater speed.

The white sky through the opening before him grew rapidly in size, until he was finally swept through into the open air.

Mountains soared above him and the dead sky spread its hateful whiteness above the dark rocks of Medrengard as Uriel was spat out of Khalan-Ghol hundreds of metres above the ground.

He tumbled downwards through the air towards a repulsive, scum-frothed pool, catching a glimpse of armoured warriors crawling from the water as he fell. The breath was driven from him by the impact as he slammed into the surface of the pool and he swallowed great mouthfuls of rank water.

Uriel spun through the murky liquid, kicking out, though he had no idea of which direction was up and which was down. He felt hands upon him and surrendered to their grip, feeling himself hauled upwards and dragged from the water. He retched, spewing huge mouthfuls of foamed, oily water and rolled onto his side as hands slapped him on the back.

He looked up to see the filthy, streaked face of Ardaric Vaanes, bleeding and battered.

'You made it out then?'

'Only just,' coughed Uriel, feeling as though he had done a dozen sparring sessions with Captain Agemman, leader of the Ultramarines veterans company. He sat up, feeling a measure of his strength returning with each stale breath he took. He took a moment to survey his surroundings, seeing that the deep pool sat in a

high-sided basin of rock at the base of a tall peak of
glistening rock, the water bubbling and swirling with
treacherous currents. One side of the basin was a sheer
face of smooth rockcrete, a vertical slab of stone with
the pouring outflow they had fallen from hundreds of
metres above them.

He looked around to see who else had survived the
horror of Khalan-Ghol, feeling a cold hate suffuse
him as he saw that the escape from the dungeons of
the Iron Warriors had cost them dear. Ardaric Vaanes
had survived, as had two other Space Marines, a Wolf
Brother named Svoljard and a White Consul, whose
name Uriel did not know. He let out a great sigh of
relief as he saw Pasanius sitting on the wet rocks at
the side of the pool. Such was his joy that it took him
a moment to realise that his sergeant's arm ended
just above the elbow, that his forearm had been
removed. A crusted mass of knotted scar tissue
graced the stump of his arm, and though the wound
must surely have been painful, Pasanius gave no sign
of it.

'What happened to you?' he asked.

'Those monsters cut it off,' said Pasanius. 'Hurt like a
bastard.'

Despite himself, Uriel laughed at such masterful
understatement.

Leonid and Ellard were also amongst the living, but
Uriel could see that Sergeant Ellard was grievously
wounded, a terrible gash running across his stomach.
Uriel was no Apothecary, but even he could see the
wound would soon be mortal.

'You are a survivor, colonel.'

'I would be dead were it not for Pasanius,' said
Leonid, cradling Ellard's head and staring at his
friend's terrible wound. 'But I don't think...'

Uriel nodded in understanding and said, 'No... but I am glad you are alive.'

Putting the wounded sergeant from his mind for now, Uriel turned to face Ardaric Vaanes. 'Where are we? Do you know this place?'

'Aye,' said Vaanes, 'and we should be away quickly.'

'Why?'

'Because this is the hunting ground of the Unfleshed,' said Vaanes, looking to the ridges surrounding the pool.

Uriel felt a thrill of fear as he remembered the malformed, red-skinned monsters that had devoured the wretched inhabitants of the Iron Warriors' flesh camp.

'You're right,' he said, pushing himself unsteadily to his feet and gripping the filmy hilt of his golden sword. 'We need to get out of here.'

'Too late,' said Leonid, pointing towards the ridge that ran along the circumference of the basin. 'They're already here...'

Uriel followed Leonid's pointing finger to the top of the ridge and the breath caught in his throat as he saw the silhouetted forms of perhaps a hundred of the Unfleshed surrounding them.

CHAPTER SIXTEEN

Uriel watched the silhouetted shapes resolve into clarity as they descended the high slopes of the ridge above. They came quickly, scrambling their way over the jagged rocks with great speed despite their horrifically malformed limbs. Great intakes of breath heaved from wide chests as they scented their prey on the air and drooling jaws parted to reveal huge, yellowed fangs. Blackened claws slid from meaty fingers.

As hideously deformed as the beasts they had seen attack the flesh camp, these monsters were a similar horror of insane anatomies. Limbs turned inside out, pulsing organs grown and mutated through warped external skeletons, heads and chests fused with metastasised bone sinews, siamese twins wrapped together with fleshy streamers and some with grossly swollen bellies that resembled the daemonic mothers that had brought them into being.

'From one death sentence to another,' observed Ardaric Vaanes sourly, unsheathing his lightning claws.

'Shut up, Vaanes!' snapped Uriel as he drew his sword and the blade leapt to fiery life. The members of the warrior band who had retained hold of their weapons drew them and readied themselves for battle. It would be an uneven fight, but it was a fight they would make nonetheless. Leonid left the wounded Ellard and picked up a jagged rock.

The Unfleshed closed the noose about them, grotesquely muscled and swollen limbs propelling them rapidly across the rocky floor of the basin, hungry for the taste of warm, bloody meat in their mouths. The nearest beast splashed into the foetid water of the pool, the noise of the waterfall from the outflow not enough to cover its bestial grunts of monstrous appetite. Its muscled forelimbs formed powerful fists as it prepared to attack. Uriel and the others formed a circle as the creatures loped forwards, ready to die on their feet, facing their deaths like warriors.

'You meat...' hissed the Unfleshed as it waded through the water towards them.

Uriel started in surprise, amazed the creature could speak. Vaanes had told him that these beasts were the by-blows of the Iron Warriors and until now he had believed them to be nothing more than failed experiments carried out by the Savage Morticians, similar to the creature, Sabatier.

But seeing them up close and having been fed to the wombs of the daemonculaba himself, he now knew better. He pictured the children being sutured into the daemon wombs alongside him and knew that such an imperfect method of hot-housing Chaos Space Marines must result in more failures than successes...

'Emperor's blood,' whispered Uriel as the realisation of his shared kinship with the Unfleshed sank in. He glanced up at the outflow pipe high on the rockface above them, understanding how these beasts came to be in the mountains.

He returned his attention to the Unfleshed as the beast reared up to its full height and bellowed its challenge. Uriel felt a burst of adrenaline dump into his system at the size of the thing. Its barrel chest was crisscrossed with imperfectly grafted folds of skin, pinned to its muscular frame by shards of bone and its head was a vast, hydrocephalic nightmare with multiple, yellowed eyes and a distended jaw filled with blunt fangs. Perfect for grinding his bones to digestible mush.

'Blood,' said the monster, nodding its elephantine head and licking its lips.

The remaining creatures held back as the lead beast approached, and Uriel sensed a tribal, pack mentality at work.

Uriel stepped towards the beast and held his sword, two-handed, before him.

'What are you doing?' said Pasanius.

'I think this is the alpha male of the group,' said Uriel. 'Perhaps if I can kill it, the others won't attack.'

'Or they'll tear us to pieces all the quicker,' said Leonid.

'True,' allowed Uriel, 'but I don't think we have much choice.'

'Give it your best shot,' said Vaanes, sheathing his claws.

The beast watched Uriel approach, flexing the huge muscles of its upper body. He tried to read its expression, but its blunted features gave him no clue as to its thoughts.

'Come on then. Come and get me if you want to eat me!' he roared.

The monster sprang forward and Uriel barely avoided a swinging blow that would have taken his head off had it connected. He ducked beneath the punch and dodged around the side of the Unfleshed, swinging his sword for its back. The blade sliced barely a centimetre into its flesh and Uriel felt the shock of the blow up his arms, horrified that the lethal energies of his weapon had failed to cut the monster in two. Before he recovered from his surprise, the beast was upon him, its meaty fists clubbing him down. Uriel collapsed into the water, rolling from a thunderous stamp that sent up a geyser of brackish water.

'Uriel!' shouted Pasanius, stepping forward to help.

'No!' shouted Uriel, scrambling away from the monster on his backside and into the downpour of rushing water driving down from the Halls of the Savage Morticians. 'If you help me, they will all attack!'

Uriel pushed himself clear of the foaming torrent and lunged forward, stabbing for the monster's groin. The tip of the blade barely penetrated the Unfleshed's hide before sliding clear without further injury. It roared and picked him up in one fist, snapping its jaws shut on his side. Uriel shouted in pain and twisted in its grip, saving himself from being disembowelled and stabbed his sword for the monster's head.

The blade scraped across its eyeballs, drawing a howl of pain from the monster. Its claws spasmed and Uriel fell from its hand. He landed before the Unfleshed and thrust his sword straight forward with a roar of anger, putting his entire strength behind the blow.

He yelled in triumph as the point of the blade punched through a weaker section of the monster's flesh and he drove the blade clean through its body. A heavy fist smashed into his shoulder and Uriel was driven to his knees in the water. He felt his collarbone crack and released his grip on the sword hilt. He looked up into the Unfleshed's weeping-blood eyes and knew that he could not defeat it. Despite a crackling blade impaling its belly, the monster gave no indication that it even felt the wound.

Uriel had stood before the might of a star god, had destroyed the heart of a tyranid hive ship, had faced the unimaginable power of a rogue psyker and now he was to die at the hands of this monster that was kin to him at a genetic level. Its clawed hands reached for him, but before they closed on his head and crushed his skull to splinters, a bellowing roar echoed from the sides of the basin and, as one, the Unfleshed that surrounded them drew back in fearful respect.

A stillness fell, a sudden peace, and Uriel watched as a terrible beast, larger than the others, descended slowly into the water-filled depression. The Unfleshed Uriel had just fought was a gargantuan, swollen monstrosity, but this beast was an order of magnitude greater than that. Its physique was colossal and rippled with abnormal growths of fierce muscle, a powerhouse of primal, destructive energy. Red and raw, its body was a glistening mass of wet, exposed musculature, sinews bulging and contracting as it moved. If there was an alpha male of the Unfleshed, then surely this must be it. Uriel recognised the thing as the creature that had led the attack against the huddled slaves at the flesh camp.

Its head was lodged low between its shoulders, a red skull face with burning yellowed eyes set within a prosaic arrangement of gory features. Without the guise of flesh, its features were dead and expressionless, its mouth lipless, its nose a torn gash in the centre of its face. Unlike many of its brethren, it retained a measure of its humanity in its form, though massively built beyond even what the ancient legends told of the primarchs.

But worst of all, Uriel could see a gleam of intelligence lurking within its calculating gaze. Where the others of its kind might be spared the awful knowledge of their fate and the horror of their existence, Uriel knew that this terrible creature knew full well how the fates had damned it.

It descended into the valley with a guttural series of grunts and roars, the Unfleshed that surrounded them backing away from what must surely be their lord... the Lord of the Unfleshed. Uriel shivered as he conjured the phrase, grimacing at its appropriateness.

It stomped and splashed through the pool towards him and pushed the creature with Uriel's sword still lodged in its belly aside. It crouched in the water, its head still metres above Uriel and hauled him to his feet, dragging him close to its horrific features.

Uriel struggled against it, but its strength was beyond even that of a dreadnought and he was held firm. He was lifted from the water and held close to the Lord of the Unfleshed's face, the ragged flaps of skin around its nasal cavity fluttering as it smelled him.

A thick tongue slid from its mouth and Uriel gagged at the monster's corpse-breath as the leathery appendage licked the skin of his face. Before he could do more than retch, the Lord of the Unfleshed dropped him back into the water, and he grunted in pain as the splintered ends of his collarbone ground together.

The massive creature turned to the Unfleshed around the pool.

'Not meat yet! Maybe they Unwanted like us. Smell and taste flesh mother meat on him,' it said, its words twisted and guttural.

The Unfleshed threw back their heads and gave voice to a plaintive howling that echoed from the high peaks of the mountains, and Uriel could not decide whether the ululating cry was a gesture of welcome or a desperate cry of pity.

THE HALLS OF the Savage Morticians still echoed to the pounding beat of the Heart of Blood, the air still stank of desperation and the psychic deadness still draped the soul. But for all that it remained the same, there was a subtle shift in the dynamic of the chamber. Honsou had not noticed it at first, but as he followed the bronze-legged Savage Mortician through the paths of the dying, he noticed it in the downcast skull-faces of each of the black-robed monsters...

'Have you noticed...' whispered Obax Zakayo, reading his master's features.

'Aye,' replied Honsou. 'They are afraid, and that doesn't happen often.'

They had good reason to be afraid, though, thought Honsou. Prisoners entrusted to their destruction by the master of Khalan-Ghol had killed two of their number and escaped. Obviously dark memories of the fortress's last master still burned in the minds of the Savage Morticians and Honsou found himself relishing their apprehension as he reached the mortuary circle where the Space Marines who followed Ventris had been shackled.

In the centre of the circle were the mangled, dismembered remains of two Morticians; their flesh hacked to carven, grey chunks. Honsou knelt beside the nearest, pulling the dead arm bearing a vicious drill from the ruin of its head.

'I fear I may have underestimated this Ventris and his band,' he said.

'You think he might be more than one of Toramino's mercenaries?'

Honsou nodded. 'I'm beginning to think that he might not have anything to do with Toramino at all, that he might be here for reasons of his own.'

'What reasons?'

Honsou did not answer at first, but snapped his fingers and indicated that one of the hissing, dark surgeons approach. A tall beast with wide, bladed legs and clicking hydraulic claws for arms stooped to face him, its gleaming jaws centimetres from Honsou.

'You put Ventris in the daemonculaba?' he asked.

'Yes. Stitched him in. Into the womb with the others. He should not be alive.'

'No,' agreed Honsou. 'He very definitely should not. Show me.'

'Show master of Khalan-Ghol what?' hissed the Savage Mortician.

'Show me where you implanted him,' ordered Honsou. 'Now.'

The creature nodded and reared up to its full height, stalking off between the barrels of viscera and blood towards the nearest ramp that led to the gantries of the daemonculaba. Honsou and Obax Zakayo followed, noting with interest some of the more cruel and unusual experiments in pain that were being carried out in the quest for deathly knowledge.

'With all due respect, my lord,' began Obax Zakayo. 'Is it wise to concern yourself with a fate of a few renegades? The armies of Lord Berossus are at the gates of Khalan-Ghol.'

'And?'

'And they are within days at most of breaching the walls...'

'Berossus will not get in, I have plans for him.'

'Any you want to share?'

'Not with you, no,' said Honsou as they reached the top of the ramp. 'Understand this, Obax Zakayo, you are my servant, a mere functionary, and nothing more. You served a master who had forgotten why we fight the Long War, a master who had allowed the bitter fires of the False Emperor's treachery to smoulder instead of burning brightly in his breast. Have you forgotten how our Legion was almost destroyed piece by piece by his uncaring, unthinking betrayals? Have you forgotten how he allowed us to stagnate and become little more than gaolers? The False Emperor drove us to this fate, condemning us to suffer an eternity of torment in the Eye, and while Forrix forgot that, I did not.'

'I only meant–' began Obax Zakayo.

'I know what you meant,' snapped Honsou, making his way along the gantry past the heaving masses of flesh that rippled in agony with new life. 'You think I don't know of your entreaties to Toramino and Berossus? You have betrayed me, Obax Zakayo. I know everything.'

Obax Zakayo opened his mouth to protest, but Honsou turned and shook his head. 'You can say nothing. I don't blame you. You saw an opportunity and you took it. But to think that someone like you could outwit me... please!'

The servo claws hunched at Obax Zakayo's shoulders reared up, snapping like the jaws of evil, mechanical snakes, and the giant Iron Warrior gripped his toothed axe tightly.

Honsou smiled and again shook his head as a pair of Savage Morticians loomed behind Obax Zakayo. The axe was snatched from his hands and broken like a twig as bronze claws snapped shut on his limbs and crackling, piston driven pincers cut the mechanised arms from his back.

'No!' shouted Obax Zakayo as he was lifted from his feet. 'I know things you need to know!'

'I don't think so,' said Honsou. 'Toramino is not so stupid as to trust you with anything of importance.'

Honsou nodded to the Savage Mortician and said, 'Do with him as you will.'

He turned away as Obax Zakayo screamed curses upon his name and was carried away by the Savage Morticians to his no doubt bloody fate. Honsou had not been surprised by Obax Zakayo's treachery; indeed it had proven to be extremely useful. Soon Berossus and Toramino would learn the price for trusting such a poor traitor.

Putting Obax Zakayo from his mind he walked along the grilled gantry to where a wheezing mass of blubbery, torn flesh was being prodded and cut further by the creature that had led him here. The pain-filled features of the daemonculaba stared at him in mute horror, its glassy eyes rolling in unspeakable pain. Honsou ignored its suffering and leant down to examine its torn belly, where recently sutured flesh had been rudely torn open.

'From the inside…' noted Honsou. 'He climbed out himself.'

The Savage Mortician bobbed its head, though Honsou could clearly see its confusion at such a thing.

'How could Ventris have done this?' asked Honsou.

'Not knowing. Daemonculaba tasted him, fed him soporifics. Should not have happened,' rasped the Mortician.

'And yet it did,' mused Honsou, pulling back the greasy folds of flesh from the daemonculaba's ruptured belly. The slippery innards of the great beast heaved and shuddered at his touch and Honsou drew back as the creature went into a violent seizure, its entire frame shuddering. Though it had no voice to call its own, a high, keening wail ripped from its ruined throat and a flood of gore gushed from the open wound.

'What's happening to it?' demanded Honsou.

'Womb ready to expel its issue,' explained the moribund surgeon.

More blood and amniotic fluids poured from the daemonculaba's belly and the Savage Mortician reached in to hack at its internal structure with long, sword-like limbs. Hissing, gurgling tubes carried away dead fluids and Honsou heard the crack of bone and the sharp twang of severed sinews from within the daemonculaba's body.

The Mortician cut the wound wider and with a final splash of blood and blue and purple viscera, the daemonculaba's offspring spilled out onto the floor.

He landed with a wet, meaty thump; powerfully muscled and hot-housed far beyond the callow youth he had been when implanted. Honsou knelt beside the quivering newborn, the skinless body shivering with the violence of its delivery. Even wrapped in a mutated length of glistening umbilical cord, Honsou could see that this birth was perfect – no need to flush him into the pipes with the rest of the discards.

Filmy, acidic residue coated his muscles and he began weeping in pain as the Savage Mortician lifted him from the ground.

'Wait,' said Honsou, stepping forward and wiping handfuls of bloody, matter-flecked slime from the newborn's gleaming red skull and clearing the birth fluids from his skinless features.

The newborn lifted his head at Honsou's touch, looking into his face with a fierce earnestness. Honsou held the newly born Chaos Space Marine towards its dark, clawed midwife.

'Clean him and then clothe him in fresh skin,' he ordered. 'Give him Obax Zakayo's armour and bring him to me when he becomes ready.'

The Savage Mortician nodded and dragged away the mewling newborn.

And the master of Khalan-Ghol laughed, realising that the Gods of Chaos could sometimes have a sense of humour after all.

WHETHER THE MANUFACTORY facility had fallen into disuse and then been colonised by the Unfleshed or whether they had taken it by force was unknowable, but judging by the state of disrepair and wreckage strewn around, either explanation was possible. Uriel had been shocked at the hideousness of the Unfleshed he had seen on the surface of Medrengard, but they were nothing compared to the horrors of those who remained below in the darkness. How such things could live baffled Uriel, but even as he felt revulsion at their terrible forms, he felt a great pity for them. For they too were victims of the Iron Warriors' malice.

Uriel had no way of measuring, but reckoned on the passing of perhaps ten or twelve hours since they had escaped the dungeons of Khalan-Ghol. Led by the Lord of the Unfleshed on a gruelling march into the high peaks of mountains, they had set off to an unknown destiny, though it had been impossible to tell whether they had been taken as brothers-in-arms or prisoners. Uriel and Pasanius had bound Ellard's wound and carried him with them, despite Vaanes's protestations that the man was as good as dead and should be left behind.

Upon leaving the pool at the base of the cliffs where their lunatic flight from the depths of Khalan-Ghol through the sewage pipes had carried them, Uriel had seen that they were indeed many kilometres from the fortress. After covering many more, the warrior band had eventually been led to a great crack in the mountainside where noxious clouds of vapour gusted and spoil heaps of refuse and bones were gathered.

Descending into the stygian darkness of the mountainside, the rock passageway had eventually opened into a wide chamber where perhaps some underground earthquake had ripped an underground manufactory apart. Buckled, iron columns supported a bowing ceiling on vast, riveted girders, and beams of murky light speared down through shattered coolant towers that pierced the roof and illuminated the echoing space. Twisting bridges of knotted rope connected the forests of columns and a great pit had been dug or drilled in the centre of the manufactory floor where something unseen glittered and twisted in the dim light.

Piles of shattered machinery lay rusting in pools of moisture and groups of the Unfleshed, hundreds of them, gathered around them, their red bodies wet and glistening. These Unfleshed were the true monsters, so mutated and deformed as to be unable to hunt, or – in some cases – even move. Piles of altered flesh, twisted limbs without number and warped symbiotes of fused flesh that gibbered and howled in constant pain.

'So many of them…' said Uriel.

Further comment had been prevented as they were herded down into the depths of the manufactory and the Lord of the Unfleshed indicated that they should sit in the lee of a great pressing machine, with hammers the size of a battle tank.

'You. Not move.'

'Wait,' said Uriel. 'What do you want with us?'

'Tribe needs talk. Decide if you Unwanted like us or just meat. Probably we kill you all,' admitted the Lord of the Unfleshed. 'Good meat on your bones and fresh skin to wear.'

'Kill us?' snapped Vaanes. 'If you're just going to kill us, then why the hell did you bother to bring us here, you damn freak?'

'Weak of Tribe need meat,' rasped the monster, staring at Ellard with undisguised appetite. The sergeant had surprised them all by surviving the journey, though Uriel saw that he surely could not live much longer. Blood soaked the makeshift bandage of his tattered uniform jacket and his face was deathly pale. 'They cannot hunt, so we bring meat to them.'

'You had to ask,' growled Pasanius.

Vaanes shrugged and slumped to the ground with his back to the Ultramarines.

The Lord of the Unfleshed had then departed, making his way down to the floor of the manufactory to rejoin his tribe, leaving them in the company of a dozen gigantic monsters, each larger than a dreadnought and equipped with a fearsome array of gnashing fangs and long, dripping talons.

Since then, they had waited for hours in the stinking twilight as their captors – or brethren – debated whether to kill them or not. The creature Uriel had fought in the outflow pool was one of their guards, though it still appeared not to care about the weapon lodged in its flesh.

'Damn it, but I wish I knew what they were doing,' said Uriel, turning from the creatures that surrounded them.

'Do you?' said Pasanius. 'I'm not so sure.'

'We can't stay here. We have to get back to that fortress.'

'Back to the fortress?' laughed Ardaric Vaanes. 'Are you serious?'

'Deadly serious,' nodded Uriel. 'We have a death oath to fulfil, to destroy the daemonculaba or die in the attempt.'

'You'll die then,' promised Vaanes.

'Then we die,' said Uriel. 'Have you heard nothing I have said to you, Vaanes?'

'Don't you dare lecture me about honour and duty, Ventris,' warned Vaanes. 'I have seen enough of what your honour has to offer. Most of us are already dead, and for what?'

'No warrior ever died in vain who died for honour in the service of the Emperor.'

'Spare me your borrowed wisdom, Ventris,' sneered Vaanes. 'I have had my fill of it. If we survive this, there's no way I'm going anywhere near that fortress again. I am done with your heroics and will leave you to die.'

'Then I was wrong about you, Vaanes,' said Uriel. 'I thought you had honour left within you, but I see now that you do not.'

Vaanes ignored Uriel and stared sullenly at the lumpen, misshapen beasts that watched over them.

Uriel turned to Pasanius and said, 'Then we are on our own, my friend.'

'So it would seem,' agreed Pasanius, slowly, and Uriel could see that his friend was struggling to speak – burdened by the terrible weight of guilt.

An awkward silence fell between the two friends, neither knowing the right way to break it or how to begin to say what needed to be said.

'Why didn't you tell me?' said Uriel at last.

'How could I?' sobbed Pasanius. 'I was tainted. Touched by evil and corrupted!'

'How? When?' asked Uriel.

'On Pavonis, I think,' said Pasanius, the words, now undammed, pouring from him in a rush of confession. 'You remember that I hated the augmetic arm the moment the artificers of the Shonai cartel grafted it to me?'

'Aye,' nodded Uriel, remembering how Pasanius had complained that the arm could never be as good as one grown strong through a lifetime of war.

'I didn't know the half of it,' continued Pasanius. 'After a while I got used to it, even began to appreciate the strength in the arm, but it was when we fought the orks on the *Death of Virtue* that I first realised something was wrong.'

Uriel well remembered the desperate fighting to destroy the ork and tyranid infested space hulk that had drifted into the Tarsis Ultra system and heralded the great battle against a splinter fleet of bio-ships from Hive Fleet Leviathan.

'What happened?'

'We were fighting the orks, just before you killed their leader, you remember? One of the greenskins got behind me, nearly took my damn head off with his chainsaw.'

'Yes, you took the blow on your arm.'

'Aye, I did, and you saw the size of that blade. My arm should have been hacked in two, but it wasn't. It wasn't even scratched.'

'But that is impossible,' said Uriel.

'That's what I thought, but by the time we got away and were back at the Thunderhawk, it was as good as new, not a scratch on it.'

'I remember...' whispered Uriel, picturing Pasanius's arm reaching down to haul him to safety when their demolition charges had begun to tear the space hulk apart. 'It shone like silver.'

'I know,' agreed Pasanius, 'but it didn't register on me until we were back aboard the *Vae Victus* that my arm should have been pulverised. I thought maybe I'd imagined how hard I'd been hit, but now I know I didn't.'

'How is it possible? Do you think the adepts of Pavonis had access to some form of xeno tech?'

'No,' said Pasanius, shaking his head. 'The silver-skinned devils we fought beneath Pavonis, the servants of the Bringer of Darkness, they could do the same thing. No matter how hard you cut, stabbed or shot them, they could get back up again, their bodies putting themselves back together right before your eyes.'

'The necrontyr,' spat Uriel.

Pasanius nodded. 'Aye, necrontyr. I think maybe part of the Bringer of Darkness went into me when it cut off my arm, something corrupt that waited and then found a home in the metal of my new arm.'

'Why did you say nothing?' said Uriel. 'It was your duty to report such a thing.'

'I know,' said Pasanius, dejectedly. 'But I was ashamed. You know me, it's always been my way to deal with things myself. I've been that way since I was a boy on Calth.'

'I know, but you should still have reported it to Clausel. I will have to report it when we get back to Macragge.'

'You mean *if* we get back,' reminded Pasanius.

'No,' said Uriel, emphatically. 'When.'

Uriel turned as he heard footfalls approaching. Colonel Leonid, his face gaunt and worn stood behind him and said, 'Sergeant Ellard is dead.'

Uriel looked over to where the big man lay, and stood, placing his hand on Leonid's shoulder. 'I am sorry, my friend. He was a fine man and a good soldier.'

'He shouldn't have had to die like this, alone in the darkness.'

'He wasn't alone,' said Uriel. 'You were with him at the end.'

'It's not right though,' whispered Leonid. 'To have survived so much and then to die like this.'

'A man seldom has the choice in the manner of his death,' said Uriel. 'It is the manner in which he lives that is the mark of a warrior. I did not know Ellard well, but I believe he will find a place at the Emperor's side.'

'I hope so,' agreed Leonid. 'Oh, and you're wrong, by the way.'

'About what?'

'About having to get back into Khalan-Ghol on your own. I will come with you.'

Uriel felt his admiration for Leonid soar and said, 'You are an exceptional man, colonel, and I accept your pledge of courage. Though you should know that Vaanes is almost certainly right, this will, in all likelihood, be the death of us.'

Leonid shrugged. 'I don't care any more. I have been living on borrowed time ever since the 383rd was ordered to Hydra Cordatus, so I plan to spit in death's eye before he takes me.'

A slow clapping sounded and Uriel's anger flared as he saw Vaanes sneering at them. The renegade Raven Guard shook his head.

'You are all fools,' he said. 'I will say a prayer for you if we don't get killed by these monsters.'

'Be silent!' hissed Uriel. 'I will not have any prayers from the likes of you, Vaanes. You are not a Space Marine any more, you are not even a man. You are a coward and a traitor!'

Vaanes surged to his feet, hate flaring in his violet eyes and his lightning claws snapped from his gauntlet. 'I told you that people never called me that twice!'

Before blood could be spilled, a great shadow fell across the company and the mighty form of the Lord of the Unfleshed blotted out the light. A coterie of hideously deformed creatures accompanied him, and a hunchbacked monster with its head fused into its spine limped towards Ellard's corpse.

It dipped a long talon into the sergeant's torn belly and raised its bloody digit to its slit of a mouth.

'Deadflesh,' it said. 'Still warm.'

The Lord of the Unfleshed nodded its thick head. 'Take it. Meat for Tribe.'

'No!' shouted Ellard, as the hunchback effortlessly lifted the sergeant's body.

Pasanius reached out with his remaining arm and held Leonid back, hissing, 'No, don't. That's not your friend any more, it's just the flesh he wore. He's with the Emperor and there's nothing these monsters can do to him now. You will only get yourself killed needlessly.'

'But they are going to eat him!'

'I know,' said Uriel, standing before the struggling man. 'But you have pledged yourself to our death oath and if you break it, you break it for all of us.'

'What?' spluttered Leonid.

'Aye,' nodded Uriel. 'We are all bound to this quest now. Pasanius, me and now you.'

Leonid looked set to argue, but Uriel could see that the fight had gone out of the man as he realised the pact he had made with the Ultramarines. He nodded numbly and his struggles ceased as the Lord of the Unfleshed loomed above them.

'You come now,' said the monster.

'Where?' said Uriel.

'To the Emperor. He decide whether you die or not.'

CHAPTER SEVENTEEN

THE EMPEROR'S ARMOUR was filthy, stained with the residue of uncounted millennia of industry, the eagle on his breastplate a series of rusted bronze strips. Beaten metal shoulder guards hung from his mighty shoulders and a pair of beatific wings of stained metal flared from his back. Over twenty metres tall and suspended by thick, iron chains within the great pit at the centre of the manufactory, it was a creation of supreme devotion.

Uriel felt like a child against its immensity, remembering the first time he had seen a statue of the Emperor in the Basilica Konor on Calth. Though the statue there had been masterfully carved from beautifully veined marble quarried from the deep wells of Calth, this one – for all its crudity – was no less impressive.

The Unfleshed's Emperor hung over the blackness of the pit, its armour and limbs fashioned from whatever scrap and machinery had been left behind when the manufactory had been abandoned.

Whereas some zealous preachers of the Ministorum might find it blasphemous that such hideous creatures had created such a crude idol of the Emperor, Uriel found it curiously touching that they had done so.

'May the Emperor preserve us!' hissed Pasanius as he laid eyes upon the suspended statue.

'Well we're about to find out,' replied Uriel as he realised his first impression had been correct when he had felt like a child before this idol.

Who knew how long the Unfleshed had lived beneath the surface of Medrengard or what their memories were of the time before their abduction and implantation within the horror of the daemon-culaba?

But one thing was clear: of the innocent children who had been transformed into the Unfleshed, one memory had survived – constant and enduring: the immortal and beneficent Emperor of Mankind.

Through all the vileness that had befallen the Unfleshed, they still remembered the love of the Emperor and Uriel felt an immense sadness at their fate. No matter that they had been horrifically altered to become monsters, they still remembered the Emperor and fashioned his image to watch over them.

Uriel and the others were pushed roughly to the edge of the great pit as the Unfleshed painfully drew near. Uriel saw that there were hundreds of them – many unable to walk on their mutated legs, corkscrewed bones or fleshy masses that had once been limbs, and so were helped by their brethren.

'God-Emperor, look at them!' said Vaanes. 'How can such things be allowed to live?'

'Shut up, Vaanes,' said Uriel sadly. 'They are kin to you and I, do not forget that. The flesh of the Emperor is within them.'

'You can't be serious,' said Vaanes. 'Look at them. They're evil.'

'Are they? I'm not so sure.'

A ripple of hunger and self-loathing went round the pit as the Lord of the Unfleshed turned and drew himself up to his full height. He reached back and pulled Uriel forwards, lifting him easily from the ground. Powerless to resist, Uriel felt the ground beneath him fall away as he was dangled over the bottomless pit.

'Smelled mother's meat on you,' roared the Lord of the Unfleshed. 'You washed out from mountain of iron men, fell from the Wall. But you not look like us. Why you have skin?'

Uriel's mind raced as he tried to guess what response would not see him cast into the pit. The yellowed eyes of the monster bored into his and Uriel saw a desperate longing within them, a childlike need for... for what?

'Yes!' he yelled. 'We came from the mountain of the Iron Warriors, but we are their enemies.'

'You are Unwanted too? Not friends with iron men?'

'No!' cried Uriel, shouting so that the Unfleshed around the pit could hear him. 'We hate the iron men, came to destroy them!'

'Saw you before,' snarled the Lord of the Unfleshed. 'Saw you kill iron men in mountains. We took much meat then.'

'I know. I saw.'

'You kill iron men?'

'Yes!'

'Mother's meat on you, yes?'

Uriel nodded as the creature spoke again. 'Iron men's flesh mothers made us ugly like this, but

Emperor not hate us like iron men, he still love us. Iron men try to kill us. But we strong and not die, though dying be good thing for us. Pain stop, Emperor make pain go away and make us whole again.'

'No,' said Uriel, finally understanding a measure of this creature that, for all its massive strength and colossal size, was but a child within its monstrously swollen skull. It spoke with a child's simplicity and clarity of the Emperor's love, and as Uriel looked into its eyes, he saw its deathly craving to atone for its hideousness.

'The Emperor loves you,' he said. 'He loves all his children.'

'Emperor speaks to you?' said the Lord of the Unfleshed.

'He does,' agreed Uriel, hating himself for such deception, but understanding its necessity. 'The Emperor sent us here to destroy the iron men and the dae... the flesh mothers that made you like this. He sent us to you so that you might help us.'

The creature pulled him close and Uriel could sense its suspicion and hunger warring with a deep-seated desire to take revenge on its creators, those that had made it into this warped form.

It smelled him once more and Uriel just hoped that the stench of the daemonculaba that had stayed its hand at the outflow pool was still strong on him.

But the Lord of the Unfleshed roared in anguish, drawing back his arm, and Uriel cried out as he was hurled out across the pit.

URIEL SAILED THROUGH the air, his vision spiralling in a kaleidoscope of images: warped beasts that had once been children, a rusted iron chain, silvered panels of beaten metal and the black, depthless void of the pit. He slammed into the hanging effigy of the

Emperor and the breath was knocked from him by the impact.

He snatched at the metal, scrabbling for a handhold, feeling his ragged fingernails break off on rivets as he slid down the rough iron. The black hole of the pit yawned before him, promising death, but his fingers closed on a panel of beaten iron, not quite flush with the giant statue's body. Portions of its edges were sharp and he felt the tip of his middle finger slice off on the jagged metal. The panel bent and screeched, peeling away from the statue's body, but it slowed his descent enough for him to be able to secure a handhold on the bronze eagle on the Emperor's breastplate.

Uriel hung over the great depths of the pit, holding on for dear life with one hand, swinging above the darkness of the pit as the Unfleshed roared and – those that were able – stamped their feet, shouting, 'Tribe! Tribe! Tribe!'

Now that he had a better grip on the statue, Uriel pulled himself up the strips of metal that formed the eagle and swung himself onto the Emperor's shoulder guards, his breath coming in great gasps.

The Lord of the Unfleshed stood immobile at the edge of the pit, and Uriel had no idea what to do next. He watched as the Unfleshed took hold of the remains of the warrior band, dragging Pasanius, Vaanes, Leonid and the other Space Marines to the edge of the pit.

'No!' he shouted, risking standing upright and leaning on the swaying statue's giant helm. 'No!'

Then the miracle happened.

Whether it was some long-dormant mechanism within the battered machine forming the statue's helmet – given a brief resurgence of life by Uriel's movement – or the power of the Emperor himself,

Uriel would never know, but at that moment, a radiant light burst from the crudely-formed visor.

A bass hum, like a charging generator, built from beneath the helmet and the Unfleshed drew back in terror from the great effigy as the glow intensified. Uriel felt the metal of the helmet grow hot to the touch and though he had no idea as to what was happening, was not about to let such a chance go by.

He shouted over to the Lord of the Unfleshed. 'See! The Emperor wants you to help us! Together we can destroy the flesh mothers and the iron men!'

The great beast dropped to its knees, its wide jaws open in rapture as a terrible moaning and wailing built from the throats of the Unfleshed gathered around the pit.

Hot sparks leapt from the metal of the helmet and Uriel realised he was going to have get off the statue soon or risk being electrocuted by whatever was doing this. He edged along the Emperor's shoulder guards, begging the Master of Mankind's forgiveness for such base treatment of his image as he worked his way over to the nearest of the supporting chains.

No sooner had he clambered onto the chain, lying across its thick links and pulling himself away from the helmet – which now shone with a fierce, blinding glow – when a great thunderclap boomed and it exploded in an arcing shower of blue lightning.

The Unfleshed wailed in fear as the statue of the Emperor plummeted into the darkness of the pit, the chains supporting it flopping with a great clang against its sheer sides. Uriel swung on the chain, bracing his legs for impact against the side of the pit and feeling the ceramite plates of his armour buckle with the force of it.

Uriel spun crazily above the depthless chasm, knuckles white as he held onto the flaking links of the chain.

He hung there until he had got his breath back and carefully began the long climb to the top.

As he climbed he suddenly felt the chain being pulled from above. Able to do nothing else, Uriel awaited whatever fate had in store for him. He looked up in time to see the massive, raw hand of the Lord of the Unfleshed reach down and lift him from the chain.

He was lifted up and deposited roughly on the earthen ground beside Pasanius and Ardaric Vaanes, both of whom looked at him with expressions of fearful awe. Uriel shrugged, too breathless to speak.

The Lord of the Unfleshed knelt beside him and said, 'Emperor loves you.'

'I think that maybe he does...' gasped Uriel.

The Lord of the Unfleshed nodded and pointed to the pit. 'Yes. You still alive.'

'Yes,' gasped Uriel. 'You are right, the Emperor does love me. Just as he loves you.'

The creature nodded slowly. 'Will help you kill iron men. Flesh mothers too. Should not be more of us.'

'Thank you...' hissed Uriel.

'Emperor loves us, but we hate us,' said the Lord of the Unfleshed, painfully. 'We did nothing, did not deserve this. Want to kill iron men, but not know how to get into mountain. Cannot fight over high walls!'

Uriel pulled himself breathlessly to his feet and, despite his brush with death, smiled at the Lord of the Unfleshed as a portion of their journey into Khalan-Ghol returned to him with a clarity that was surely more than mere memory.

'That doesn't matter,' said Uriel. 'I know another way in.'

KHALAN-GHOL SHOOK with the fury of the renewed bombardment, shells exploding like fiery tempests against its ancient walls. Armies of heavy tanks and entire corps of soldiers mustered at the base of the gigantic ramp that led to the mountainous plateau which was all that remained of the fortress's outer defences and the spire of the inner keep.

Temporary, yet incredibly robust, revetments and redoubts had protected the workers and machinery constructing the ramp and now that it was complete, Berossus began his final assault.

A marvel of engineering, it climbed thousands of metres up the side of the mountain, beginning many kilometres back from the rocky uplands of its base. Paved with segmented sheets of iron, rumbling tanks climbed in the wake of a pair of monstrous Titans, their armour stained red with the blood of uncounted thousands of sacrifices, the thick plates still dripping and wet. Equipped with massive siege hammers, pneumatic piston drills and mighty cannon, these colossal land battleships also carried the very best warriors from Berossus's grand company. These warriors would lead the assault through the walls of the fortress and tear it down, stone by stone.

A gargantuan-mouthed tunnel led into the bedrock of the ramp, huge rails disappearing into the darkness and running to the very base of the mountain itself. Great mining machines had travelled through the tunnel and even now prepared to breach the underside of the fortress, burrowing into the very heart of Honsou's lair. Tens of thousands of soldiers waited in the sweating darkness of the tunnel to invade the fortress from below. The traitor, Obax Zakayo, had provided precise information regarding the best place to break into Khalan-Ghol and together with the frontal assault, Honsou's life could now be measured in hours.

Confident that this was to be the last battle, Berossus himself led the attack at the head of a pack of nearly a hundred blood-maddened dreadnoughts.

The final battle for Khalan-Ghol was about to begin.

'WE CANNOT STOP this attack,' said Onyx, watching as the Titans of Berossus began their inexorable advance up the ramp to the fortress. Though still many kilometres away from the top, the scale of their daemonic majesty was magnificent. 'Berossus will sweep us away in a storm of iron and blood.'

Honsou said nothing, the ghost of a smile twitching at the corner of his mouth. He too watched the huge force coming to destroy them. Hundreds of screeching daemonic warriors spun and looped in the sky above phalanxes of weapon-morphing monsters whose flesh seethed and bubbled with mecha-organic circuitry. Scores of howling, spider-limbed daemon engines clanked and churned their way up the ramp, jetting noxious exhaust fumes, the hellish entities bound to their iron bodies eager for slaughter now that they were free of their cages.

Clad in his dented and battered power armour, with a reckless look of battle-hunger creasing his pale features, and sporting a gleaming silver bionic arm in place of the one his former master had gifted him with, Honsou seemed unfazed by their approaching doom.

Onyx was puzzled by this, but had long since realised that the inner workings of Khalan-Ghol's newest master were a mystery to him – the half-breed did not resemble or behave like any of the warsmiths he had served in his aeons of servitude to the masters of this fortress.

'You do not seem overly concerned,' continued Onyx.

'I'm not,' replied Honsou, turning from the cracked ramparts of the topmost bastions of the spire. A hot wind was blowing, tasting of ash and metal. Honsou took a deep breath, at last turning to face his champion.

'Berossus hasn't let me down this far,' said Honsou, staring out at the great tunnel that led into the ramp and, no doubt, beneath his fortress. 'And I hope he won't now. Not at the last.'

'I don't understand.'

'Don't worry, Onyx, I know your concern is for your own essence, not my life, but you don't need to understand. All you need to do is obey me.'

'I am yours to command.'

'Then trust me on this,' grinned Honsou, and looked down to the level below, where smoke and crackling lightning conspired to obscure his own Titans and the masterful works he had prepared for Berossus. He stared up into the featureless white sky and the sun that burned like a black hole above him. 'I have fought the Long War almost as long as Berossus and Toramino and have stratagems of my own.'

'For your sake, I hope so,' said Onyx. 'Even if we manage to stop this attack, there is still the matter of Lord Toramino. His army is yet to be blooded.'

Honsou glanced to the glow of fires and forges beyond those of Berossus's encampments, where Toramino waited, unseen and unknown. Here, at last, Onyx caught a flash of unease.

'He waits for Berossus to grind us and his own warriors to dust before marching in to take Khalan-Ghol and become lord of its ruins.'

'And how will we stop him?'

Honsou laughed. 'One problem at a time, Onyx, one problem at a time.'

* * *

THE HATEFUL SOUND of massed artillery fire was muted and distant, though Uriel knew it must be perilously close to be heard this far beneath the mountains. Dust drifted in lazy clouds from the tunnel roof, and fine pebbles skittered and danced upon the floor. The darkness was absolute, even his enhanced vision had difficulty piercing the gloom.

Heat filled the tunnel along with the hot, foetid stink of animals, though these were no animals. They were, or at least had once been, human.

Hundreds of the Unfleshed filed along the fearful passages beneath the mountains, their winding route taking them through echoing crystal chambers, disused manufactorum and up dizzyingly steep stone channels hacked into the rock. Their massive bodies filled the passageways as they led Uriel and the others back towards Khalan-Ghol.

They travelled through dark and secret ways under the mountains, forgotten by all save them, the hidden, abandoned culverts and the lost, forgotten passageways that led towards their fate.

Behind Uriel, Pasanius grunted with effort, his journey made all the harder by virtue of his limb's amputation, but wherever he had encountered difficulty, the Lord of the Unfleshed reached back and lifted him onwards.

The giant creature led the way through the darkness, his huge form easily filling the width of the passage, and were it not for his hunched shoulders and stooped head, he would surely have dashed his skull open on drooping stalactites.

The Lord of the Unfleshed marched with newfound purpose, his long, loping stride setting a fearsome pace through the secret mountain paths. Uriel winced with every step, his breath painful in his single functioning

lung and the pain of his cracked collarbone and ribs
stabbing into him without the balms of his armour's
dispensers to dull them.

Further back, a twisted creature with a withered twin
fused to its back carried Leonid, the stunted sibling
clutching the grimacing colonel tightly in its embrace.
And further back yet came Ardaric Vaanes and his two
surviving Space Marine renegades.

When the rapture of the Emperor's coming to life
before the Unfleshed had died down, the creatures had
embraced Uriel's cause with all the zeal and fervour of
a crusade, mustering those who could hunt and fight
to join them. It had made Uriel want to weep at the
holy joy that infused every one of them and made his
deception of them even harder to bear.

As he had gained his feet before the Lord of the
Unfleshed, it had beckoned to one of its tribe, and
another of the beasts loped towards him. Uriel saw
that it was the creature he had fought in the outflow
pool, his sword still jammed in its belly.

'Take blade,' said the Lord of the Unfleshed and Uriel
nodded, gingerly gripping the hilt of the weapon. He
had pulled, muscles straining as he fought the suction
of flesh, bracing his feet on the floor of the manufactorum to gain better purchase. The sword was wedged
tightly in the beast's body, and he was forced to twist
the blade to allow it to move. At last, it slid grudgingly
from its sheath of flesh, the creature remaining stolidly
silent throughout. As it came free, the giant beast
moved to join the remainder of its awed brethren.

'Thank you,' said Uriel.

The Unfleshed nodded respectfully and Uriel had
felt a glowing ember of hope fan to life in his heart.

But his initial relief and elation at such a turn of
events had soon turned sour when he had been

reunited with his comrades and Ardaric Vaanes spoke to him.

'They will kill you when they discover you have lied to them,' said the renegade as the Unfleshed had girt themselves for war, gathering crude iron cudgels. Most needed no weapons however, their horrific mutations equipping them for killing without the need for such things.

'Have I?' Uriel had said, guardedly. 'I do the Emperor's work, and so now do they.'

'The Unfleshed?' said Vaanes, aghast. 'You think the Emperor would work through such beasts? Look at them, they're monsters. How can you think that such creatures are capable of being instruments of His will? They are evil!'

'They carry the flesh of the Emperor within them,' snapped Uriel. 'The blood of ancient heroes flows in their veins and I will not fail them.'

'Don't think you can fool me, Ventris,' sneered Vaanes. 'You are no messenger of the Emperor, and I can see in your eyes that you know you're not either.'

'It does not matter what I believe any more,' said Uriel. 'What do *you* believe?'

'I believe that I was right about you.'

'What does that mean?'

'That I knew you were trouble the moment I saw you,' shrugged Vaanes. 'It doesn't matter anyway. As soon as we get to the surface, myself and the others will leave you and your motley band.'

'You are really going to turn your back on us? After all that has happened, all the blood spilt, the death and the pain? Can you really do that?'

'I can and I will,' snarled Vaanes. 'And who would blame me? Look around you, look at these monsters. They are all going to be dead soon, and their blood will be on your hands. Think about it, you're going to

try and storm a besieged fortress with a tribe of cannibalistic mutants, a dying Guard colonel and a sergeant
with one arm. I am a warrior, Ventris, plain and simple, and there is nothing left to me except survival. To
go back to Khalan-Ghol is madness, and attacking that
fortress isn't my idea of courage, it's more like suicide.'

Vaanes gripped Uriel's shoulder and said, 'You don't
have to die here. Why don't you and Pasanius come
with me. You're pretty handy in a fight and I could use
a warrior like you.'

Uriel shrugged off the renegade's arm and said, 'You
are a fine warrior, Ardaric Vaanes, but I was wrong to
have thought you might regain your honour. You have
courage, but I am glad that I do not go into battle with
you again.'

Hatred flared in the renegade's eyes and his expression became hard as stone.

Without another word, Vaanes stalked away.

Uriel put the renegade from his mind as he saw a
patch of bright light coming from ahead and realised
that the noise of battle was swelling in volume as well.
With renewed vigour, he climbed after the Lord of the
Unfleshed and emerged, blinking into the harsh while
light of Medrengard.

The noise of the battles raging around Honsou's
fortress was tremendous, and Uriel saw that the secret
paths of the Unfleshed had brought them out into the
rocky uplands near the base of Khalan-Ghol itself, the
plains before the fortress hundreds of metres below
them.

High above, the ramparts of the fortress were
wreathed in the fires of battle, and Uriel saw that they
were going to have to ascend into the very heart of the
maelstrom raging above them.

* * *

MANY KILOMETRES AWAY, the clang of picks and shovels echoed in the hot, lamp-lit confines of the mineworks beneath the great ramp. A wide gallery had been excavated, some nine hundred metres wide and with a gently sloping floor. A warrior in stained iron armour watched as hundreds of slaves and overseers hauled vast flatbed wagons bearing drums of explosives and fuel to be packed into the length of the excavations.

The long gallery was almost full, packed with enough explosives to level the mountain itself, knew Corias Keagh, Master of Ordnance to Lord Berossus himself. The tunnels to reach the underside of Khalan-Ghol would be his masterwork. It had been hard, slow work and cost the lives of thousands, but he had succeeded in getting the complex web of tunnels to exactly the right spot. It was almost a shame to blow such a perfect example of siege mining apart.

Thirty metres above him – if his calculations were correct, and he had no reason to doubt them, for Obax Zakayo had been very precise in his treachery – were the catacombs of the fortress, where the revenants of previous masters of Khalan-Ghol were said to haunt its depths. Keagh knew that such tales were probably nonsense, but in the Eye of Terror it never paid to scoff at such things too openly.

But word of these tales had filtered back to the thousands of human soldiers who had spent the last few months billeted in the garrison tunnels he had constructed within the body of the great ramp, and he had heard ill-favoured mutterings concerning this attack. He had ritually flayed these doomsayers, but a pervasive sense of dread had already taken hold.

Despite this, all the soldiers were armed and ready to begin the assault upon the opening of Khalan-Ghol's belly, and Keagh was eager to finally get to grips with the foe.

His armour thrummed in the heat, its internal systems struggling to keep his body temperature even.

The heat in the tunnels was fearsome – more than Keagh would have expected at such a depth – but he paid it no mind, too intent on the spectacle of destruction he was about to unleash.

THE BATTLEMENTS WERE aflame, gunfire and steel scything through men and stone in devastating fusillades of heavy calibre shells. Mobile howitzers moving in the midst of the armoured column approaching the top of the ramp rained high explosive shells within the last line of bastions, filling the air with spinning fragments of red-hot metal.

Men died in their hundreds, ripped apart in the devastating volleys or flamed from the wall by incendiary shells fired from the upper bastions of the approaching Titans.

But Berossus was not going to take Khalan-Ghol without a fight and Honsou's Titans and revetted artillery positions had laid-in targeting information and punished the approaching column terribly. Tanks exploded as armour-penetrating shells slashed down from above and tore through their lighter upper armour. Such casualties were bulldozed aside without mercy, tumbling down the steep sides of the ramp to smash to pieces on the rocks below. But no matter how many Honsou's gunners killed, the column continued its relentless advance.

Honsou gripped onto a splintered corbel of rock and watched the approaching army with a mixture of exhilaration and dread.

Logistically Berossus had the upper hand, and he was using it to strangle the life from the defenders of his fortress – or what was left of them. Onyx was right, they could not defeat this army conventionally.

But Honsou did not intend to fight conventionally.

'Come on, damn you!' he shouted into the deafening crescendo of noise. He struggled to penetrate the gunsmoke, but could see nothing through the acrid fog.

Onyx looked at Honsou in confusion, but said nothing as more shells landed nearby. Whizzing shrapnel ricocheted from the walls and Onyx leapt before Honsou, allowing several plate-sized blades of metal to hammer into his daemonic flesh rather than shred his master.

'Onyx!' called Honsou, dragging the daemonic symbiote to its feet. 'Look towards Berossus's army and tell me what you see!'

Onyx staggered over to the edge of the wall and shifted his vision patterns until he could see clearly across the entirety of the battle. Streamers of fire and starbursts of explosions flickered like distant galaxies, but his eyes pierced the chaos and confusion of the battle with ease.

The lead elements of Berossus's army had smashed their way onto the spire's plateau and were less than a hundred metres from the last wall that stood between them and final victory. Dreadnoughts howled in battle fury and the Titans strode behind them like avatars of the gods of battle, weapons roaring with prayers to their dark masters.

'Berossus is at the wall!' shouted Onyx. 'He will be upon us in moments!'

'No! The ramp!' returned Honsou. 'What's happening at the end of the ramp!'

'I see tanks, hundreds of tanks,' yelled the daemonic symbiote, barely audible over the concussive booms of artillery fire. 'They are gathered beside the entrance to the mineworkings at the base of the ramp and are simply awaiting their turn to begin the climb.'

'Excellent,' laughed Honsou. 'Oh, Berossus, you are even more of a fool than I took you for!'

SATISFIED THAT THERE was just the right amount of explosives, shaped and arranged to explode upwards into the fortress, Corias Keagh retreated swiftly from the gallery beneath Khalan-Ghol, unwinding a long length of insulated cable from the servo-rig on his back. Darting pincer arms mounted on the rig kept the cable from fouling and ensured that it remained straight and level.

'Here should do it,' he said to no one in particular as he turned into the armoured bunker he had constructed for just this moment.

The pincer arms cut the cable and craned over his shoulder to hand him the brushed copper end of its length. Synchronous timers had been calibrated from his armour's own power unit and he hooked the end of the cable into a power port on the chest of his breastplate. A winking red light on his helmet's visor turned to gold and he felt a physical stirring as the charges he had set armed.

He opened a channel to his lord and master and said, 'Lord Berossus, the charges beneath the fortress are set and ready to be detonated.'

'Then detonate them now,' came the familiar growling rasp of his master's voice. 'We are almost at the head of the ramp.'

Pausing to savour this moment of his greatest triumph, Keagh allowed the dim silence of the tunnel to enfold him before sending a pulse of energy along the length of the cable.

THE MOUNTAIN ITSELF shook with the force of the blast far below, thousands of tonnes of ordnance and fuel exploding in one simultaneous blast that instantly atomised a whole swathe of the bedrock of Medrengard. Honsou staggered and fell to his knees as the shockwave rippled throughout the fortress. Tall towers that had stood for millennia crashed down to ruin and every fighting man was knocked from his feet.

Tanks, and even one of Berossus's Titans, tumbled from the ramp as the shockwave fanned upwards from below. Cracks split the stonework of the battlements and hundreds died as they fell to their deaths upon shattered ramparts. The main wall crumbled, torn like paper and breached in a dozen places by the shear forces twisting the mountain.

Aftershocks continued to rumble, shaking Khalan-Ghol to its foundations and Honsou heard a deep, answering roar, as though the fortress itself cried out in rage at this violation.

His fortress had been breached, but Honsou felt nothing but elation as the growling tremors that gripped his fastness began to fade.

'Now I have you, Berossus!' he snarled. 'Iron Warriors, ready yourselves!'

PART FOUR

THE ENEMY OF MY ENEMY...

CHAPTER EIGHTEEN

CORIAS KEAGH FELT the thunderous roar of the explosion force its way down his tunnels like the bellow of an angry god. He braced himself against the wall of his underground bunker, confident that his works would survive this violence he had unleashed. He heard the metal of his tunnel supports groan in protest at the power of the shockwave, but Keagh had been digging mines and bringing ruin to fortresses from below for thousands of years and knew his craft well.

Only when the temperature readout on his visor leapt upwards did he realise that something was amiss.

He heard it first as a whooshing rush of superheated air, forced through the tunnels ahead of something unimaginably hot. He rushed out into the tunnels as a terrible fear suddenly seized him.

Leaping from tunnel to tunnel, a flashing cloud of incandescent vapours foamed along the length of his workings. Behind it came a roaring, seething orange glow of molten metal and Keagh heard the screams of the soldiers as the lethally hot steam boiled the flesh from their bones.

He knew then that every one of the thousands of men in the tunnels beneath the ramp was going to die. His tunnels had not breached the sepulchres of Khalan-Ghol, but somewhere else entirely.

But how could that be, when the location of Keagh's breaching gallery had come straight from Obax Zakayo...?

In the split second Keagh had left of life, he realised that that they had been horribly deceived – that all they had striven for was ruined.

He turned to run, but even one as enhanced as an Iron Warrior could not outrun millions of tonnes of roaring molten metal as it spilled from the forges of Khalan-Ghol, destroying everything before it and liquefying the earth of the ramp as it went.

Keagh was engulfed in the rushing torrent of fire and had the exquisite horror of a last few seconds of life before his armour was melted away and his flesh vaporised.

URIEL FELT THE immense power of the subterranean explosion spread through the landscape and stumbled, gripping the sharp rocks of Khalan-Ghol's peak tightly as the tremors shook the foundations of the world itself. Plumes of glowing, orange steam geysered from the foot of the mountain and, as he watched, more and more began bursting from channels cut into the monstrous ramp.

'What in the Emperor's name?' breathed Uriel as he looked up and saw the top of the ramp sag and collapse upon itself as though the weight of earth supporting it was being steadily removed.

'A countermine?' shouted Pasanius.

'It would need to have been colossal to cause such damage,' said Uriel, shaking his head.

'Emperor angry at iron men,' roared the Lord of the Unfleshed. 'Strikes them from heaven!'

'He does indeed,' nodded Uriel, risking a glance at the gory features of the creature and feeling immense relief that Vaanes was not here to see the expression on his own face.

The renegades had turned their backs on them, spitting on this last chance for redemption and had marched away without a single word as soon as they had reached the surface. Uriel had watched them go, his heart heavy at their betrayal of what it meant to be a Space Marine, but relieved that he himself had been tested and not been found wanting.

Truth be told, there was some merit in what Vaanes had said. Perhaps this was a suicide mission and would see them all dead. And perhaps as well there was merit in survival, for where was the glory or honour to be had from their deaths?

But Uriel knew that for a true warrior of the Emperor there was no terror of death, only the fear that he might die with his works unfulfilled.

The death oath placed upon them by Marneus Calgar remained to be honoured and even should they fail in their quest, their deaths would respect the chance their Chapter Master had given them, so long ago it seemed, on Macragge.

As he watched Vaanes and the renegades depart, Uriel knew that though he was probably going to his death, his was the better choice.

'We fight iron men now?' asked the Lord of the Unfleshed. 'Show us way in!'

The primal ferocity in the Lord of the Unfleshed's face reminded Uriel just how precarious their situation was. There was no guarantee that his plan would succeed and he did not want to think of the consequences should the Unfleshed decide that he no longer spoke with the Emperor's voice.

'Soon,' said Uriel, resuming his climb of the rocks that led to the fighting above.

HONSOU TOOK THE steps from the high spire that led to the main wall quickly, thinking that the swelling roars of hate he could hear were a fine hymn upon which to wage war. He and Onyx and a coterie of his finest warriors emerged onto a cracked series of barbican ramparts, arranged in a saw-toothed pattern, freshly constructed behind the main walls.

Smoke wreathed the breaches and the Khalan-Ghol's main gate hung in splinters, a pack of frenzied dreadnoughts smashing through it. At their head, Honsou saw Lord Berossus, his mechanised arms hurling warriors before him in sprays of blood. A wild, orgiastic howling screeched from his vox-amp and Honsou grinned ferally as he knew that he would not allow Berossus to survive this battle.

Billowing clouds of scalding steam and the crack of splintering stone from beyond the ruined walls told him that the top of the great ramp was no more, the stone and earth running molten and collapsing under the strain of supporting Berossus's armoured column.

Virtually everything metal within the fortress had been smelted down and the forges had burned constantly to ensure that when Berossus's engineers breached the fortress from below – as Honsou had known they would – they would be tunnelling into a great reservoir of molten metal and not the catacombs they expected.

Honsou knew that a warsmith as gullible as Berossus did not deserve to live; his very existence weakened the Iron Warriors. To have believed that Honsou would not have known of Obax Zakayo's treachery and use him against his paymasters was ludicrous, but had proven to be his salvation.

Gunfire and explosions filled the interior space of the barbican as the vanguard of Berossus's army swarmed through the gate, though Honsou realised that it was no longer the vanguard, but its entirety. Now the odds were evened and Berossus would learn what it was to fight Honsou of the Iron Warriors.

Dreadnoughts charged towards the sandbagged gun pits, shrugging off weapon impacts and ripping men apart with wild bursts of weapons' fire. But behind the gun pits, disciplined teams of Iron Warriors picked off the armoured fighting machines with calm efficiency, their smoking hulks soon outnumbering those that still fought.

A dark shadow loomed above the fortress walls as the surviving Titan gripped the ruined battlements and began ripping them down with great sweeps of its piston-driven hammer arms. Blocks of stone the size of buildings crashed down amongst the warriors of both armies, killing a dozen men or more each time.

Huge assault ramps smashed down on the massive piles of rubble and debris, and Iron Warriors bearing the black and gold banner of Berossus charged from the shoulder bastions of the Titan.

'Iron Warriors!' shouted Honsou. 'Now is your time to show these bastards who is the master of Khalan-Ghol!'

His warriors roared in adulation, following their master down into the heat of the battle. The Iron Warriors of Berossus fought their way down the rubble of the breach, firing as they went and Honsou saw that they were warriors of courage and iron as volley after volley of lethally effective weapons' fire took a horrific toll on their numbers, but they did not falter.

The space between the smashed wall and the bunkers and saw-tooth walls Honsou had constructed was a killing ground: nothing could cross it and live. But with no way back, the Iron Warriors of Berossus had no choice but to advance into the teeth of Honsou's guns, and the carnage was awe-inspiring in its savagery.

More rubble fell from the main wall as the Titan smashed its way inside now that its cargo of warriors had disembarked. A shoulder-mounted cannon blasted a great crater in the centre of Honsou's defences and the warriors of Berossus cheered as they fought their way forwards once more.

Before it could fire again, a huge explosion ripped the cannon from the Titan's shoulder and a line of white fire stitched itself across its bloody carapace. From the smoke either side of the attacking Titan came a pair of similarly massive forms, Titans bearing the dread banners of the Legio Mortis. No longer required to guard the inner sanctum of Khalan-Ghol, the two terrifying daemon engines stalked from the rubble and smoke of the fortress's interior to do battle.

Berossus's last Titan roared at such worthy adversaries and turned its guns upon its new foes, leaving the Iron Warriors it had carried to look to their own battles. The ground shuddered at the tread of these mighty daemon machines, and whole sections of the walls were pulverised as they grappled with white-hot blades and screaming chainfists.

All subtleties and stratagems were meaningless now; the outcome of this storming would be decided at the end of a smoking bolter or upon the roaring blade of a chainsword. Iron Warriors charged one another, the battle degenerating into a close-range firefight and swirling melee of savage killers.

A fierce exhilaration pounded through Honsou's veins at the visceral thrill of such slaughter. He hacked his axe through the arm of an Iron Warrior, spinning on his heel to behead him before leaping the smoking corpse of a dreadnought to find more foes. Onyx followed him, killing any who dared come near the master of the fortress with casual swipes of his bladed fists.

Honsou saw the awesomely powerful form of Berossus through the swirling smoke and shouted, 'Onyx! To me!'

URIEL KNEW THEY did not have much time. The battle above was seething with the ferocity of a tempest, the screams of men in battle echoing from the high peaks. He climbed with all the speed he could muster, but their destination seemed always tantalisingly out of reach.

He did not want to get caught up in the fighting, but knew they had to reach the site of the battle before too much time had passed.

'Come on!' he shouted. 'We have to hurry!'

The Lord of the Unfleshed roared, 'You slow! Not fast like me!'

'I know!' shouted Uriel. 'But we cannot climb any faster!'

'We go faster!' said the Lord of the Unfleshed and reached out to grab Uriel's wrist, swinging him around and onto his shoulders so that he was being carried in much the same fashion as Colonel Leonid.

The ground swung dizzyingly below Uriel and he gripped onto the clammy, glistening flesh of the creature as it scaled the rocky flanks of Khalan-Ghol with terrifying speed.

He turned his head to see Pasanius scooped up in the same manner, and the speed of their ascent doubled.

'Go faster now!' promised the Lord of the Unfleshed. 'Tribe! On!'

Hundreds of the red, skinless creatures followed the Lord of the Unfleshed and Uriel was suddenly seized by a wild sense of abandonment.

They might be heading to their deaths, but what an end they would make for themselves!

He returned his gaze to the smoke-wreathed peak of the fortress, amazed at how different it now looked. When he had first laid eyes upon it, it had seemed utterly impregnable, fashioned from dark madness and impossibly hewn stone, and placed upon the highest peak. Now little of its lower reaches remained, save as blasted, dusty boneyards and its upper spire looked in danger of falling at any moment.

But having seen what happened to the huge ramp, Uriel knew that Honsou was not going to let his fortress fall without a damn hard fight.

He did not know exactly what had happened to the ramp, but watched in wonder as entire sections of its upper reaches cracked, and the tanks and men who climbed towards the fortress were swallowed whole.

Streaming lines of smoking, orange liquid boiled from cracks in the side of the ramp, pouring down its sides like lava spilling from the crater of an erupting volcano. A vast, oozing lake of molten metal poured from the mouth of the tunnel at the base of the ramp, growing larger with every passing moment.

Hundreds of vehicles had mustered here and were caught in the flash flood of killing liquid. Uriel watched tanks burn and explode as their fuel and ammunition cooked in the awful heat.

Madly revving tanks barged into one another, crashing together in their desperation to escape, but succeeding only in forming an impenetrable logjam. Soon an army of fighting vehicles was reduced to molten slag without so much as a shot being fired.

'No,' whispered Uriel, as Honsou's fortress drew ever closer. 'You are certainly not going without a fight.'

CHUNKS OF STONE and flesh were thrown skyward as wreckage and debris from the Titans' battle smashed into the ground. Another bunker was flattened and Honsou knew that, one way or another, this battle would soon be over. An Iron Warrior slashed a huge, crackling fist towards his head and he rolled beneath it, swinging his axe in a backhand sweep that cut the legs from beneath his opponent.

The warrior screamed and collapsed, clutching the stumps of his thighs as Onyx removed his head in the wake of his master, but Honsou carried on towards Berossus as the warsmith finally saw him coming.

'Half-breed!' roared the dreadnought, raising his arms in challenge. Though he was no longer a warrior of flesh and blood, Berossus had lost none of the ferocity he had displayed in life, his bronze-skulled sarcophagus blazing with diabolical energy.

The giant dreadnought braced its legs and lowered its monstrous drill ringed with heavy calibre cannons. Onyx leapt forwards as the cannons spooled up

to firing speed, slashing his claws through the barrels
in a shower of bright sparks.

For such a massive machine, Berossus was still inhu-
manly quick and his mighty, piston-driven siege
hammer smashed into the daemonic symbiote and
sent him spinning through the air.

'Now you die, half-breed!' screamed the dreadnought, bringing the monstrous hammer back for
another blow and taking a crashing step towards him.
Honsou struck out at Berossus's sarcophagus, but the
thick, mechanical arms that sprouted from his
armoured shell snatched out and deflected the blow, a
screaming breacher drill stabbing for his chest.

Honsou spun around, the tip of the drill scoring
across his breastplate and drawing blood before hammering his axe into the dreadnought's thick leg. The
axe clanged from the limb, ricocheting from its thick
armour and sending ringing shockwaves up Honsou's
arms.

Another explosion rocked the ground and Honsou
was pitched from his feet by the blast. The giant dreadnought barely shook and a great, clawed foot slammed
down, centimetres from his head. Honsou rolled
between the armoured legs as the battle raged around
them, Iron Warriors cutting each other down with furious savagery.

Berossus spun on the axis of his waist and a pair of
his augmetic limbs slashed the ground. Honsou rolled
backwards, the tip of Berossus's clawed arm catching
the edge of his armour and spinning him off balance.

He felt a stinging blow to his leg and roared in pain
as Berossus's breacher arm stabbed through his thigh.
The drill ripped a great wad of bloody flesh from his
leg and Honsou dropped to one knee. The dreadnought stepped close and its clawed arm closed on

Honsou's shoulder guard, lifting the struggling warrior high into the air.

'You have cost me dear, mongrel, but it ends now,' snarled Berossus. 'Your fortress is mine, no matter what happens.'

'Never!' shouted Honsou, fighting to free himself from his captor's grip, but Berossus had him firm and wasn't about to let go.

The dreadnought stabbed his breacher drill towards Honsou's face.

The master of Khalan-Ghol hurled his arm in front of the blow, the screeching of tearing metal and white-hot shavings spraying the air as the drill pierced the silver metal of Honsou's arm.

But instead of shearing straight through the arm and skewering Honsou's skull, the metal ran like liquid, reknitting itself as quickly as Berossus's arm attempted to destroy it. The dreadnought watched amazed as the drill stuttered and jammed within Honsou's arm. Even as Berossus paused, a black-armoured blur streaked through the air, twisting to land upon the upper mant-let of the dreadnought's carapace.

Onyx landed gracefully on one knee and powered both bronze claws down into the armoured shell of the dreadnought. The terrible machine roared in pain, its arms spasming and dropping Honsou to the cratered ground.

Honsou rolled away from the thrashing dread-nought as he heard a thunderous crashing behind him and the headless form of Berossus's Titan crashed through the last remaining portion of the main wall, hurling stone and blazing streamers of plasma through the air. One of his own Titans fell with it, shorn practically in half, and the impact to the two armoured leviathans sent shockwaves through the earth that were almost the equal of the blast beneath the ramp.

A great cry of dismay went up and Honsou knew that he could end this now. Berossus fought to dislodge Onyx, his clawed arms slashing and stabbing the daemonic symbiote repeatedly. Honsou gripped his axe and sprang to his feet, not about to waste the chance his champion had gained him.

With a roar of hate, he charged forwards while the dreadnought's attention was fixated on Onyx and hammered his axe with all his strength into the now-unguarded portion of the dreadnought's leg where the armour was weakest.

Screaming, warp-forged steel met ancient metal crafted by forgotten technologies in a blazing corona of flaring energy. Berossus roared and smashed to the ground, slamming down on his back as Onyx leapt gracefully clear of the toppled machine.

'Call me half-breed now, you bastard!' screamed Honsou, stepping in and hammering his axe against the dreadnought's sarcophagus. The ancient metal split and Berossus wailed in agony as the daemon weapon tore into his iron body.

'Still think you're better than me?' yelled Honsou as he hacked at the dying dreadnought's body. Metal and sparks flew as the master of Khalan-Ghol butchered his iron foe. Berossus fought to right himself, but Honsou and Onyx gave him no chance, darting away from his clumsy blows and hacking his uselessly flailing limbs from his body.

'You're nothing, Berossus, nothing! Do you hear me?'

A grainy wash of static-laced, incoherence blared from Berossus's vox-amp, and Honsou vaulted onto the dreadnought's sarcophagus yelling, 'Perhaps you can't hear me through all that iron.'

He raised himself triumphant on the warsmith of the attacking army and brought his axe down again and again on the grinning skull-faced sarcophagus, finally splitting it apart with his fifth blow.

The sounds of battle faded and, for the first time in months, the fighting stopped as the battling Iron Warriors paused to watch the unfolding drama being played out before them.

Honsou knelt atop Berossus's sarcophagus and punched his pristine silver arm into the dreadnought. With a grunt and wrench, he ripped something clear in a welter of black blood and amniotic fluids.

He held up his arm and shouted, 'Your warsmith is dead!'

In his hand he held a monstrously swollen skull and dripping spinal column, fused wires like veins dangling from the last mortal remains of Warsmith Berossus.

The tension was palpable and Honsou knew he had to cow the scores of enemy warriors or risk this slaughter becoming a battle of mutually assured destruction. With a roar of hate, he swung the spinal column like a club and smashed Berossus's skull to splinters of bone against the ruptured iron shell that had once housed it.

'Your warsmith is dead!' he repeated, hurling away the remains. 'But you do not need to die! Berossus is gone and by right of conquest I offer any warrior who wants it a place in my army. You have proved yourselves warriors of courage, and I have need of such men.'

No one moved, and for the briefest second Honsou thought he had made a grave error.

But then a warrior in heavily tooled armour of burnished iron and sporting a burnt and tattered back banner of gold and black stepped forwards.

The warrior's armour was bloody and scored from the hard fighting. He removed his cracked helmet, revealing scarred and pitted features topped with a close-cropped mohawk.

'Why should we join you, half-breed?' he shouted. 'You may have defeated Berossus, but Toramino will wipe you and your fortress from the face of Medrengard.'

'What is your name, warrior?' said Honsou, jumping from the broken carcass of the dreadnought and marching purposefully towards the Iron Warrior.

'I am Cadaras Grendel, Captain of Arms of Lord Berossus.'

Honsou stood before the bloody warrior, seeing the defiance in his eyes.

'Aye,' agreed Honsou, raising his voice so that all the warriors gathered in the ruins of his fortress could hear him. 'You may be right, Cadaras Grendel. Toramino has the strength of arms to destroy me, I cannot argue with that. But ask yourself this... why has he not blooded his warriors yet?'

Honsou turned to address the rest of the assembled warriors, raising his arms and punctuating his words by punching the air with his axe. 'Where was Toramino while you all fought and bled to get here? You know who built this place and you know that only the bravest of warriors could take it. Where was Toramino while you were dying in your hundreds to storm this fortress?'

He could see his words were having the desired effect. Honsou felt a hot rush of adrenaline race around his body as he saw that he had correctly anticipated the rancour these brave Iron Warriors must have felt at the bloody work they did while Toramino's warriors watched them die.

'Toramino hung you out to dry and laughed while he did it. Even if you had succeeded here, do you think the spoils of Khalan-Ghol would be yours to plunder? Toramino has betrayed you, just as the Emperor betrayed the Iron Warriors in the ancient days. Will you be used like that or are you men of iron?'

'We are men of iron!' shouted Cadaras Grendel, the shout taken up by his surviving warriors.

'Then join me!' bellowed Honsou, gripping Grendel's shoulder guards. 'Join me and avenge this betrayal!'

Months of bitterness at the deaths of his men rose to the surface on Grendel's face and he nodded. 'Aye. Toramino will pay for this. My warriors and I are yours to command!'

Honsou turned and with Cadaras Grendel beside him roared, 'Iron within!'

'Iron without!' came the answering bellow from every Iron Warrior, shouted over and over again.

And Honsou knew he had them.

URIEL WATCHED THE two Titans collapse and, amazingly, heard the sounds of battle fade away. Had Khalan-Ghol fallen or had Honsou defeated the escalade? It was impossible to tell, and they would only know when they reached the top.

Their ascent up the cliff-face had been heart-poundingly fraught, as the Unfleshed had carried them swiftly up slopes Uriel would have sworn were unclimbable. Their strength was prodigious and their endurance phenomenal.

In the sudden silence, Uriel could hear the crackling flames from the burning vehicles at the foot of the mountain and the occasional explosion from a shell as it detonated in the heat. The infrastructure of

Berossus's army burned and as the quietness stretched on, Uriel guessed that the attack had failed to take the fortress. Warriors who had fought their way through a breach were so fuelled on adrenaline and rage that looting and slaughter usually followed in the wake of a successful storming.

But silence… that was new to Uriel.

The Lord of the Unfleshed clambered over an overhanging splinter of rock, swinging his massive body up and over the lip of the plateau and Uriel had his first look at the bloody ruin of the final assault.

'Emperor preserve us!' breathed Pasanius as he joined Uriel.

'Even the storm of the citadel was nothing compared to this…' added Leonid as the fused twins deposited him next to the Space Marines.

The wreckage of a destroyed army lay strewn before the shattered remains of the spire's defensive wall, itself no more than jagged stumps of black stone jutting from the ground like rotten teeth in a diseased gum. Blazing tanks and bodies were strewn about the plateau; some crushed flat, others hollowed out by explosions. Pyres of ammunition sparked and blew, and the remains of the Titans burned with a bright glare of plasma.

Gun barrels the size of cooling towers lay cracked and useless amid the debris and even had anyone been keeping watch on the battlefield, the smoke and flames would conceal them from detection.

'Who won?' asked Leonid.

'I'm not sure…' said Pasanius, following Uriel through the corpse-choked rubble.

He bent to retrieve a fallen bolter with his remaining hand and checked its load before saying, 'Find yourself a weapon, colonel, and scavenge as much ammunition as you can carry.'

Leonid nodded and scooped up a battered, but serviceable lasgun, some charged clips and a bandolier of grenades. As he did so, his chest hiked in pain and he was bent double by a coughing fit. He wiped his hand across his mouth, seeing brackish, matter-flecked blood coat his palm before wiping it clear on what remained of his dusty, sky-blue uniform jacket.

The Unfleshed capered across the battlefield, stooping to feed amid the cadavers, tearing limbs from bodies and devouring the still-warm meat straight from the bone. The Lord of the Unfleshed lifted the limbless corpse of an Iron Warrior and tore off its breastplate, biting into the chest and tearing off a great mouthful of flesh.

Even though it was the body of an enemy, Uriel was appalled and said, 'No, do not eat this meat.'

The Lord of the Unfleshed turned, his face alight with horrid appetite and savage glee at this chance to feast on an Iron Warrior. 'Is meat. Fresh.'

'No!' said Uriel, more forcefully.

'No?' replied the Lord of the Unfleshed. 'Why?'

'It is corrupt.'

Seeing the creature's incomprehension, he said, 'It is bad.'

'No... is good,' said the Lord of the Unfleshed, holding out the opened corpse of the Iron Warrior. The ribcage had been bitten through and the warrior's internal organs were laid bare.

Uriel shook his head. 'If you love the Emperor, you will not eat this meat.'

'Love the Emperor!' bellowed the Lord of the Unfleshed and Uriel winced, thinking that the creature's voice could be heard even through the fury of a battle.

'Many iron men dead,' growled the Lord of the Unfleshed, angrily. 'Much meat.'

'Yes, but we are not here for meat,' said Uriel. 'We are here to kill iron men and flesh mothers, yes?'

The Lord of the Unfleshed looked set to argue the point, but with an angry snarl dropped the half-eaten body and said, 'Kill iron men now?'

'Yes, kill iron men,' said Uriel as he heard the sound of approaching engines from within the fortress. 'But we need to get to the heart of the fortress first.'

Uriel turned as Pasanius and Leonid approached, bearing guns, ammunition and grenades. Pasanius unslung a bolter from his shoulder and handed it to Uriel together with several magazines of shells.

'It galls me that we must use the weapons of the Enemy,' said Uriel as he slammed a magazine home in the bolter.

'I suppose there's a certain poetic justice in using their own guns against them,' said Pasanius as he awkwardly loaded and cocked the weapon.

'What's that noise?' asked Leonid as he finally heard the rumbling engine sound drawing yet closer.

'It is our way in,' said Uriel, gesturing to the bodies surrounding them. 'I want you to conceal yourself amongst the dead Iron Warriors. We will lie close to one another, but must make sure we're amongst the dead.'

Uriel turned to face the Lord of the Unfleshed and hurriedly said, 'Have the tribe lie down with the dead iron men. You understand? Lie with the dead.'

'Lie down with meat?'

'Yes,' confirmed Uriel. 'Lie down with the iron men, and when we get up we will be where we need to be.'

The Lord of the Unfleshed nodded slowly and made his way through the tribe, grunting and pointing to piles of corpses.

As the Unfleshed began lying down amongst the dead Chaos Space Marines, Pasanius said, 'You know they'll feed on the bodies.'

'I know,' said Uriel, 'but there is little we can do about it.'

'Truly the Emperor does work in mysterious ways,' added Leonid.

Uriel tried to put aside the thought of the Unfleshed's cannibalistic tendencies as they located a group of shredded Iron Warriors arranged on the edges of a shell crater, and secreted themselves amongst their corpses.

Even as he dragged an Iron Warrior's body over his own he saw their way into the fortress emerge from the rolling banks of smoke that hugged the ground.

Huge bulldozers, red and hateful, with tall banner poles hung with eight-pointed stars and iron tenders hitched behind them came from the Halls of the Savage Morticians.

They came to gather up the dead for crushing and feeding to the daemonculaba.

CHAPTER NINETEEN

DEAD EYES IN a skull with the top blown off stared at him, sightless and fixed in an expression of surprise. No matter where Uriel turned in the blood-filled container, he could not escape the staring eyes of the dead. Scooped up with the rest of the corpses by the daemonic bulldozers, he had been unceremoniously dumped in the tender by the growling machine as it performed its automated and graceless coroner's task.

Bodies piled upon bodies, blood and entrails spilling to the sloshing floor and Uriel fought to claw his way to the surface, lest he drown in the stagnant blood of the fallen. He coughed red as he pushed his way clear of the bodies, keeping his head below the level of the tender's railings for fear of discovery.

The hot stink of blood filled his nostrils and slippery bodies jostled him as the trailer bumped over the uneven ground. He rolled onto his back, craning his neck left and right to see as much as he could without raising his head too far. He saw the shattered remains of a high wall pass, its fabric riddled with shell impacts and looking as though it had been struck by an orbital bombardment. Smoke curled, fat and black, from pyres and Uriel could hear chanting voices shouting from afar.

They had penetrated the walls of Khalan-Ghol and now just had to stay concealed until these bulldozers took them back to the nightmare Halls of the Savage Morticians and the daemonculaba.

A cadaver bobbed from beneath the blood and Uriel made to push it away when it blinked at him.

'Imperator! I thought you were a corpse!' exclaimed Uriel when he saw it was Pasanius.

'Not yet,' grinned Pasanius, spitting blood.

'Where is Leonid?'

'Here,' said a voice from the other side of the tender. 'By the High Lord's balls, this is almost worse than being flushed from the chambers below.'

Uriel raised an eyebrow and Leonid shrugged. 'Well, maybe not.'

'If I'm right, these will take us right where we want to go,' said Uriel. 'We just have to bear it for a little longer.'

'How long do you think it'll take to get there?' asked Leonid, almost afraid of the answer.

Uriel shook his head. 'I do not know for sure, but I do not believe these machines will be confounded by the magicks protecting this place, so not long would be my guess.'

Leonid nodded resignedly and shut his eyes, trying to block out the dreadful smell of the dead bodies.

As it transpired, the bulldozers' journey through the twisting interior of Khalan-Ghol took perhaps another hour, travelling along grisly thoroughfares of sacrificial altars, winding between dark-armoured bunkers and through the maze of manufactorum that the warrior band had become so lost in.

The vast shadow of the gate of the tower of iron at the centre of the fortress passed over them, and once again they were deep in the heart of Honsou's lair. Distant hammer blows and the grinding clanking of nearby machines filled the gloom, and Uriel heard the clicking footsteps of unseen creatures as they filed past the growling bulldozers. Sickly yellow light came and went as they passed along wide, rockcrete tunnels lit by flickering lumo-strips.

Eventually, Uriel heard the thudding beat of a monstrous heart growing louder and shared an uneasy glance with his companions. The booming bass note was all too familiar.

'The Heart of Blood,' said Pasanius.

Uriel nodded, his muscles tensing as he heard clicking and wheezing mechanical footsteps approaching. The bulldozer ground to a halt with a juddering lurch. A tall silhouette loomed over the edge of the tender and Uriel snapped his eyes shut, recognising the dead skin features of one of the Savage Morticians.

He remained utterly immobile as he felt metal pincers jab into the tender. Hissing claws turned bodies within the pooled and now sticky blood. Corpses rolled and flopped in the tender as the Savage Mortician inspected the dead for some unknown purpose.

He fought back a gasp of revulsion as he felt a claw close on his leg and turn him over, fighting to remain still as his flesh was jabbed and probed.

The Savage Mortician clicked and whistled in its incomprehensible language, presumably to another of its fell, surgical kin, before releasing his limb and

clanking off on some other errand. Uriel kept his eyes
shut and his breathing shallow until the bulldozer set
off once again and they had put some distance
between them and the hellish surgeons.

'Holy Throne,' he whispered, sickened by the Savage
Mortician's touch.

Their nightmarish journey continued into the chamber of screams, the terrible beat of the daemonic Heart
of Blood dulling his senses once more. Even over the
heavy thuds of the Heart of Blood, Uriel heard the
rumbling whine of heavy machinery as well as the
grinding crack of bones and wet squelch of pulverised
flesh.

'Be ready!' he hissed. 'I think we have arrived!'

Pasanius and Leonid nodded as Uriel slid himself
over the carpet of bodies and raised his head slowly
over the edge of the tender.

Sure enough, they were close to the great crushing
machine that ground up the dead Chaos Space
Marines and transformed them into genetic matter for
the daemonculaba to feast upon.

But as before, his gaze was drawn upwards to the
centre of the chamber, to the massive form of the
Heart of Blood, the daemonic creature that hung suspended above the lake of blood on a trio of great
chains.

He tore his eyes from the imprisoned daemon and
saw that they were part of a great, curving procession
of red bulldozers parked next to the iron ramp that led
up to the gantry of the great, daemonic wombs. Their
hellish conveyance was but one of perhaps a dozen or
more of the bulldozers, lurching in fits and starts
towards the blood-smeared conveyor that led to the
sticky crushers and rollers. A pulsing forest of pipes
pumped a pinkish, gristly matter from the machine to

the cages of the daemonculaba and Uriel felt his gorge rise at such a blasphemy against what had once been the sacred flesh of the Emperor's body.

Vacuum-suited servitor mutants on a raised platform stabbed wide hooks attached to lengths of chain into the dead flesh in the tenders then wound the chains through heavy pulley mechanisms. They worked quickly and efficiently, loading the corpses onto the conveyor in a manner that spoke of many years of repetition.

Beside the conveyor, Uriel saw a cruciform frame holding what looked like a rack of meat, positioned close enough to be spattered by blood spraying from the grinding rollers. Uriel paid it no mind as he searched for any of the dark-robed monsters that were macabre lords of this place.

Seeing none, he eased his body up and over the edge of the tender, dropping lightly to the wet, churned ground.

He tapped the tender and said, 'Come on.'

Pasanius clambered to join him, cleaning blood from the action of his weapon and wedging the bolter between his knees to rack the slide. Leonid followed suit, wiping blood from his eyes and scouring the vent-breech of his lasgun.

The three warriors crouched in the shadow of the tender, breathing heavily and clearing their bodies of as much coagulated blood as they could.

'Well, we're in,' said Leonid. 'Now what?'

Uriel glanced around the edge of the tender. 'First we destroy that machine. If the Iron Warriors cannot feed the daemonculaba genetic material…'

'Honsou will not be able to create more Iron Warriors!' finished Leonid.

'And there will be no more of the Unfleshed,' added Pasanius.

Uriel nodded. 'And after that, well, we make for the ramp behind us and slay as many of the daemonculaba as we can before the Savage Morticians kill us.'

His companions were silent until eventually Leonid said, 'Good plan.'

Uriel grinned and said, 'Glad you approve.'

Pasanius put down his bolter and offered his left hand to Uriel, saying, 'No matter what happens, I regret nothing that has led us here, captain.'

Uriel took his friend's hand and shook it, touched by the simple affection of the sentiment, and said, 'Nor I, my friend. No mater what, we will have done some good here.'

'For what it's worth,' said Leonid. 'I wish I'd never even heard of this damn place, let alone been dragged here. But I am here, and that's the end of it, so what are we waiting for? Let's do this.'

Uriel racked the slide on his own bolter and nodded.

But before he could do anything more, he heard a great, bestial howl that was answered by a demented chorus of roars and bellows that echoed from the chamber's ceiling.

He rushed to the edge of the tender in time to see the Lord of the Unfleshed rear from hiding in a fountain of blood and limbs, and tear one of the mutant butchers in two with his bare hands.

THE UNFLESHED ERUPTED from the blood-filled tenders in a thrashing mass of knotted, deformed limbs, ripping into the mutants feeding the crushing machine with the frenzy of predators who had held their anger and hunger in check for far too long.

Uriel watched as the Lord of the Unfleshed's massive jaws snapped shut on a screaming mutant, biting him in two at the waist and silencing his screams forever.

The beast Uriel had fought at the outflow pulled the arms from another foe before hurling its victim into the crushers of the grinding machine. The Unfleshed slaughtered a score of the servants of the Savage Morticians in the blink of an eye, and Uriel was horrified and grateful at the same time for their savagery.

'Damn it,' cursed Uriel. 'There goes the element of surprise!'

'Now what?' asked Pasanius.

'It will only be a matter of time until the Savage Morticians come to investigate, so come on. We don't have long.'

Uriel and the others broke from cover, running over to the roaring machine that had a potent aura of malice and hunger to it, its dark purpose imbuing it with a loathsome evil. The sooner it was destroyed the better, knew Uriel, as he drew near and a clawing sickness built in his gut.

Leonid staggered as he approached and coughed a flood of gristly vomit, the daemon machine's vile presence too much for his cancer-ridden body to bear.

'Uriel!' he shouted, holding out the bandolier of grenades he had taken from the ruin of Berossus's army on the mountainside.

Uriel snatched the grenades and ran towards the machine, passing the cruciform frame that held the dripping rack of meat, sparing it but a glance as he did so.

He pulled up short and turned to face it as he realised that it was not a rack of meat at all.

It was Obax Zakayo.

URIEL FELT NOTHING but revulsion at the sight of Obax Zakayo's ruined, mutilated body, but part of him wondered at the cruelty of creatures that could do this to another living soul. The Iron Warrior – or what was left of him – was pinned to the frame and drooled thick ropes of saliva from the corner of his twisted lips. Trailing clear tubes pumped life-sustaining chemicals into his ravaged frame.

'Guilliman's oath,' whispered Uriel as the Iron Warrior raised his beaten and bruised face towards him.

'Ventris…' he gasped, sudden hope filling his watering eyes. 'Kill me, I beg of you.'

Uriel ignored Obax Zakayo as Pasanius attempted to form the Unfleshed into some kind of defensive perimeter, and snapped grenade after grenade from the bandolier. The machine roared as he approached, filthy blue oilsmoke venting from corroded grilles and an angry bellow growling from its depths.

The gnawing sensation in his gut increased, but Uriel suppressed it and began attaching the grenades to the machine at power couplings, axle joints and even climbing on top of the machine to place one at the base of the forest of gurgling feed tubes. He worked swiftly, but methodically, ensuring that the machine would be comprehensively wrecked upon the grenades' detonation.

Uriel climbed down from the machine in time to see Leonid standing before Obax Zakayo, his lasgun shouldered and aimed squarely between the Iron Warrior's eyes.

'Do it!' wept the broken Obax Zakayo. 'Do it! Please! They feed me piece by piece to the machine and make me watch…'

Leonid's finger tightened on the trigger, but he released a shuddering breath and lowered the weapon.

'No,' he said. 'Why should you get off easy after you tortured so many of my soldiers to death? I think I like the idea of you suffering like this!'

'Please,' begged Obax Zakayo. 'I… I can help you defeat the half-breed!'

'The half-breed?' said Uriel.

'Honsou, I mean Honsou,' wheezed Obax Zakayo. 'I can tell you how you can see him dead.'

'How?' asked Leonid, stepping in and slamming the butt of his lasgun against the Iron Warrior's chin. 'Tell us!'

'Only if you promise that you will kill me,' leered Obax Zakayo, spitting teeth.

'Uriel!' shouted Pasanius from the barricades of the tenders. 'I think they're coming!'

'We don't have time for this, traitor,' snapped Uriel. 'Tell us what you know!'

'Swear, Ultramarine. Give me your oath.'

'Very well,' nodded Uriel. 'I swear I will see you dead, now speak!'

'The Heart of Blood,' began Obax Zakayo. 'It is a daemon of the Lord of Skulls and the half-breed's former master imprisoned it beneath Khalan-Ghol and fattened its essence with the blood of sorcerers.'

'What has this to do with Honsou?' demanded Uriel.

'Know you nothing of your enemies?' mocked Obax Zakayo. 'The Lord of Skulls is the bane of psykers and the Heart of Blood was driven mad by such polluted blood. The warsmith's sorcerers channelled their most potent null-magicks through the imprisoned creature, using its immaterial energies to cast a great psychic barrier around the fortress that no sorcerer has been able to breach in nearly ten thousand years!'

Obax Zakayo coughed and said, 'I have your oath that you will end my suffering?'

'Yes,' said Uriel. 'Keep talking.'

The Iron Warrior nodded and said, 'Lord Toramino has some of the most powerful sorcerers in the Eye of

Terror to command and, though they have great power, they cannot breach the ancient barrier of the Heart of Blood. Destroy it and they will raze this place to the ground!'

Uriel looked into Obax Zakayo's eyes for any sign of a lie, but the Iron Warrior was beyond such deception, too immersed in his own misery and need for death. He felt the guiding hand of providence in the traitor's presence now, for here was a chance to fulfil his death oath and deny the Omphalos Daemonium its prize.

'Very well,' pressed Uriel. 'How do we destroy it?'

'The awls,' said Obax Zakayo. 'The silver awls that pierce its daemonic flesh and hold it fast above the lake of blood...'

'What of them?'

'They are hateful artefacts, stolen from your most sacred reclusiam or taken from those whose inquisitions delved too deep into the mysteries of Chaos. They are more than just physical anchors; they bind it to this place. Remove or destroy them and its dissolution will be complete.'

Uriel took a step back from Obax Zakayo and looked up into the darkness of the chamber above the hissing lake of blood where the huge daemon hung suspended in its writhing madness. He saw three gleaming silver pinpricks of light impaled through its scaled flesh, each attached to a chain that was anchored in the bedrock of the chamber's walls.

His eyes followed the line of the chains from the daemon and squinted as he sought where the nearest was embedded. Uriel turned back to Obax Zakayo and raised his bolter, saying, 'I will kill you now.'

'No!' said Leonid grimly. 'Let me do it. I owe this bastard a death.'

Uriel saw the thirst for vengeance in Leonid's eyes and nodded. 'So be it. Once he is dead, set the timers on the grenades and get clear. The Savage Morticians are coming, so stay close to the Unfleshed. They will try to protect you if you are near them, but you have to hold the enemy at bay for as long as you can.'

'I understand,' said Leonid. 'Now go.'

Uriel nodded and ran towards Pasanius.

Leonid watched as Uriel hurriedly outlined his plan to Pasanius and the two Ultramarines set off up the iron ramps that led towards the daemonculaba.

'Now, slave,' hissed Obax Zakayo. 'Ventris told you to kill me.'

Leonid raised his lasgun and shot Obax Zakayo in the gut. He smelled burned flesh and nodded to himself, satisfied that the Iron Warrior was in pain, but still alive.

Obax Zakayo raised his head and roared, 'Shoot me again, I'm not dead yet!'

Leonid stepped close and spat into Obax Zakayo's face. 'No,' he said calmly.

'An oath was given!' screamed the Iron Warrior. 'Ventris swore he would see me dead!'

'Uriel gave his word, but I didn't,' snarled Leonid. 'I want you to live in agony then die in pain when this place is brought down!'

Obax Zakayo wept and cursed him, but Leonid ignored his pleadings as he removed the grenade attached to the crushing machine that was nearest the Iron Warrior and slipped it into his uniform jacket's breast pocket.

'Don't want you dying by accident, now do we?' he said.

Without another word, Leonid turned and walked away.

* * *

URIEL POUNDED UP the ramp and ran past the heaving bodies of the daemonculaba, wishing he could stop to end each one's suffering. He knew that they had a better chance to end their torment if they could enable Honsou's enemies to do the job for them. He and Pasanius ran around the circumference of the chamber to reach one of the three awl-chains that pierced the Heart of Blood's body and kept it bound to Khalan-Ghol.

If they could pull even one of the awls from the terrible daemon, then it would be something...

'Great Emperor of Mankind, grant me the strength of your will to do this for you,' he prayed as he ran, his eyes tracing the line of the chain that ran from the daemon's body.

He saw it was higher than this level of daemonic womb-creatures, and as they reached the point on the gantry directly below the chain, he heard the explosive destruction of the crushing machine and the bestial roars of the Unfleshed echoing through the chamber. This was quickly followed by the bark of lasfire and the screech of the Savage Morticians.

'We'll need to climb,' said Pasanius.

Uriel nodded and turned to watch the battle below, seeing bodies flying through the air and leaping arcs of blue lightning as the denizens of this awful place fought against the Unfleshed.

'Emperor watch over you,' whispered Uriel as he gripped the iron bars of one of the daemonculaba cages and began to climb. The thick chain was some ten metres above them, and even in the dim light he could see it was firmly embedded in the chamber's wall with a rockcrete plug.

'I'll need a hand,' said Pasanius as Uriel reached the top of the cage, sounding thoroughly ashamed to be asking for help.

Uriel turned back, mortified that it hadn't occurred to him that Pasanius might have difficulty in reaching the chain with only one arm until this moment. He reached down and helped his sergeant climb to join him.

Rusted struts and long-abandoned scaffolding pierced the rock below the plug, presumably left behind by those who had put it there in the first place.

He heard a piteous, mewling cry of anguish from below him and looked down through the mesh of the cage roof into the weeping face of the daemonculaba.

Uriel knelt as close as he could to the tormented creature. 'I will see your suffering ended,' he promised. Her eyes closed slowly and Uriel thought he detected an almost imperceptible nod of her bloated head.

'There is not enough suffering in the galaxy to make the Iron Warriors pay for what they have done here,' said Pasanius, his voice choked with emotion.

'No,' agreed Uriel, 'there is not, but we will make them suffer anyway.'

'Aye,' agreed Pasanius as they climbed onto the roof of the cage and made their way further up the sides of the shadowed chamber, their goal nearing with every heave upwards.

The sounds of battle continued to rage from below as they clambered over the protruding scaffolding spars wedged into cracks in the rock and pulled themselves level with the chain.

As thick as Pasanius's forearm, it stretched off towards the centre of the chamber and the Heart of Blood.

'Ready?' asked Uriel.

'Ready,' nodded Pasanius, spitting on his palm.

Taking a firm grip on the flaking, rusted chain, the two Space Marines pulled with all their strength to wrench the awl-chain from the Heart of Blood's body.

LEONID SPRAYED A burst of full auto lasfire towards the skulking, vacuum-suited mutants taking cover behind a row of blood-filled barrels. His bolts punctured the containers, spilling crimson arcs from their sides. He knew he hadn't killed any of them, but it kept their heads down. He'd seen the mutant creature, Sabatier with the armed slaves of the Savage Morticians and dearly desired to put a bolt through that monster's head.

Damn, but it felt good to fire a weapon in anger again! The chaos of the bloody struggle swirled and raged around him, the Unfleshed battling with a primal ferocity against their creators and their slaves to give the Ultramarines more time to bring down the Heart of Blood.

The Lord of the Unfleshed bellowed as he slew, his powerful fists bringing death to his enemies with every blow. A black-robed monster reared up on great pneumatic legs equipped with shrieking blades, but another of the Unfleshed, a gibbering horror of limbs and mouths, landed upon it and tore its legs off with savage jerks.

Leonid rolled into the cover of the smoking remains of the crushing machine to reload as the Savage Mortician collapsed and its killer leapt for another victim. The limbless form of Obax Zakayo screamed, 'Kill me!' from his cruciform rack, but Leonid ignored him, too intent on the battle around him.

As ferocious as the Unfleshed were, the Savage Morticians had been practitioners of the art of death for uncounted millennia, and if there was one thing they knew, it was the weaknesses of flesh. Even when it was as resilient as that of the Unfleshed.

Flying razor discs lopped off thick limbs and heavy darts coated with poisons that could only exist in the Eye of Terror stabbed into pounding veins to slay their victims before they were even aware they were hit.

Creatures were dying and even the relentless fire of the Savage Morticians' servants was taking its toll, volley after volley cutting down the Unfleshed where they fought.

Leonid rose from cover and saw a Savage Mortician with massive chainblades for fists scuttle behind the Lord of the Unfleshed as he tore the torso from the mechanised track-unit of yet another foe. Leonid swung the barrel around and squeezed off a burst of bright lasbolts.

His aim was true and the Savage Mortician's head exploded, its twitching form slumping to the ground behind the Lord of the Unfleshed. The massive creature spun as he heard it fall, his confusion at its death turning to savage joy as he saw who had saved him. He beat his fists on his chest and roared, 'Now you Tribe!'

Even as Leonid ducked back into cover, he heard the thump of booted feet behind him. He spun, bringing the barrel of his lasgun up, seeing half a dozen mutant slave warriors armed with cudgels and billhooks bearing down upon him. An iron-tipped club slashed for his head and he hurled himself backwards, too slow, the tip of the weapon thudding against his temple.

He dropped his lasgun, hands flying to his head as the world spun crazily and bright starbursts exploded before his eyes. The ground rushed up to meet him and he slammed into the hard rockcrete, closing his eyes as he waited for the killing blow to land.

The shadow of something hot and heavy fell across him and warm blood splashed him.

He opened his eyes and shook his head, regretting it the moment he felt hammerblows of concussion reverberate inside his skull. The Lord of the Unfleshed towered above him, his thickly-muscled body pierced by a score of long blades and burned by innumerable lasburns. The creature reached down to lift him to his feet, and Leonid saw the bodies of those who had been about to kill him.

They looked like an explosion in an anatomist's collection, a mass of severed limbs and burst-open bodies.

'Thank you,' managed Leonid, wiping blood from the side of his head and bending to retrieve his fallen weapon.

'You Tribe,' replied the Lord of the Unfleshed as though no other explanation was needed. Without another word, the creature hurled itself back into the fray. Scores of the Unfleshed were dead, but the remainder fought on, unrelenting in their savagery. More and more of their foes were pouring into the chamber and Leonid knew it would not be long until they were overwhelmed.

He looked up towards the gantries surrounding the chamber, willing Uriel and Pasanius to hurry.

THE VEINS ON Uriel's arms stood out like steel hawsers as he pulled on the chain. Bracing themselves against the raised edge of the scaffolding before him, they hauled with all their might on the chain.

Uriel's booted feet slipped and he spread his stance to gain better leverage. The grinding pain in his chest and neck from his cracked bones tore into him as he pulled, but he focussed his mind, using all the discipline he had been taught at Agiselus and in the Temple of Hera to shut it out.

'Come on, damn you!' he yelled at the chain, hearing the ferocious sounds of battle and knowing that the Unfleshed were dying for him.

He could not let them down, and redoubled his efforts.

Pasanius strained at the chain also, sweat popping from his brow as he hauled on the chain. The sergeant was much stronger than Uriel, but had only one arm with which to heave at the chain.

Together, they put every ounce of their hatred for the Iron Warriors into their efforts.

Uriel roared in pain and frustration as he kept on pulling.

And suddenly he felt give…

Yelling in triumph, the two Ultramarines pulled even harder, feeling tendons tear in their shoulders and arms, but pushing their bodies to the limits of power.

Without warning, the awl-chain tore loose and Uriel saw a flaring spurt of white fire as the silver spike ripped free of the ancient daemon's flesh.

The red-scaled creature dropped, silver-white flashes exploding against its body where its falling weight tore the other two silver awls from its body.

It landed in the lake of blood with an enormous splash, sending a tidal wave of crimson spilling throughout the chamber. It vanished beneath the churning surface of the lake and Uriel felt a prescient sense of inevitability seize him as he watched the hissing red pool.

'We did it!' shouted Pasanius.

'Yes,' agreed Uriel, watching as the surface of the lake parted and the massive daemon reared up to its full height, arc lightning playing about its lustrous, scarlet flesh, 'but I am beginning to wonder if we should have.'

* * *

HIGH UP IN the tower of iron, Onyx cried out as though struck and dropped to his knees, clutching his head as his soulless silver eyes blazed with sudden awareness. Honsou saw the movement and looked up, irritated at having his battle-planning with Cadaras Grendel interrupted.

Then he saw the look of alarm on Onyx's face.

'What is it?' he demanded.

'The Heart of Blood!' hissed the daemonic symbiote.

'What about it?'

'It's free...' said Onyx.

CHAPTER TWENTY

THE HEART OF Blood threw back its horned skull and roared in lunatic pain, its bellow of rage and madness filling the chamber at a pitch that pierced the soul and drew screams of primal fear from almost every living thing within it. The lake of blood boiled where it stood and its eyes burned with white fire that blazed with ancient malice.

Its shaggy, horned head twisted as it surveyed its surroundings, as though seeing them for the first time, and its bloated body threw off great bolts of dark lightning that exploded with red fire.

The Heart of Blood's flesh was scaled and thick tufts of shaggy, matted hair ran down the length of its spine. The great wounds on its back, where the Savage Morticians had removed its wings, smoked with a liquid, red bloom, like a cloud of ink released underwater.

359

Its chest heaved violently, the thudding echoes of its
heartbeat filling the chamber as it ripped away the
pulsing red tube that pierced its chest and fed it the
tainted blood of psykers. The flood of vital fluid
gushed into the lake.

'Guilliman preserve us!' breathed Pasanius as the
daemon stepped forwards, striding purposefully to the
shore, the spark of its hoofed feet on the lakebed
throwing up gouts of flaming blood.

'A daemon,' said Uriel. 'One of the fell princes of
Chaos…'

'What do we do?' said Pasanius.

Uriel drew his sword as the huge daemon reached
the edge of the lake of blood and reared up to its full
height.

'We ready our souls for the end,' he said simply.

HONSOU WATCHED THE sky around his fortress burn
with an actinic blue light. Hundreds of pillars of pellucid blue flame surrounded Khalan-Ghol, spearing
kilometres upwards from the plain below, like oil-
wells gushing with precious fuel. The azure fire seethed
and Honsou could see living nightmares swirling
within the flames, the dreadful power and malice of
the warp contained within them.

'What's happening?' he demanded.

'The towers!' said Onyx.

'Towers? What towers?'

'The ones we saw when we made that sortie into
Berossus's camp,' said Onyx. 'Tall, baroque towers of
iron that were saturated with psychic energy. You
remember?'

Honsou nodded, recalling the unsettling sight of their
arcane geometries and the chanting groups of gold-
robed figures who danced around them, anointing

them with the blood of sacrifices. He had put them from his mind after the raid, confident that the power of the Heart of Blood could resist their magicks.

He rounded on Onyx, raising his axe and saying, 'You told me that no sorcerous powers could defeat the Heart of Blood!'

'And none can, but it is free now and not bound to Khalan-Ghol any more.'

'We are defenceless?' asked Cadaras Grendel.

Onyx shook his head. 'No. The fortress's own sorcerers can maintain the barrier for a while, but without the power of the Heart of Blood, it is only a matter of time until Toramino's magicks break through and destroy us.'

'Blood of Chaos!' swore Honsou, heading for the great doors that led from his inner sanctum and waving his chosen warriors to follow him. 'How could the daemon get free?'

'The warsmith bound the Heart of Blood with three defiled awls, and it could only be freed if someone were to remove them.'

'But who would dare risk such a thing?'

Honsou pulled up short as Onyx said, 'Ventris and his warrior band?'

'Of course!' snapped Honsou. 'I should have known Toramino would never have stooped so low as to employ renegades just to fight for him. He and Ventris must have planned this whole thing! Free the Heart of Blood and then destroy us with sorcery. I'll have those bastards' entrails fed a piece at a time to the Exuviae.'

'Then Toramino never intended to blood his army here!' snarled Cadaras Grendel.

'No,' agreed Onyx. 'It would seem not.'

'How long do we have before the barrier falls?' demanded Honsou, setting off into the darkness of the

tower of iron and towards the Halls of the Savage Morticians.

His warriors followed him, bolters and swords at the
ready.

'I do not know for sure,' admitted Onyx, 'but it will
not be long.'

'Then we'd better hurry!' said Honsou. 'I want to kill
Ventris before Toramino brings Khalan-Ghol to ruin!'

URIEL DROPPED TO the gantry that ran the circumference of the chamber, thumbing the activation rune on
his sword's hilt and slashing its bright blade through
the air. Pasanius landed beside him and together they
hurriedly made their way to the chamber's floor as the
Heart of Blood stepped from the lake, red liquid running from its crimson body in grisly runnels.

It towered above them, fully four or five metres tall,
its powerfully muscled physique running with hot
streamers of light that snaked beneath its flesh like
fiery veins. It looked down on the bloody ground
before it – at the corpses of the Unfleshed, the Savage
Morticians and their servants – and a bloody leer split
its bestial face. The surviving mutants fled before its
terrifying power and even those Savage Morticians the
Unfleshed had not killed backed away from this diabolical presence in their midst.

Only the Unfleshed stood their ground, too ignorant
of the horrifying power of a daemon prince to fear it.
Though they felt its abominable power, they had no
concept of the threat it represented.

The Lord of the Unfleshed stood before the mighty
daemon, his chest puffed out in challenge, and it
regarded him with as much interest as a man might
notice an ant. The Lord of the Unfleshed roared and
charged the daemon, but before he could so much as

land a blow, the Heart of Blood swatted him aside with a casual flick of its scaled arm.

The monstrous leader of the Unfleshed smashed into the side of the cavern with a bone-crunching thud and Uriel knew that the force of the impact must have shattered every bone in his body.

Seeing their leader so easily defeated, the Unfleshed howled and scattered before the horrendous daemon, seeking shelter in the dark nooks and crannies of the deathly cavern.

Uriel and Pasanius watched as the Heart of Blood turned from the fleeing Unfleshed, the tremendous booming of its vital organ diminishing now that sorcerous magicks were no longer pouring into it. Uriel felt his senses becoming sharper, the smothering numbness lifted now that the daemon was free.

Leonid hurried over to where they stood and shouted, 'I thought it was supposed to be destroyed when the awls came out!'

'So did I,' replied Uriel as the Heart of Blood threw back its head and gave vent to a terrible roaring that overwhelmed the senses, not through its volume, but by the sheer sense of loss and fury that it contained. Its hunger pierced the wall of the dimensions and echoed across the vast gulf that separated universes.

Uriel and every living thing in the chamber fell to the ground, shaken to the very core of their being by the daemon's cry.

'What's it doing?' yelled Leonid.

'Emperor alone knows!' cried Pasanius.

Uriel picked himself up, his hands clamped to the side of his head in an effort to shut out the monstrous noise of the daemon's howl. Something in the tone of the long, ululating cry spoke to Uriel of things lost and things to be called back. He realised what it was as he saw a twisting blob of dark light appear in the air before the daemon.

'It is a cry of summoning…' he said.

Pasanius and Leonid looked strangely at him as the daemon's roar ceased and the fragile veil of reality pulled apart with a dreadful ripping sound, as of tearing meat. A black gouge in the walls separating realities opened, filling the air with sickening static, as though a million noxious flies had flown through from some vile, plague dimension.

Awful knowledge flooded Uriel as he stared into the portal opened in the fabric of the universe. He saw galaxies of billions upon billions of souls harvested and fed to the Lord of Skulls, the Blood God.

'Emperor's mercy,' wept Uriel as he felt each of these deaths lodge like a splinter in his heart. New life and new purpose had once filled these galaxies, but now all was death, slaughtered to sate the hunger of the Blood God… whose fell name was a dark presence staining the coppery wind that blew from the portal, a stench of deepest, darkest red, whose purpose was embodied in but a single rune and a legend of simple devotion: Blood for the Blood God… *Khorne… Khorne… Khorne…*

A single shriek of dark and bloody kinship, a pact of hate and death. It echoed from the portal and grew to shake the dust from the ceiling. And there was an answering roar of bloody welcome, torn from the Heart of Blood's brazen throat.

Light blazed from the portal as an armoured giant, clad in burnished iron plates of ancient power armour stamped down into the chamber, the portal sealing shut behind it as it marched to stand before the Heart of Blood.

Taller than a Space Marine, its vile presence was unmistakable, its malice incalculable. White light, impure and corrupt, spilled like droplets of spoiled milk from beneath its horned helmet and its shoulder guards bore stained chevrons that marked the figure as an Iron Warrior.

The daemonic warrior carried a great, saw-toothed blade and a gold-chased pistol, both weapons redolent with the slaughter they had inflicted. Powerful and darkly magnificent, Uriel knew that this… thing was the most consummate killer imaginable.

Uriel caught a glimpse of a shambling shape limping towards the passageway that led from the cavern, recognising it as the vile creature, Sabatier. Barely had he registered its presence when the iron-armoured warrior snapped up its pistol and fired.

The bolt caught Sabatier high in the back, exploding through its chest and blasting a great crater in its body. Sabatier grunted and toppled over and Uriel felt sorry that it hadn't suffered more before it died.

'We can't fight both of them,' said Pasanius.

'No,' agreed Uriel, 'but maybe we will not have to. Look!'

The armoured figure dropped to its knees before the Heart of Blood, but Uriel could see that it was no simple a gesture of abasement. The daemonic Iron Warrior dropped its weapons and raised its arms, a blood-red glow spilling from every joint of its armour and bathing the Heart of Blood in its light.

'I return to you!' shouted a high voice from beneath the armoured warrior's helmet.

The Heart of Blood raised its arms, mimicking the warrior's pose and, piece-by-piece, the iron armour detached from the kneeling figure and floated through the air towards the massive daemon.

'Now what the hell's it doing?' said Leonid, barely keeping the terror from his voice.

'Oh no...' whispered Uriel as he remembered a tale he had been told not so long ago by Seraphys of the Blood Ravens in the mountains. A tale of how the Heart of Blood had forged for itself a suit of armour into which it had poured all of its malice, all of its hate and all of its cunning, a suit of armour so full of fury that even the blows of its enemies would strike them down.

Truly it was the avatar of Khorne, the Blood God's most favoured disciple of death.

Iron armour floated from the figure who now diminished as each piece deserted it. Though the Heart of Blood was larger by far than the armoured warrior, each piece somehow moulded itself to the daemon's form, darkening from the colour of iron to a dark and loathsome brass. Its greaves and breastplate clanged into place and, unbidden, the warrior's weapons leapt from the ground, writhing in midair to change from a pistol and sword to a moaning axe and snaking whip of rippling, studded leather.

Lastly, the iron helm was snatched by invisible hands from the warrior's head and placed upon the Heart of Blood's great, horned skull.

Where once had knelt a fearsome, armoured giant, there was now only a waif-like figure of a woman in a filthy and tattered sky-blue uniform of the Imperial Guard.

'383rd!' exclaimed Leonid.

'What?'

'That jacket,' pointed Leonid. 'It's the uniform of my regiment!'

'It can't be,' said Uriel. 'Here?'

'I know my own regiment, damn it,' snapped Leonid. 'I'm going to get her!'

'Don't be a fool,' said Pasanius, gripping Leonid's jacket.

'No!' protested Leonid, struggling in the sergeant's grip. 'Don't you understand? Along with me, she's probably the last survivor of the 383rd! I have to go!'

'You'll die,' said Uriel.

'So? I'm dying anyway,' shouted Leonid. 'And if I have to end my days here, I want it to be with a fellow Jouran. Remember your words, Uriel! We all die bloody, all we get to do is choose where and when!'

Uriel nodded, now understanding Leonid's desperation, and said, 'Let him go.'

Pasanius released his grip on Leonid, and they watched as he ran towards the swaying woman, gathering her up in his arms as another set of thick, curling, bronze-tipped horns ripped through the metal of the daemon's helmet. The Heart of Blood's eyes shone with renewed purpose and awareness as it lifted its head and sniffed the air, grinning with terrible appetite.

'Psykers…' it roared, turning towards the upright iron sarcophagi that surrounded the lake of blood.

THE IRON-MESHED cage sped downwards into the depths of Khalan-Ghol, ancient mechanisms and sorcerous artifice combining to make the journey as quick as possible, oily sheets of beaten iron slicing past at tremendous speed. But Honsou knew it was still not fast enough. The mystical barrier protecting his fortress was still holding firm against Toramino's sorcerers, but it wouldn't last much longer unless they could somehow re-imprison the Heart of Blood.

He and his chosen warriors, deadly killers loyal only to him, journeyed into the depths of the fortress, ready to kill whatever they encountered. Onyx stood backed into the corner of the speeding elevator cage, his silver eyes and veins dulled and sluggish in his features.

'What's the matter with you?' snapped Honsou as the daemonic symbiote moaned.

'The Heart of Blood is powerful…' hissed Onyx.

'And?'

'It could snuff out my essence in the blink of an eye,' snarled Onyx, his dead eyes shining with murderous lustre. 'And if it commanded me, I could not resist its imperatives.'

'You mean it could turn you against me?' asked Honsou.

'Yes,' nodded Onyx. 'It knows my true name.'

Honsou turned to Cadaras Grendel and said, 'If this creature so much as makes a move towards me, kill it.'

'Understood,' said the mohawked Iron Warrior, his scarred features alight with relish at the thought. 'I never killed one that's possessed before.'

Honsou looked down through the grilled floor of the cage, seeing only a dimly glowing shaft roaring upwards. Its end was lost to perspective, but as he watched, the dark square of the tunnel's base rushed up to meet them.

With a gut-wrenching sensation of nausea, the iron cage slowed and ground to a halt with a shriek of ancient metal. The grilled door squealed open, but before Honsou could step through, he was knocked from his feet by a tremendous impact and felt the crash of falling masonry from far away, accompanied by the distant boom of massed artillery.

'What the hell?' he roared, climbing to his knees as he heard the clang of metal on stone, and an approaching, crashing din.

Onyx dropped to his knees, screaming in pain and clutching his head with his dead-fleshed hands.

'The barrier is down!' he yelled. 'Gods of Chaos, the barrier is down!'

Honsou pulled himself to his feet and looked up as he pinpointed the source of the approaching noise.

'Out of the elevator!' he shouted, diving and rolling into the tunnel as he saw thousands of tonnes of rubble plummeting down the shaft. His warriors moved quickly, but some not quickly enough, as a torrent of massive chunks of stone and rockcrete hammered into the base of the shaft and crushed the elevator cage flat. Roiling banks of choking dust and smoke billowed from the wreckage.

The impact and deafening noise disoriented Honsou, but he quickly gained his feet, seeing that nearly half his warriors were missing, crushed beneath the deadly rain of debris.

Onyx stood unsteadily before him, the threatening form of Cadaras Grendel close by.

'If the barrier is down–' began Grendel

'Then that means Toramino is attacking!' finished Honsou.

Just saying the words gave Honsou a curious sense of reckless abandonment as he realised that this was probably the end. There was no way Khalan-Ghol could stand against Toramino's army and he had no more stratagems left to employ.

There was nothing left but vengeance for hate's sake and malice for the sake of spite.

If that was all he had left, then so be it.

It would be enough.

URIEL PULLED LEONID into the scant cover offered by one of the corpse bulldozers and helped him get the muttering woman he had dragged to safety into a seated position. Tears of joy streaked the colonel's face and he kept repeating the name of his regiment over and over again.

'Come on, hurry,' urged Uriel, desperate to keep Leonid out of the way of the Heart of Blood's murderous rampage. The mighty, armoured daemon was making sport in the centre of the lake of blood, ripping gold-robed sorcerers from their exsanguination coffins, toying with them in numerous terrible ways before slaughtering them with its axe or powerful, fanged maw.

It waded through the blood, letting the terrified magickers tear themselves to pieces as they desperately fought to free themselves from their coffins. Not one amongst them survived the daemon's predatory malice and it inhaled their deaths like a fine wine.

'Psykers!' it bellowed. 'The food of the gods!'

Uriel returned his attention to the wan, lean-faced woman Leonid had rescued from the clutches of the daemonic armour. Her hair was long, lank and falling out in patches, while her features spoke of horrors endured and a mind on the very brink of sanity.

'All dead, all dead, all dead, all dead…' she repeated, over and over.

'Who is she?' asked Pasanius.

Leonid fished out rusted dogtags from beneath her uniform jacket and turned them over to examine them in the chamber's dim light.

'Her name is Lieutenant Larana Utorian of the 383rd Jouran Dragoons,' he said proudly.

'Do you know her?'

Leonid shook his head. 'No, I don't. Her tags say she was part of Tedeski's lot in Battalion A and he didn't like other officers mingling with his soldiers. He was old school you see.'

'How in the Emperor's name did she end up here?'

'I don't know,' wept Leonid, holding her in a tight embrace. 'Perhaps the God-Emperor didn't want me to die alone without someone from the old homeworld next to me.'

Uriel nodded and locked eyes with Pasanius as he gripped his sword hilt tightly. 'Aye, perhaps you're right, my friend. If a man has to die, it should be with his friends.'

THE DEAD, WHITE sky burned with magickal energies, whipping plumes of blue fire shooting up into the heavens from the geomantic towers Toramino's sorcerers had constructed around Khalan-Ghol. Monstrously powerful energies had been unleashed, and now that the eternal barrier that had kept Honsou's fortress safe from the fell powers of the warp was no more, it suffered terribly under the immaterial assault.

Black lightning speared from the cloudless sky, blasting colossal slabs of rock from the mountain and fearsome red storms of bruised, weeping clouds hammered the few remaining towers and bastions with mutating rains that dissolved fortifications which had stood invincible for ten thousand years.

Great, ravening beasts of the warp swooped and dived around the high reaches of the fortress, tearing apart the flying creatures that circled the topmost towers, and a fog of magickal energies enveloped the redoubts and bunkers that Honsou had only recently rebuilt in the wake of his victory over Lord Berossus.

Nor was the fortress attacked only by sorcerous powers, for Toramino's grand artillery batteries were finally unleashed to bring explosive ruin upon the mountain of their master's enemy. Thousands of tonnes of ordnance rained down on Khalan-Ghol, smashing apart the very mountain itself.

Huge columns of soldiers and an entire grand company of Iron Warriors, led by Toramino himself, marched upon Khalan-Ghol, a host of thousands that would destroy whatever of the half-breed's force might survive the furious assault now wracking the mountain.

Khalan-Ghol's final doom was upon it.

URIEL FELT A familiar churning sensation in his stomach, hearing a chiming, splintering sound of glass breaking, and a terrible sensation of powerlessness gripped him. He experienced sickening vibrations deep in his bones as a restlessness rippled through the ground. A powerful vision of jagged stumps of bone jutting through the ground gripped him, and a mad howling built from the air, piercing and vile, with an unimaginable thirst for revenge.

He blinked as a fiercely painful sensation built within his skull, as though hot needles were being pushed out through his eyeballs.

'Oh, no…' he whispered, as he realised what was happening, and looked up into the face of Leonid, whose gaze betrayed the same knowledge that had just come to Uriel.

'God-Emperor, no,' wept Leonid. 'Not again, please no, not again!'

'What is it?' said Pasanius.

Before Uriel could answer, they heard the Heart of Blood roar in sudden awareness, sounding like a cry of unexpected pleasure.

'My old nemesis…' it rasped as the very air in the chamber became saturated with an electric tang of ozone and sulphur. Uriel felt his stomach heave and gripped onto the side of the bulldozer as the Hall of the Savage Morticians seemed to… *shift…*

The ground now felt soft and loamy underfoot, a weeping red fluid seeping upwards where his weight had forced it from the dark earth. Uriel looked up, already knowing what he would see.

Above him, a lacerated crimson sky, flecked with cancerous, melanoma clouds boiled, wheeling carrion creatures circling and awaiting their chance to feed. A familiar mad screaming, like the wails of the damned, echoed painfully, but it was nothing compared to the misery he had already seen in this place, and he pushed it aside.

Fleshless, bony hands reached up through the dark earth and Leonid kept his eyes shut tightly, holding onto Larana Utorian. Rippling spirals of reflective light coiled from the walls of the chamber, twisting the image of the rock behind like a warped lens. The walls seemed to stretch, as though being sucked into an unseen vortex behind, until there was nothing left but a rippling veil of impenetrable darkness, a tunnel into madness ringed with screaming faces.

Brazen rail tracks coated in crusted blood ran from the previously impermeable walls of the chamber, streamers of multi-coloured matter oozing from the cracked rock.

With no eternal barrier to stop it from reaching its hated rival, the Omphalos Daemonium manifested within the walls of Khalan-Ghol.

CHAPTER TWENTY-ONE

ROARING FROM THE mouth of the tunnel like a dark force of nature, the Omphalos Daemonium thundered into the Halls of the Savage Morticians. The armoured leviathan's mad structure was doubly hateful to Uriel now that a suspicion that had been nagging at the back of his head was horribly confirmed.

'It knew...' he snarled.

'Knew what?' said Pasanius, shouting to be heard over the howling roar of the Omphalos Daemonium's arrival. Uriel ducked back as the swirling red tendrils of smoke that were the hallmarks of the Sarcomata slashed past, carried onwards by the passing of the colossal daemon engine. It came to a halt before a newly-raised platform of bloodstained rockcrete with the sound of squealing iron and brazen roars, hissing souls escaping from its billowing stacks in shrieking waves of pain.

'It knew we would try to defy it,' said Uriel, sick with the realisation that they had been used. 'It knew we would try and destroy the Heart of Blood.'

'Then why did it send us here?'

'Because now that the psychic barrier Obax Zakayo spoke of is down, it can manifest within Khalan-Ghol. Remember the tale Seraphys told us? These daemons are ancient enemies and now the Omphalos Daemonium will wreak its vengeance upon the Heart of Blood for trapping it within that daemon engine.'

Pasanius turned as the Heart of Blood stepped from the crimson lake, its slaughter of Honsou's psykers complete and the promise of battle with its ancestral foe drawing it towards the seething engine. The brazen machine heaved with power and red mist writhed around its thick plates as the heavy door to the interior heaved open and the Slaughterman stepped onto the platform, the thick, clanking iron plates of his armour dripping with a black, oily residue.

The daemonic Iron Warrior was as huge as Uriel remembered it, its bulk made all the more massive by the extra plates of armour welded and bound to its fabric over the millennia. It still wore its charred and blackened apron, stiffened with ancient blood and reeking of cooked flesh and blood.

A crown of dark horns sprouted from its battered helmet and Uriel was not surprised to see that it still carried its murderous, iron-hafted billhook, the blade broad and crusted with aeons of bloodshed.

The Heart of Blood roared with mirth as the Slaughterman stepped into the Hall of the Savage Morticians.

'Is this what you are reduced to?' it bellowed. 'To wear the flesh of your gaoler?'

'Only liveflesh left to me,' barked the Slaughterman. 'Enough words. I rip your warpself apart!'

The Heart of Blood broadened its stance and raised its enormous axe, cracking its whip and roaring its bloody challenge to the Slaughterman. Thick red tendrils of smoke coalesced around the gigantic Iron Warrior, becoming solid things of dead flesh and immaterial energies.

'Sarcomata!' snarled Uriel, seeing the featureless daemon creatures that had carried them aboard the Omphalos Daemonium's horrific daemon engine. Eight of them attended their daemonic master, each wearing a grey, featureless boiler-suit and knee high boots with rusted greaves protecting their shins. They carried knives, hooks and saws and, from the loathsome snapping of their jaws, looked eager to use them.

Their disgusting faces were red and raw, like the Unfleshed, but where the Unfleshed still possessed qualities that were human, even if they were only rudimentary, the Sarcomata were utterly flensed of the mask of humanity. Their eyeless faces were crisscrossed with crude stitches above their fanged mouths, and their narrow, questing tongues licked the air.

Uriel expected some form of retort from the Heart of Blood, but words were not part of the equation when it came to daemons of the Blood God. The Heart of Blood cracked its whip again, the barbed tip scoring across the Slaughterman's chest in a slash of sparks. The iron-armoured daemon roared and hurled itself from the platform and the Heart of Blood leapt to meet it, the two mighty creatures hammering together in a blazing corona of fiery warp energy.

Machinery was crushed and great, iron pillars were smashed aside as the two powerful daemons tore at one another with a hate that had burned for uncounted aeons. Deafening shrieks of diabolical weapons echoed as the cavern shook with the violence of their battle.

Uriel hunkered down against the bulldozer, realising that more than just the daemonic battle was destroying this place. He felt a bass thump, thump of impacts against the rock and smiled to himself as he knew what was happening.

'Honsou's fortress is under yet another bombardment,' he shouted.

Pasanius looked doubtful. 'The shelling must be incredible to be felt this deep.'

'Indeed,' agreed Uriel. 'Toramino must be attacking with everything he has.'

Rock and machinery flew, hurled aside as the two daemons fell back into the lake of blood. Geysers of flaming blood and flesh were thrown into the air and a foul red rain began to fall as the daemons tore at one another.

'Come on!' yelled Uriel over the din. 'We should get out of here. Toramino's army will destroy this place soon and I do not want to be anywhere near these two creatures while they fight!'

'Where do we go?' asked Pasanius as chunks of rubble fell from the walls of the chamber, smashing to the ground and throwing up huge clouds of debris and smoke.

'Anywhere but here,' said Uriel, nodding to the long passageway that led to the elevator cage that had brought them here from Honsou's chambers. 'If that elevator is still working, we can get back to where that silver-eyed daemon thing brought us into the fortress.'

He knelt beside Leonid and said, 'We are going now, colonel. Come on.'

Leonid looked up through his tears and Uriel saw that the colonel was at the end of his endurance. The colonel shook his head. 'No. You go. I will stay here with Larana Utorian.'

Uriel shook his head. 'We will not leave you here. A Space Marine never leaves a battle-brother behind.'

'I am not your battle-brother, Uriel,' coughed Leonid sadly. 'Even if she and I get out of this place we will not survive more than a few days. The cancers the Mechanicus infected us with are growing stronger every day. It is over for us.'

Uriel placed his hand on Leonid's shoulder, knowing the man was right, but hating the feeling of betrayal that settled on him as he accepted Leonid's decision.

'The Emperor be with you,' said Uriel.

Leonid looked down into the face of Larana Utorian and smiled. 'I think He is.'

Uriel nodded and turned from Leonid as Pasanius said, 'Die well, Leonid. If we survive, I will light a candle for your soul to find its way home.'

Leonid said nothing, cradling Larana Utorian's wasted frame and rocking back and forth.

Knowing there was nothing more for them to say, the Ultramarines turned and ran towards the entrance to the cavern as more of the Savage Morticians' domain was brought down by the battling daemons.

Behind them, Colonel Mikhail Leonid and Lieutenant Larana Utorian of the 383rd Jouran Dragoons held each other tight and waited for death.

PASANIUS FLINCHED AS a huge cascade of rocks crashed down beside him, hurling him off balance and wreathing him in powdery dust. He coughed and shouted for Uriel as everything became obscured in banks of smoke.

'Here!' shouted Uriel, and Pasanius made his way towards the source of the shout.

He tripped on something on the ground and rolled, putting his arm down to push himself back to his feet and falling flat as he remembered that there was no arm to take his weight. He cursed himself for a fool, then saw what he had tripped over.

The gurgling form of Sabatier painfully pulled itself towards safety, its twisted, deformed body, dusty and covered in contusions. A great crater had been gouged in its back where the creature that had stepped through the portal had shot it, but Pasanius was not surprised to see that Sabatier still lived. After all, it had survived Vaanes snapping its neck like a dry branch.

Bone still protruded at its neck from that wound and Pasanius flipped the repulsive creature onto its back as it mewled in pain and fear.

'Not so proud now, are you?' said Pasanius.

'Leave Sabatier! He never did any harm!'

'No,' snarled Pasanius. 'He just gloated while my friends were butchered like animals!'

The huge sergeant knelt on Sabatier's chest, his weight alone cracking the hideous creature's ribs. A horrid gurgling burst from Sabatier's throat, but Pasanius felt no remorse for its suffering. It had stood and laughed as Space Marines were killed and for that Pasanius knew it had to die.

Keeping it pinned with his knee, he gripped Sabatier by the neck with his remaining hand and heaved.

The mutant's neck stretched and Pasanius heard the crack of splitting tendons before he wrenched Sabatier's head clean off. Sabatier's mouth still flapped, but no sound came out.

Pasanius had no idea whether he had killed Sabatier, but didn't care. To have struck back at it was enough. He stood and spat on the twitching body, stamping repeatedly on its altered limbs to crush the bones to powder before turning and hurling the mutant's head back towards the lake of blood.

If Sabatier could live through this, it would have nothing left of its body to return to.

'What was that?' said Uriel, emerging from the cloud of dust and beckoning him onwards towards the entrance to the tunnel.

'Nothing,' said Pasanius. 'Just some rubbish.'

LEONID STROKED LARANA Utorian's cheek, tears spilling down his face as the burning pain that had been his constant companion since he had been taken from Hydra Cordatus sent another spasm of hot fire into his belly. He knew that he did not have much time left – the cancers had devoured most of him already – and, looking at Larana Utorian, she did not have much time left to her either.

They were the last of the 383rd and the fact that they would die together gave him great comfort. He thought back to the men and women of his regiment and the last time he had fought beside them at the fall of the citadel. They had been magnificent.

Castellan Vauban, a courageous and honourable warrior. Piet Anders, Gunnar Tedeski and Morgan Kristan; his brother officers. And not forgetting Guardsman Hawke, the worst soldier in the regiment, whose unexpected depths of courage had very nearly saved them all.

They were all dead, and soon he and Larana Utorian would be with them again.

Colonel Leonid looked up, hearing a sibilant hissing, and drew a sharp intake of breath as he saw the two daemons stagger from the lake of blood. Both were ravaged and battered, their armours torn and rent by the mighty blows they laid upon one another. The violence of their struggle had devastated much of the cavern and portions of it continued to rain down in avalanches of rocks and rubble.

The Heart of Blood reeled from a terrible blow done to it by the Omphalos Daemonium… the Slaughterman… Leonid was not even sure he understood the distinction between these two beings, or that he wanted to even if there was one.

The daemonic Iron Warrior hammered its long bill-hook against the Heart of Blood's unguarded flank and hurled it backwards into a giant pile of mortuary tables and swinging cadavers. Bodies and debris clattered down amid the ongoing destruction and Leonid saw the Slaughterman turn and cast its gaze around the chamber.

No, Ultramarines, you do not escape my vengeance so easily…

Leonid cried out as he heard its filthy, loathsome voice in his head.

The Sarcomata shall feast on your souls for all eternity!

Leonid saw the eight daemons that were the servants of the Slaughterman dissolve once more into their smoky aspects, swirling in the air for a moment before speeding after Uriel and Pasanius.

'No!' shouted Leonid in rage. 'You will not have them!'

The Sarcomata ignored him, too intent on their prey, until he remembered their hunger for corruption. Leonid pulled the frayed collar of his uniform jacket away from his skin, slashing the rusted edge of Larana Utorian's dogtags across a swollen, cancerous melanoma growing on the pulsing artery of his neck.

Polluted, dirty blood spilled down his skin, pooling in his collarbone and soaking his uniform jacket. He smelled its coppery, unclean stink and shouted, 'Over here, you daemon spawn! This is what you want, isn't it?'

Almost as soon as his polluted blood sprayed out, the smoky comets of the Sarcomata twisted in the air and sped towards him, scenting the malignancies devouring his body as the choicest sweetmeats.

Colonel Leonid slumped to his haunches and pulled Larana Utorian tight, reaching into his breast pocket and removing something round and flat.

'All dead, all dead, all dead, all dead...' whispered Larana Utorian.

'Yes,' agreed Leonid. 'We are.'

Red mist enfolded them, sickening and moist, then vanished in an instant, leaving the two Jourans surrounded by the cancer-hungry Sarcomata, their writhing-maggot touch stroking their swollen sicknesses.

The daemons bit and tore at their flesh and he cried out in pain.

For the briefest instant, his eyes met those of Larana Utorian, and he saw the last fragment of her mind reach out to him.

She smiled at him and nodded.

Leonid pressed the detonation stud of the grenade he had taken from the crushing machine next to Obax Zakayo, obliterating them and the Sarcomata in the white heat of a melta blast.

'No way out this way, Ventris,' said Honsou, gripping his axe and widening his stance ready for combat. The master of Khalan-Ghol and a score of Iron Warriors had emerged from the passageway just as the Ultramarines had reached it, and Uriel saw that there was no way past them. The silver-eyed daemon-thing that had called itself Onyx stood apart from the Iron Warriors, its movements tentative.

An Iron Warrior with the brutal face of a killer and a mohawk stood next to it, a huge gun that resembled a bolter with an underslung melta pointed at the daemonic symbiote.

The cavern continued to rumble as the two daemons fought at its heart, but a stillness held sway here, as though the universe held its breath and awaited the outcome of this particular drama.

'It is over, Honsou,' said Uriel. 'Your fortress has fallen.'

'I can build another,' shrugged Honsou. 'This one wasn't really mine anyway.'

'True, but it's Toramino's now,' shouted Pasanius.

'Yes, or at least whatever his sorcerers and artillery leave of it once they have pounded it to rubble,' said Honsou.

The Iron Warrior pointed towards the ugly red skies overhead. 'Tell me though, is this your doing as well, or another of your master's sorceries?'

'My master?'

'Come on, Ventris!' laughed Honsou. 'The time for games is long past. Toramino!'

'We have no master save Lord Calgar and the Emperor,' said Uriel.

'Even now you play your games,' sighed Honsou. 'Well, no matter, it ends now.'

'Aye,' agreed Uriel, raising his sword before him. 'It ends with your death, traitor.'

'Perhaps, but you'll follow me into hell a heartbeat later.'

Uriel shook his head. 'You think that matters, amid all this? I will fight you and I will kill you. That will be enough for me.'

'Fight me?' said Honsou, spreading his arms to encompass his warriors. 'You think we're going to fight a duel? My warriors and I outnumber you ten to one! What makes you think I'd give you a chance to trade blows with me?'

The Iron Warriors aimed their weapons at them, knowing that blood was soon to be spilled here, but waiting for their master's command before unleashing death.

Pasanius leaned close to Uriel and said, 'You take the ten on the right and I'll take the ten on the left.'

Despite himself, Uriel chuckled and stood back to back with his oldest comrade.

'Courage and honour, my friend,' said Uriel.

'Courage and honour,' repeated Pasanius.

The two Ultramarines prepared to charge as the Iron Warriors cocked their bolters.

THE HEART OF Blood fell to its knees, the Omphalos Daemonium's billhook tearing into its warp-spawned flesh and opening a great gash in its body. Dark ichor spilled down its armour and its strength was fading; too long imprisoned within the depths of Khalan-Ghol had robbed it of much of its diabolical vigour and power. Another blow smashed into its chest, sending it hurling across the width of the chamber.

'Eternity awaits you!' roared the Omphalos Daemonium. 'An age trapped in fire will be nothing to torments you will suffer!'

Smoke and rubble fell in a constant rain from the walls, crushing anything exposed on the cavern floor.

'You cannot destroy me. I am the Heart of Blood!'

The Omphalos Daemonium ran towards it, fierce, vengeful hunger burning in its eyes. The Heart of Blood sprang to its feet and lashed out with its whip.

The blow struck its foe's head, drawing a bellow of pain and a spray of dark blood as it severed one of its gnarled antlers.

The Heart of Blood staggered away in the respite its lucky blow had gained, wading back into the lake of blood, feeling the invigorating fluid enter its immaterial flesh and new strength seep into its essence. But this was poor, stagnant blood, polluted with the taint of psychic energies and devoid of the hot, urgent nourishment it needed to defeat its foe.

As the Omphalos Daemonium came after it, memories thrashed and screamed in the Heart of Blood's skull, though it had not the faculties left to recall them. The lunacy that had consumed it during its incarceration had robbed it of any clarity of thought save that it needed blood, desired blood... craved blood!

A powerful vision of a great fortress swam across the fluid landscape of its memory – no, not its memory, the blood-soaked memories of the Avatar of Khorne, the creature the armour had become in its absence...

A battle alongside the Iron Warriors, a sorcerous foe in yellow armour – one of the corpse-god's followers – and a howling gale of gore that thundered like a hurricane and fed its spirit with unimaginable power.

Something in this memory was the key it needed to defeat its rival and drive the Omphalos Daemonium back to the fiery prison the Heart of Blood had confined it to for an age.

A single word penetrated the Heart of Blood's fug of amnesia and lunacy.

Bloodstorm...

THE FIRST BOLT took Uriel low in the gut as he charged, tearing through the knotted mass of scar tissue that covered the wound dealt to him by the tyranid Norn Queen.

He was too close and the bolt was moving too quickly for it to detonate within him, but it exploded a fraction of a second after punching out through his lower back and peppered his flesh with searing fragments.

The second shattered on one of the few remaining portions of his armour, the hot shrapnel scoring upwards across his cheek, and the third blasted a chunk of his side to red ruin.

He staggered, but kept going, hacking his fiery-bladed sword through the neck of the Iron Warrior that had shot him. Pasanius was hit four times, his armour deflecting the majority of the impacts, but unable to save him completely.

The sergeant fell, dragging down the Iron Warrior before him and breaking his neck with a loud cracking noise.

Another round hit Uriel and he fell to the hard ground.

Bolter rounds filled the air. Uriel heard a cry of pain and surprise.

Yelling voices and more shots.

He tried to push himself to his feet, feeling sharp pain flare as he moved, and wondered why he was not dead.

Bellowing roars of hatred echoed from all around them, howls of furious anger and anguish. Even over the stench of blood and death that filled this place, Uriel could make out the stink of wet, raw flesh and realised what was happening.

Blood sprayed from a ragged stump of an Iron Warrior's neck and Uriel shouted in triumph as he saw the battered but unbowed form of the Lord of the Unfleshed hurl the grisly trophy to one side before leaping onto another Iron Warrior who fired wildly into the attacking monsters.

'Iron men die!' he roared as the surviving creatures of the Unfleshed fell upon Honsou's warriors.

The mohawked warrior shot down the fused twins, the white-hot blast of his gun obliterating the creature with a hiss of superheated air. Onyx nimbly dodged the brutal, clubbing blows of a pair of the Unfleshed, spinning around them and hamstringing them as he danced aside from their attacks.

Uriel saw Honsou retreat from the attack of the Unfleshed, and rolled onto his side, dragging his bolter around.

He realised how much he missed the ministrations of his armour as the pain from the burning fragments of the bolter shell stabbed into his back. Pasanius lay atop a dead Iron Warrior, two large exit wounds blasted through his back.

'Pasanius!' called Uriel.

His sergeant turned his head, and Uriel saw his face was deathly pale, his cheeks ashen and sunken.

'Don't you dare die on me, sergeant!' shouted Uriel, putting down his sword and bringing his bolter to a firing position.

'Aye, captain,' said Pasanius, weakly.

Smoke and the thrashing combatants conspired to obscure Uriel's aim, but eventually he was able to draw a bead on Honsou.

'Now you die, traitor!' whispered Uriel as he squeezed the trigger and a crash of rubble and smoke exploded beside him.

But in the instant before he lost sight of Honsou, he had seen the master of Khalan-Ghol pitched backwards, his helmet spraying ceramite fragments and an arc of crimson.

* * *

BLOODSTORM...

The two daemons faced each other in the depths of the lake of blood, their shared hatred a physical thing between them. Swirling eddies of power gusted around them, the energies both had expended in their battle having drained them almost to the point of extinction.

There were no more words to be said. What could two beings that had been enemies since the dawn of time have to say to each other at this moment?

Words were now only for mortals and those with a future to remember them.

The Omphalos Daemonium had prepared for this moment ever since it had been freed by the random actions of two mortals, and its strength was by far the greater.

But the Heart of Blood and the Avatar of Khorne were once again the same creature, and the blasted armour had feasted on the death of an entire galaxy of souls. Both daemons were evenly matched, but none could yet see the other destroyed.

Bloodstorm…

The Heart of Blood spread wide its arms and gave vent to a shout of hatred that parted the vital fluid of the lake and sent a tidal wave of blood spilling outwards from its centre. A rippling whirlwind of raw, red hunger swept from the Heart of Blood's armour, spreading throughout the chamber like the pressure wave of an explosion.

A lashing storm of hate-fuelled energy roared around the ruined domain of the Savage Morticians, lashing like a blind, insensate monster and driving the Omphalos Daemonium back from the Heart of Blood with its unstoppable power.

The bloodstorm enfolded the few, cowering mutants that had hidden beneath the shattered machines and rubble of the chamber. It scythed through their flesh and blew them apart.

The bloodstorm tore into the mutilated ruin of Obax Zakayo, finally ending his suffering in an explosion of red bone.

The bloodstorm streaked past the fleshy wombs of the daemonculaba and, one by one, they exploded like great fleshy balloons filled with blood.

The bloodstorm hurtled around the circumference of the chamber, an ocean of blood swept up in the etheric whirlwind as it howled back to the Heart of Blood at its epicentre.

The mighty daemon swelled to monstrous proportions, its armour and weapons blazing with barely-contained power as it sought to master the energies ripped from the ocean of ripe blood it had just feasted upon.

Now it was ready.

Now all things would end.

CHAPTER TWENTY-TWO

HOWLING RED WINDS swept through the Halls of the Savage Morticians, the harsh metallic reek of blood catching in the back of Uriel's throat. He rolled onto his side and scooped up his sword as the fury of the hurricane scouring the air swirled around them, tearing at their flesh with harsh lashes.

The Iron Warriors dived for cover as the etheric whirlwind tore through the cavern and the Unfleshed were hurled from their feet by its power. The desperate battle broke apart as the combatants found shelter or held onto giant boulders to prevent themselves from being swept away.

Uriel gasped as the very life was leeched from him, feeling as powerless as one of the weakling newborns left to die on the mountains of Macragge. But at the edge of the cavern the power of the bloodstorm was at its weakest and they were spared the horrors of those closer to the Heart of Blood.

Pasanius grunted in pain and Uriel watched as the clotted blood on his back liquefied and was snatched into the air by the vampiric storm. His own wounds ran freely as they fed the terrible daemon at the heart of the chamber.

'Not like this…' he hissed. 'Not like this!'

Then, it was gone – the sudden silence unnerving after the tempestuous violence of the diabolical storm. Uriel pushed himself to his knees, grimacing in pain as those around him began to recover from the hellish experience.

The Unfleshed howled in pain. Without the protection of skin to save them from the worst effects of the bloodstorm, their bodies looked wasted and gaunt, pale and anaemic.

Uriel used a fallen surgical table to pull himself to his feet, the pain from his gunshot wounds and cracked bones sharp and biting. His enhanced metabolism had clotted the blood and already formed scar tissue over the wounds, but he was still terribly injured.

'Come on,' he urged Pasanius. 'There's no way out here. We have to find another way.'

'I don't know that I can,' said Pasanius, but Uriel did not give him a chance to argue further, pulling the sergeant upright over his groans of pain. Eventually, Pasanius nodded slowly and said, 'All right, all right, you're worse than Apothecary Selenus.'

Painfully, Pasanius sat himself against a pile of rubble, freshly-clotted blood gummed on his chest from multiple bolter wounds.

THE SOUNDS OF the battle raging in the centre of the chamber continued to echo, but there was a renewed fury to the roars and clash of weapons. As the bloodstorm abated, Uriel heard savage laughter, brazen and malicious, and felt a sick sensation in his bones as his soul recoiled from its evil.

Through the swirling dust and cascades of rock, Uriel saw the furious climax of the two daemons' battle, the sight of such incredible power taking his breath away. The Heart of Blood towered above the Omphalos Daemonium now, swollen to three times its size, and its sheer physicality was like nothing he had ever seen before.

Even the Bringer of Darkness had not awed him as much with its dark majesty. Its nightmarish presence had filled his thoughts with tormented visions of his own darkness, but this…

This was something else entirely.

Where the Heart of Blood walked, death followed. A red mist came in its wake, a bloody veil that glistened with wetness, and its weapons clove the air with every stroke, leaving dark trails that split the very world open. The daemonic Iron Warrior fell back before it, battered and broken, the armour torn from its body and its wounds spewing ichor from every cut.

Each mighty blow of the Heart of Blood forced it to retreat, its parries growing more clumsy with each backwards step it took. It desperately fell back towards the hissing daemon engine that had brought it here, its screaming stacks billowing shrill screams of anguish.

But the Heart of Blood was not to be cheated of victory and its whip lashed out, snapping around the armoured daemon's arm and tearing it off in a fountain of black blood. The Omphalos Daemonium fell to its knees and bellowed in angry defiance, but it was in vain as the Heart of Blood stepped close and hammered its axe down against its shoulder, cleaving its head from its body with one mighty blow.

The armoured daemon collapsed, a flood of gore spilling from the mortal wound and the Heart of Blood raised its weapons to the heavens with an ear-splitting roar of triumph to the Blood God that shook the very walls of the chamber.

Dark energies swirled from the destroyed daemon and the Heart of Blood convulsed as it drank of the essence of its ancient foe, its limbs shuddering with the inherited power.

Even as it savoured the spoils of its victory, the red sky that had come into being at the arrival of the Omphalos Daemonium began to fade and the screaming souls trapped in the damned metal of its engine howled with renewed vigour.

Hissing bone-pistons ground upwards as the monstrous daemon engine built power to escape its dying master and the collapsing cavern.

Then, as though the battle and sheer power its victory had unleashed were too much for the terrible creature, it dropped to its knees, sated and overwhelmed with dark energies. The axe and whip fell from the Heart of Blood's clawed hands as it toppled onto its side, the lustre of its red flesh deepening to a hot vermilion that smoked and hissed like that of an electrocution victim.

With the collapse of the two abominations, the discordant shriek of clashing daemon weapons was silenced, replaced by the omnipresent thunder of artillery from outside. The battle within Khalan-Ghol might be over for now, but the violence unleashed by Toramino was still very much ongoing.

Uriel held his breath, afraid that even the slightest motion would bring the daemon surging to their feet again. But nothing of the sort happened and he let out a great, shuddering breath as the Lord of the Unfleshed limped over to him and leaned down so that its head was level with his.

'We kill iron men!' he said.

'Yes,' said Uriel, wearily. 'We did.'

'Emperor happy?'

Uriel looked around the ruins of the Halls of the Savage Morticians, seeing that there was nothing recognisable left of it, everything had been destroyed in the cataclysmic battle of the two daemons. The surgical horrors enacted here were gone, the suffering victims of the bizarre experimentations finally granted the Emperor's peace. The lake of blood was now nothing more than a dusty crater, the gantries where the daemonculaba had been housed reduced to twisted masses of mangled iron.

Of the daemonculaba themselves, there was nothing but sad piles of ruined flesh and Uriel felt a great weight lift from his shoulders as he saw that their death oath had been fulfilled. The creatures Tigurius had seen in his vision and Marneus Calgar had charged them to destroy were no more.

'Oh, yes,' said Uriel. 'The Emperor is happy. You made the Emperor very happy.'

The Lord of the Unfleshed reared up to his full height and beat his chest with his massive fists. The few of his surviving brethren did likewise and howled their joy to the fading red skies.

'Tribe! Tribe! Tribe!' they shouted, over and over.

Uriel nodded and copied the enormous creature, hammering his fists on his chest and yelling, 'Tribe! Tribe! Tribe!' at the top of his voice. Pasanius looked oddly at him, but Uriel was too caught up in the primal exultation of the Unfleshed to care.

As the chant faded, the Lord of the Unfleshed returned his attention to the few surviving Iron Warriors who began picking themselves up now that the fury of the bloodstorm had abated.

The Lord of the Unfleshed twisted his hungry head towards Uriel and asked, 'Meat?'

Uriel's heart hardened as he slowly nodded.

'Meat,' he agreed.

These Iron Warriors had been the mightiest of Honsou's grand company, but even they could not stand before the fully-unleashed savagery of the Unfleshed. The ground was littered with the dead, both Iron Warriors and their monstrous by-blows, but it was only a taster of the slaughter that followed.

Armour was broken open and limbs were torn from their sockets as the Unfleshed feasted on the still-living bodies of their hated creators.

Uriel helped Pasanius to his feet as he saw the daemon-thing, Onyx, surrounded by a pack of the Unfleshed. The dark-armoured warrior cut and stabbed with furious speed, but the Unfleshed fought on, uncaring of wounds that would have slain a lesser opponent thrice over.

Uriel felt no pity for Onyx, it was a thing of the warp, an abomination and, as it was borne to the ground beneath a roaring mass of the Unfleshed, he turned away.

'So what do we do now?' asked Pasanius, leaning against a shattered pile of rockcrete slabs and wiping dust and blood from his face.

'I am not sure,' answered Uriel honestly. 'We did what we set out to do. We fulfilled our death oath.'

Despite his obvious pain, Pasanius smiled, and the sullen weight his friend had carried since the last days on Tarsis Ultra seemed to slide from his face.

'It is good to see you smile again, my friend,' said Uriel.

'Aye, it's been a while since I've felt like it.'

'Our honour is restored,' said Uriel.

'You know,' said Pasanius. 'I don't think we ever really lost it.'

'Perhaps not,' agreed Uriel. 'If only there was some way we could tell them that on Macragge.'

'I don't suppose they'll ever hear of what happened here.'

'No, I do not suppose they will,' said Uriel. 'But that does not matter. We know, and that is enough.'

'Aye, I think you're right, captain.'

'I told you before, you do not need to call me that.'

'Not before,' pointed out Pasanius, 'but we've honoured our death oath, and you are my captain again.'

Uriel nodded. 'I suppose I am at that.'

The two warriors shook hands, pleased to be alive and enjoying the sensation of having achieved what they set out to do. No matter that they were still trapped on a nightmarish daemon world, thousands of light years from home. Their success felt good by the simple virtue of its accomplishment.

No matter what happened now, they were done. It was over.

The Lord of the Unfleshed approached, thick ropes of clotted blood dangling from his jutting, fanged jaws.

'We go now?' he said. 'Leave now?'

'Leave?' said Uriel. 'How? There is nowhere to go. The passage to the elevator cage is impassable and hundreds of tonnes of rock have shut off the outflow pipe. There is no way out.'

The Lord of the Unfleshed gave him a lopsided look, as though he couldn't believe that Uriel was being so dense. He pointed over Uriel's shoulder and said, 'Big iron man's machine leaves!'

For a second, Uriel was mystified until he followed the Lord of the Unfleshed's pointing finger and saw the dark shape of the armoured leviathan that had carried the Slaughterman here. It ground towards one of the skull-wreathed tunnels it had created to manifest within the cavern. The red-lit door to its interior was still open and though the masterless machine was slowly building speed, there was still time get aboard.

'Brought big iron man here,' said the Lord of the Unfleshed. 'Take us away too!'

Uriel shared a look with Pasanius.

'What do you think?' said Uriel, a ghost of a smile playing at the corners of his mouth.

'I think that wherever the thing takes us, it's got to better than here, captain,' said Pasanius, pushing off the rocks and clutching his wounds.

'I hope you're right.'

'Well, it's either that or we stay and get flattened by Toramino's artillery.'

'Good point,' agreed Uriel, turning to the Lord of the Unfleshed. 'Gather the Tribe. We are leaving.'

The Lord of the Unfleshed nodded, its massive shoulders heaving with the motion. It threw back its head and let out a rising howl.

Within seconds, the Unfleshed broke off from their grisly feasting and joined their leader. Less than a dozen of them still lived, and Uriel was shocked at how few had survived the mission to Khalan-Ghol. Ardaric Vaanes had been right when he said that most, if not all, of them would die here.

Uriel nodded. 'All right, let's get the hell out of here.'

FOR A MOMENT Honsou thought he was dead.

Once he realised he wasn't, he thought he was blind.

All he could feel was pain and all he could hear were heavy thumps of artillery impacting somewhere above him. He sat up, feeling a stinging in his eyes and reached up to the vacuum seals on his armour's gorget. They were cracked and useless, so he wrenched his helmet off, realising that he wasn't blind after all, but simply had clotted lumps of blood in his eyes.

Honsou scooped the clumps of sticky matter from his face and spat out a mouthful of dirt.

He wiped his face again, angry that he still couldn't see out of one eye. As he probed further he realised there a was good reason for this. Part of his head had been pulverised by the impact of the bolt round, and the left side of his face was a burned and bloody ruin, his eye a glutinous, fused mess.

Dizziness and nausea swamped him, but he put his silver arm out to steady himself, giving a short bark of laughter as he saw that it was smooth and unblemished despite the fury of the battles he had fought since it had been grafted to him.

'Damn you, Ventris, that's twice you've blinded me with my own blood.'

Honsou clambered to his knees, trying to piece the last few moments of the battle together. He remembered facing Ventris, and the Ultramarines' desperate charge that had ended in a hail of bolter fire.

Or, at least, it should have ended that way. The luck of the damned was with them and they had survived long enough to kill a pair of his warriors. As foolishly heroic as their charge had been, it had bought them moments at best.

But then the monsters had attacked.

Honsou still felt a shiver of revulsion as he thought back to their unimaginable hideousness. Their corpses were strewn all around him and as he pulled himself free of the rubble that buried his legs and swayed unsteadily to his feet, he was amazed that such incredibly abhorrent creatures could live.

He had heard of the Unfleshed, but had never dreamed they could have been so fearsome as to almost be his undoing.

The last thing he remembered was catching a snapshot of Ventris aiming a bolter for his head and twisting to get out of the way. Honsou remembered seeing the muzzle flash, a sensation of bright, burning pain in his face, then... then nothing until this moment.

'Iron within!' he shouted.

There was no answer and he knew that all the warriors who had accompanied him to the Halls of the Savage Morticians were dead. He put them from his mind and admiringly surveyed the destruction around him.

Nothing remained of the chamber, its entire structure laid waste by the daemonic battle and the continuous bombardment from Toramino's grand batteries.

A flash of movement caught his eye and he picked up his axe before making his way unsteadily towards its source. An Iron Warrior, trapped beneath the half-devoured corpse of another, moaned in pain.

Honsou lifted the body from the buried Iron Warrior and saw that it was his newest lieutenant, Cadaras Grendel. The armour of the warrior's legs had been torn away and great bites had ripped away a chunk of his quadriceps muscle.

'Still alive, Cadaras Grendel?' said Honsou.

'Aye,' replied the warrior. 'I don't die easily. Help me up.'

Honsou reached down and pulled Cadaras Grendel to his feet. The grim-faced killer retrieved his weapon from the ground and checked its action before saying, 'It's over then?'

Honsou shrugged. 'Maybe. I don't know. It looks like it, though.'

Cadaras Grendel nodded. 'What about Toramino?'

'What about him?'

'I still want to kill him.'

'Don't we all?' said Honsou, looking through a great rent torn in the side of the mountain. Blue fire still hammered his fortress from the sorcerous towers that surrounded it. Toramino's artillery captains were thorough, thought Honsou, to have broken open a mountain.

He turned towards a gleaming pile of twitching metal lying beside the entrance to the passageway that had led to the elevator cage. Recognising a discarded set of bronze claws that lay beside the pile, he strode over towards the jumble of metal.

As he drew closer he saw that it was no simple debris, but the still-living remains of his champion. Onyx lay twitching on the ground, his black armour cracked and shorn from his body, his daemonic flesh ripped from the metal of his skeleton by the monsters.

The daemonic symbiote's immaterial flesh had housed a scion of the warp and without a body, it had been cast from its shell. All that remained of Honsou's champion was a collection of loosely connected, silvered limbs, brass pistons and a bronze skull with a slowly dulling silver light weeping from the eye-sockets.

'Are you in there, Onyx?' asked Honsou.

'For now,' answered Onyx, his voice little more than a rasping whisper.

'What happened to you?'

'The monsters…' hissed the creature, only just holding off its dissolution. 'They unfleshed me, gave the daemon in me nowhere to hide. It fled and left me like this…'

Cadaras Grendel joined Honsou and said, 'This the daemon thing you wanted me to watch out for?'

'Aye,' nodded Honsou.

'Don't look like much now.'

'No, he doesn't, does he?' said Honsou, turning away and limping towards the centre of the chamber.

'What you want me to do with it?' shouted Cadaras Grendel after his retreating back.

'Get rid of it,' said Honsou with a dismissive wave.

He clambered painfully over the many piles of rubble and bodies that littered the cavern, hearing the hot flash of Cadaras Grendel's melta gun and knowing that Onyx was no more.

The centre of the cavern looked like the epicentre of some great orbital bombardment, the ground torn up and gouged with the fury of the battle that had taken place. Bodies and wreckage filled the place, so smashed and unrecognisable as to give no clue as to what they had been in life.

A shorn suit of power armour, gigantic in its proportions, lay at the edge of a deep crater and before it lay the Heart of Blood. The massive daemon's body was a dull, smouldering red, the colour of threatening embers that can leap to life in an instant. Its chest heaved with sated lust and as Honsou watched, the fiery streaks of its veins pulsed with renewed life.

The axe lying next to the daemon was twice as tall as Honsou and though he knew it was unfeasible, he felt an undeniable urge to try and lift it. His own axe growled in his hand and he knew that it was the daemonic presence within the Heart of Blood's weapon that was calling to him.

Honsou marched over to the Heart of Blood's recumbent body and delivered a thunderous boot to its horned skull.

'Come on!' he yelled. 'You are free now, and there are sorcerers to kill! Up!'

The daemon's lava-hot veins flared and its eyes flickered open, a soulless white fire, like dying suns, burning from its skull. Shaking off the satiety of its victorious engorgement, the Heart of Blood raised itself to its full height, its gargantuan axe and whip leaping to its great, taloned hands.

'That's better,' snarled Honsou as the daemon towered above him.

'Who dares rouse me from my blood-reverie?' bellowed the daemon.

'I am Honsou. Half-breed. Master of Khalan-Ghol.'

The colossal daemon loomed over Honsou, but he stood his ground, determined that he would show no fear before this creature.

'You are touched by the warp,' said the Heart of Blood. 'You have been flesh for one of my kind.'

Honsou nodded. 'Yes, I was once briefly blessed with the touch of a daemon of Chaos.'

'I still smell sorcery upon this place,' growled the daemon.

'You do,' said Honsou. 'My enemies wield powerful magicks against me and seek to destroy my fortress.'

'You are the master of this place?'

'For the moment, yes,' confirmed Honsou.

'Where are these enemies that stoop to the use of foul sorcery?' demanded the daemon.

Honsou looked out through the great breach torn in the side of the mountain and pointed to the crackling blue fires beyond.

'Out there,' he said. 'The warlord who commands the host that attacks my fortress is a sorcerer and has many magickers attending him.'

'I will kill him and rend his soul for all eternity!' promised the Heart of Blood, turning and smashing its way through the tear in the mountain of Khalan-Ghol before disappearing from sight.

Honsou clambered over to the crack torn in the rock and looked out over the smoke-wreathed mountain-side, watching with undisguised amusement as the unstoppable daemon smashed into the front line of Toramino's army.

'Yes,' he laughed. 'You go do that...'

EPILOGUE

THE SANCTUARY ECHOED with the ghosts of the dead, its empty blockhouses and bunkers deserted and abandoned. It had been that way when they had first found the place of course, but now it felt truly empty, as though the warrior band's brief occupancy had been nothing more than its last gasp of purpose.

Ardaric Vaanes knew they could not stay here now.

This place was forever tainted in his memory.

It had been here that Ventris had foisted his lie upon him and his men.

The lie of honour. The same lie that had seen him cast from his Chapter in the first place. The same lie that had almost seen him dead on this bleak, miserable shithole of a world.

Honour… What was the use of such a thing when all it got you was death and suffering? Thirty warriors had lived and fought from this place, fighting their enemies and surviving… always surviving.

Until Ventris came.

They had not had much of a life here, but it had at least been life.

'You killed them all, you bastard,' hissed Vaanes, his hatred for the Ultramarines captain burning like a slow fire in his heart as he traced spirals in the dust with his lightning claw.

Svoljard, tall and wild in his grey Wolf Brothers armour and Jeffar San, the proud and haughty White Consul, were all that was left of his warrior band, and Ardaric Vaanes knew that they would be lucky to live through the next few days.

After leaving Ventris and his ragtag band of monsters and misfits, the three of them had made their way through the mountains to the sanctuary, watching the great battles around the fortress from afar.

The spectacle had been magnificent, and during the incredible attack up the great ramp, Vaanes had unaccountably found himself hoping against hope that Honsou would see off his enemies.

When the ramp had collapsed and the army of Berossus had been all but destroyed, he had wanted to cheer.

But as spectacularly destructive as that had been it was as nothing compared to the chaos and slaughter that followed it.

The streaming pillars of blue fire that had surrounded the fortress for days now hammered it mercilessly, tearing the mountain apart piece by piece. Storms of magickal energy bludgeoned the rock with unimaginable force, smashing impregnable towers and bastions to dust in the blink of an eye. Vaanes had never seen anything like it and though the destruction was awe-inspiring to watch, he felt a flicker of regret that Honsou had not managed to pull off one last trick to defeat Toramino.

Then the Heart of Blood came, and everything changed.

It had come from the depths of the mountain like a red whirlwind of death, killing and destroying everything before it in an orgy of destruction that was staggering in its violence. Nothing could stand before this avatar of destruction – not men, not Iron Warriors, not tanks, not even Toramino's daemon engines.

Everything that came near the colossal daemon died, butchered by its screaming axe or crushed beneath its monstrous bulk. The slaughter had gone on for days, but in the end, Toramino's army had broken before the Blood God's favoured avatar, the shattered remnants quitting the field of battle while they still could and abandoning the smouldering wreck of Khalan-Ghol to the half-breed.

Honsou was still the master of Khalan-Ghol and though Vaanes had been pleased that the arrogant Toramino had been brought low, he felt an icy shiver of apprehension.

He knew that the half-breed would surely wreak a terrible vengeance on those who had attacked him. Vaanes knew that that was exactly what he would do and, from what little he knew of Honsou, he suspected that they were not so different in that respect.

That had been a week ago, and with nothing left to them, he, Svoljard and Jeffar San had remained at the sanctuary as they tried to come to terms with their new circumstances.

What were they to do? Where should they go?

Find some way to leave Medrengard and ply their trade as mercenaries once more?

Perhaps, but Vaanes had lost his taste for desperate causes and did not relish the thought of wandering the galaxy and fighting for petty tyrants once more.

He was shaken from his bitter reverie by the sound of footfalls behind him. He scuffed out the spiral he had been tracing in the dust and turned, seeing Svoljard at the door, a grim look of inevitability etched on his lupine features.

'What is it?' asked Vaanes.

'Trouble,' said the Wolf Brother.

JEFFAR SAN STOOD at the entrance to the blockhouse, his bolter carried loosely over his shoulder and his long, dirty blond hair pulled in a tight scalp-lock. The white of his armour was all but obscured by the dirt and filth of their adventure into Khalan-Ghol, but he still carried himself with an arrogant air of faded grandeur.

'What's going on?' snapped Vaanes as he and Svoljard emerged into the bright, perpetual daylight.

'Over there,' said Jeffar San, pointing to where a single vehicle sat at the end of the shadowed valley. Vaanes recognised it as a monstrously powerful Land Raider battle tank, its hard, iron sides chevroned with yellow and black stripes and its upper armour plates fringed with spikes. A disembowelled body was bound, spread-eagled, upon the tank's upper glacis, its limbs bloody and loops of its entrails wound around the tank's spikes.

Massive guns housed in armoured sponsons were aimed at the blockhouse. The power of those weapons was enormous, knew Vaanes, easily capable of demolishing the blockhouse with one shot.

So why didn't they fire? Honsou – for no other would seek them out in this place – would have no reason to come here other than to kill them.

'Why doesn't it shoot?' hissed Svoljard, thinking the same thing.

'I think we're about to find out,' said Vaanes, nodding towards the massive tank as its frontal assault ramp lowered with a great clang on the rocks.

Three warriors emerged, all liveried in the armour of the Iron Warriors and carrying their weapons before them.

'What the hell?' said Vaanes as the Iron Warriors marched from the security and strength of their vehicle and came towards them, crossing the ruined trenches and skirting the jagged remains of tank traps.

As the Iron Warriors neared, Vaanes whispered, 'Be ready to fight when I give the word.'

The other two nodded, but he could see that they had no taste for this last stand.

The lead warrior removed his helmet and Vaanes was not surprised to see the battered features of the half-breed. One side of his face was a ruined mess, a knot of augmetics covering half his skull and a glowing blue gem replacing his missing eye. The second warrior had the face of a killer, his eyes hard and cold, with a jagged mohawk running over the centre of his skull. Vaanes couldn't see the third figure; his powerfully armoured form was obscured by Honsou's body.

'You've come a long way to just to kill us, Honsou,' said Vaanes.

The half-breed laughed. 'If I'd come here to kill you, you'd already be dead.'

'Then why are you here?'

'I'll get to that soon enough,' promised Honsou. 'You fought alongside Ventris, yes?'

'Aye,' spat Vaanes. 'For all the good it did me.'

'That's what I thought.'

'What are you talking about?'

'You carry great bitterness within you, warrior, but you are a fighter, a survivor.'

'And?'

'And I need men like you now. Most of my own grand company are dead, and those of Berossus's that swore loyalty to me are few in number. I offered Ventris the chance to join me, but he spat it back at me. I now offer you the same chance, but I do not think you will do the same.'

'You want us to fight for you?'

'Yes,' said Honsou.

'For what purpose?'

'For conquest, for war and blood. And to take revenge on our enemies.'

'Ventris…' hissed Ardaric Vaanes.

'Aye,' nodded Honsou, waving forward the Iron Warrior who had been standing behind him, and who now reached up to release the clamps holding his helmet in place.

'My champion is dead,' said Honsou, 'and I need someone like you to train his newborn replacement in the art of death.'

The warrior removed his helmet and Vaanes gasped in shock as he saw the face that was revealed.

The newborn's skin was ashen and ill-fitting, raw suture wounds ringing his neck and jaw line, but there was no mistaking the patrician cast of his features nor the stormcloud grey of his eyes.

It was Uriel Ventris.

ABOUT THE AUTHOR

Hailing from Scotland, Graham narrowly escaped a career in surveying nearly five years ago to join Games Workshop's Games Development team, which, let's face it, sounds much more exciting. He's worked on loads of codexes since then, the most recent being Codex: Space Marines. As well as six novels, he's also written a host of short stories for Inferno! and takes on too much freelance work than can be healthy. Graham's housemate, a life-size cardboard cut-out of Buffy, recently suffered a terrible accident during a party and now keeps herself to herself in the spare room, scaring people who don't know she's there and plotting the best way to have her revenge on the miscreant that damaged her.

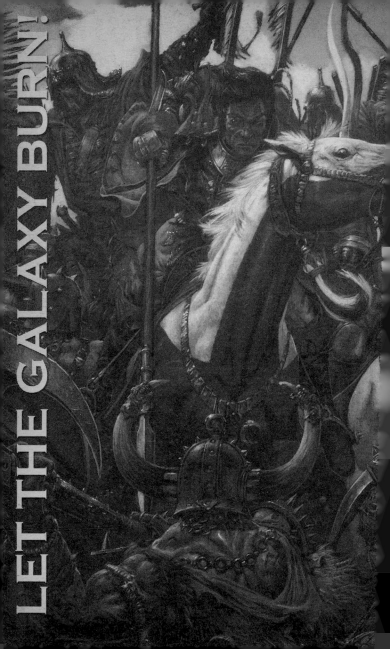

LET THE GALAXY BURN!

IN THE GRIM DARKNESS OF THE FAR FUTURE THERE IS ONLY WAR!

STORM OF IRON

A WARHAMMER 40,000 NOVEL BY GRAHAM McNEILL

WARHAMMER
40,000

Hell comes to Hydra Cordatus when the Iron Warriors invade
and lay siege to its mighty Imperial citadel. But what prize
could possibly be worth so much death and destruction?

ISBN: 1-84416-103-X

WWW.BLACKLIBRARY.COM

Graham McNeill's first two action-packed novels featuring Uriel
Ventris, Captain of the Ultramarines 4th Company.

Read till you Bleed

Do you have them all?

1 Trollslayer – William King
2 First & Only – Dan Abnett
3 Skavenslayer – William King
4 Into the Maelstrom – Ed. Marc Gascoigne & Andy Jones
5 Daemonslayer – William King
6 Eye of Terror – Barrington J Bayley
7 Space Wolf – William King
8 Realm of Chaos – Ed. Marc Gascoigne & Andy Jones
9 Ghostmaker – Dan Abnett
10 Hammers of Ulric – Dan Abnett, Nik Vincent & James Wallis
11 Ragnar's Claw – William King
12 Status: Deadzone – Ed. Marc Gascoigne & Andy Jones
13 Dragonslayer – William King
14 The Wine of Dreams – Brian Craig
15 Necropolis – Dan Abnett
16 13th Legion – Gav Thorpe
17 Dark Imperium – Ed. Marc Gascoigne & Andy Jones
18 Beastslayer – William King
19 Gilead's Blood – Abnett & Vincent
20 Pawns of Chaos – Brian Craig
21 Xenos – Dan Abnett
22 Lords of Valour – Ed. Marc Gascoigne & Christian Dunn
23 Execution Hour – Gordon Rennie
24 Honour Guard – Dan Abnett
25 Vampireslayer – William King
26 Kill Team – Gav Thorpe
27 Drachenfels – Jack Yeovil
28 Deathwing – Ed. David Pringle & Neil Jones
29 Zavant – Gordon Rennie
30 Malleus – Dan Abnett
31 Konrad – David Ferring
32 Nightbringer – Graham McNeill
33 Genevieve Undead – Jack Yeovil
34 Grey Hunter – William King
35 Shadowbreed – David Ferring
36 Words of Blood – Ed. Marc Gascoigne & Christian Dunn
37 Zaragoz – Brian Craig
38 The Guns of Tanith – Dan Abnett
39 Warblade – David Ferring
40 Farseer – William King
41 Beasts in Velvet – Jack Yeovil
42 Hereticus – Dan Abnett
43 The Laughter of Dark Gods – Ed. David Pringle
44 Plague Daemon – Brian Craig
45 Storm of Iron – Graham McNeill
46 The Claws of Chaos – Gav Thorpe
47 Draco – Ian Watson
48 Silver Nails – Jack Yeovil
49 Soul Drinker – Ben Counter
50 Harlequin – Ian Watson
51 Storm Warriors – Brian Craig
52 Straight Silver – Dan Abnett
53 Star of Erengrad – Neil McIntosh
54 Chaos Child – Ian Watson
55 The Dead & the Damned – Jonathan Green
56 Shadow Point – Gordon Rennie
57 Blood Money – C L Werner
58 Angels of Darkness – Gav Thorpe
59 Mark of Damnation – James Wallis
60 Warriors of Ultramar – Graham McNeill
61 Riders of the Dead – Dan Abnett
62 Daemon World – Ben Counter
63 Giantslayer – William King
64 Crucible of War – Ed. Marc Gascoigne & Christian Dunn
65 Honour of the Grave – Robin D Laws
66 Crossfire – Matthew Farrer
67 Blood & Steel – C L Werner
68 Crusade for Armageddon – Jonathan Green
69 Way of the Dead – Ed. Marc Gascoigne & Christian Dunn
70 Sabbat Martyr – Dan Abnett
71 Taint of Evil – Neil McIntosh
72 Fire Warrior – Simon Spurrier
73 The Blades of Chaos – Gav Thorpe
74 Gotrek and Felix Omnibus 1 – William King
75 Gaunt's Ghosts: The Founding – Dan Abnett
76 Wolfblade – William King
77 Mark of Heresy – James Wallis
78 For the Emperor – Sandy Mitchell
79 The Ambassador – Graham McNeill
80 The Bleeding Chalice – Ben Counter
81 Caves of Ice – Sandy Mitchell
82 Witch Hunter – C L Werner
83 Ravenor – Dan Abnett
84 Magestorm – Jonathan Green
85 Annihilation Squad – Gav Thorpe
86 Ursun's Teeth – Graham McNeill
87 What Price Victory – Ed. Marc Gascoigne & Christian Dunn
88 The Burning Shore – Robert Earl
89 Grey Knights – Ben Counter
90 Swords of the Empire – Ed. Marc Gascoigne & Christian Dunn
91 Double Eagle – Dan Abnett
92 Sacred Flesh – Robin D Laws
93 Legacy – Matthew Farrer
94 Iron Hands – Jonathan Green
95 The Inquisition War – Ian Watson
96 Blood of the Dragon – C L Werner
97 Traitor General – Dan Abnett
98 The Heart of Chaos – Gav Thorpe
99 Dead Sky, Black Sun – Graham McNeill
100 Wild Kingdoms – Robert Earl